This volume contains
This volume contains RANMA 1/2 PART NINE #1 through #6
(first half) in their entirety.

Story & Art by Rumiko Takahashi

English Adaptation by Gerard Jones & Toshifumi Yoshida

*

Touch-Up Art & Lettering/Wayne Truman
Cover Design/Hidemi Sahara
Graphics &Layout/Sean Lee
Assistant Editor/Bill Flanagan
Editorial Assistant/Ian Robertson
Editor/Julie Davis

*

Director of Sales & Marketing/Dallas Middaugh
Marketing Manager/Renée Solberg
Sales Representative/Mike Roberson
Editor-in-Chief/Hyoe Narita
Publisher/Seiji Horibuchi

*

Printed in Canada

*

Published by Viz Communications, Inc.
P.O. Box 77010
San Francisco, CA 94107

www.viz.com • www.j-pop.com • www.animerica-mag.com

*

10 9 8 7 6 5 4 3 2
First printing, February 2001
Second printing, October 2001

VIZ GRAPHIC NOVEL

RANMA 1/2™

17

STORY & ART BY
RUMIKO TAKAHASHI

STORY THUS FAR

The Tendos are an average, run-of-the-mill Japanese family—at least on the surface, that is. Soun Tendo is the owner and proprietor of the Tendo Dojo, where "Anything-Goes Martial Arts" is practiced. Like the name says, anything goes, and usually does.

When Soun's old friend Genma Saotome comes to visit, Soun's three lovely young daughters—Akane, Nabiki, and Kasumi—are told that it's time for one of them to become the fiancée of Genma's teenage son, as per an agreement made between the two fathers years ago. Youngest daughter Akane—who says she hates boys—is quickly nominated for bridal duty by her sisters.

Unfortunately, Ranma and his father have suffered a strange accident. While training in China, both plunged into one of many "accursed" springs at the legendary martial arts training ground of Jusenkyo. These springs transform the unlucky dunkee into whoever—or whatever—drowned there hundreds of years ago.

From now on, a splash of cold water turns Ranma's father into a giant panda, and Ranma becomes a beautiful, busty young woman. Hot water reverses the effect...but only until next time.

Ranma and Genma weren't the only ones to take the Jusenkyo plunge—it isn't long before they meet several other members of the "cursed." And although their parents are still determined to see Ranma and Akane marry and carry on the training hall, Ranma seems to have a strange talent for accumulating extra fiancées, and Akane has a few suitors of her own. Will the two ever work out their differences, get rid of all these extra people, or just call the whole thing off? And will Ranma ever get rid of his curse?

CAST OF CHARACTERS

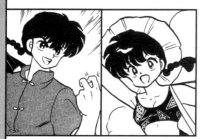

Ranma Saotome
A young martial artist with far too many fiancées. He changes into a girl when splashed with cold water.

Ukyo Kuonji
Ranma's "cute" fiancée and a master chef of *okonomiyaki* (a "Japanese omelet" or "Japanese pizza"). Ukyo runs her own restaurant, Ucchan's.

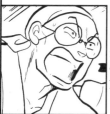

Genma Saotome
Ranma's lazy father who changes into a panda.

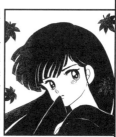

Tatewaki Kuno
Arrogant *kendo* expert who has designs on both Akane Tendo and the mysterious "pigtailed girl."

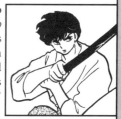

The Tendo Family

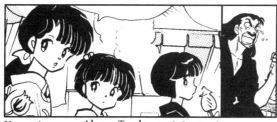

Soun Tendo
The easily excitable head of the Tendo martial arts dojo.

Kasumi Tendo
The oldest, a gentle homemaker.

Akane Tendo
The youngest daughter, a tomboy, and Ranma's fiancée.

Nabiki Tendo
The middle daughter, always out to make a few yen.

Ryoga/P-chan
A martial artist with no sense of direction, a crush on Akane, and a grudge against Ranma. He changes into a small, black pig Akane has named "P-chan." She has no idea that Ryoga is really her beloved pet.

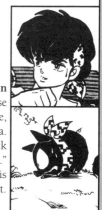

Happosai
Perverted martial-arts master who taught Soun and Genma.

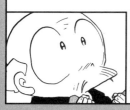

CONTENTS

Part 1
MELONHEAD

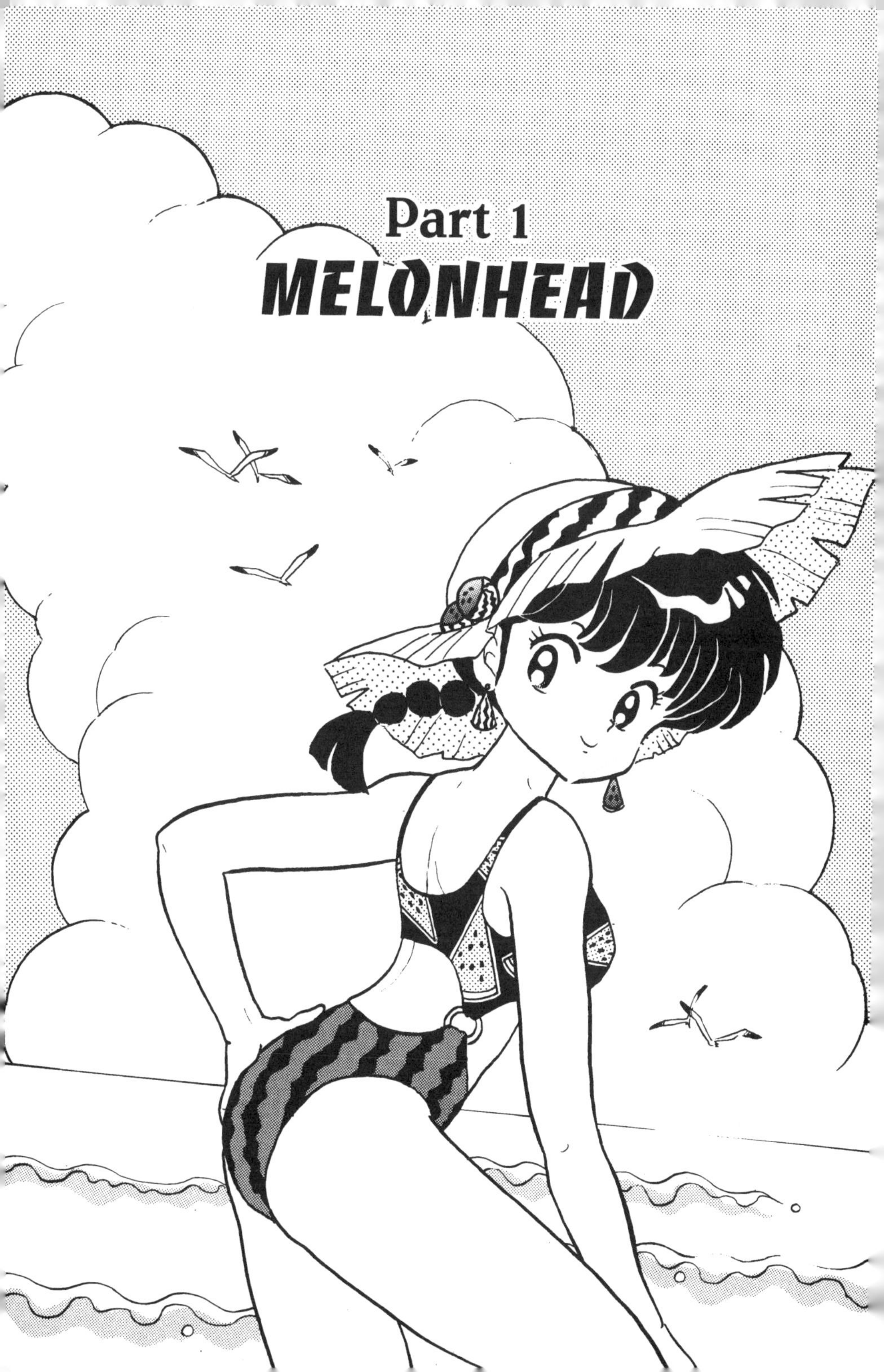

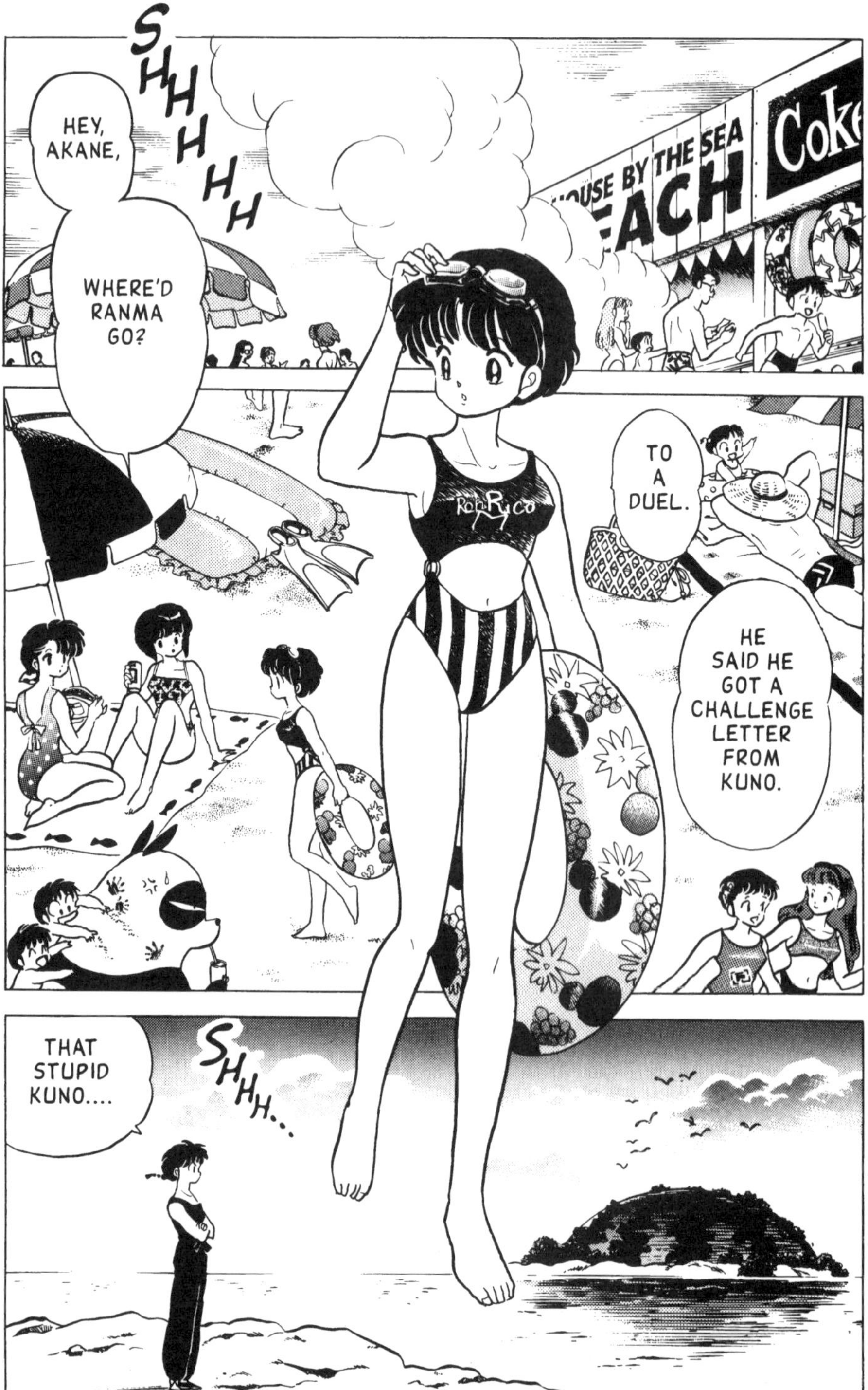
SHHHHH
HEY, AKANE,
WHERE'D RANMA GO?
HOUSE BY THE SEA
EACH
Coke
TO A DUEL.
HE SAID HE GOT A CHALLENGE LETTER FROM KUNO.
THAT STUPID KUNO....
SHHH...

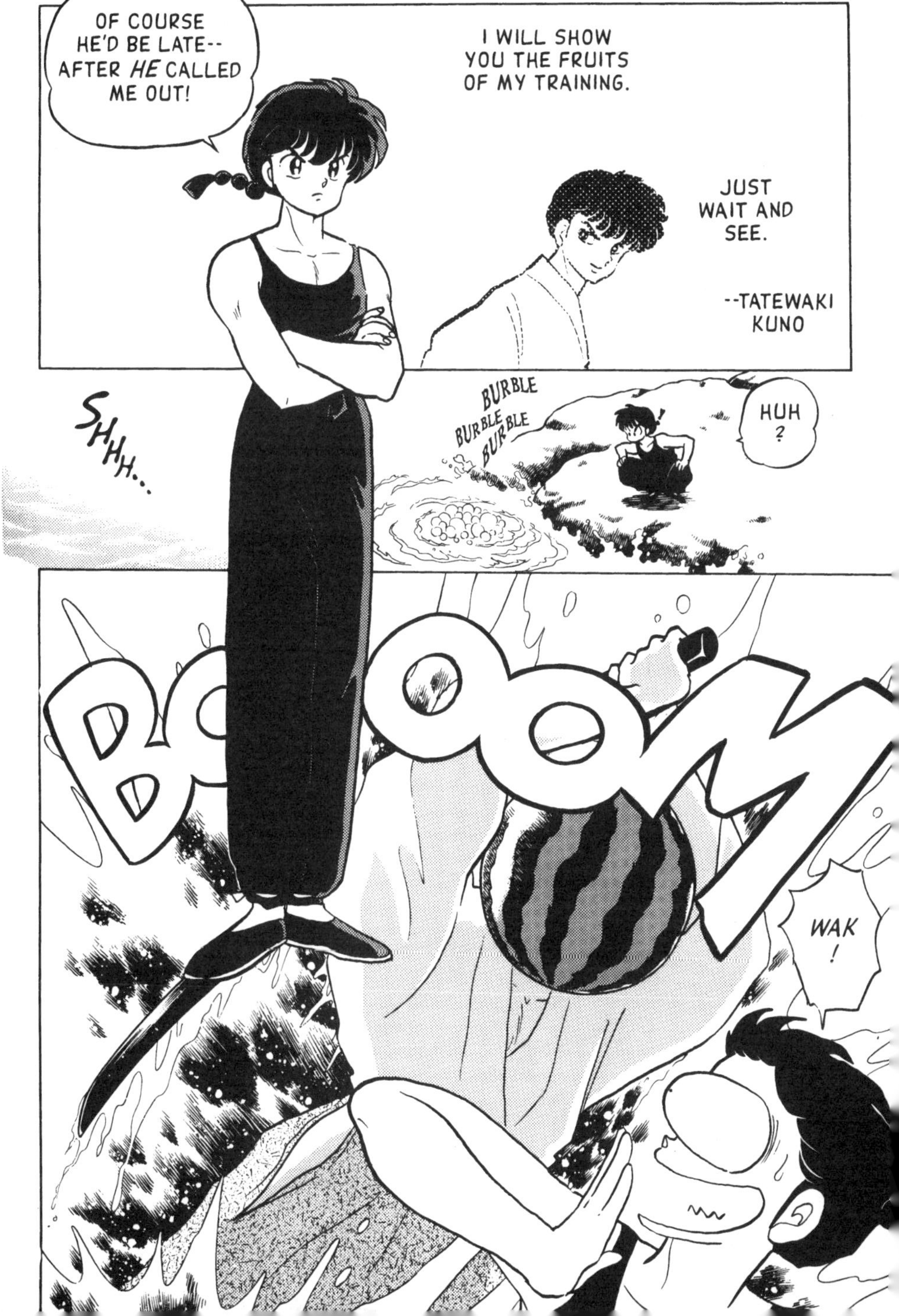
OF COURSE HE'D BE LATE-- AFTER *HE* CALLED ME OUT!
I WILL SHOW YOU THE FRUITS OF MY TRAINING.
JUST WAIT AND SEE.
--TATEWAKI KUNO
SHHH...
BURBLE BURBLE BURBLE
HUH ?
BOOOM
WAK !

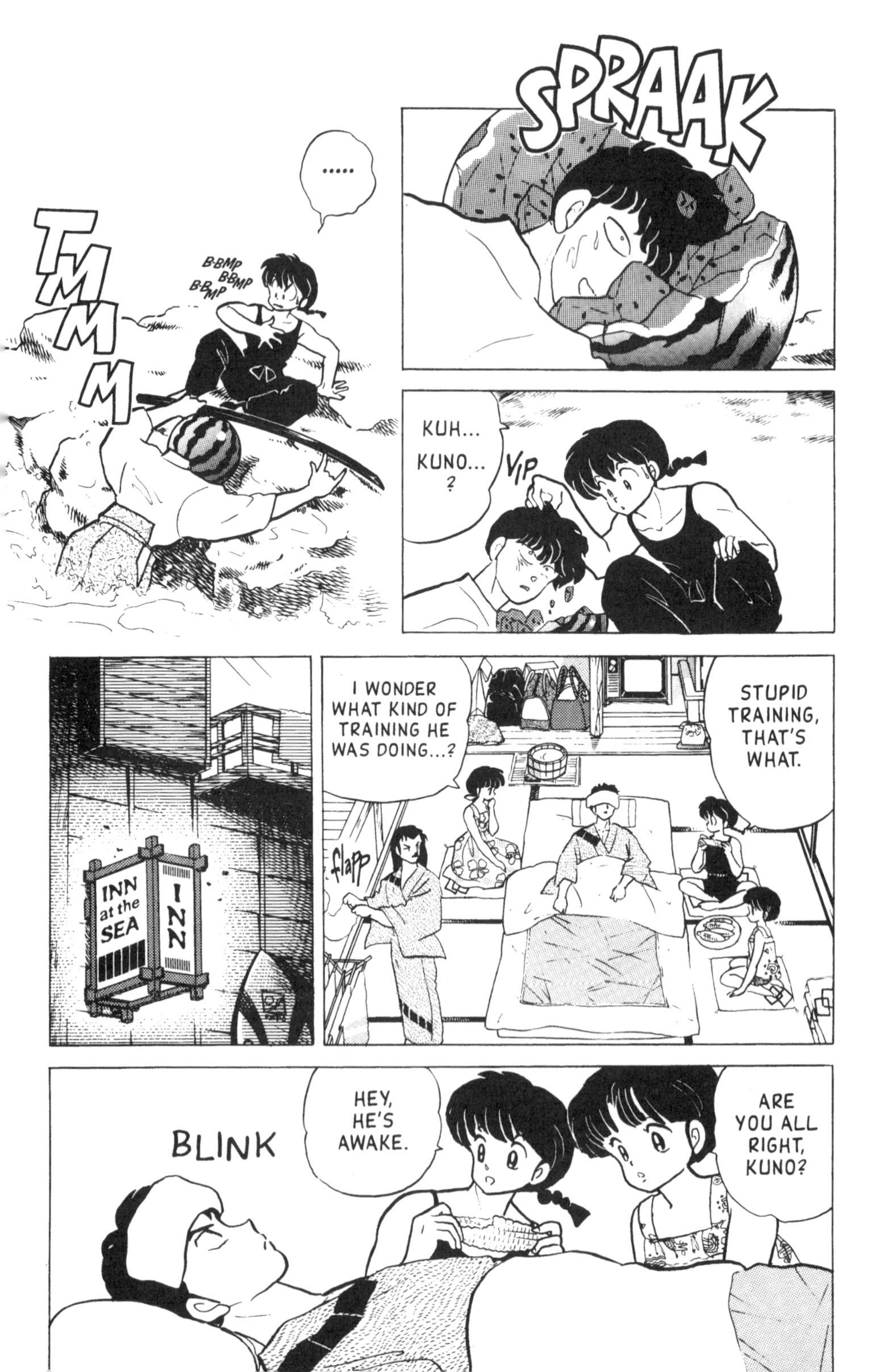

TMMM
B-BMP B-BMP B-BMP
......
SPRAAK
KUH... KUNO... ?
VIP
INN at the SEA
INN
I WONDER WHAT KIND OF TRAINING HE WAS DOING...?
flapp
STUPID TRAINING, THAT'S WHAT.
BLINK
HEY, HE'S AWAKE.
ARE YOU ALL RIGHT, KUNO?

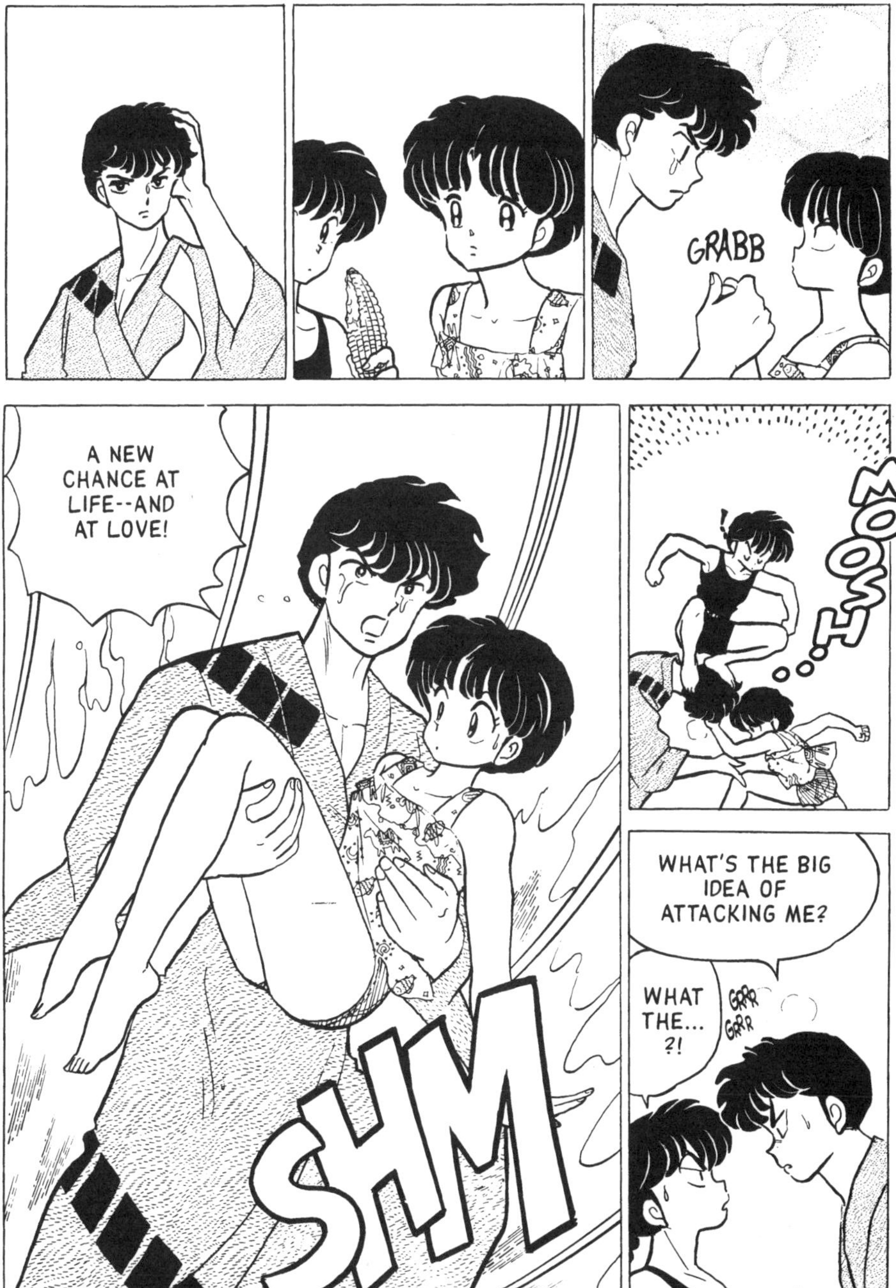
GRABB
A NEW CHANCE AT LIFE--AND AT LOVE!
SHM
MOOSH...!
WHAT'S THE BIG IDEA OF ATTACKING ME?
WHAT THE... ?!
GRRR GRRR

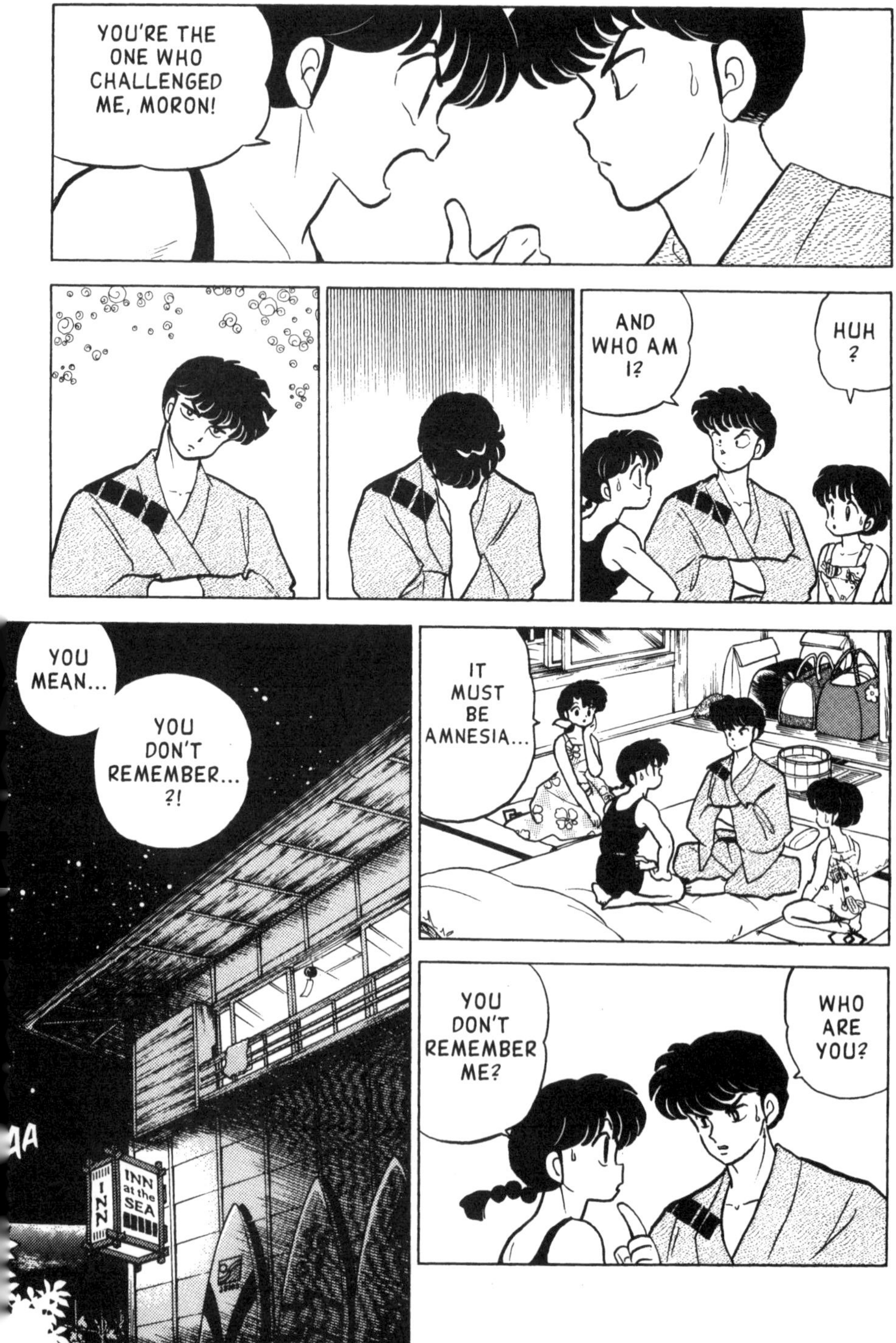
YOU'RE THE ONE WHO CHALLENGED ME, MORON!
AND WHO AM I?
HUH?
YOU MEAN...
YOU DON'T REMEMBER... ?!
INN
INN at the SEA
IT MUST BE AMNESIA...
YOU DON'T REMEMBER ME?
WHO ARE YOU?

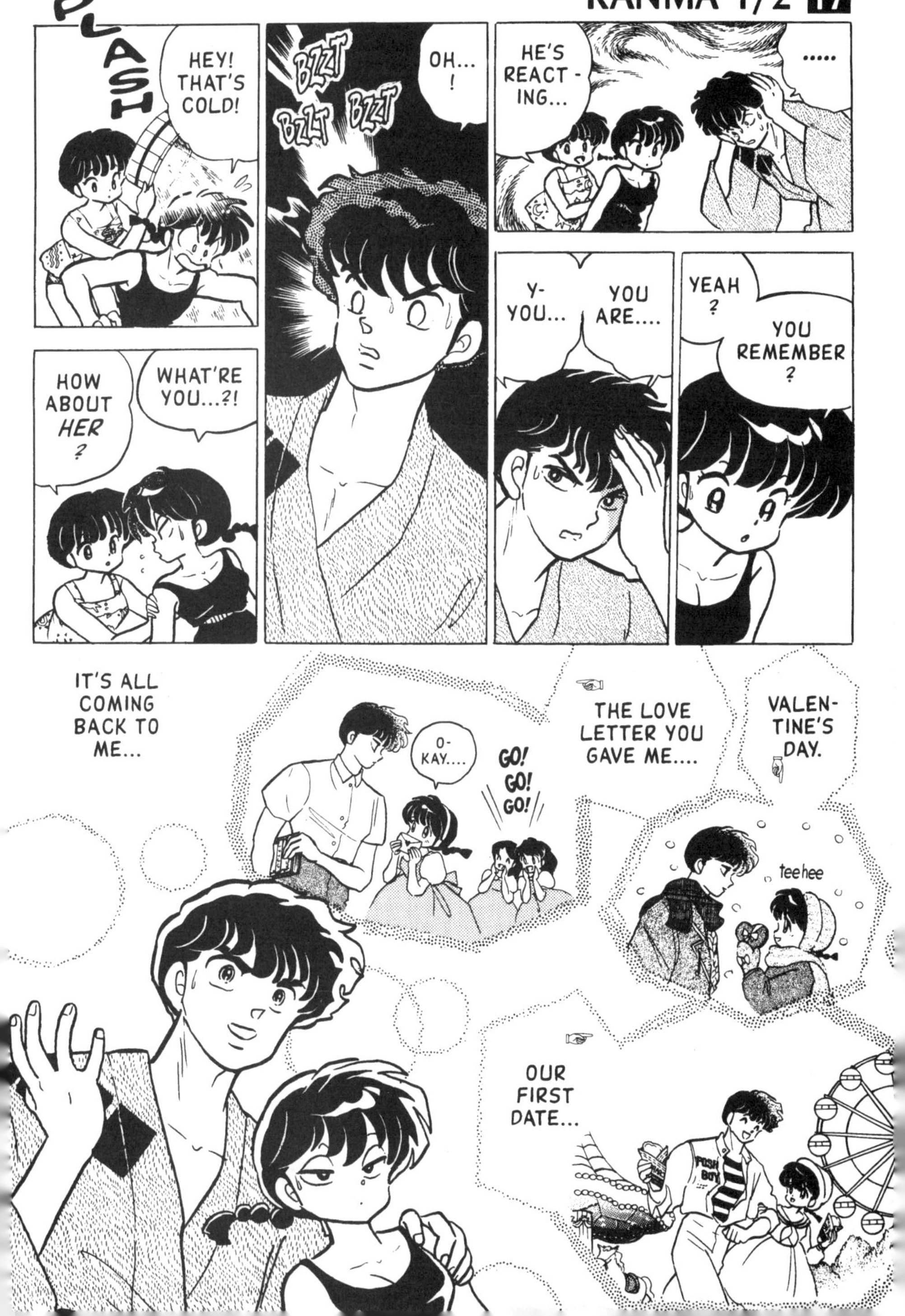
PLASH
HEY! THAT'S COLD!
BZZT BZZT BZZT
OH... !
HE'S REACT-ING...
.....
HOW ABOUT HER ?
WHAT'RE YOU...?!
Y- YOU...
YOU ARE....
YEAH ?
YOU REMEMBER ?
IT'S ALL COMING BACK TO ME...
O-KAY....
GO! GO! GO!
THE LOVE LETTER YOU GAVE ME....
VALEN-TINE'S DAY.
teehee
OUR FIRST DATE...
POSH BOY

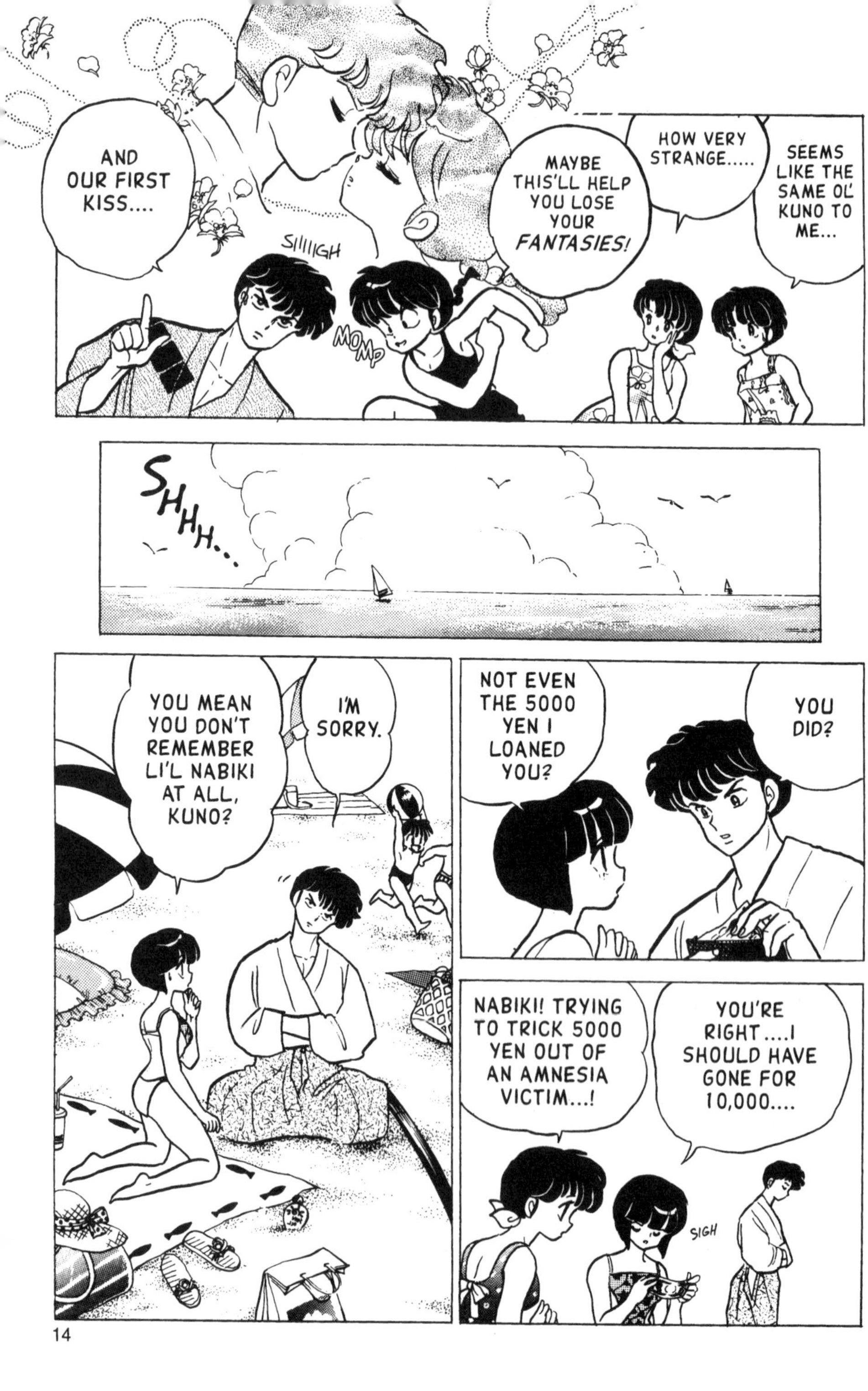
AND OUR FIRST KISS....
SIIIIGH
MAYBE THIS'LL HELP YOU LOSE YOUR *FANTASIES!*
MOMP
HOW VERY STRANGE.....
SEEMS LIKE THE SAME OL' KUNO TO ME...
SHHH...
YOU MEAN YOU DON'T REMEMBER LI'L NABIKI AT ALL, KUNO?
I'M SORRY.
NOT EVEN THE 5000 YEN I LOANED YOU?
YOU DID?
NABIKI! TRYING TO TRICK 5000 YEN OUT OF AN AMNESIA VICTIM...!
YOU'RE RIGHT....I SHOULD HAVE GONE FOR 10,000....
SIGH

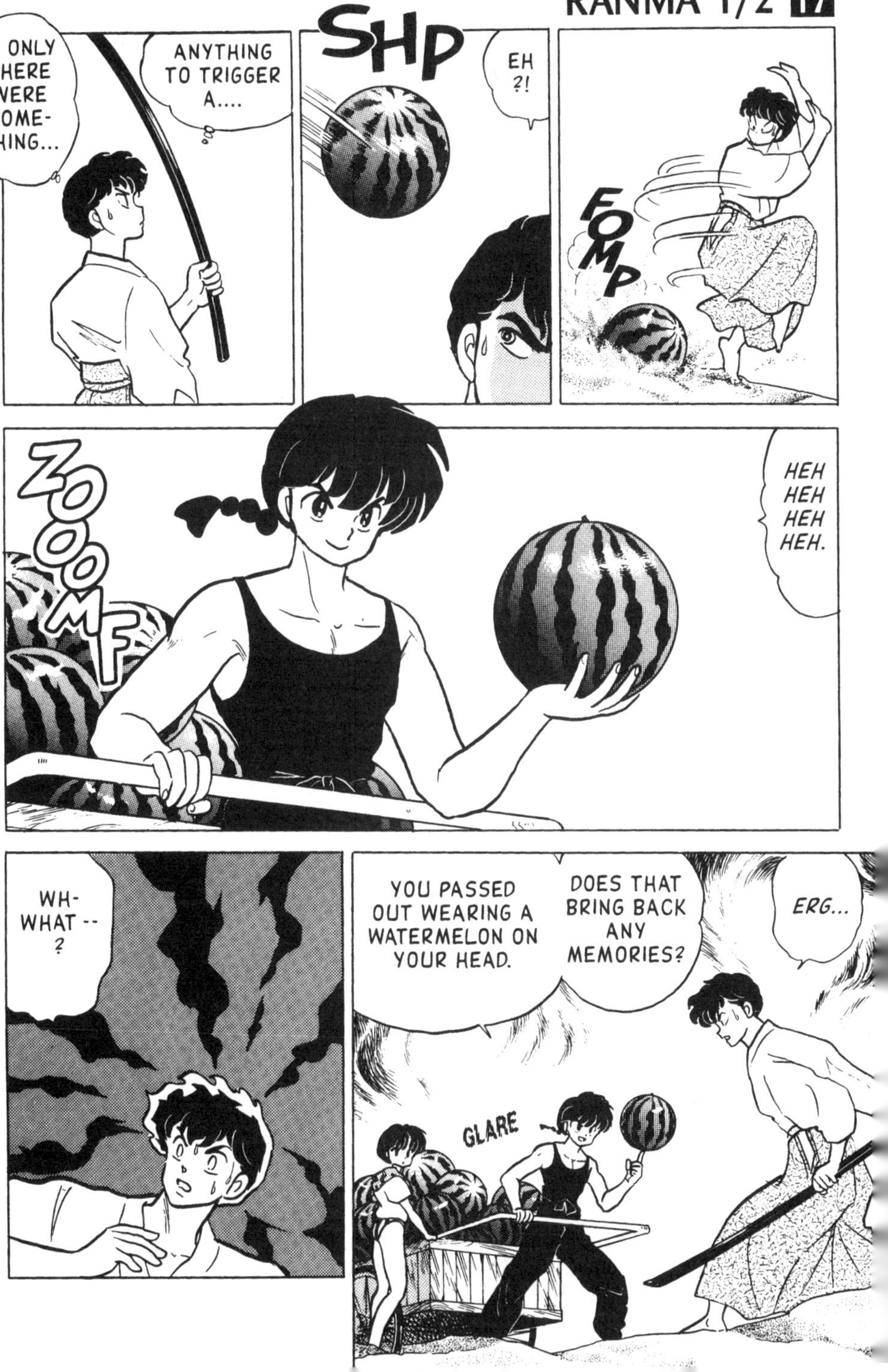
IF ONLY THERE WERE SOME-THING...
ANYTHING TO TRIGGER A....
SHP
EH ?!
FOMP
ZOOOMF
HEH HEH HEH HEH.
WH-WHAT -- ?
YOU PASSED OUT WEARING A WATERMELON ON YOUR HEAD.
DOES THAT BRING BACK ANY MEMORIES?
ERG...
GLARE

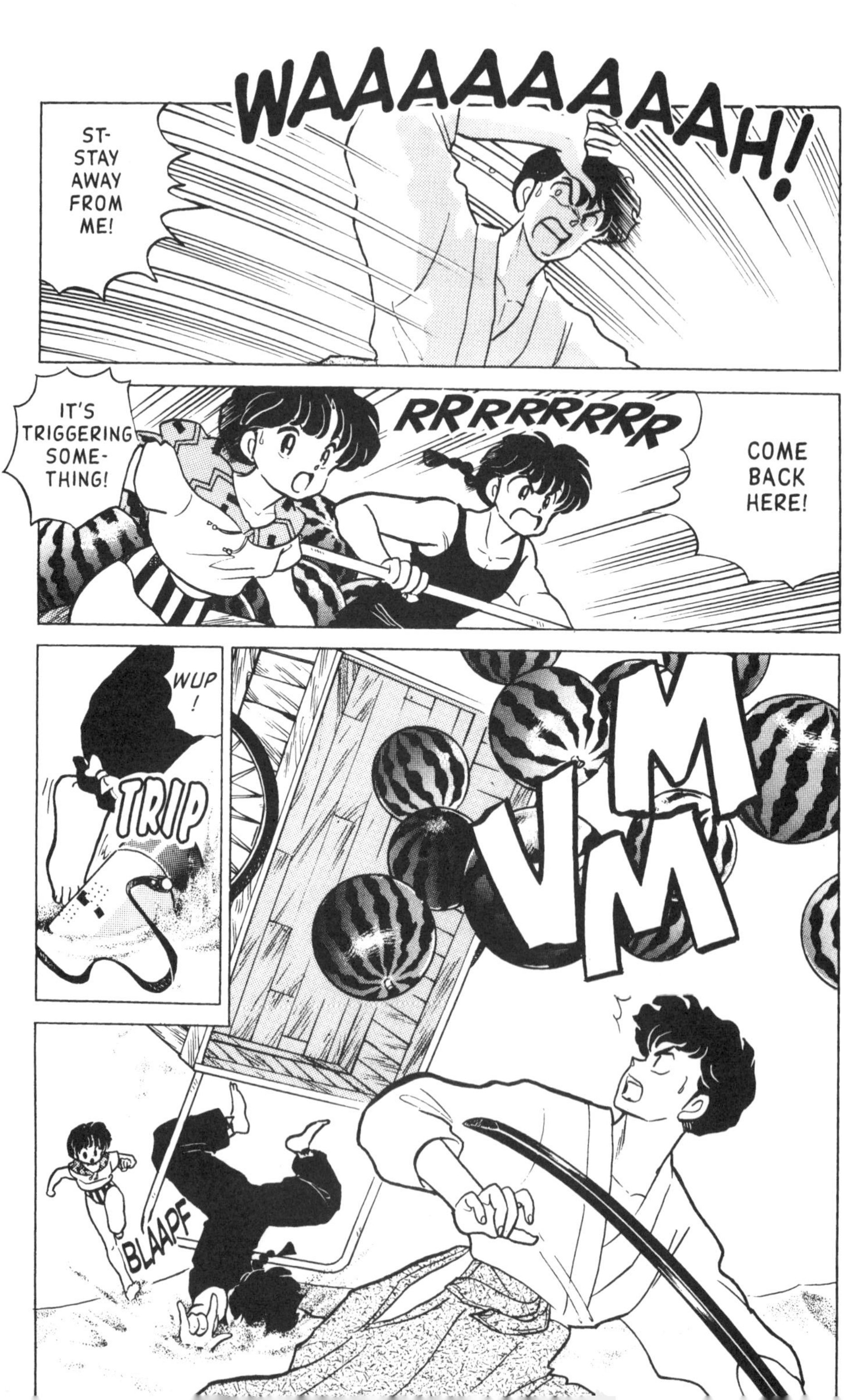
WAAAAAAAAAH!
ST- STAY AWAY FROM ME!
IT'S TRIGGERING SOME-THING!
RRRRRRRRR
COME BACK HERE!
WUP!
TRIP
VMM
BLAAPF

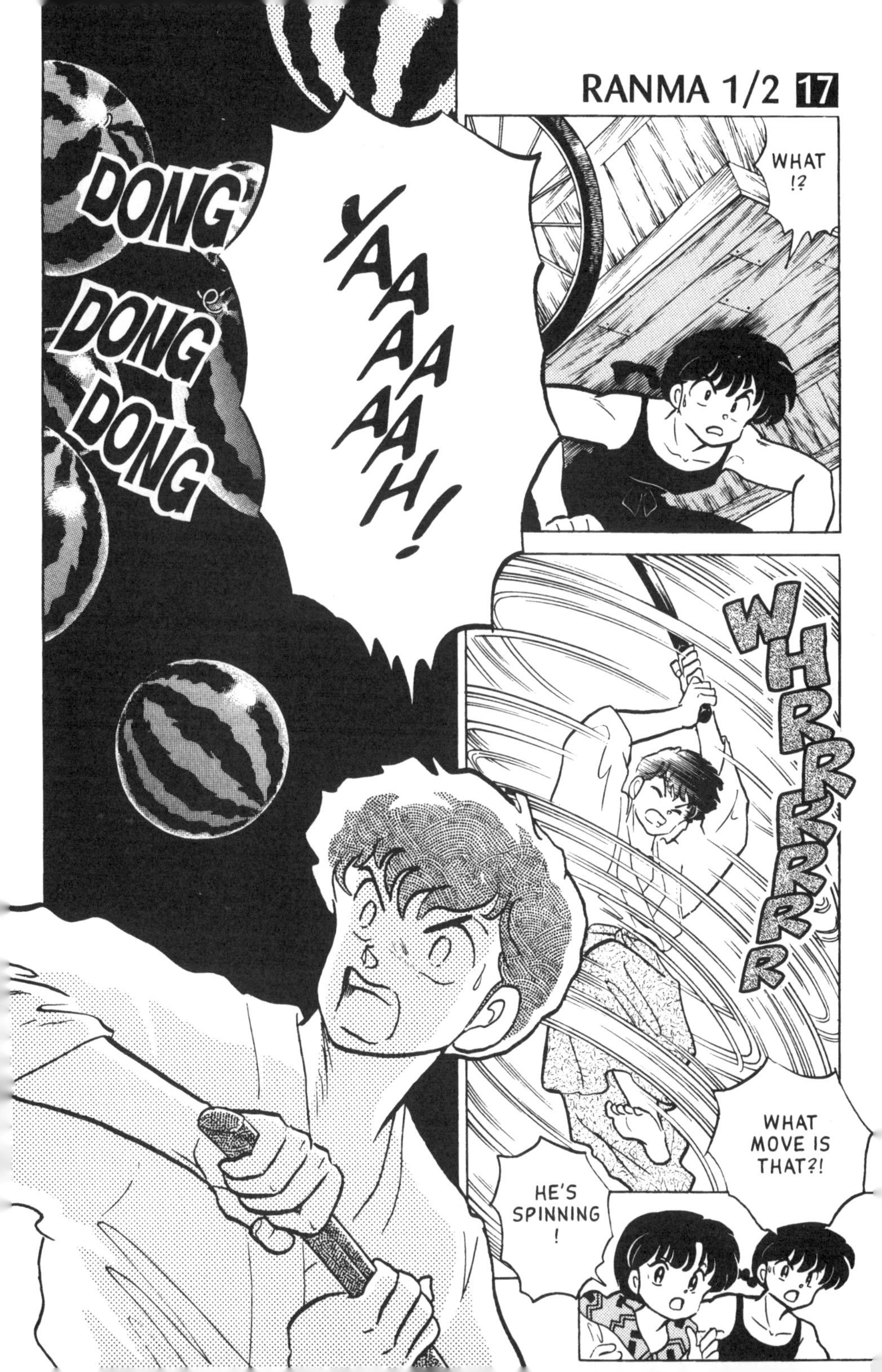
DONG
DONG
DONG
DONG
YAAAAAAH!
WHAT!?
WHRRRRRR
WHAT MOVE IS THAT?!
HE'S SPINNING!

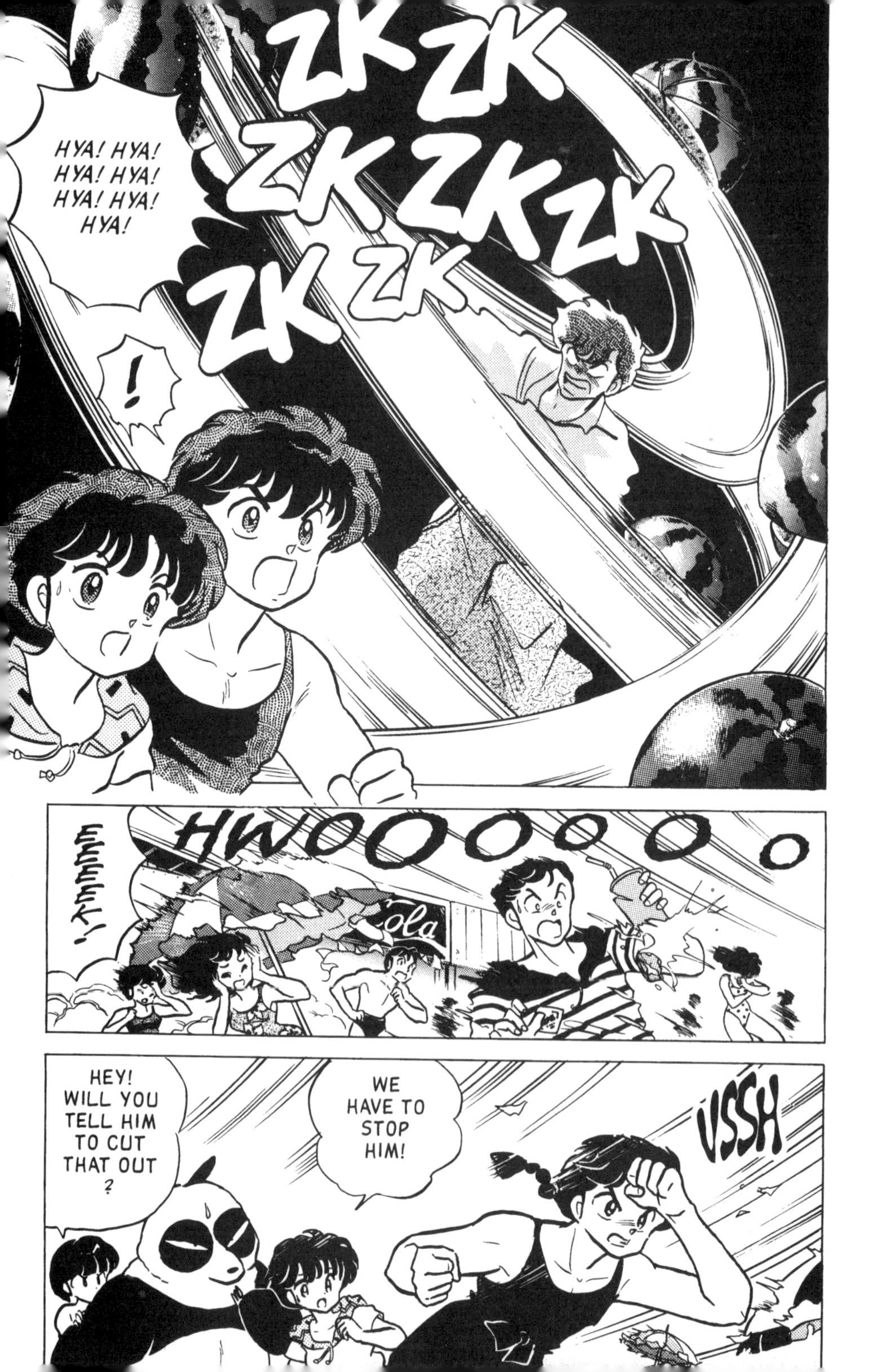
HYA! HYA! HYA! HYA! HYA! HYA! HYA!
ZK ZK
ZK ZK ZK ZK
ZK ZK
!
EEEEEK!!
HWOOOOOO
HEY! WILL YOU TELL HIM TO CUT THAT OUT?
WE HAVE TO STOP HIM!
VSSH

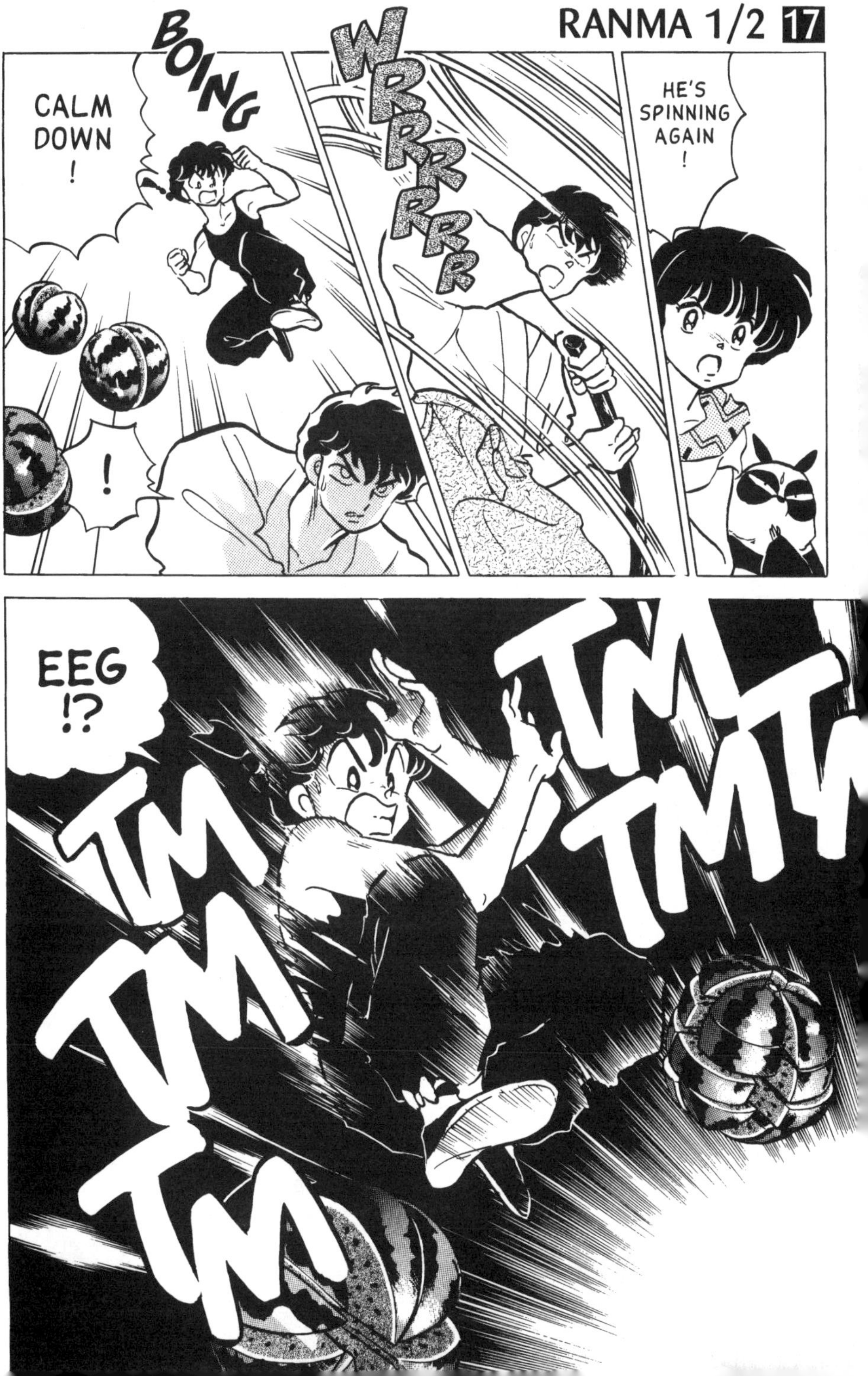
BOING
CALM DOWN !
!
WRRRRRR
HE'S SPINNING AGAIN !
EEG !?
TM
TM
TM
TM
TM
TM

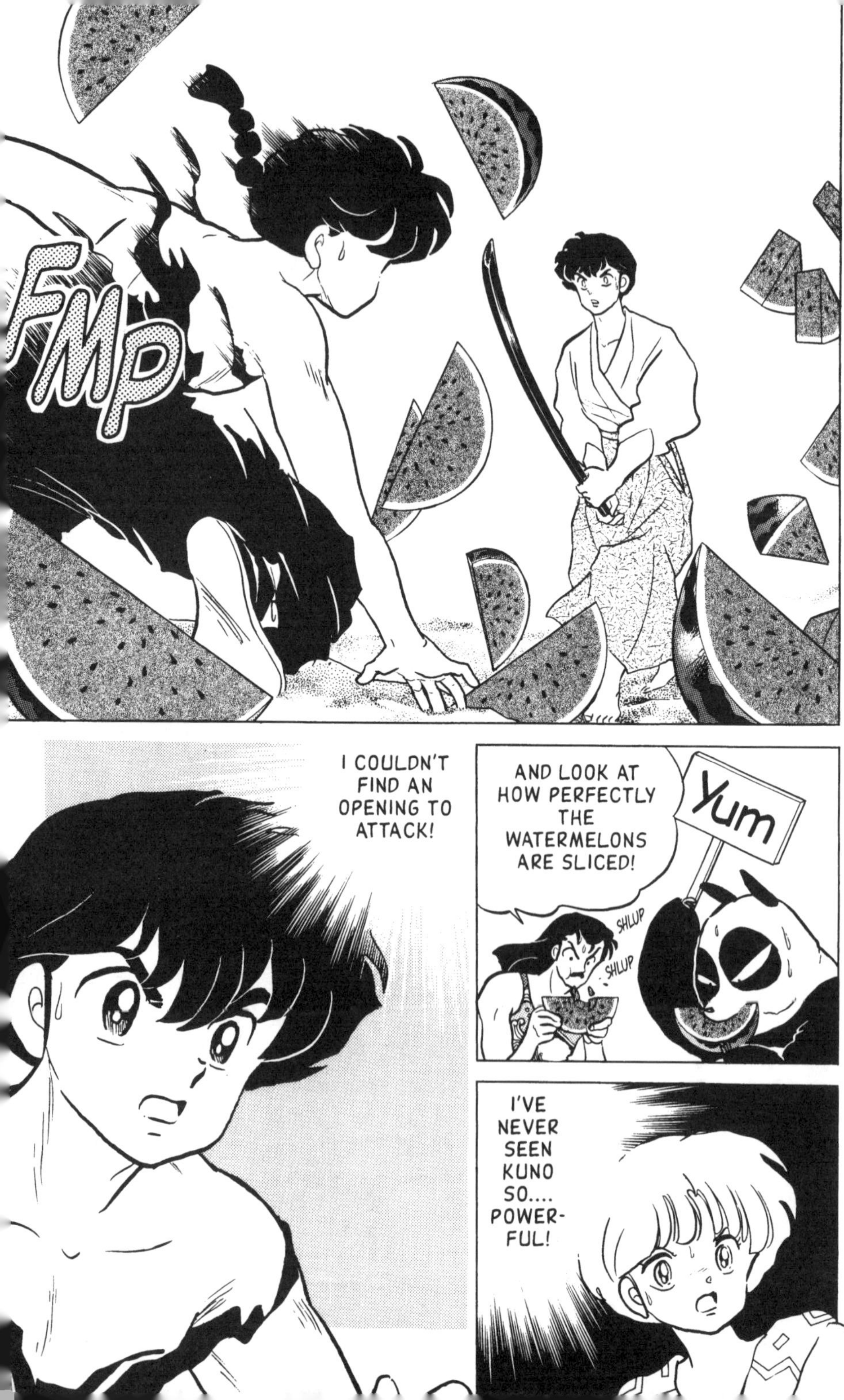
FMP
I COULDN'T FIND AN OPENING TO ATTACK!
AND LOOK AT HOW PERFECTLY THE WATERMELONS ARE SLICED!
Yum
SHLUP
SHLUP
I'VE NEVER SEEN KUNO SO.... POWER-FUL!

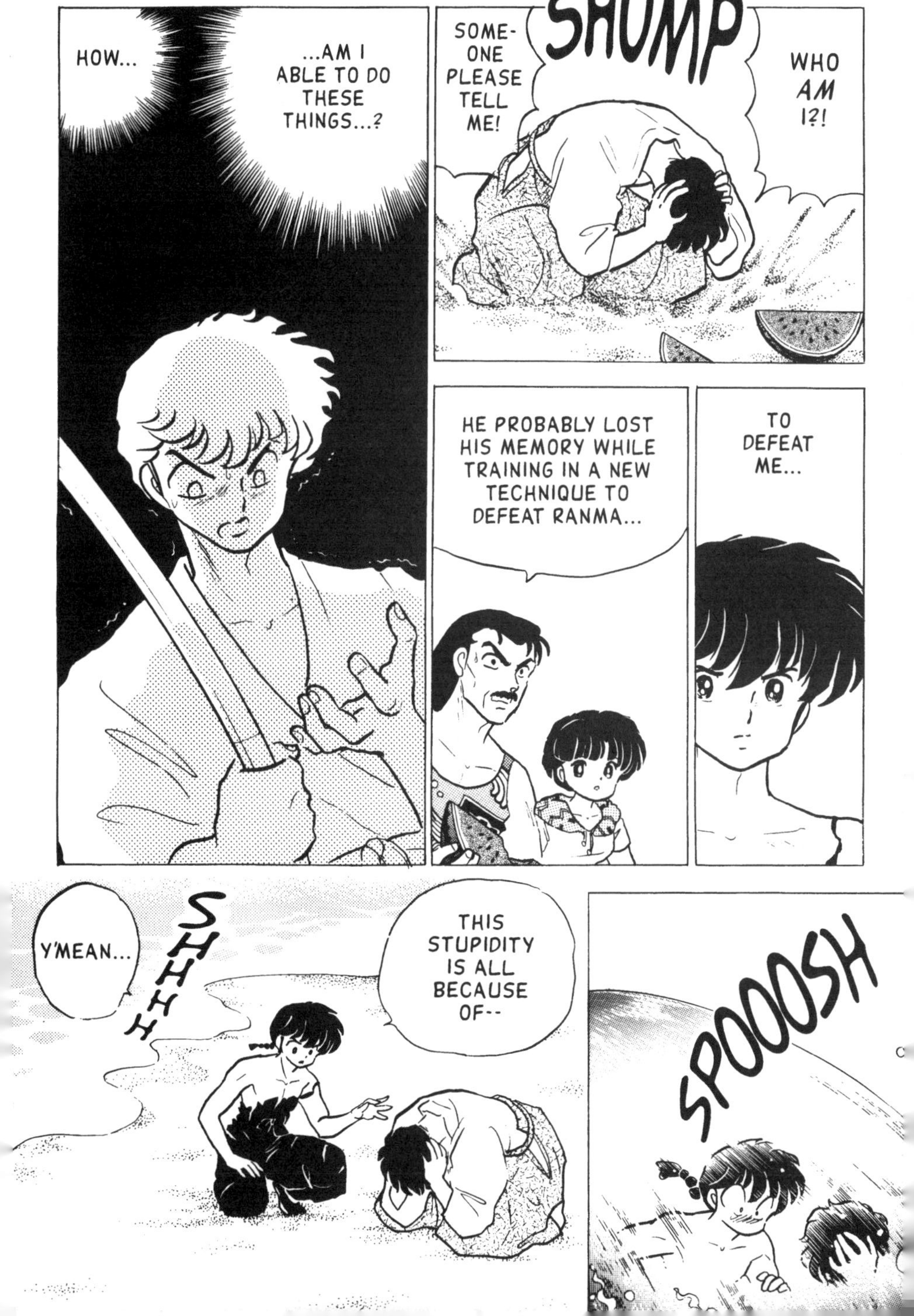
HOW...
...AM I ABLE TO DO THESE THINGS...?
SOME-ONE PLEASE TELL ME!
SHUMP
WHO AM I?!
HE PROBABLY LOST HIS MEMORY WHILE TRAINING IN A NEW TECHNIQUE TO DEFEAT RANMA...
TO DEFEAT ME...
Y'MEAN...
SHHHH
THIS STUPIDITY IS ALL BECAUSE OF--
SPOOOSH

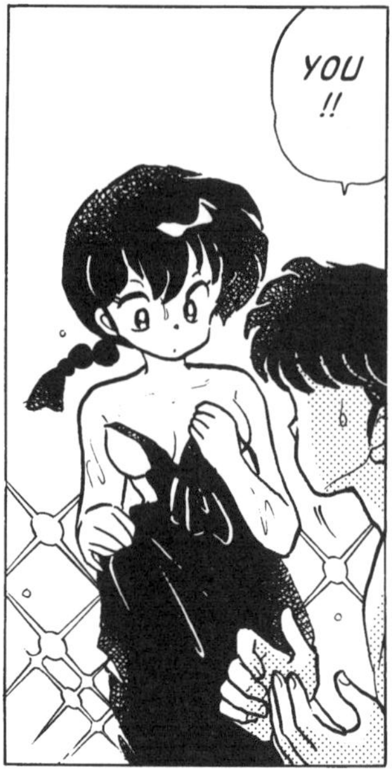
YOU !!

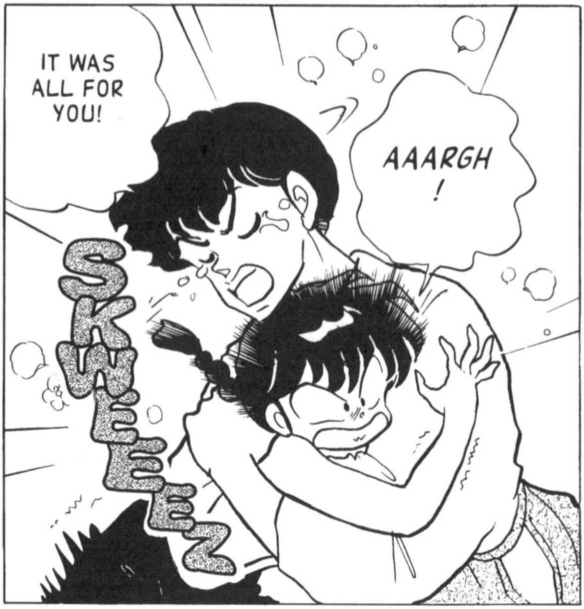
IT WAS ALL FOR YOU!
AAARGH !
SKWEEEZ

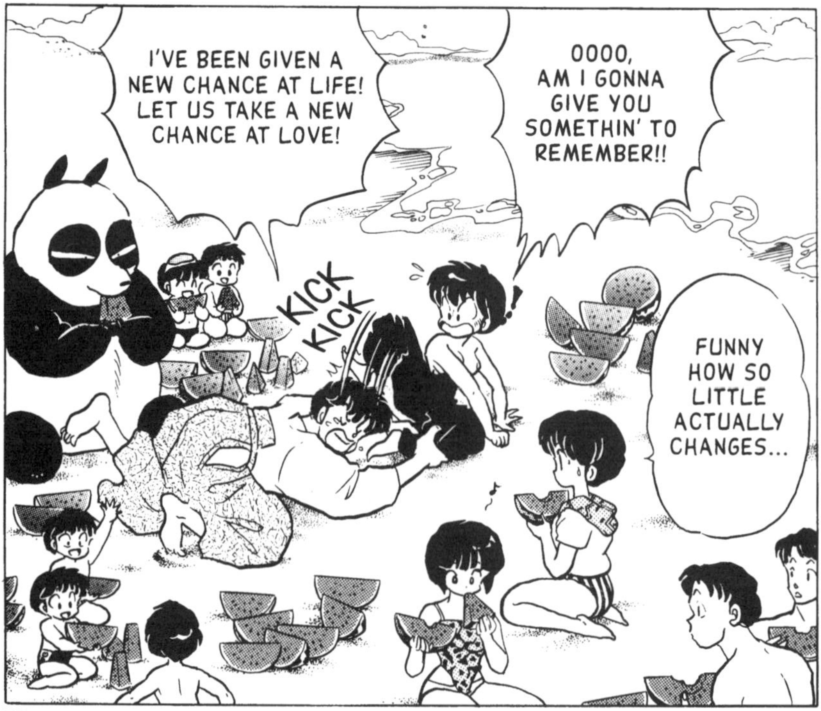
I'VE BEEN GIVEN A NEW CHANCE AT LIFE! LET US TAKE A NEW CHANCE AT LOVE!
OOOO, AM I GONNA GIVE YOU SOMETHIN' TO REMEMBER!!
KICK KICK
FUNNY HOW SO LITTLE ACTUALLY CHANGES...

Part 2

THE HORROR OF PARTY BEACH

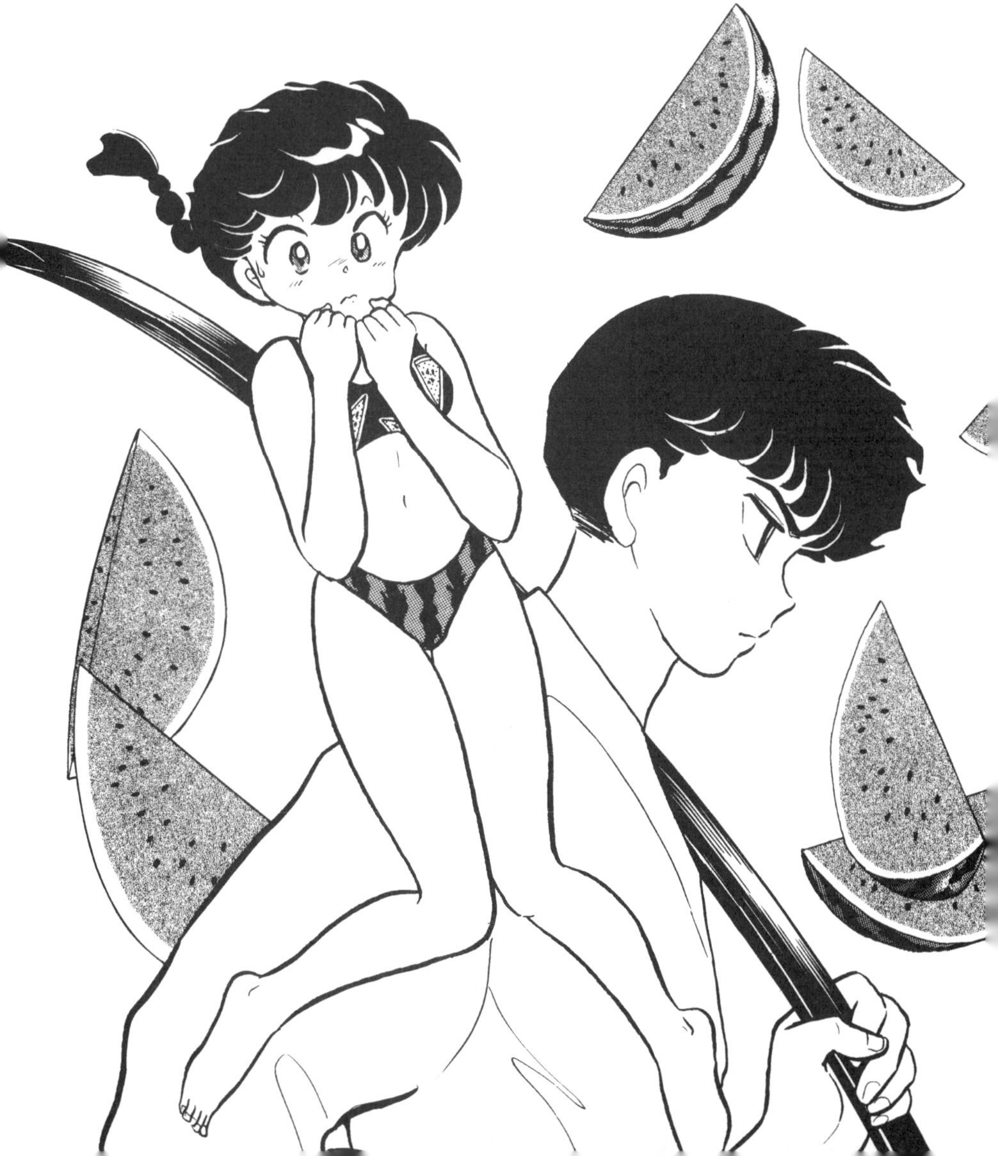

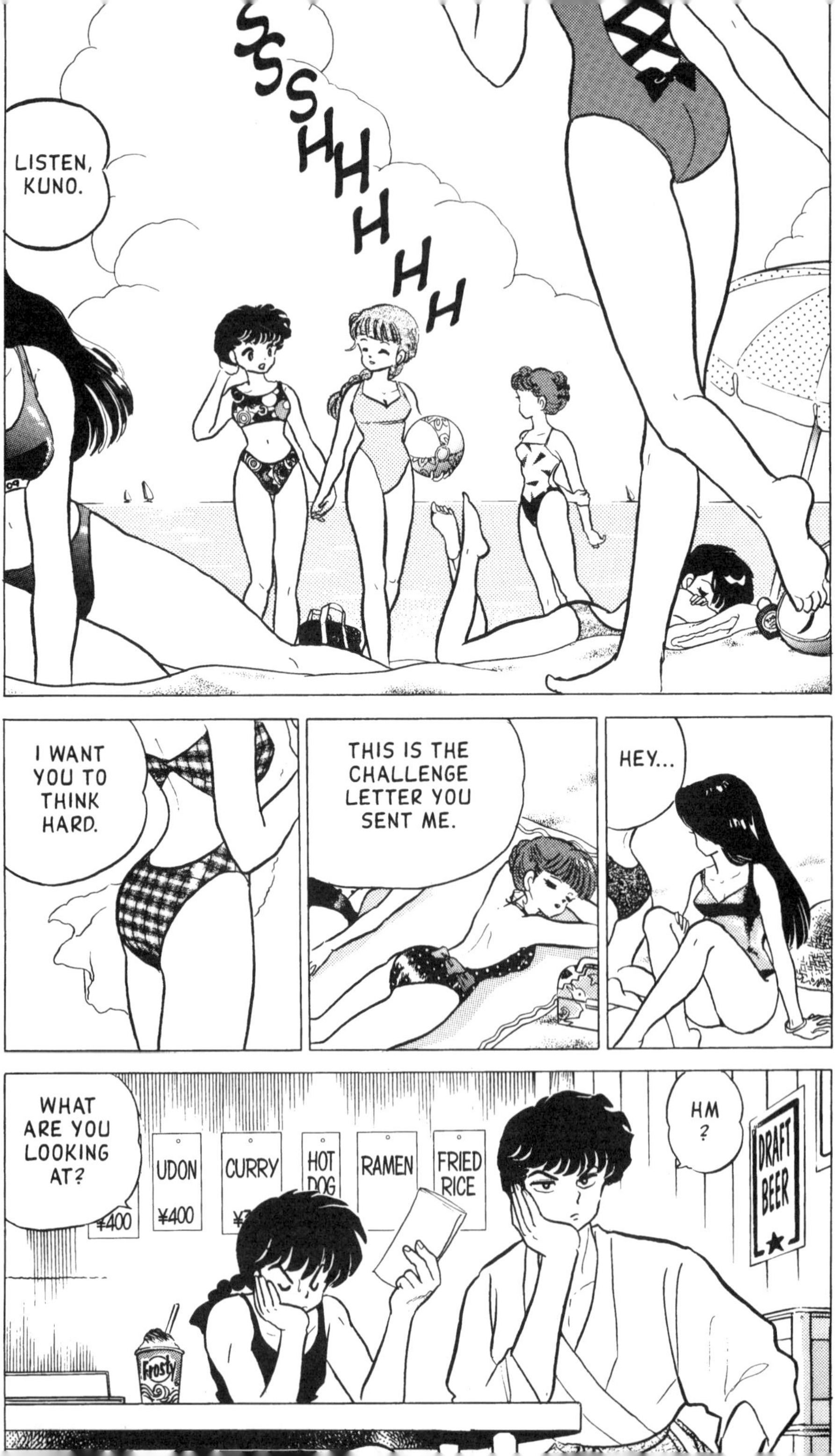
SSSHHHHHH
LISTEN, KUNO.
I WANT YOU TO THINK HARD.
THIS IS THE CHALLENGE LETTER YOU SENT ME.
HEY...
WHAT ARE YOU LOOKING AT?
UDON ¥400
CURRY
HOT DOG
RAMEN
FRIED RICE
¥400
HM?
DRAFT BEER
Frosty

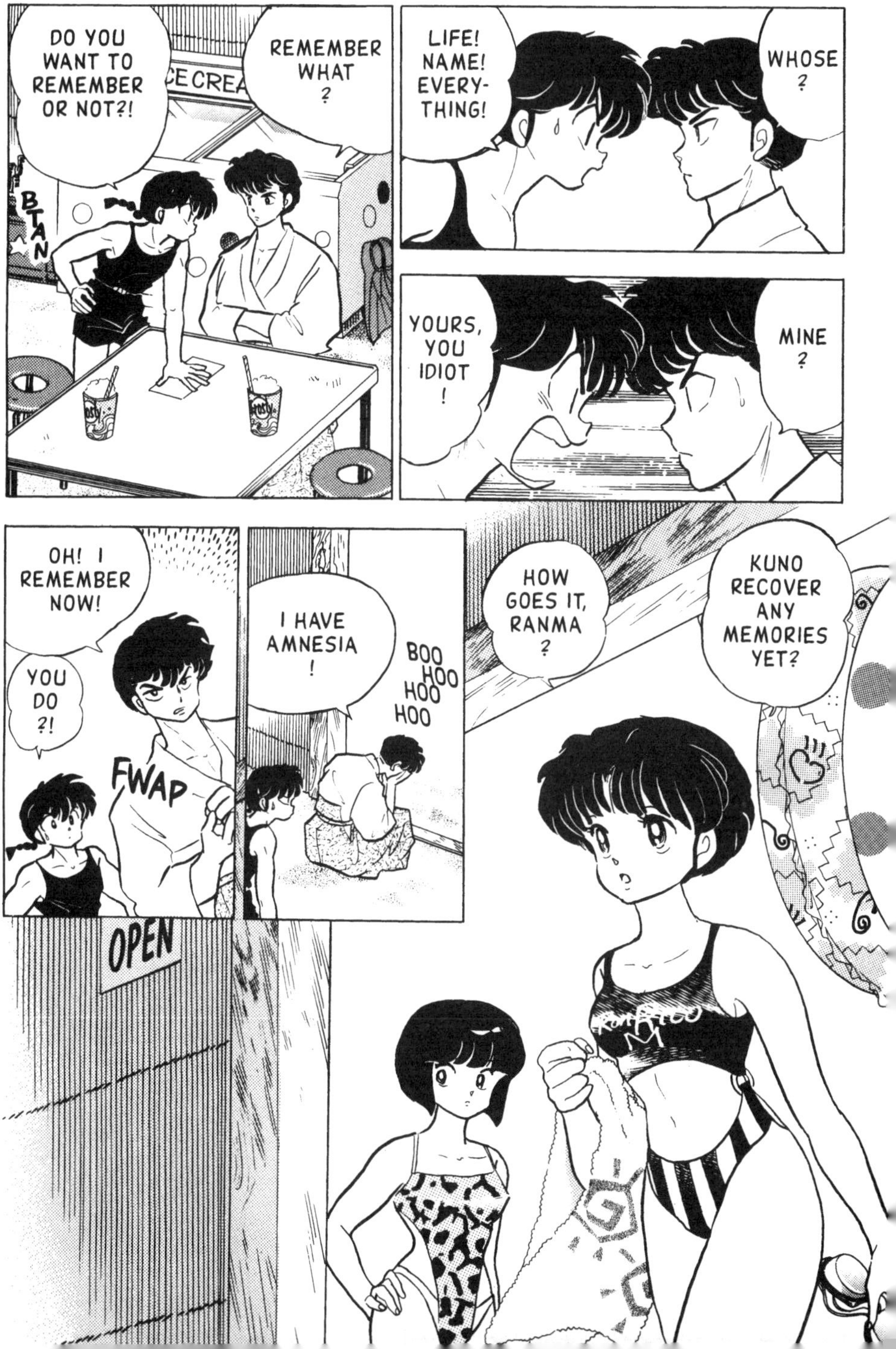
DO YOU WANT TO REMEMBER OR NOT?!
REMEMBER WHAT?
BTAN
LIFE! NAME! EVERY-THING!
WHOSE?
YOURS, YOU IDIOT!
MINE?
OH! I REMEMBER NOW!
YOU DO?!
FWAP
I HAVE AMNESIA!
BOO HOO HOO HOO
HOW GOES IT, RANMA?
KUNO RECOVER ANY MEMORIES YET?
OPEN

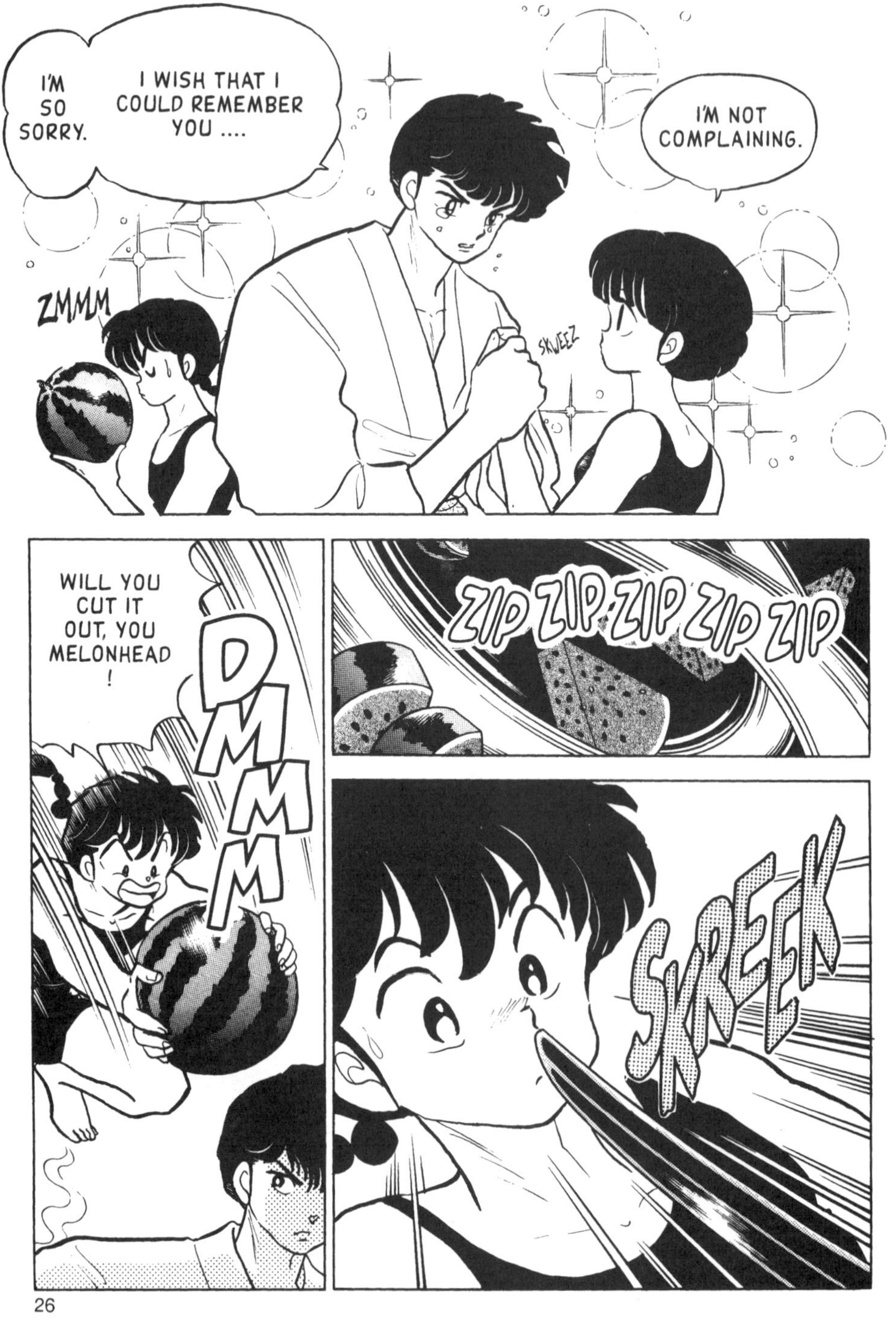
I'M SO SORRY.
I WISH THAT I COULD REMEMBER YOU ....
I'M NOT COMPLAINING.
ZMMM
SKWEEZ
WILL YOU CUT IT OUT, YOU MELONHEAD !
DMMMM
ZIP ZIP ZIP ZIP ZIP
SKREEK

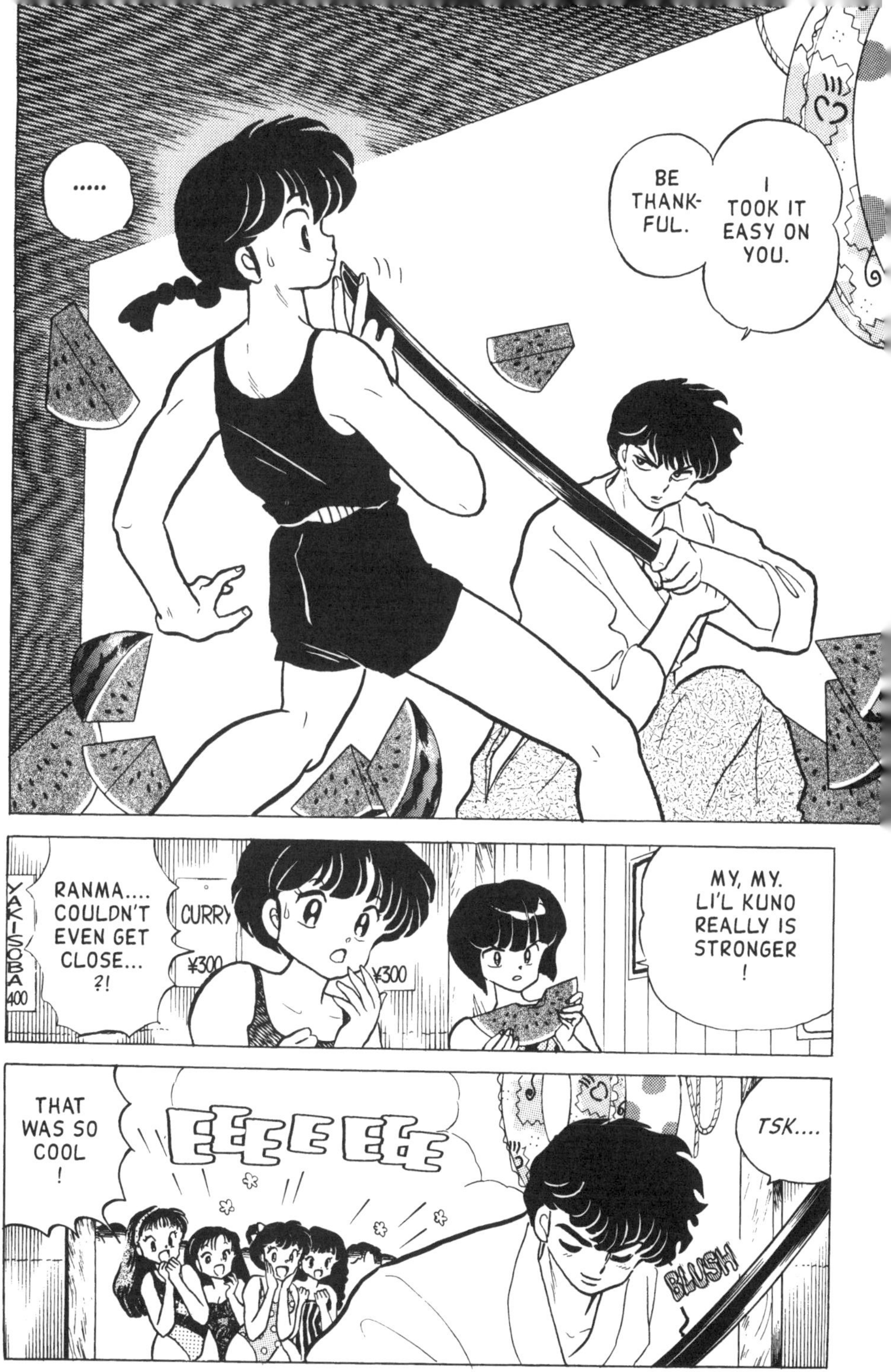
......
BE THANKFUL.
I TOOK IT EASY ON YOU.
YAKISOBA 400
RANMA.... COULDN'T EVEN GET CLOSE...?!
CURRY
¥300
¥300
MY, MY. LI'L KUNO REALLY IS STRONGER!
THAT WAS SO COOL!
EEEEEEE
TSK....
BLUSH

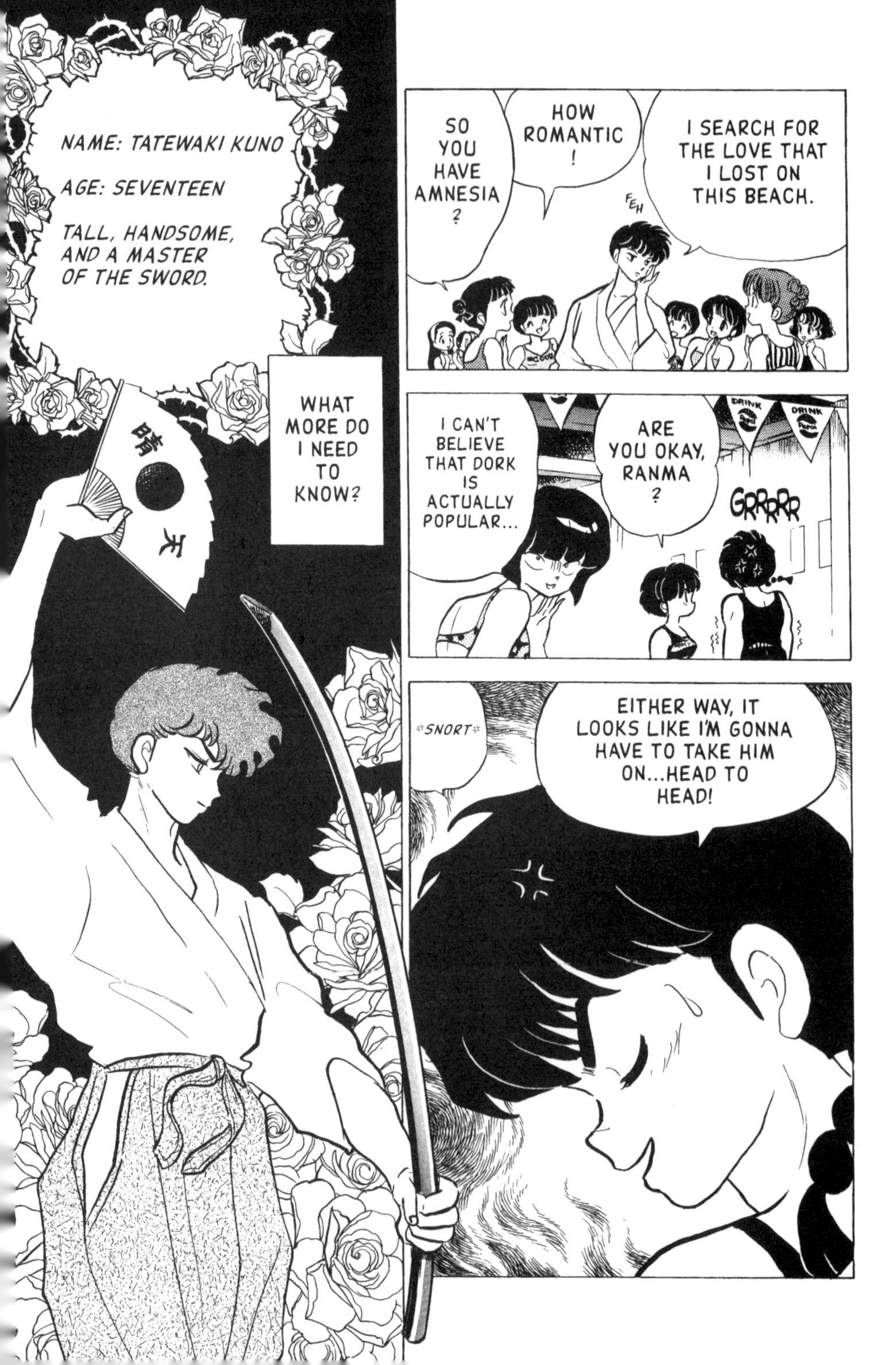

NAME: TATEWAKI KUNO
AGE: SEVENTEEN
TALL, HANDSOME, AND A MASTER OF THE SWORD.
晴
天
WHAT MORE DO I NEED TO KNOW?
SO YOU HAVE AMNESIA?
HOW ROMANTIC!
I SEARCH FOR THE LOVE THAT I LOST ON THIS BEACH.
FEH
I CAN'T BELIEVE THAT DORK IS ACTUALLY POPULAR...
ARE YOU OKAY, RANMA?
GRRRRR
SNORT
EITHER WAY, IT LOOKS LIKE I'M GONNA HAVE TO TAKE HIM ON...HEAD TO HEAD!

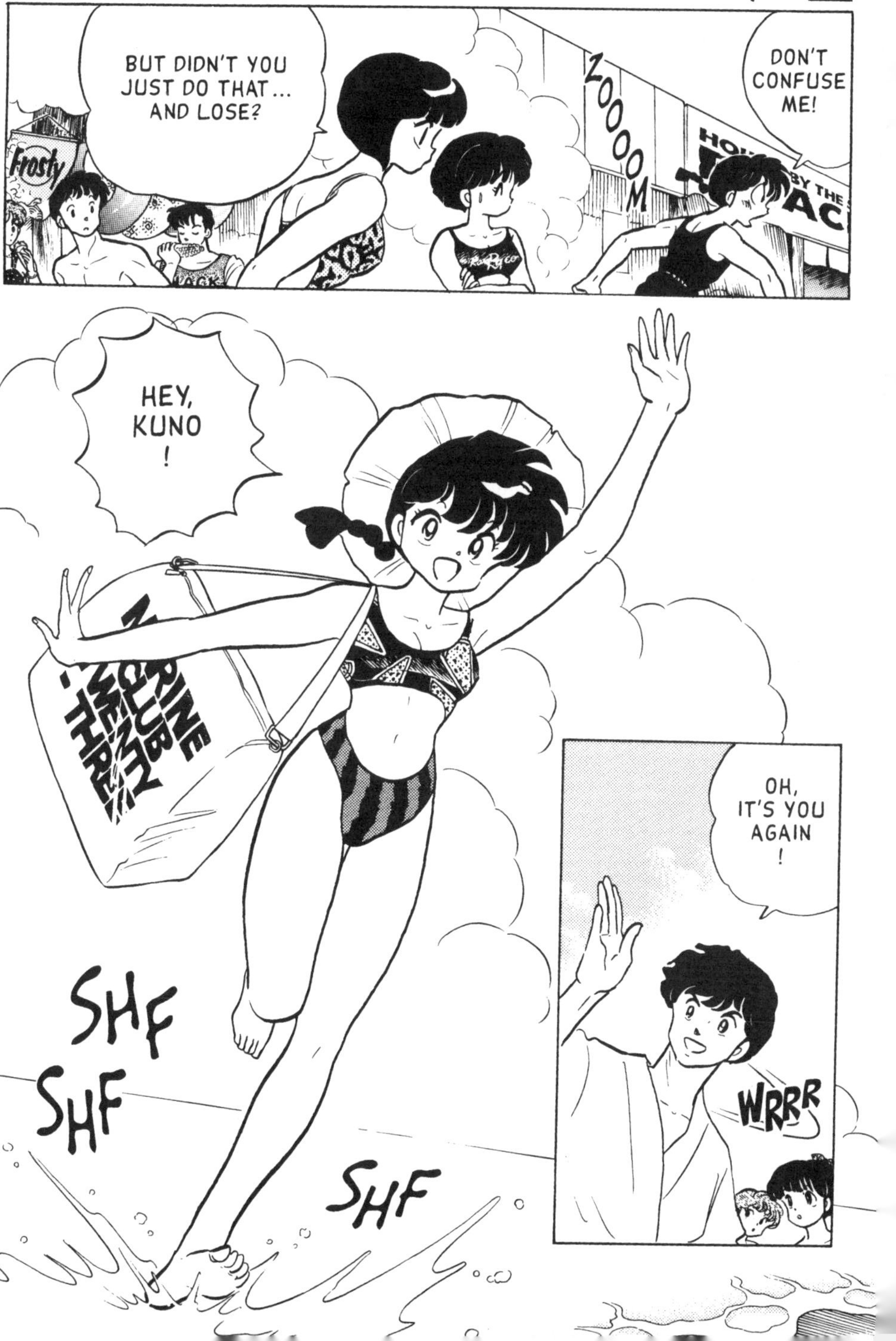
Frosty
BUT DIDN'T YOU JUST DO THAT... AND LOSE?
ZOOOOM
DON'T CONFUSE ME!
HEY, KUNO!
SHF
SHF
SHF
OH, IT'S YOU AGAIN!
WRRR

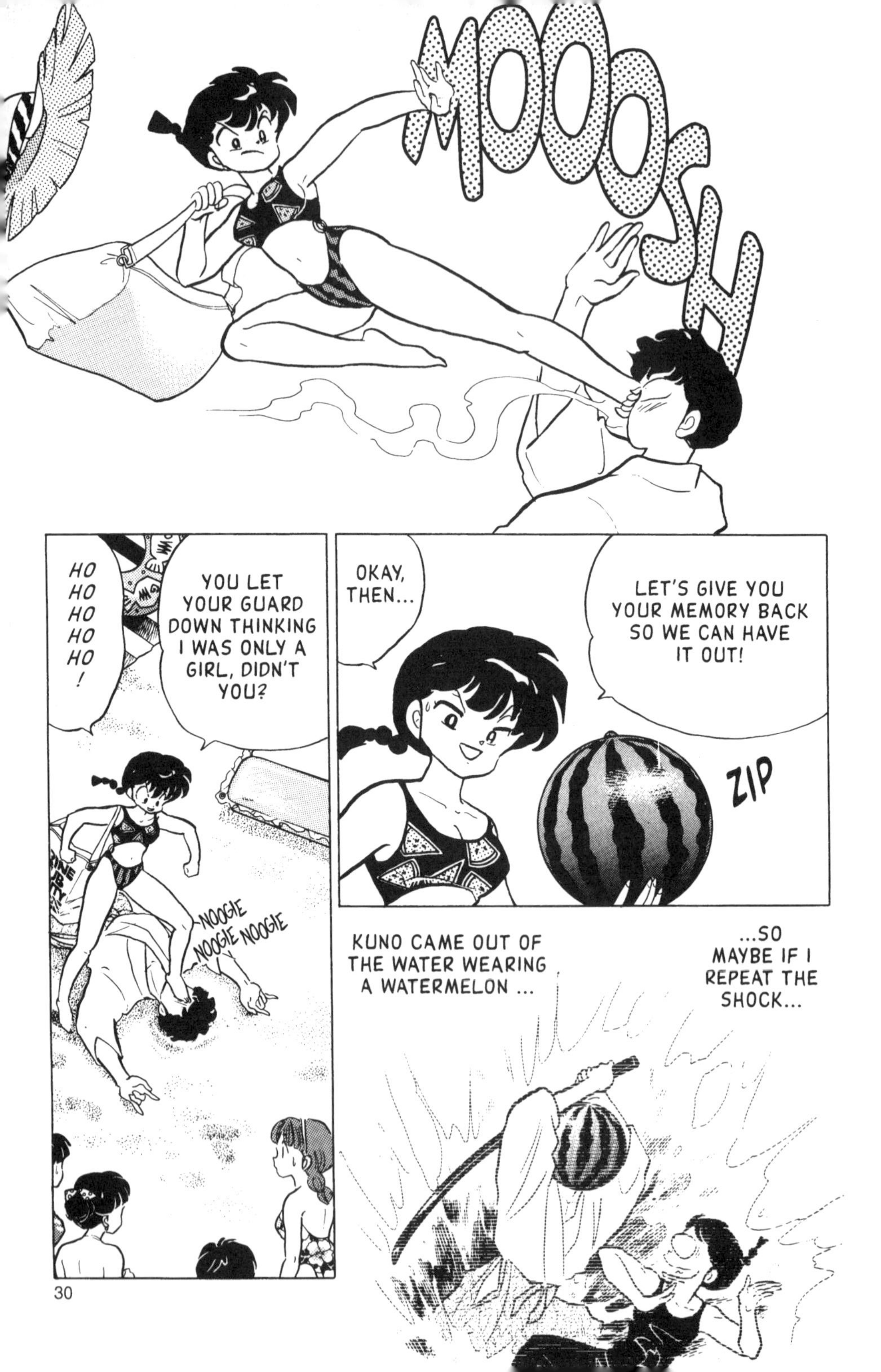
MOOOSH
HO HO HO HO HO!
YOU LET YOUR GUARD DOWN THINKING I WAS ONLY A GIRL, DIDN'T YOU?
NOOGIE NOOGIE NOOGIE
OKAY, THEN...
LET'S GIVE YOU YOUR MEMORY BACK SO WE CAN HAVE IT OUT!
ZIP
KUNO CAME OUT OF THE WATER WEARING A WATERMELON ...
...SO MAYBE IF I REPEAT THE SHOCK...

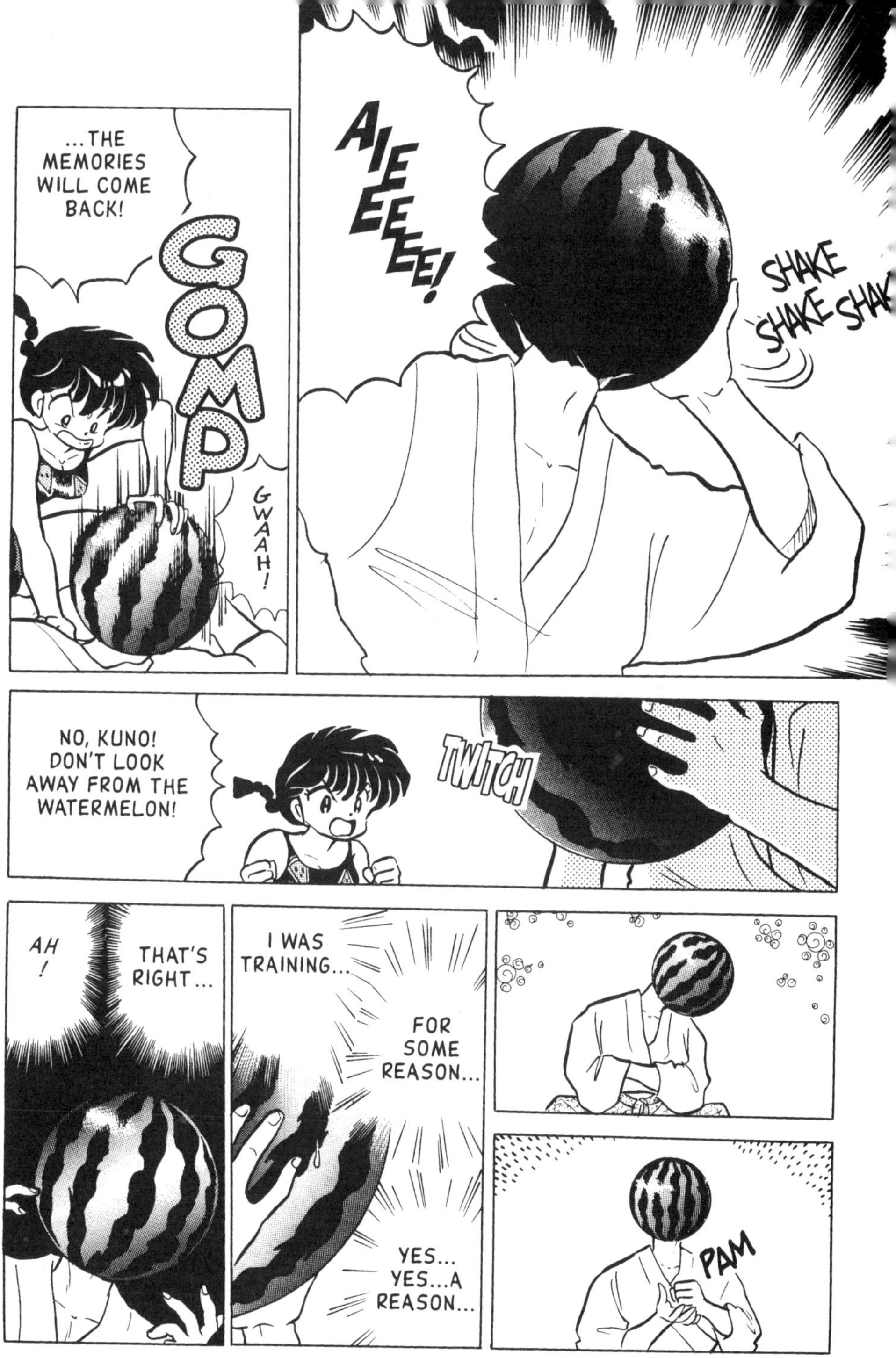
...THE MEMORIES WILL COME BACK!
GOMP
GWAAH!
AIEEEEEE!
SHAKE SHAKE SHAK
NO, KUNO! DON'T LOOK AWAY FROM THE WATERMELON!
TWITCH
AH!
THAT'S RIGHT...
I WAS TRAINING...
FOR SOME REASON...
YES... YES...A REASON...
PAM

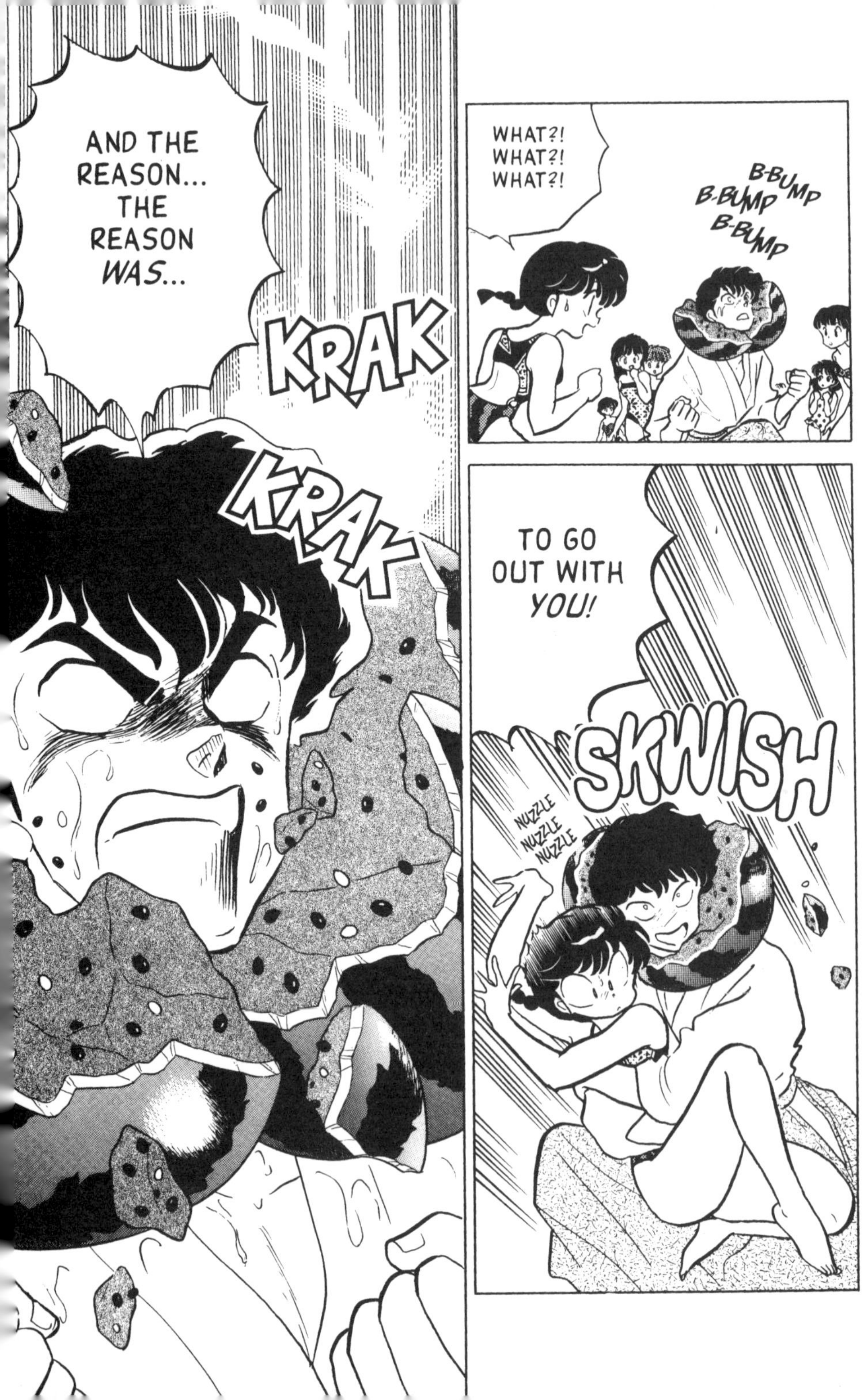
AND THE REASON... THE REASON WAS...
KRAK
KRAK
WHAT?! WHAT?! WHAT?!
B-BUMP B-BUMP B-BUMP
TO GO OUT WITH YOU!
SKWISH
NUZZLE NUZZLE NUZZLE

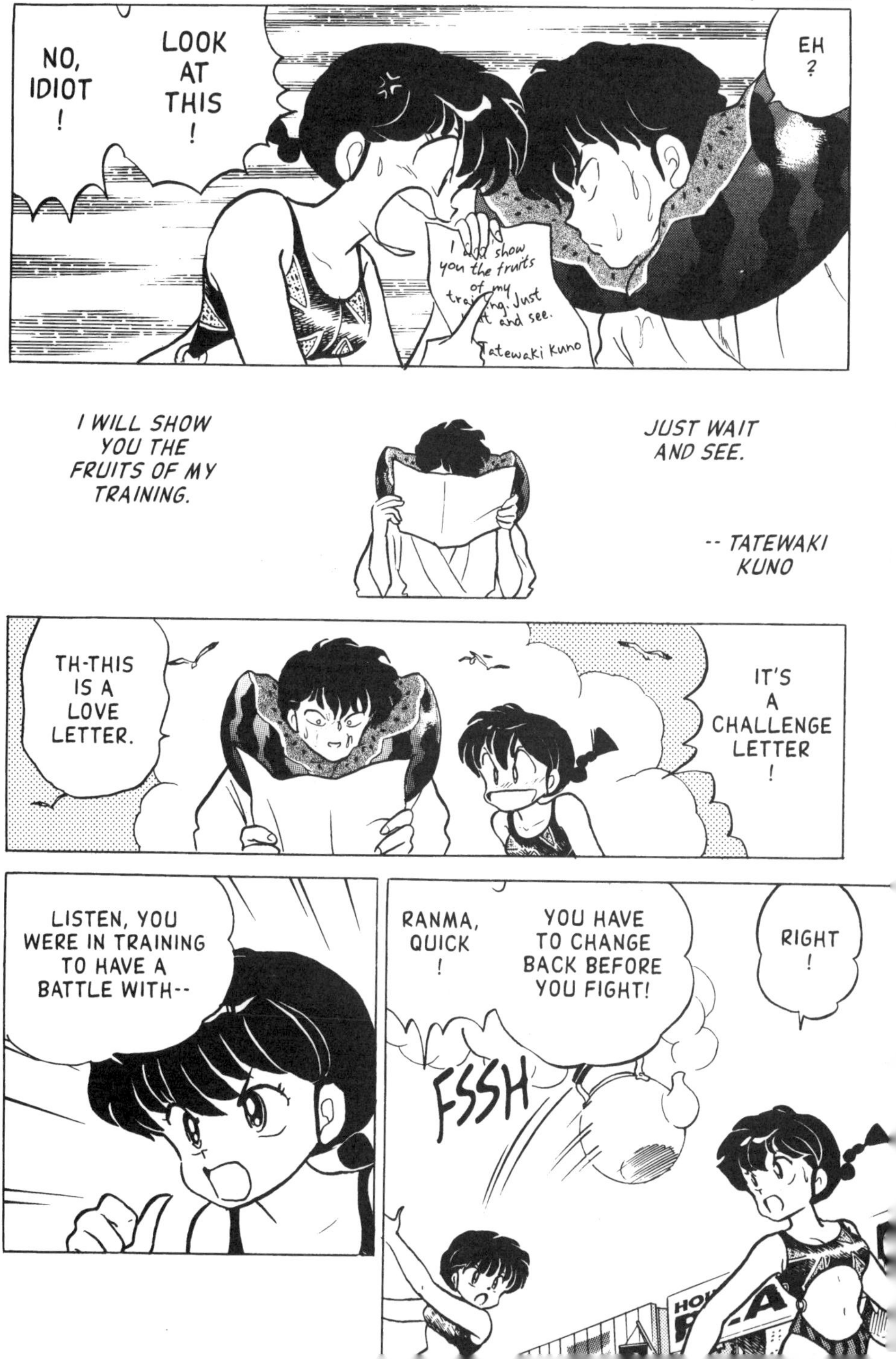
NO, IDIOT!
LOOK AT THIS!
EH?
I WILL SHOW YOU THE FRUITS OF MY TRAINING.
JUST WAIT AND SEE.
-- TATEWAKI KUNO
TH-THIS IS A LOVE LETTER.
IT'S A CHALLENGE LETTER!
LISTEN, YOU WERE IN TRAINING TO HAVE A BATTLE WITH--
RANMA, QUICK!
YOU HAVE TO CHANGE BACK BEFORE YOU FIGHT!
RIGHT!
FSSH

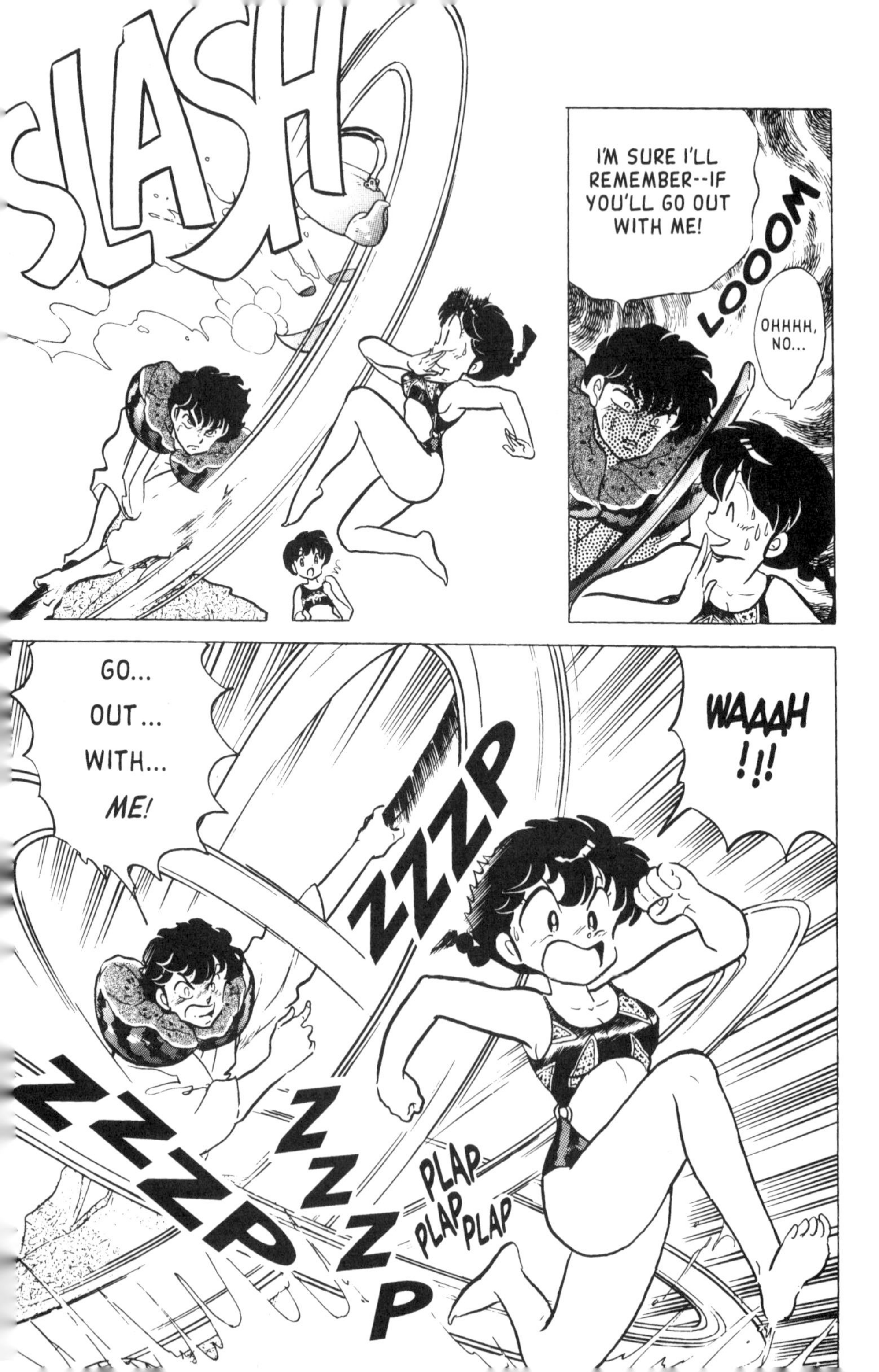
SLASH
I'M SURE I'LL REMEMBER--IF YOU'LL GO OUT WITH ME!
LOOOM
OHHHH, NO...
GO... OUT... WITH... ME!
WAAAH !!!
ZZZP
ZZZP
ZZZP
PLAP PLAP PLAP

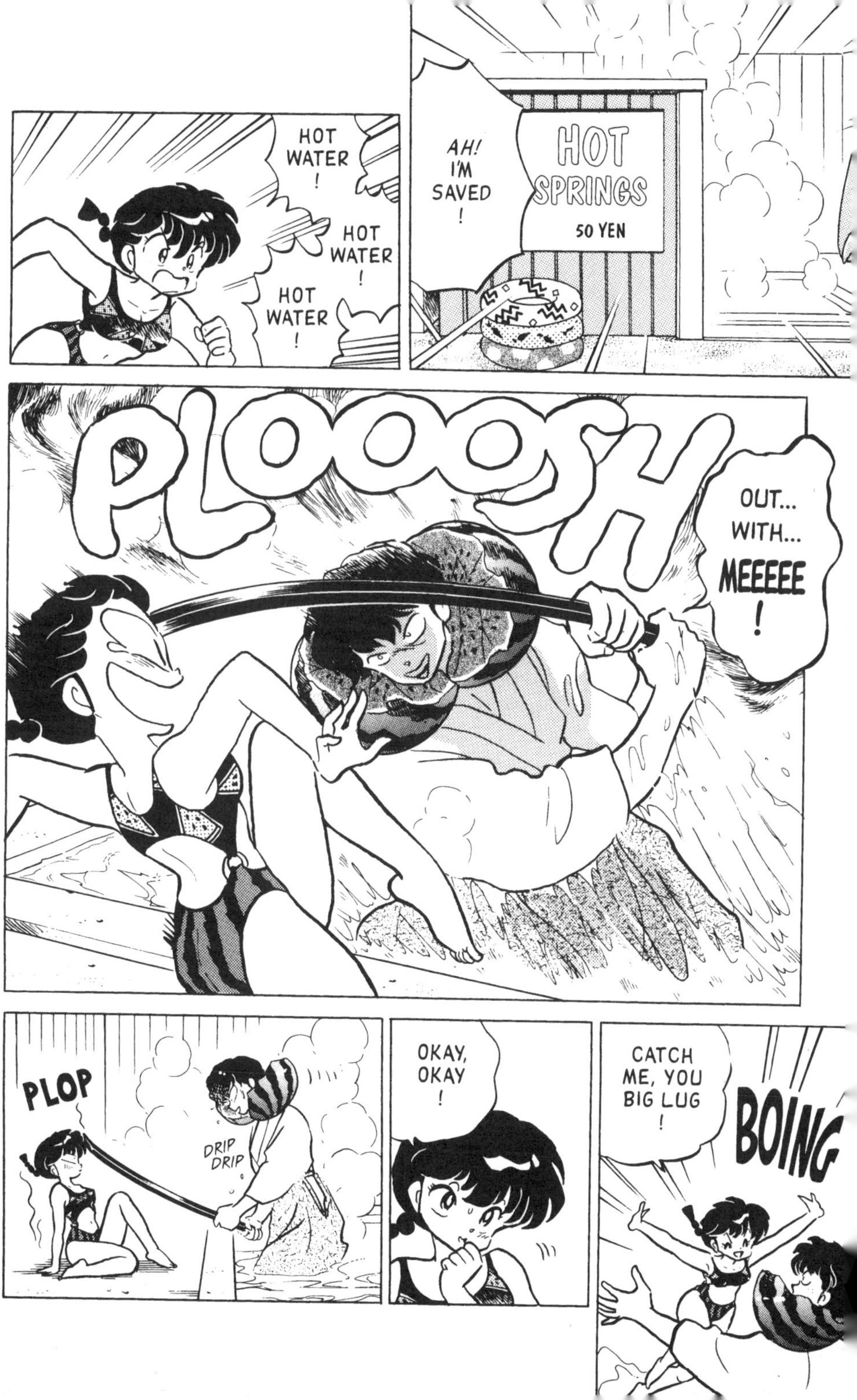
HOT WATER !
HOT WATER !
HOT WATER !
AH! I'M SAVED !
HOT SPRINGS
50 YEN
PLOOOSH
OUT... WITH... MEEEEE !
PLOP
DRIP DRIP
OKAY, OKAY !
CATCH ME, YOU BIG LUG !
BOING

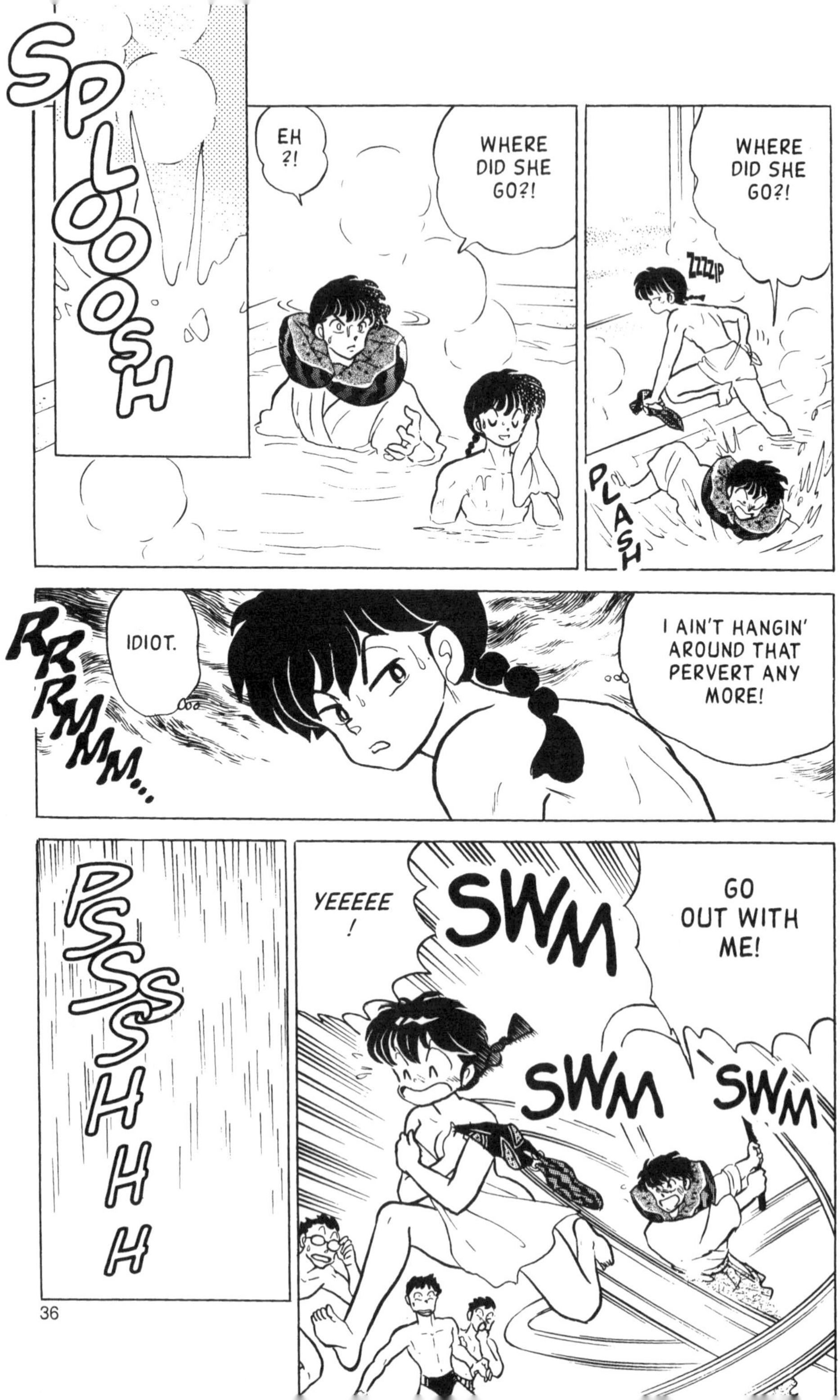
SPLOOOOSH
EH ?!
WHERE DID SHE GO?!
WHERE DID SHE GO?!
ZZZZIP
PLASH
RRRMMM...
IDIOT.
I AIN'T HANGIN' AROUND THAT PERVERT ANY MORE!
PSSSSHHHH
YEEEEE !
SWM
GO OUT WITH ME!
SWM
SWM

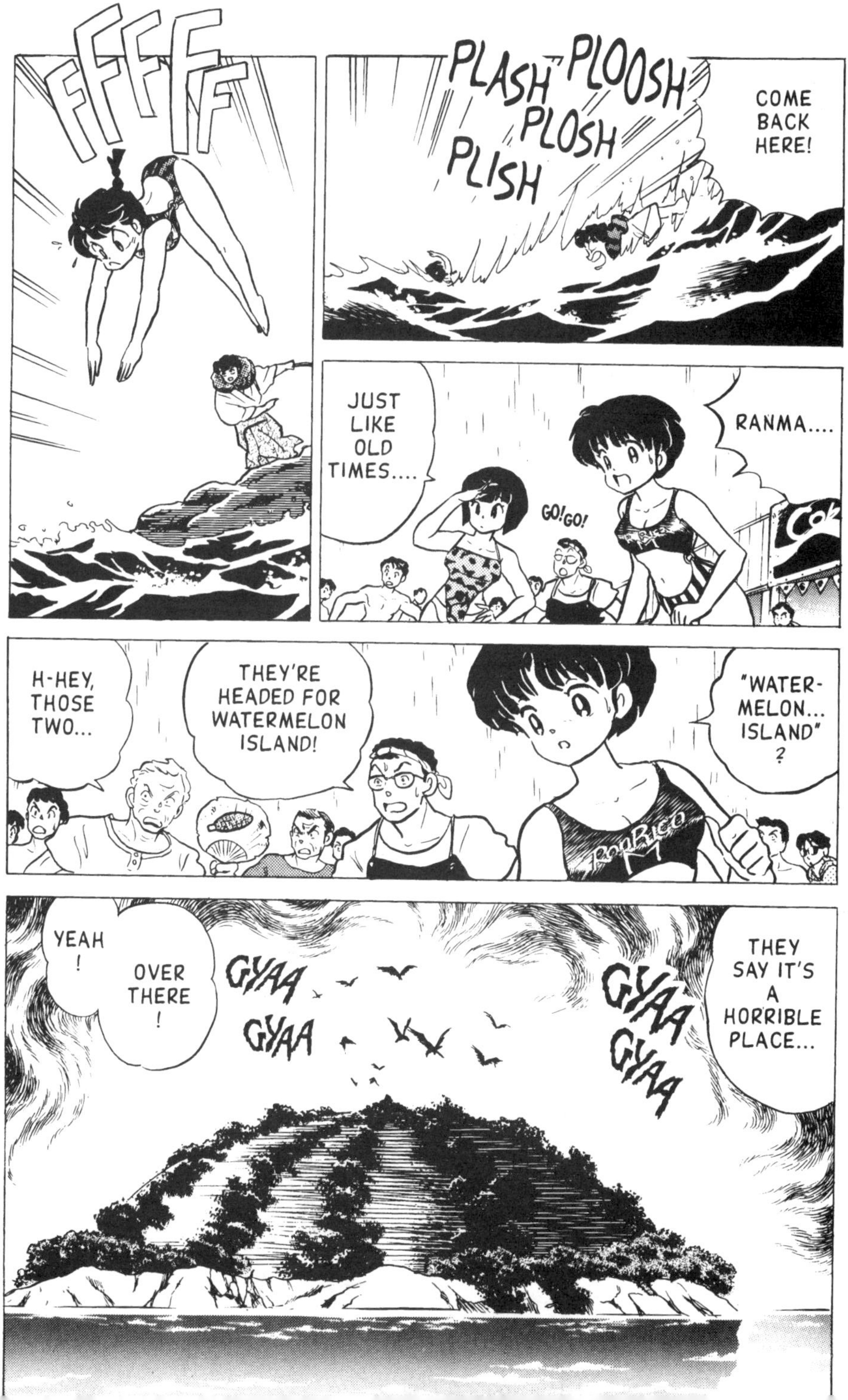
FFFFF
PLASH PLOOSH
PLOSH
PLISH
COME BACK HERE!
JUST LIKE OLD TIMES....
GO! GO!
RANMA....
H-HEY, THOSE TWO...
THEY'RE HEADED FOR WATERMELON ISLAND!
"WATER-MELON... ISLAND"?
YEAH!
OVER THERE!
GYAA GYAA
GYAA GYAA
THEY SAY IT'S A HORRIBLE PLACE...

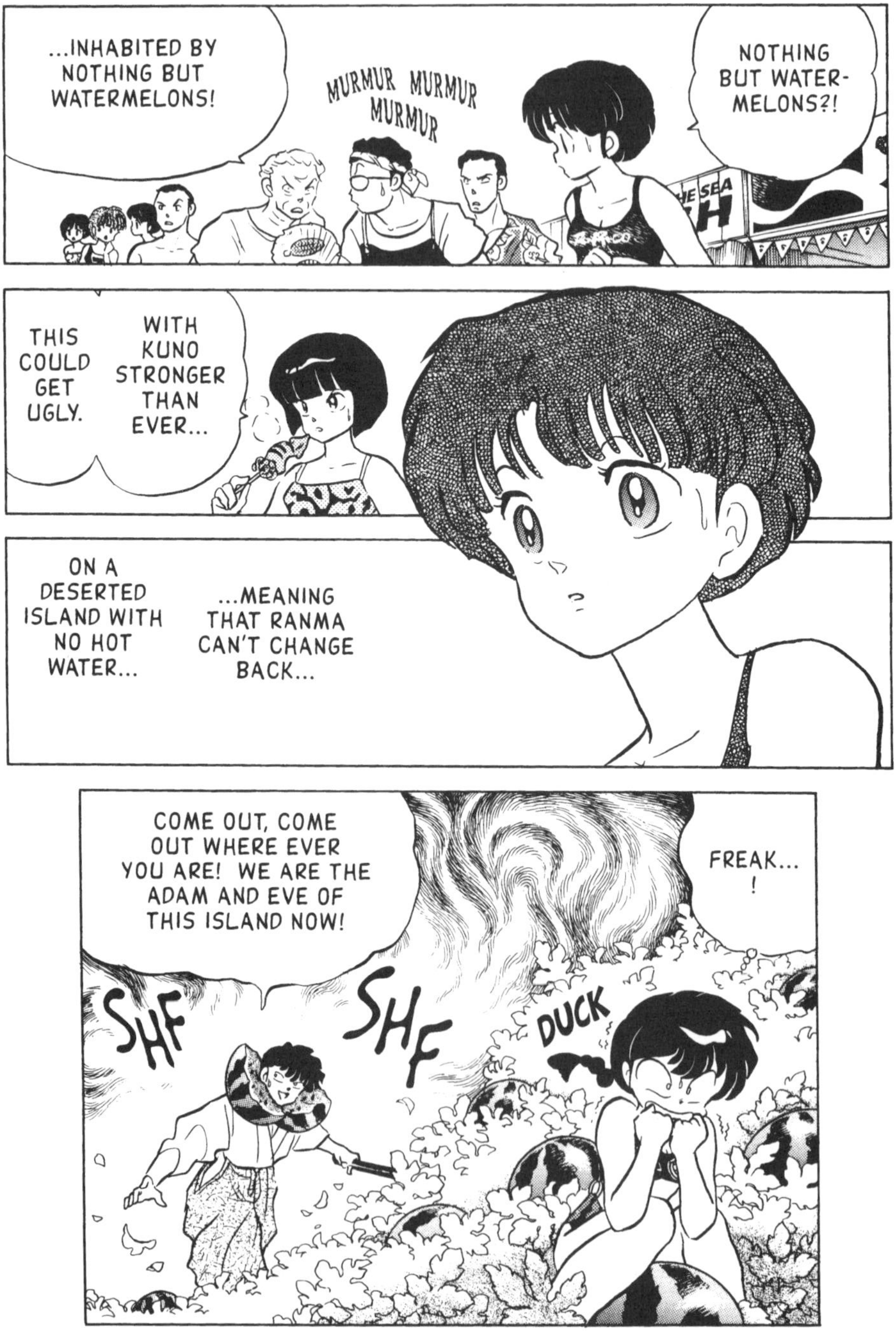
...INHABITED BY NOTHING BUT WATERMELONS!
MURMUR MURMUR MURMUR
NOTHING BUT WATER-MELONS?!
THIS COULD GET UGLY.
WITH KUNO STRONGER THAN EVER...
ON A DESERTED ISLAND WITH NO HOT WATER...
...MEANING THAT RANMA CAN'T CHANGE BACK...
COME OUT, COME OUT WHERE EVER YOU ARE! WE ARE THE ADAM AND EVE OF THIS ISLAND NOW!
FREAK... !
SHF
SHF
DUCK

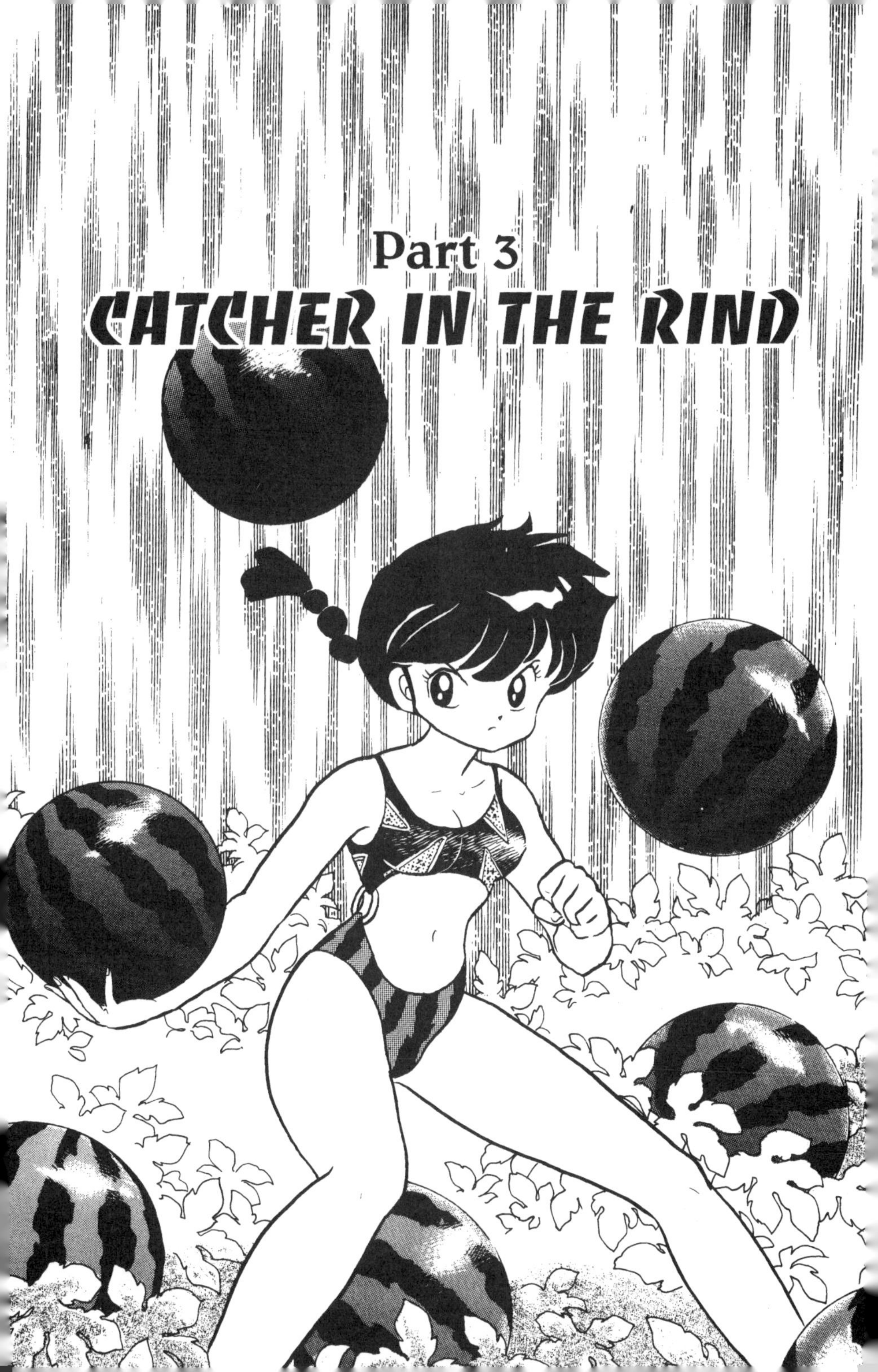
Part 3
CATCHER IN THE RIND

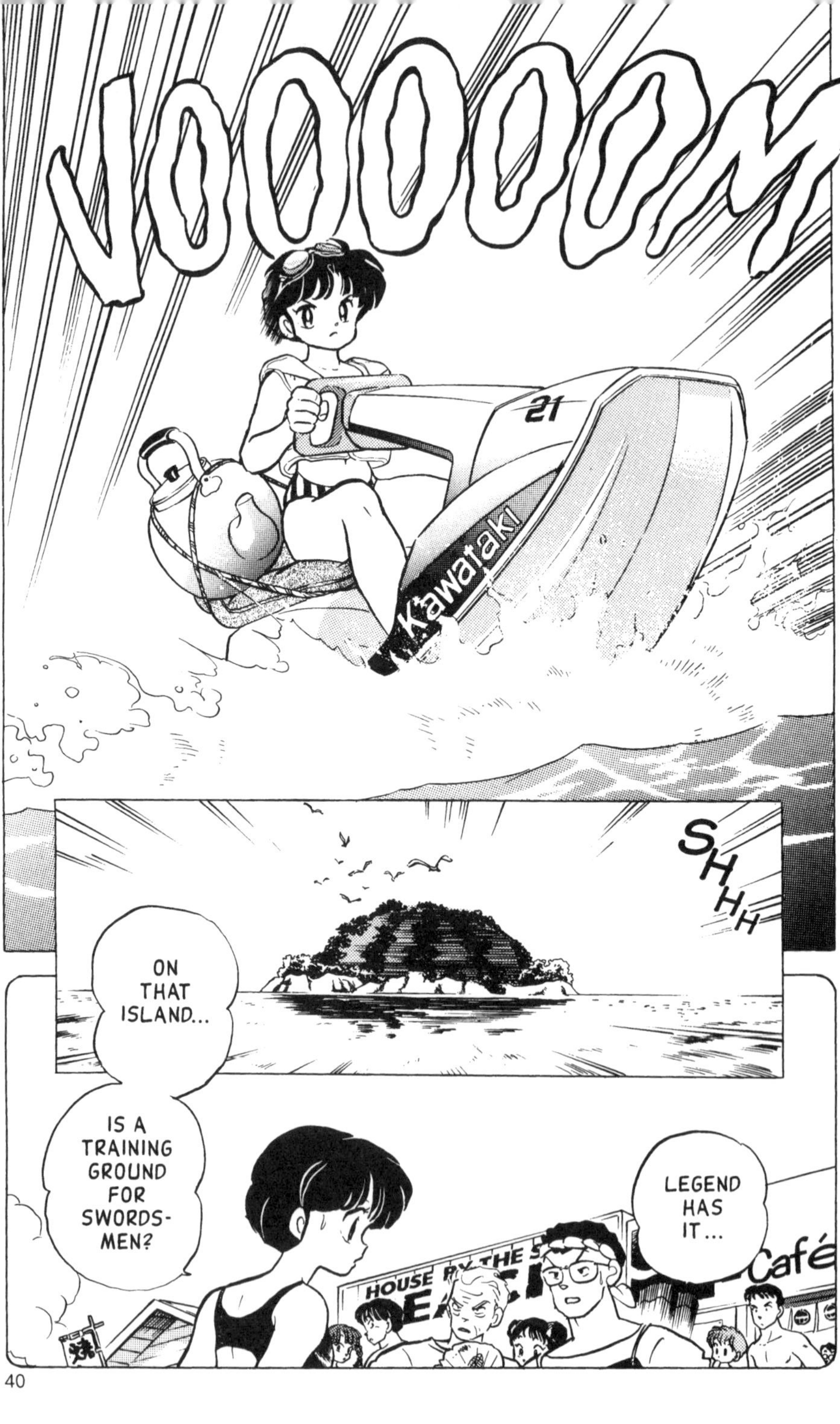
VOOOOOM
21
Kawataki
SHHH
ON THAT ISLAND...
IS A TRAINING GROUND FOR SWORDS-MEN?
LEGEND HAS IT...
Café

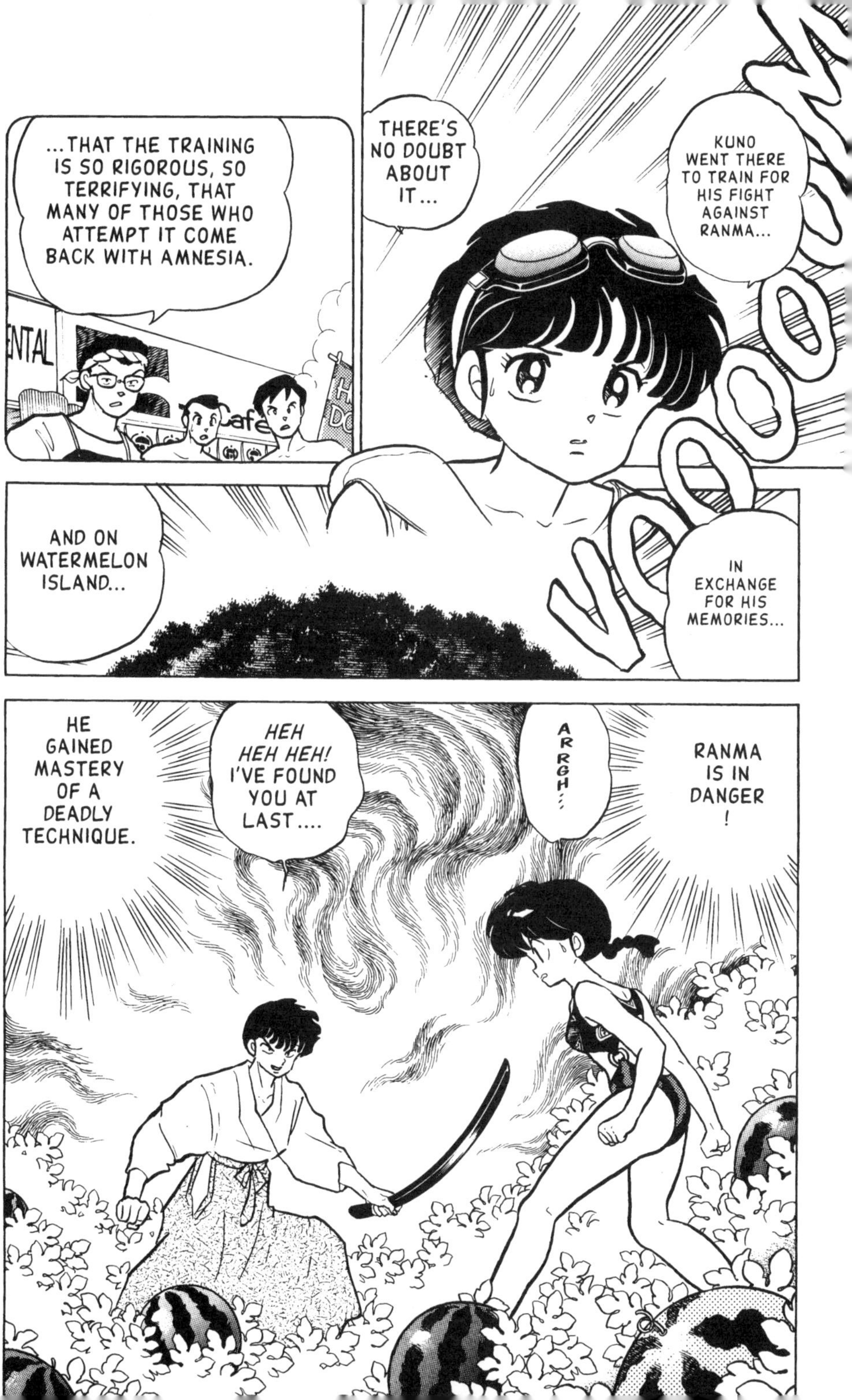
...THAT THE TRAINING IS SO RIGOROUS, SO TERRIFYING, THAT MANY OF THOSE WHO ATTEMPT IT COME BACK WITH AMNESIA.
Cafe
THERE'S NO DOUBT ABOUT IT...
KUNO WENT THERE TO TRAIN FOR HIS FIGHT AGAINST RANMA...
AND ON WATERMELON ISLAND...
IN EXCHANGE FOR HIS MEMORIES...
HE GAINED MASTERY OF A DEADLY TECHNIQUE.
HEH HEH HEH! I'VE FOUND YOU AT LAST....
ARRGH...
RANMA IS IN DANGER!

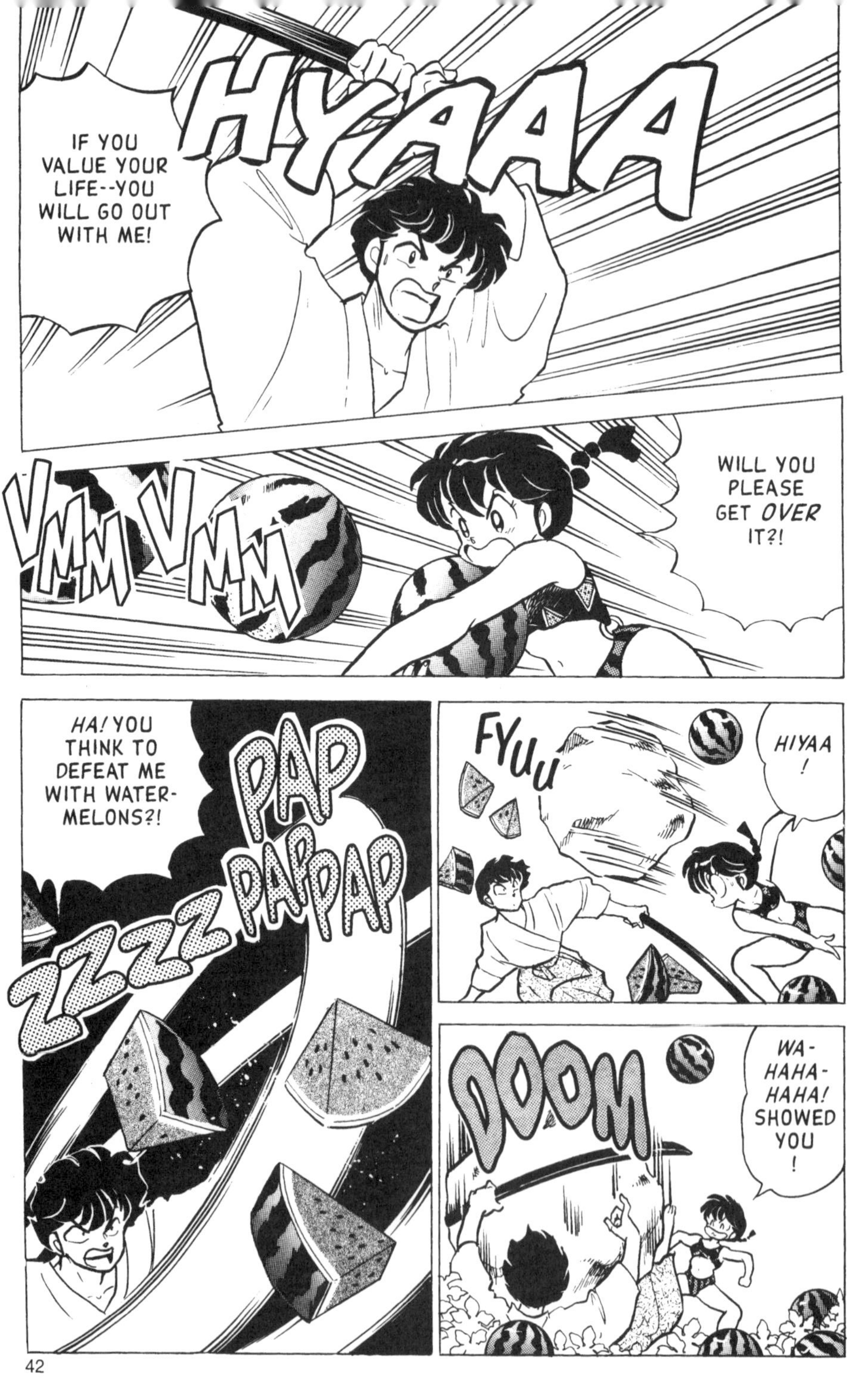
HYAAA
IF YOU VALUE YOUR LIFE--YOU WILL GO OUT WITH ME!
VMM VMM
WILL YOU PLEASE GET *OVER* IT?!
HA! YOU THINK TO DEFEAT ME WITH WATER-MELONS?!
PAP PAPPAP
ZZZZZ
FYUU
HIYAA!
DOOM
WA-HAHA-HAHA! SHOWED YOU!

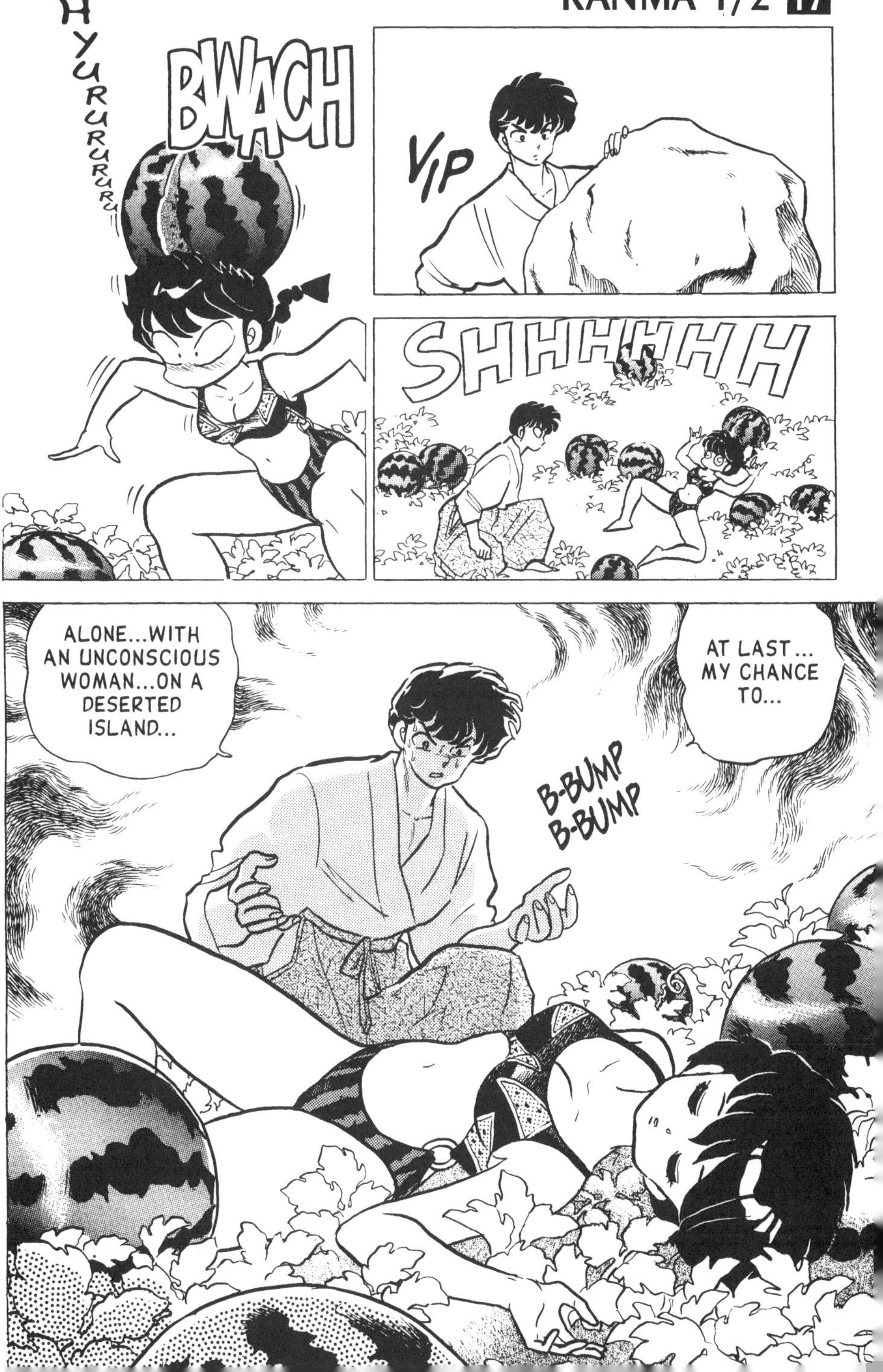
HYURURURURU
BWACH
VIP
SHHHHHH
ALONE...WITH AN UNCONSCIOUS WOMAN...ON A DESERTED ISLAND...
AT LAST... MY CHANCE TO...
B-BUMP B-BUMP

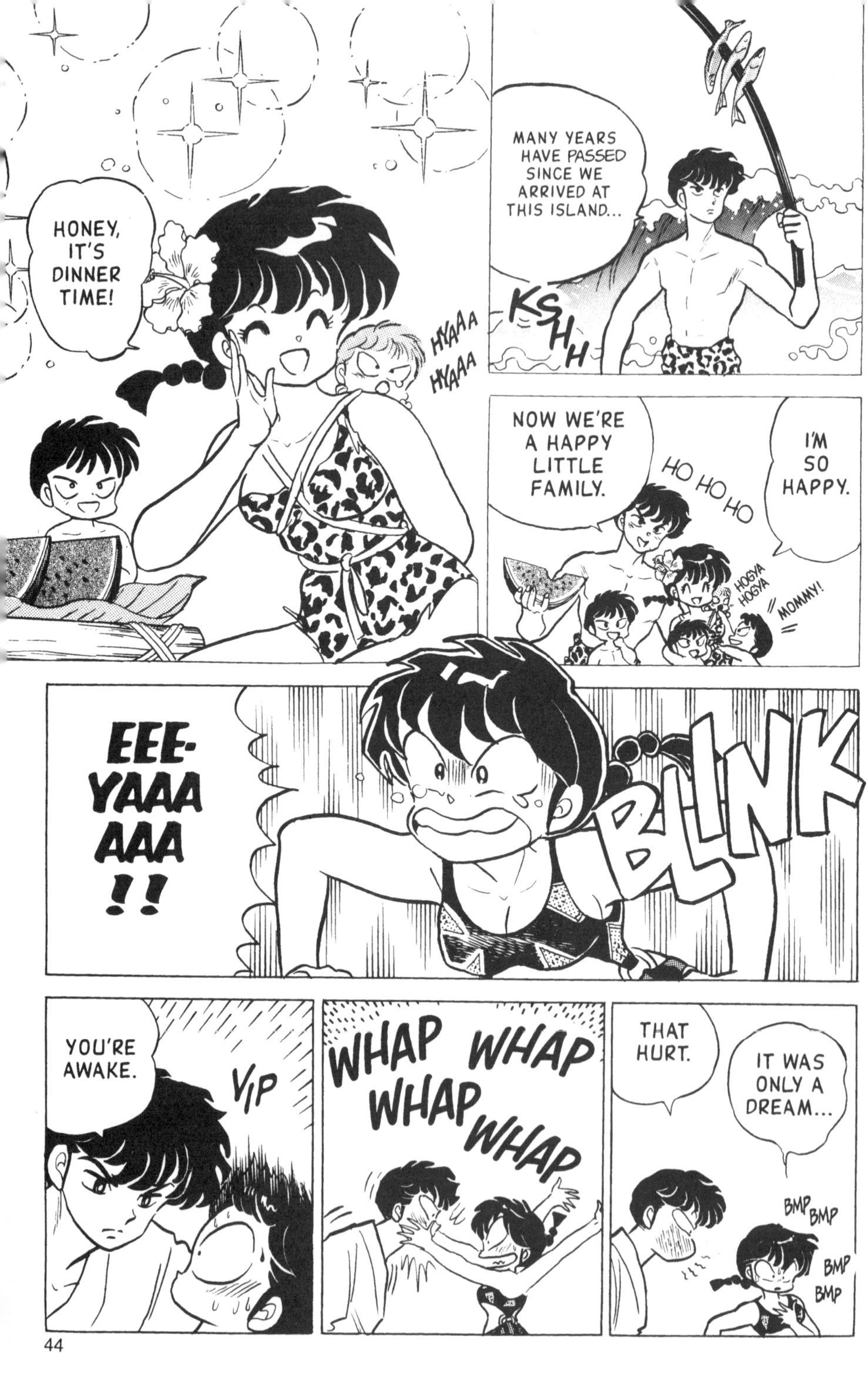
HONEY, IT'S DINNER TIME!
HYAAAA HYAAAA
MANY YEARS HAVE PASSED SINCE WE ARRIVED AT THIS ISLAND...
KSHH
NOW WE'RE A HAPPY LITTLE FAMILY.
HO HO HO
I'M SO HAPPY.
HOGYA HOGYA
MOMMY!
EEE-YAAAAAA!!
BLINK
YOU'RE AWAKE.
VIP
WHAP WHAP WHAP WHAP
THAT HURT.
IT WAS ONLY A DREAM...
BMP BMP BMP BMP

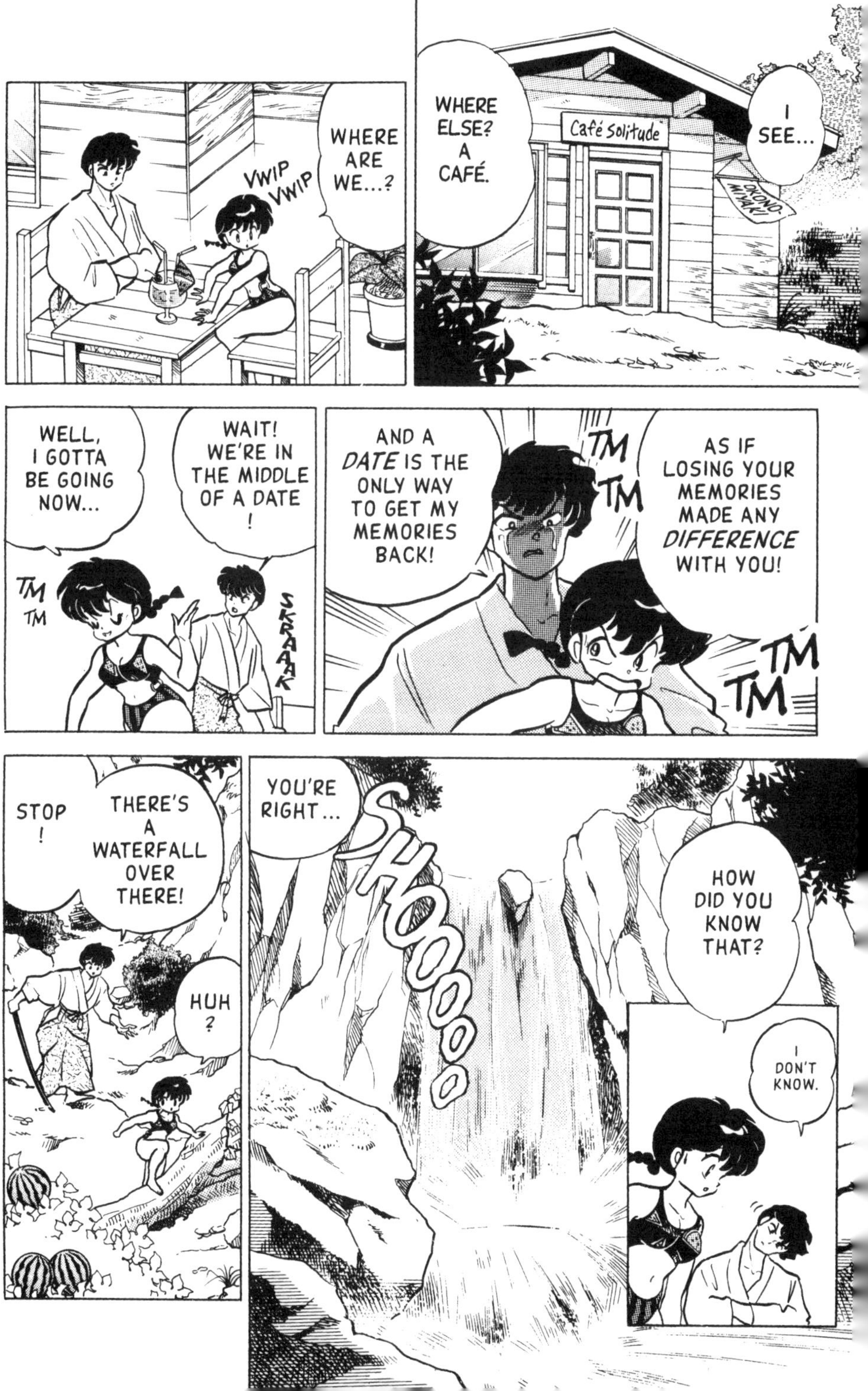
VWIP VWIP
WHERE ARE WE...?
WHERE ELSE? A CAFÉ.
Café Solitude
OKONOMIYAKI!
I SEE...
WELL, I GOTTA BE GOING NOW...
WAIT! WE'RE IN THE MIDDLE OF A DATE!
TM TM
SKRAAAK
AND A *DATE* IS THE ONLY WAY TO GET MY MEMORIES BACK!
TM TM
AS IF LOSING YOUR MEMORIES MADE ANY *DIFFERENCE* WITH YOU!
TM TM
STOP!
THERE'S A WATERFALL OVER THERE!
HUH?
YOU'RE RIGHT...
SHOOOOOO
HOW DID YOU KNOW THAT?
I DON'T KNOW.

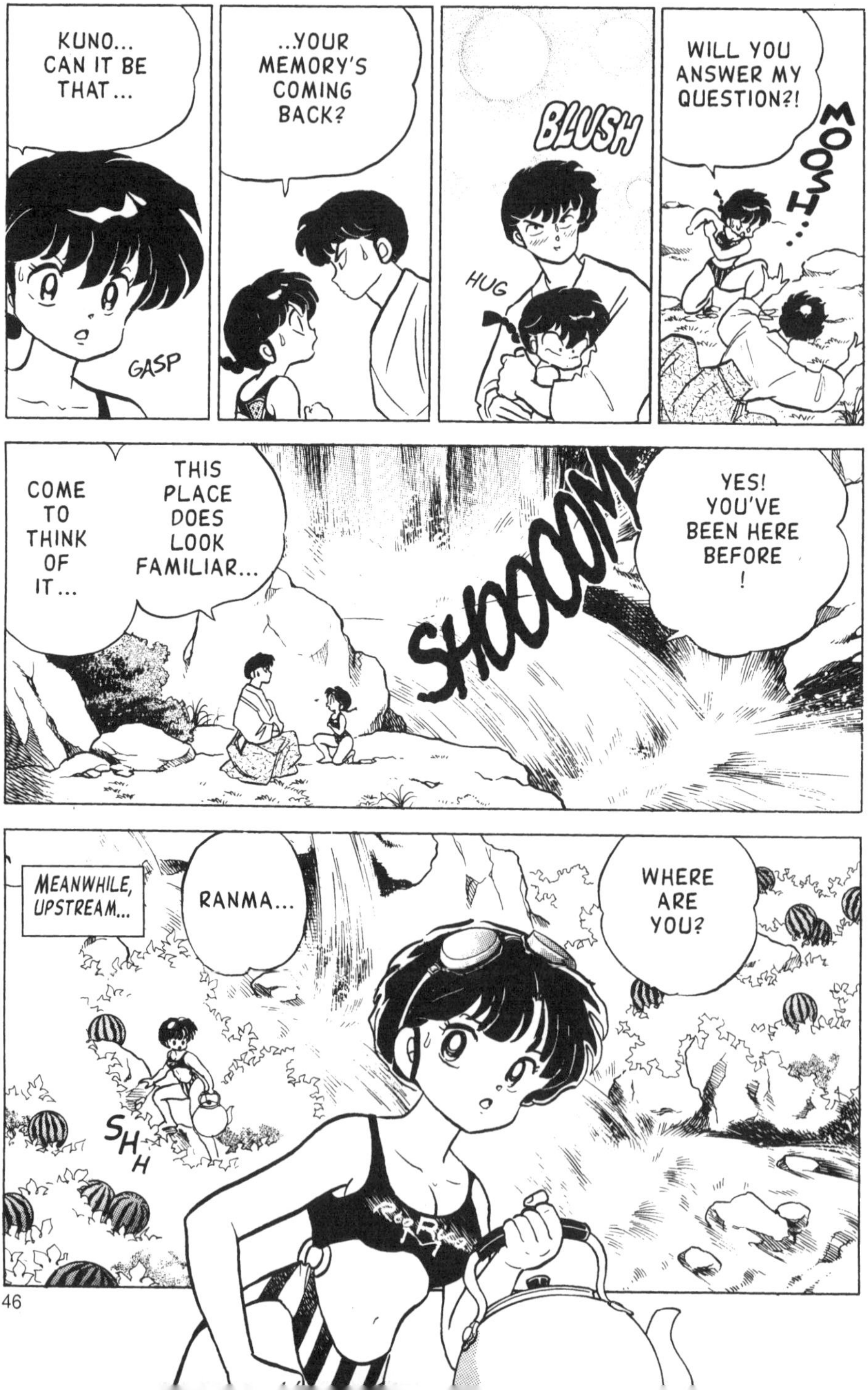
KUNO... CAN IT BE THAT...
GASP
...YOUR MEMORY'S COMING BACK?
BLUSH
HUG
WILL YOU ANSWER MY QUESTION?!
WOOOSH...
COME TO THINK OF IT...
THIS PLACE DOES LOOK FAMILIAR...
SHOOOOM
YES! YOU'VE BEEN HERE BEFORE !
MEANWHILE, UPSTREAM...
RANMA...
WHERE ARE YOU?
SHH

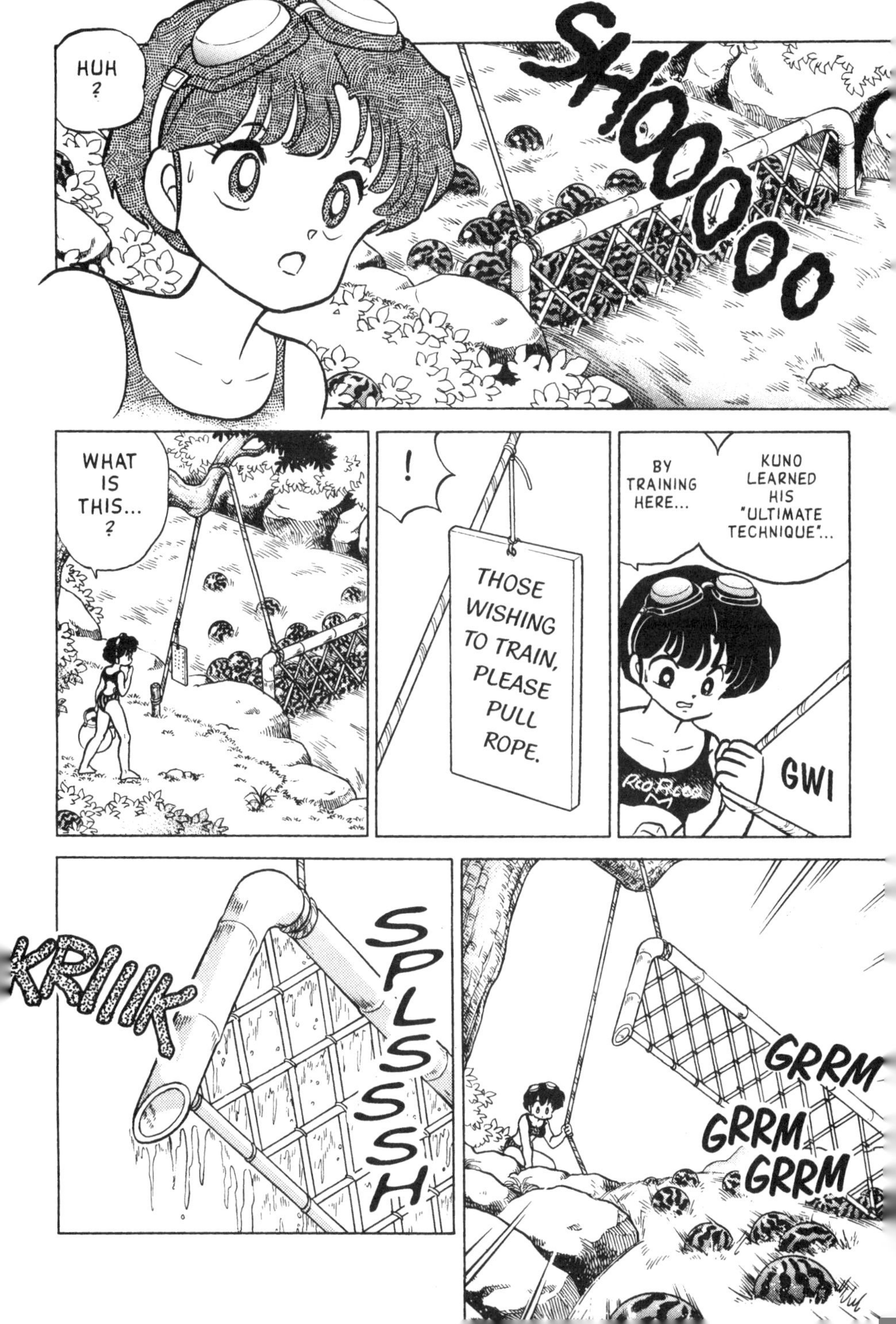
HUH ?
SHOOOOOO
WHAT IS THIS... ?
!
THOSE WISHING TO TRAIN, PLEASE PULL ROPE.
BY TRAINING HERE...
KUNO LEARNED HIS "ULTIMATE TECHNIQUE"...
GWI
KRIIIK
SPLSSSH
GRRM
GRRM
GRRM

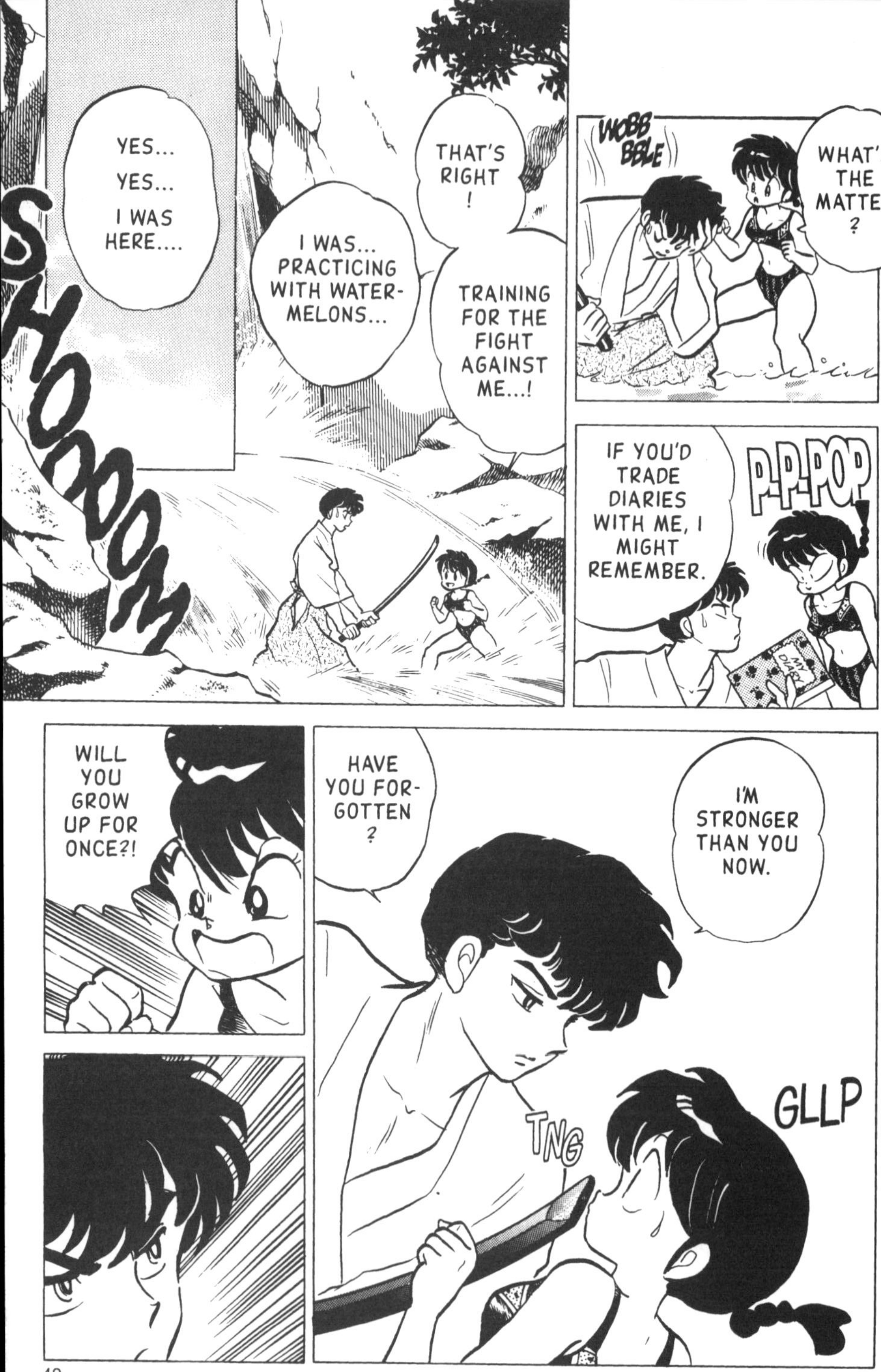
YES... YES... I WAS HERE....
SHOOOOM
THAT'S RIGHT!
I WAS... PRACTICING WITH WATER-MELONS...
TRAINING FOR THE FIGHT AGAINST ME...!
WOBBBBLE
WHAT'S THE MATTER?
IF YOU'D TRADE DIARIES WITH ME, I MIGHT REMEMBER.
P-P-POP
MY DIARY
WILL YOU GROW UP FOR ONCE?!
HAVE YOU FOR-GOTTEN?
I'M STRONGER THAN YOU NOW.
TNG
GLLP

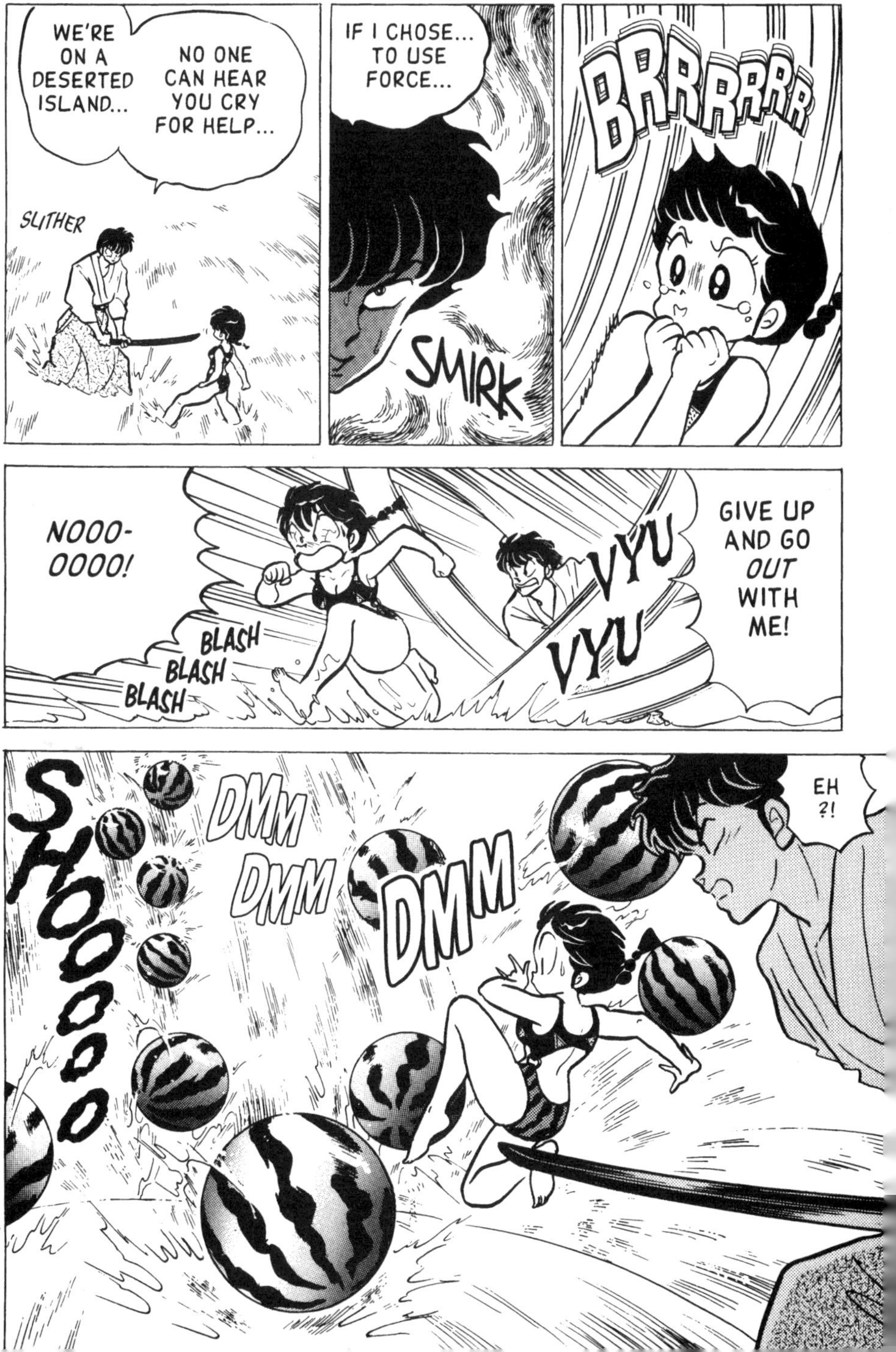
WE'RE ON A DESERTED ISLAND...
NO ONE CAN HEAR YOU CRY FOR HELP...
SLITHER
IF I CHOSE... TO USE FORCE...
SMIRK
BRRRRRR
NOOO-OOOO!
BLASH
BLASH
BLASH
VYU
VYU
GIVE UP AND GO *OUT* WITH ME!
SHOOOOOO
DMM
DMM
DMM
EH ?!

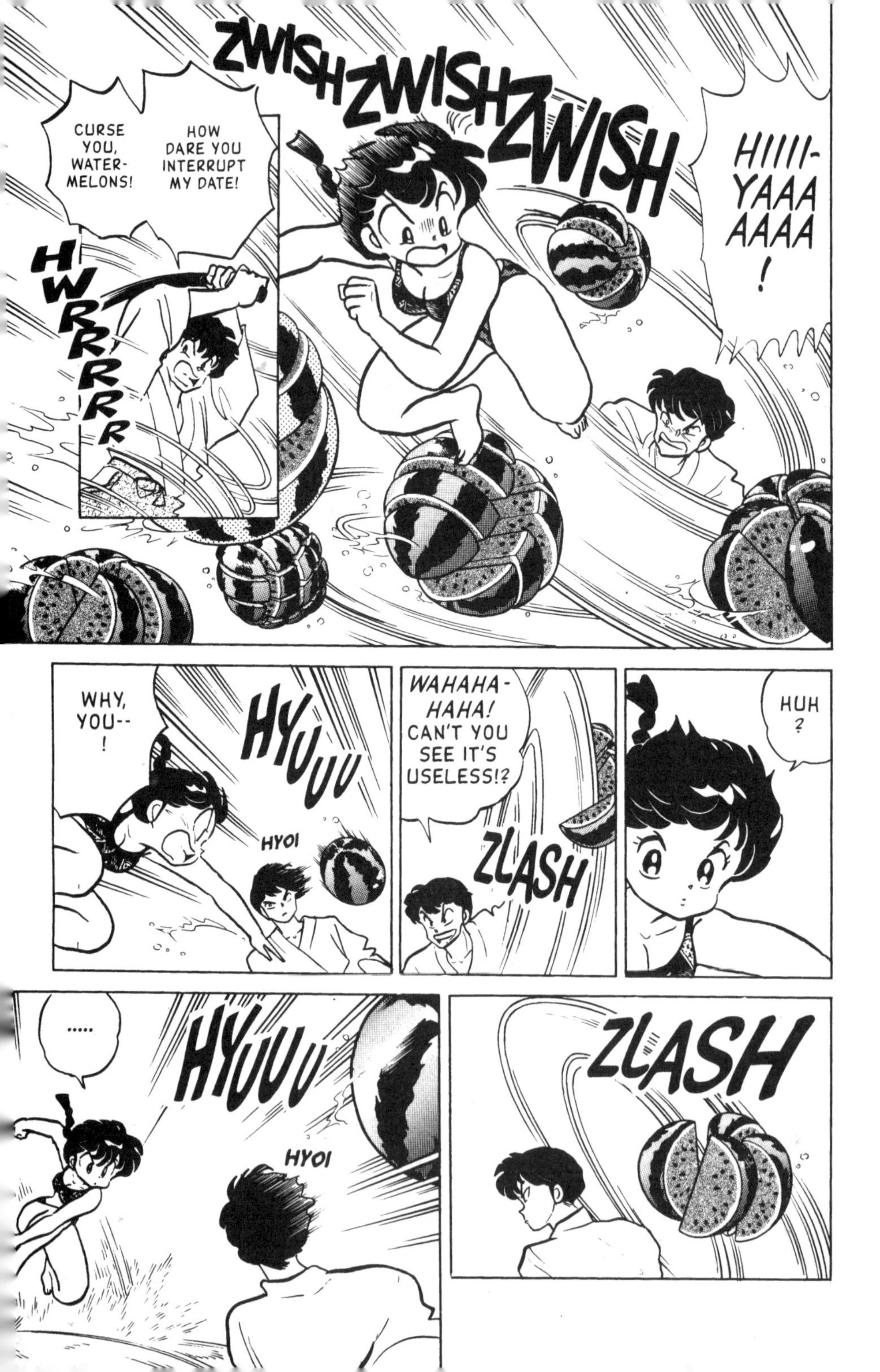
ZWISH ZWISH ZWISH
CURSE YOU, WATER-MELONS!
HOW DARE YOU INTERRUPT MY DATE!
HWRRRRRR
HIIII-YAAAAAAA!
WHY, YOU-- !
HYUUUU
HYOI
WAHAHA-HAHA! CAN'T YOU SEE IT'S USELESS!?
ZLASH
HUH?
......
HYUUUU
HYOI
ZLASH

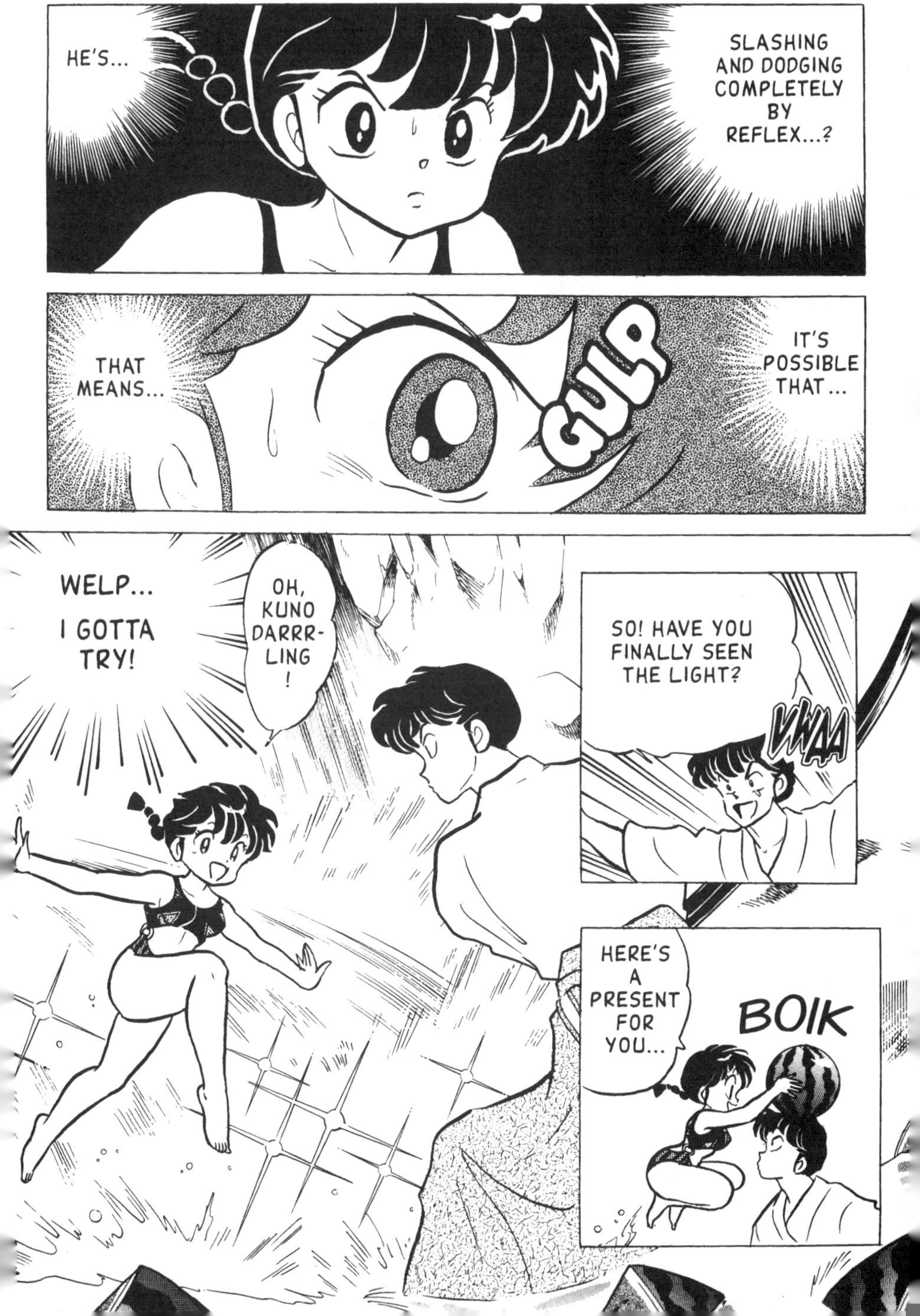
HE'S...
SLASHING AND DODGING COMPLETELY BY REFLEX...?
THAT MEANS...
GULP
IT'S POSSIBLE THAT...
WELP... I GOTTA TRY!
OH, KUNO DARRR-LING!
SO! HAVE YOU FINALLY SEEN THE LIGHT?
VWAA
HERE'S A PRESENT FOR YOU...
BOIK

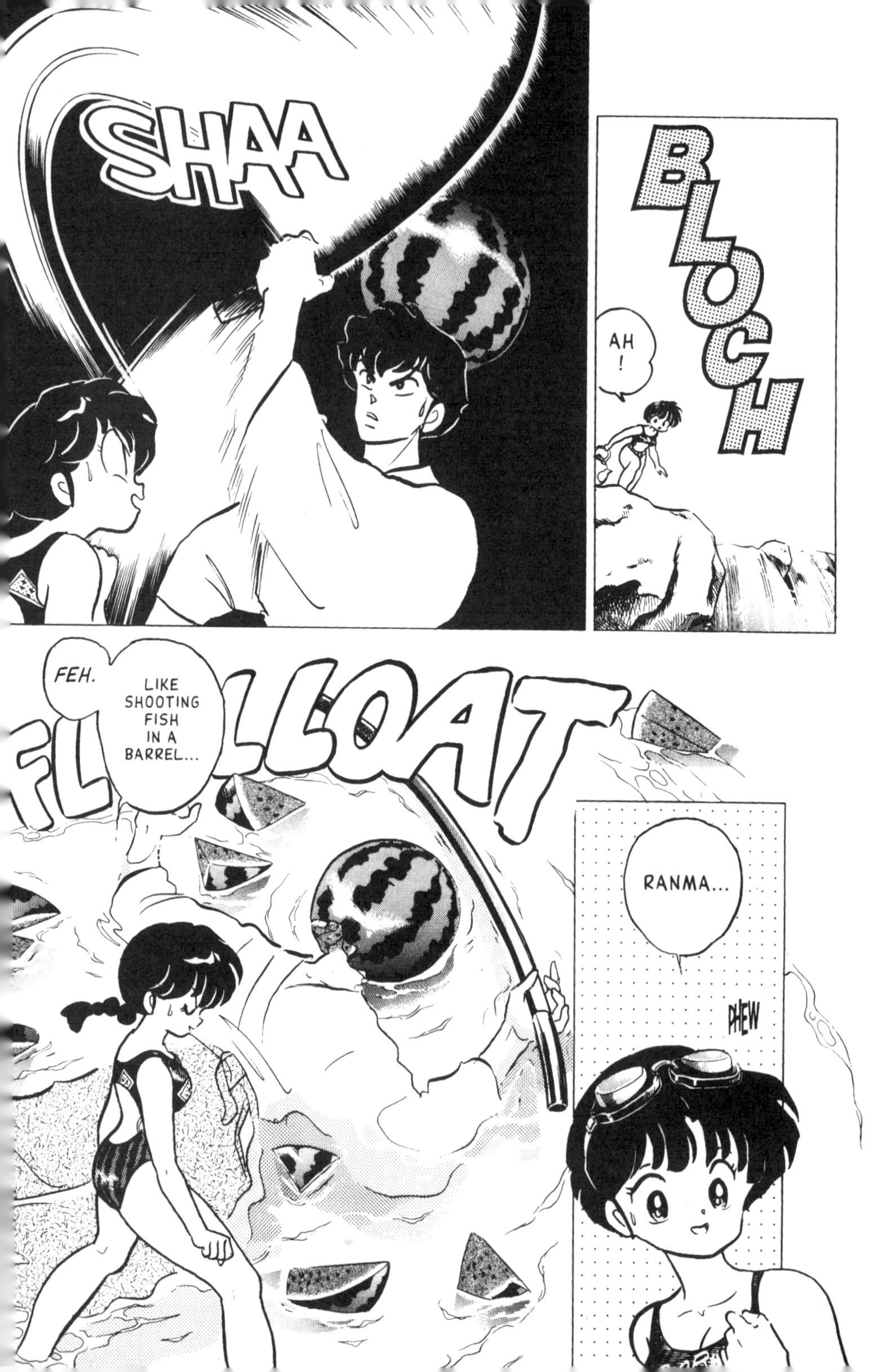
SHAA
BLOCH
AH!
FEH.
LIKE SHOOTING FISH IN A BARREL...
FLLOAT
RANMA...
PHEW

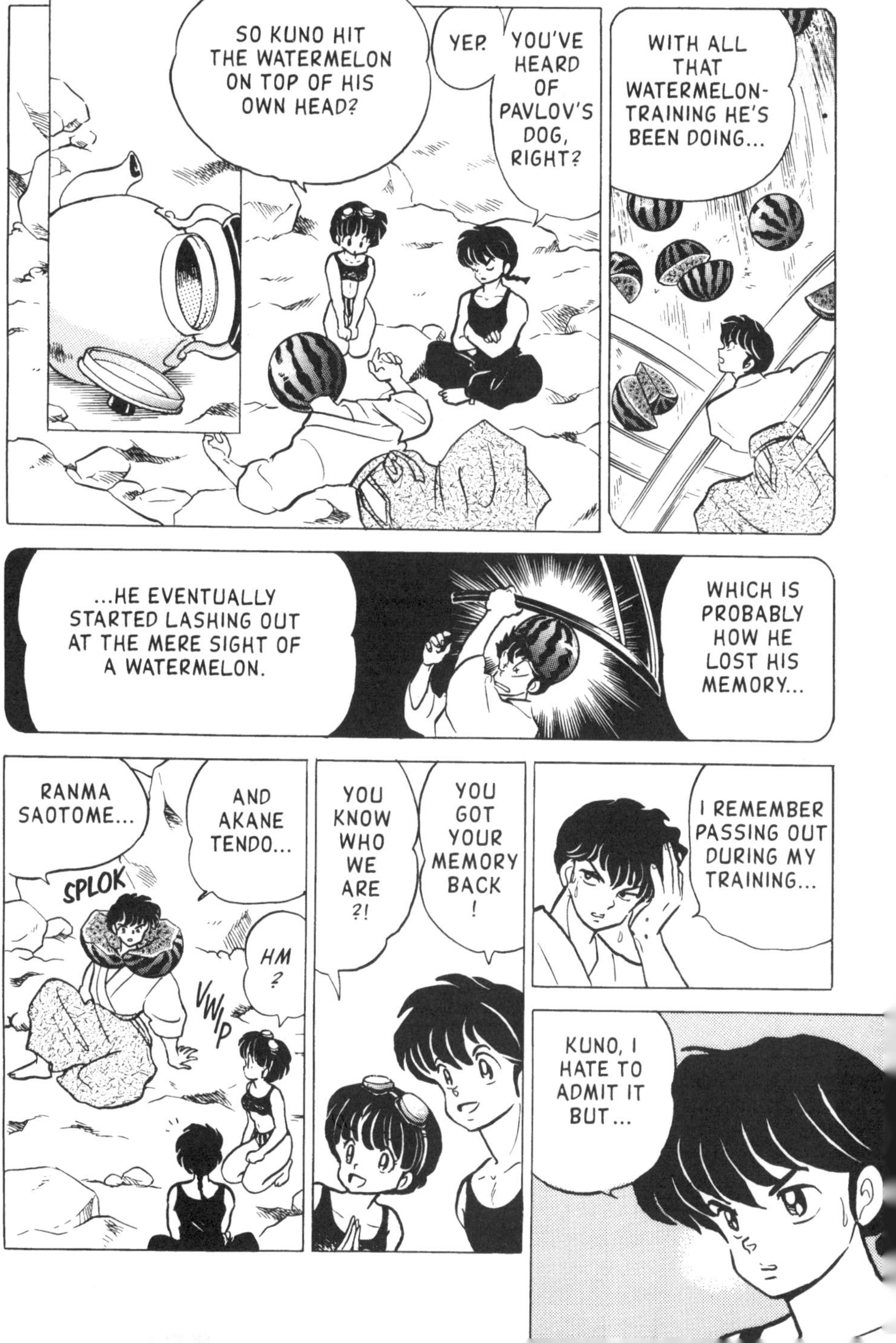
SO KUNO HIT THE WATERMELON ON TOP OF HIS OWN HEAD?
YEP.
YOU'VE HEARD OF PAVLOV'S DOG, RIGHT?
WITH ALL THAT WATERMELON-TRAINING HE'S BEEN DOING...
...HE EVENTUALLY STARTED LASHING OUT AT THE MERE SIGHT OF A WATERMELON.
WHICH IS PROBABLY HOW HE LOST HIS MEMORY...
RANMA SAOTOME...
AND AKANE TENDO...
SPLOK
HM?
VWIP
YOU KNOW WHO WE ARE?!
YOU GOT YOUR MEMORY BACK!
I REMEMBER PASSING OUT DURING MY TRAINING...
KUNO, I HATE TO ADMIT IT BUT...

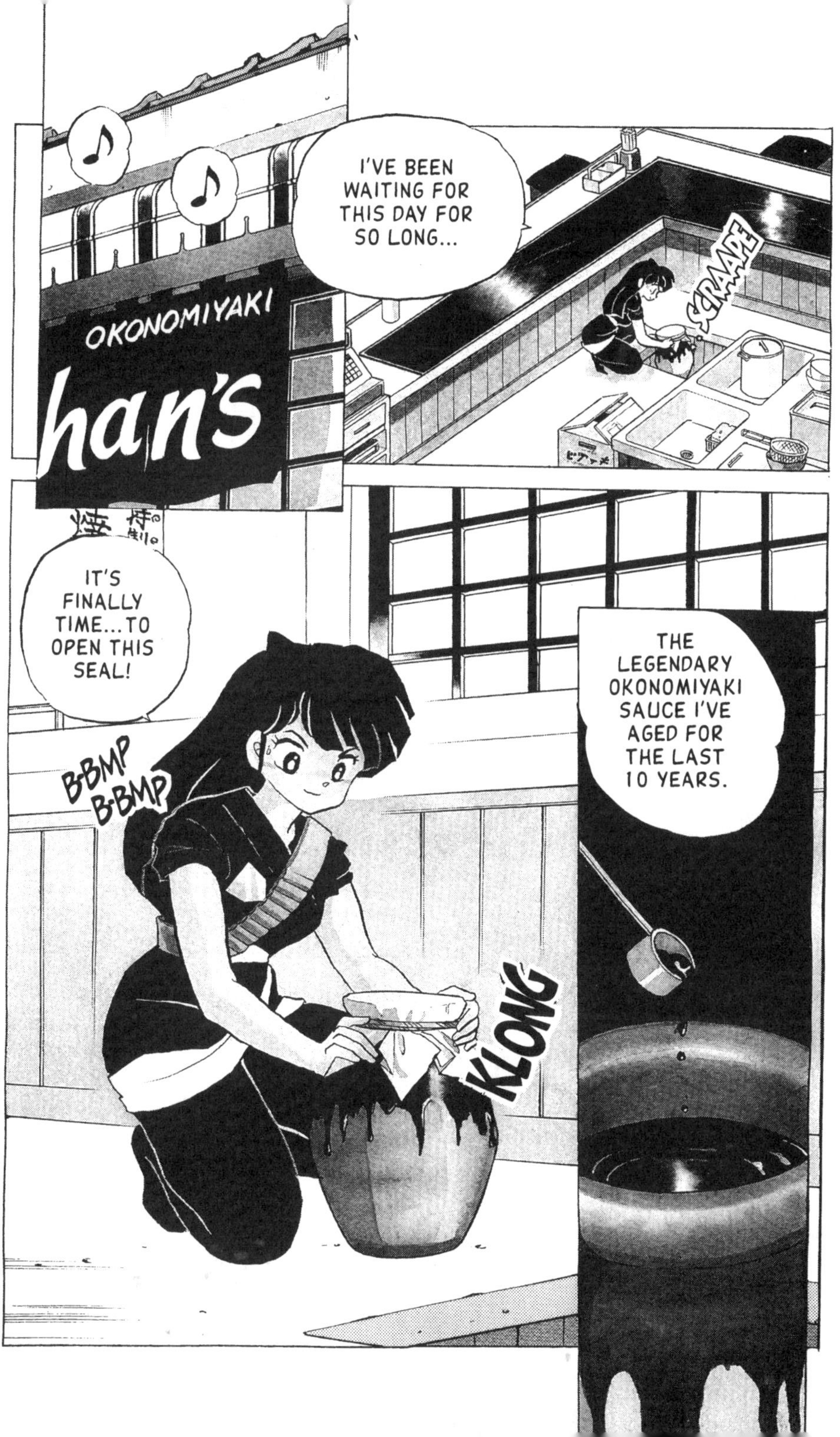
OKONOMIYAKI
han's
I'VE BEEN WAITING FOR THIS DAY FOR SO LONG...
SCRAAAPE
IT'S FINALLY TIME...TO OPEN THIS SEAL!
B-BMP B-BMP
KLONG
THE LEGENDARY OKONOMIYAKI SAUCE I'VE AGED FOR THE LAST 10 YEARS.

Part 4
THE SAUCE OF TEN YEARS

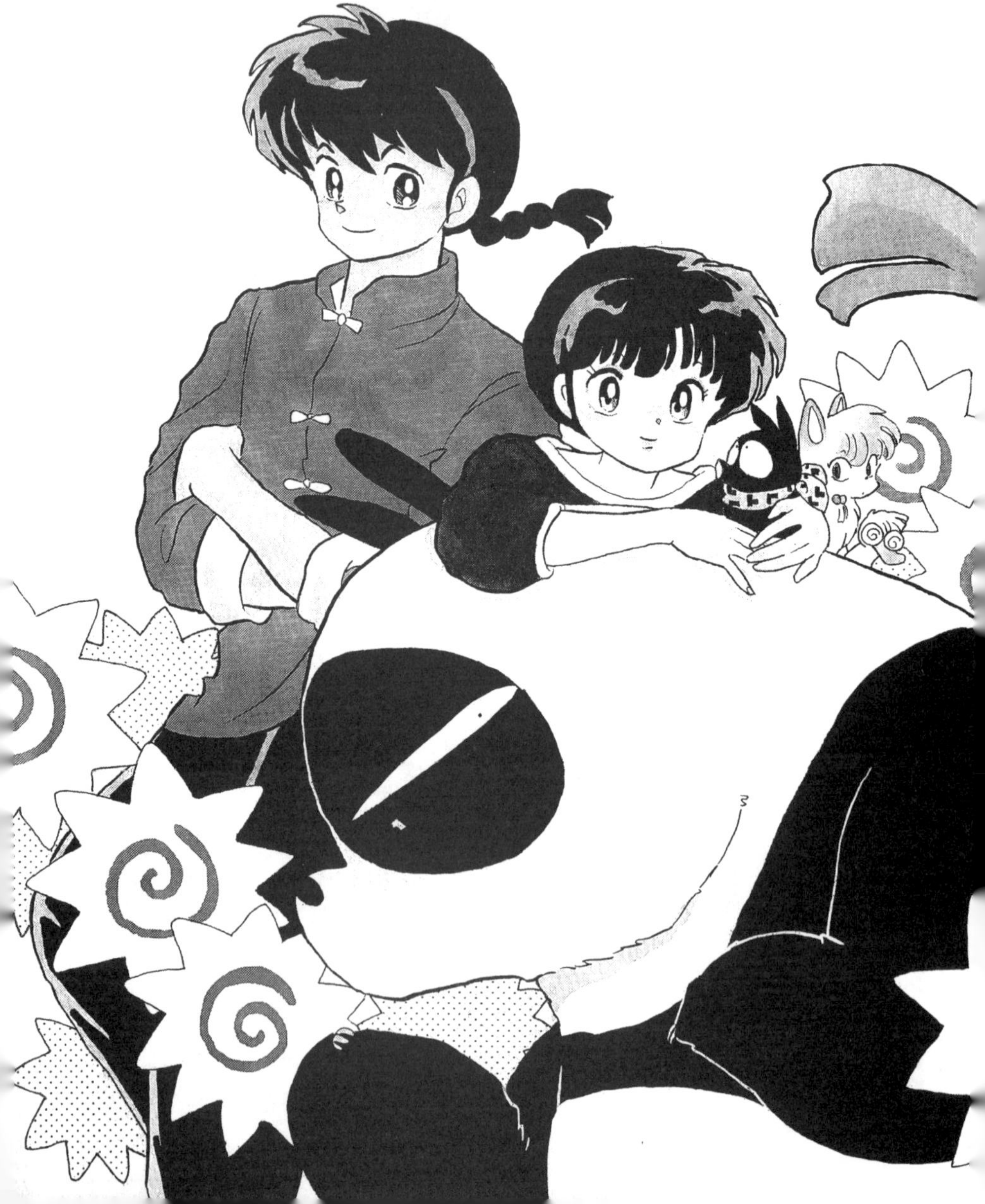

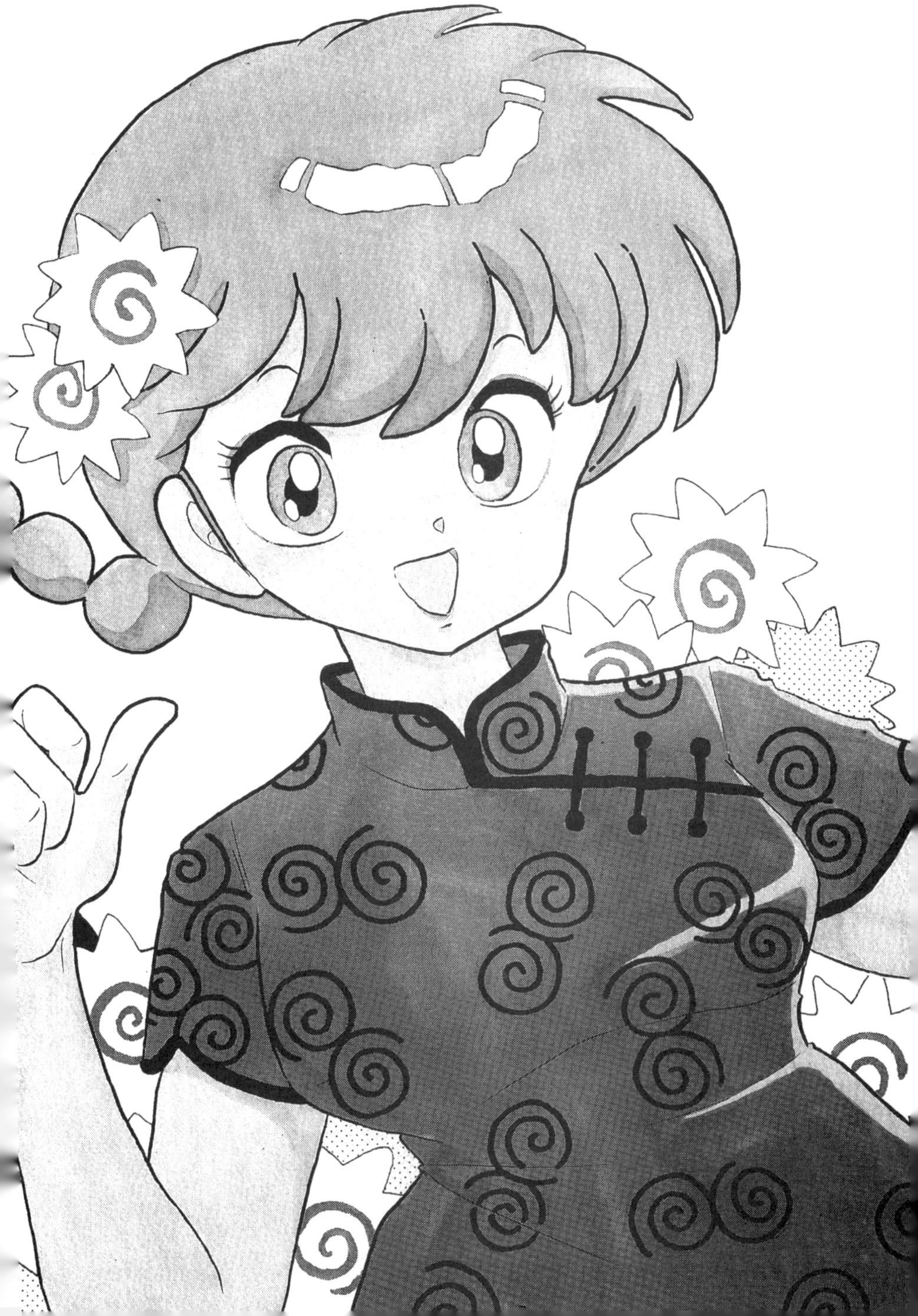

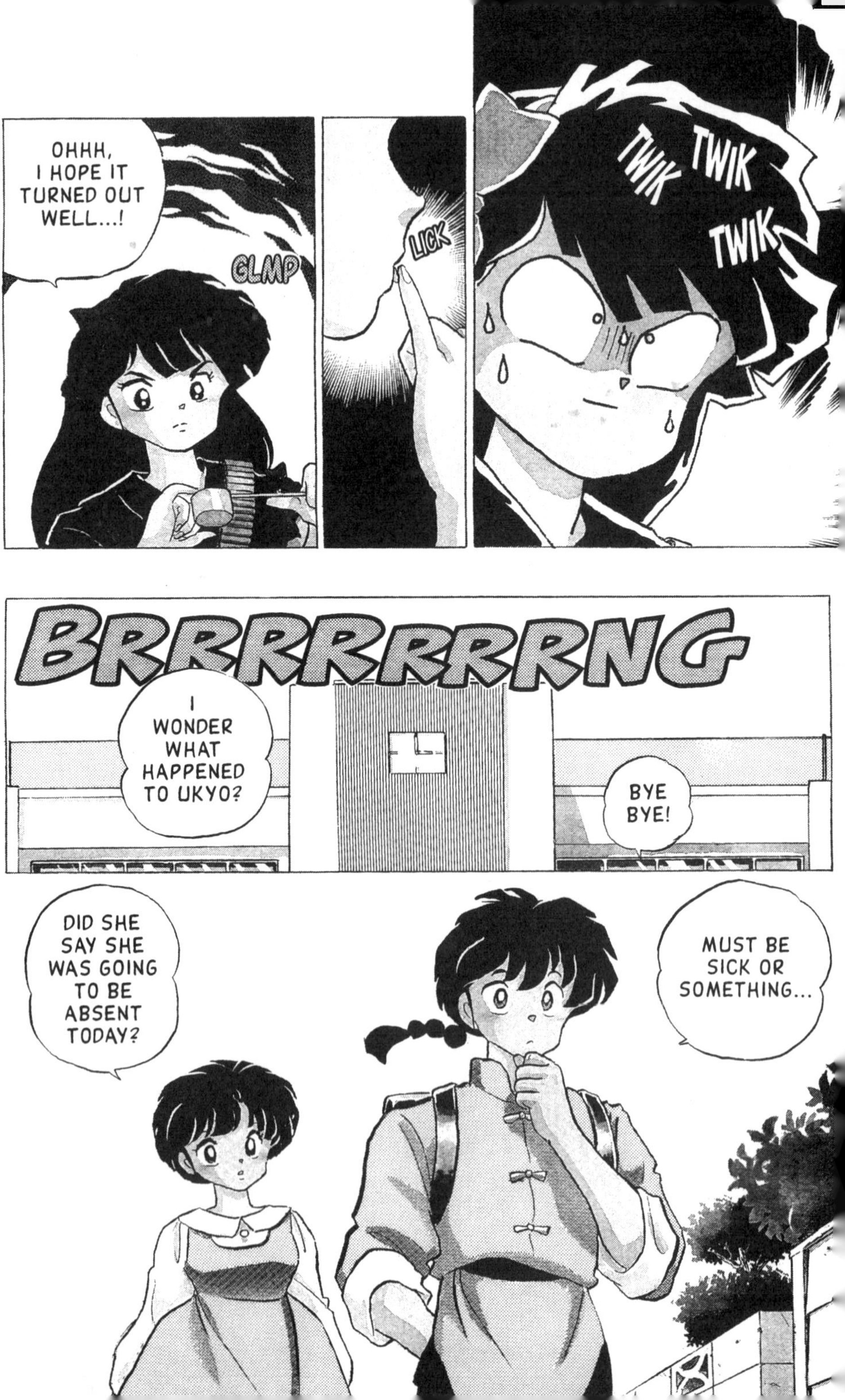
OHHH, I HOPE IT TURNED OUT WELL...!
GLMP
LICK
TWIK TWIK TWIK
BRRRRRRRNG
I WONDER WHAT HAPPENED TO UKYO?
BYE BYE!
DID SHE SAY SHE WAS GOING TO BE ABSENT TODAY?
MUST BE SICK OR SOMETHING...

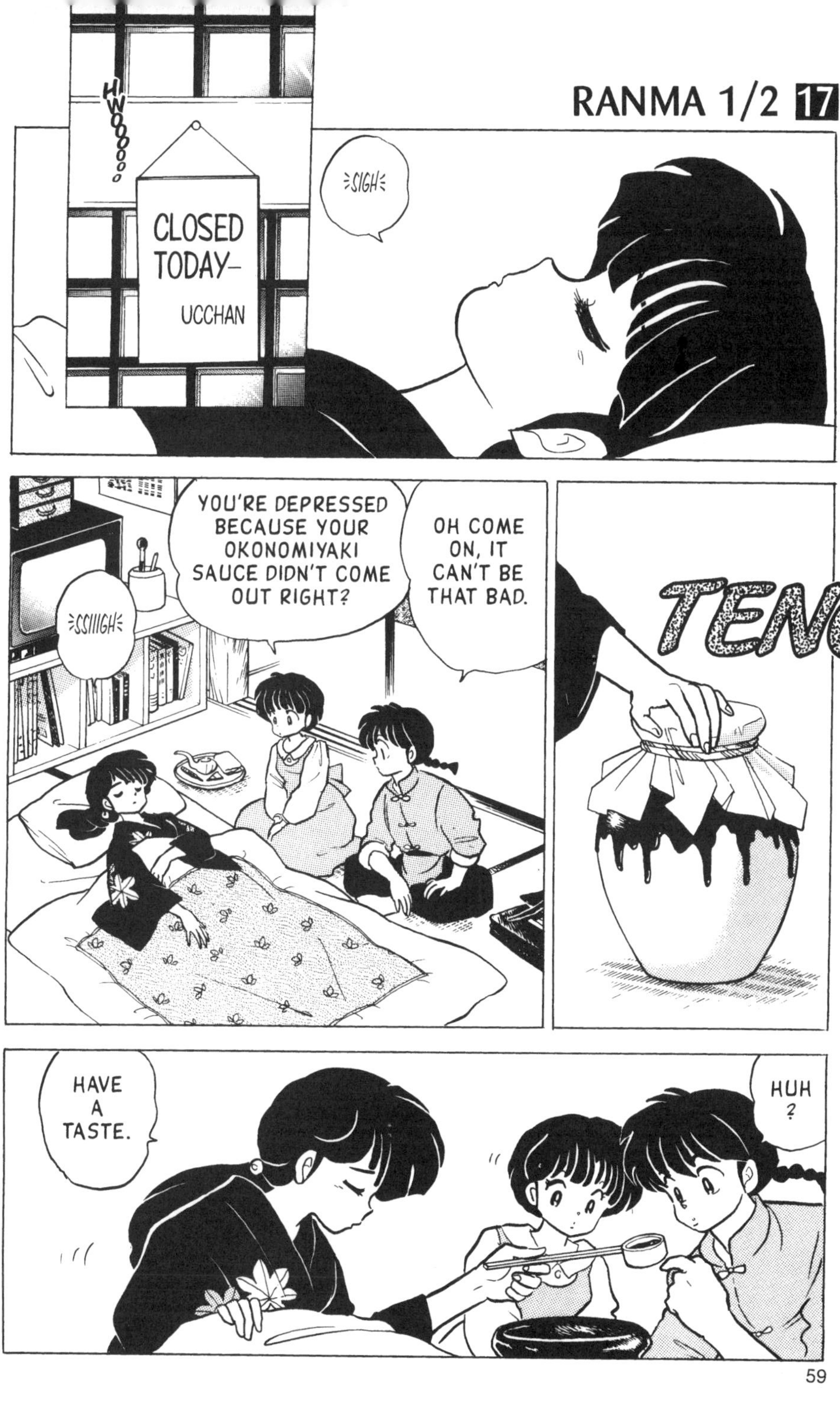
HWOOOOOO
CLOSED TODAY—
UCCHAN
SIGH
SSIIIGH
YOU'RE DEPRESSED BECAUSE YOUR OKONOMIYAKI SAUCE DIDN'T COME OUT RIGHT?
OH COME ON, IT CAN'T BE THAT BAD.
TENG
HAVE A TASTE.
HUH?

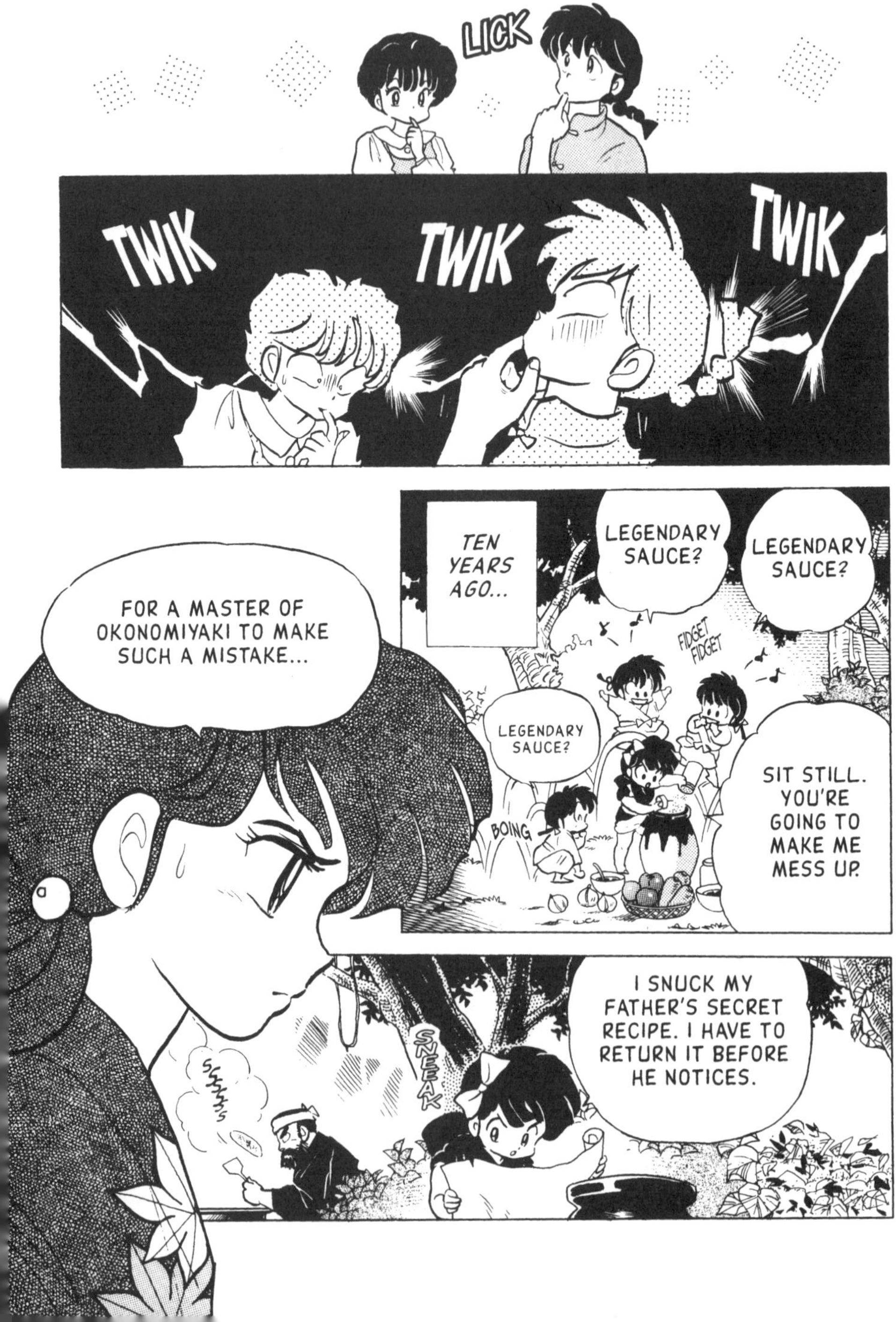
LICK
TWIK
TWIK
TWIK
FOR A MASTER OF OKONOMIYAKI TO MAKE SUCH A MISTAKE...
TEN YEARS AGO...
LEGENDARY SAUCE?
LEGENDARY SAUCE?
FIDGET FIDGET
LEGENDARY SAUCE?
BOING
SIT STILL. YOU'RE GOING TO MAKE ME MESS UP.
SNEEAK
I SNUCK MY FATHER'S SECRET RECIPE. I HAVE TO RETURN IT BEFORE HE NOTICES.

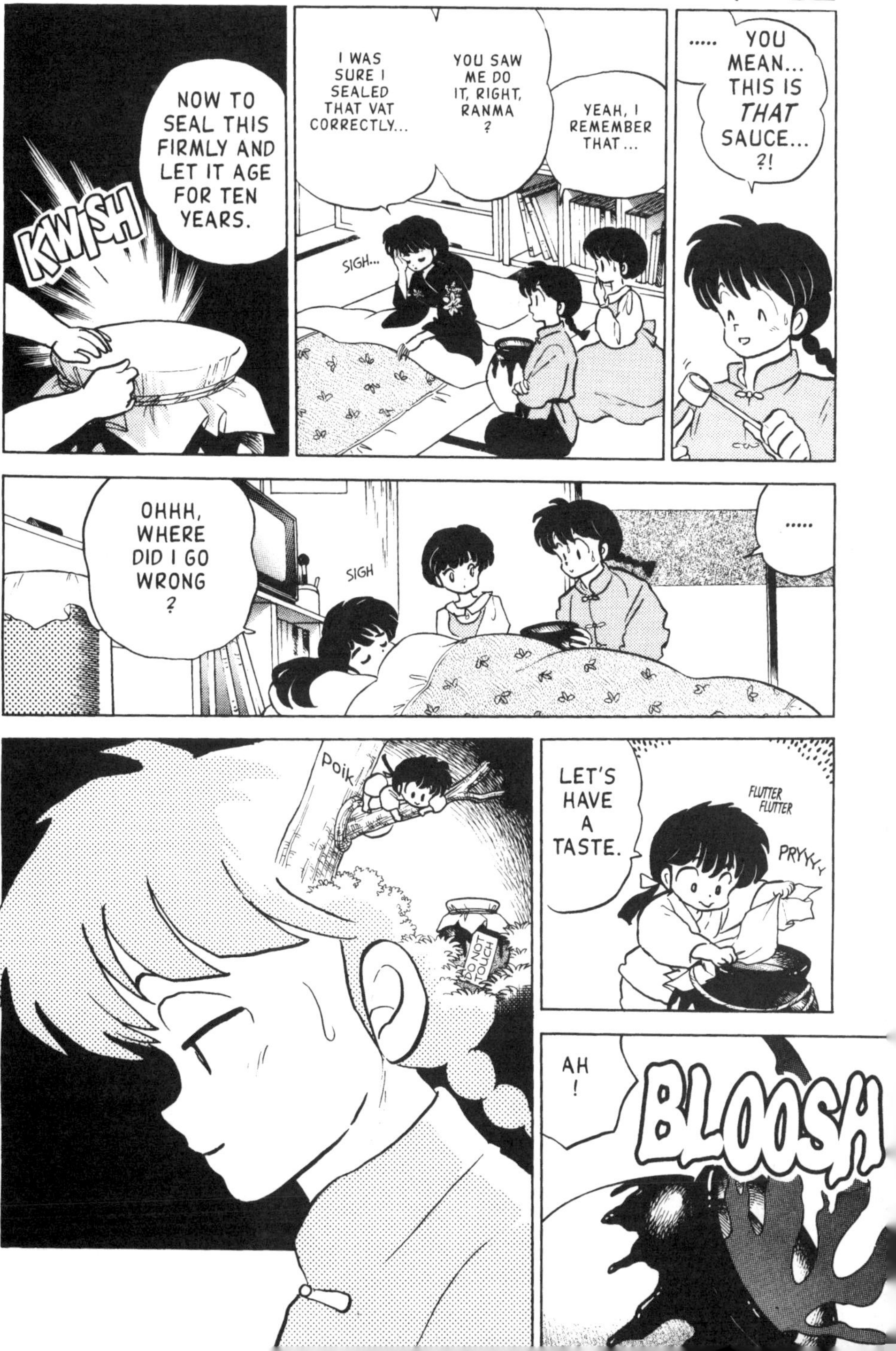
NOW TO SEAL THIS FIRMLY AND LET IT AGE FOR TEN YEARS.
KWISH
I WAS SURE I SEALED THAT VAT CORRECTLY...
YOU SAW ME DO IT, RIGHT, RANMA ?
YEAH, I REMEMBER THAT...
SIGH...
.....
YOU MEAN... THIS IS THAT SAUCE... ?!
OHHH, WHERE DID I GO WRONG ?
SIGH
.....
Poik
DO NOT TOUCH
LET'S HAVE A TASTE.
FLUTTER FLUTTER
PRYYY
AH !
BLOOSH

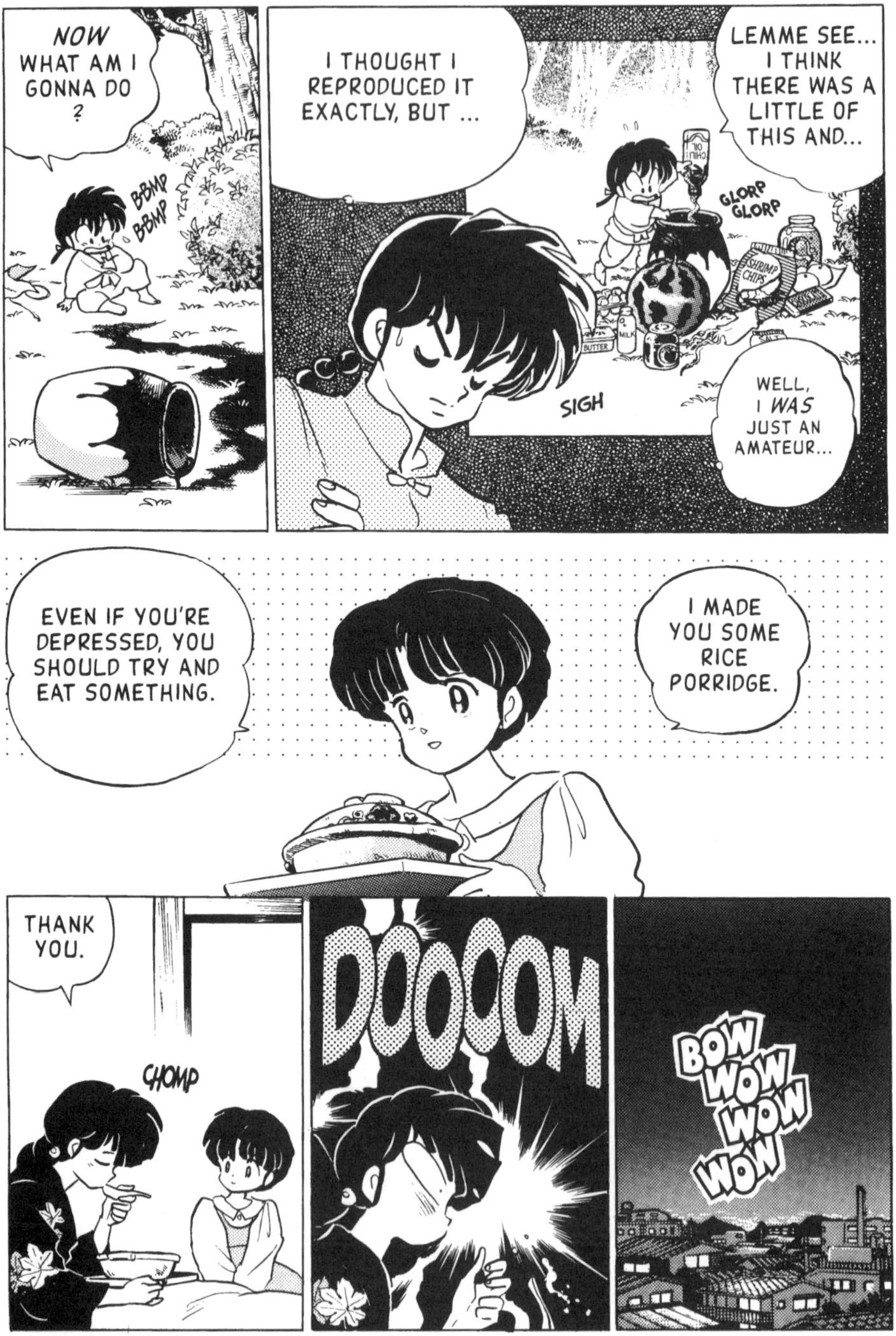
NOW WHAT AM I GONNA DO ?
B-BMP B-BMP
I THOUGHT I REPRODUCED IT EXACTLY, BUT ...
LEMME SEE... I THINK THERE WAS A LITTLE OF THIS AND...
CHILI OIL
GLORP GLORP
SHRIMP CHIPS
MILK
BUTTER
SALT
SIGH
WELL, I *WAS* JUST AN AMATEUR...
EVEN IF YOU'RE DEPRESSED, YOU SHOULD TRY AND EAT SOMETHING.
I MADE YOU SOME RICE PORRIDGE.
THANK YOU.
CHOMP
DOOOOM
BOW WOW WOW WOW

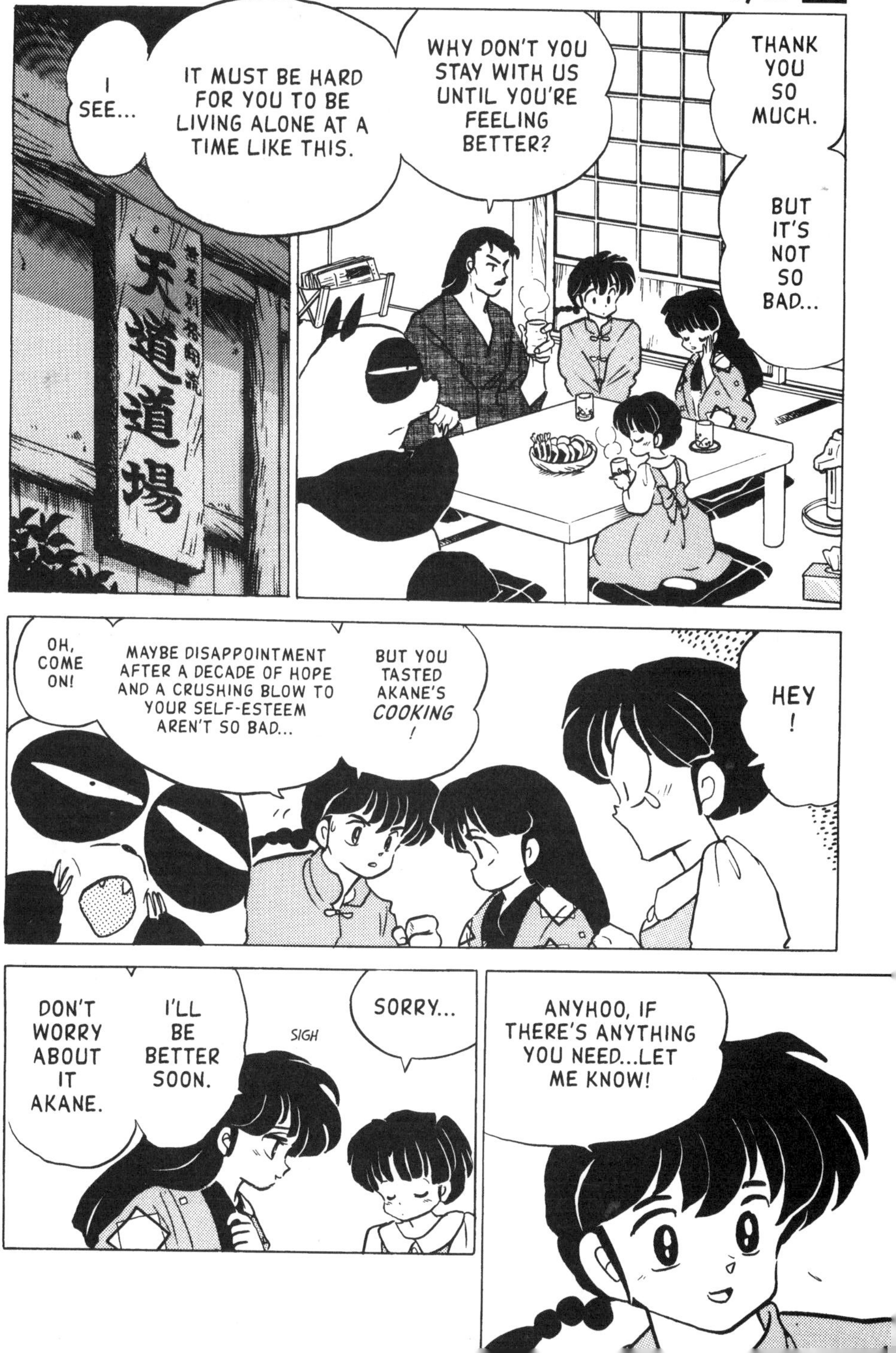
I SEE...
IT MUST BE HARD FOR YOU TO BE LIVING ALONE AT A TIME LIKE THIS.
WHY DON'T YOU STAY WITH US UNTIL YOU'RE FEELING BETTER?
THANK YOU SO MUCH.
BUT IT'S NOT SO BAD...
天道道場
OH, COME ON!
MAYBE DISAPPOINTMENT AFTER A DECADE OF HOPE AND A CRUSHING BLOW TO YOUR SELF-ESTEEM AREN'T SO BAD...
BUT YOU TASTED AKANE'S *COOKING*!
HEY!
DON'T WORRY ABOUT IT AKANE.
I'LL BE BETTER SOON.
SIGH
SORRY...
ANYHOO, IF THERE'S ANYTHING YOU NEED...LET ME KNOW!

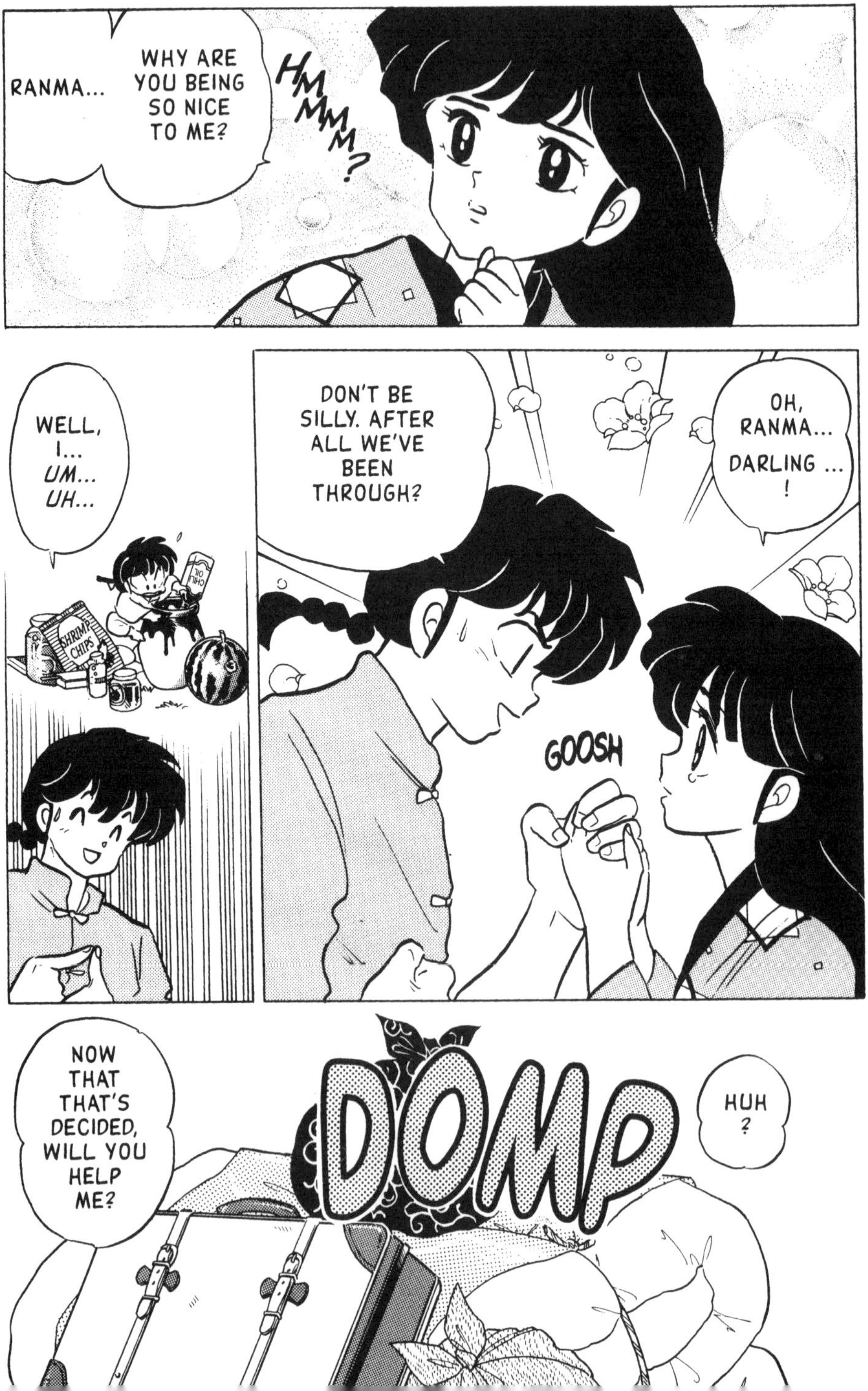
RANMA...
WHY ARE YOU BEING SO NICE TO ME?
HMMMM?
WELL, I... *UM... UH...*
SHRIMP CHIPS
CHILI OIL
DON'T BE SILLY. AFTER ALL WE'VE BEEN THROUGH?
OH, RANMA... DARLING ...!
GOOSH
NOW THAT THAT'S DECIDED, WILL YOU HELP ME?
DOMP
HUH?

65

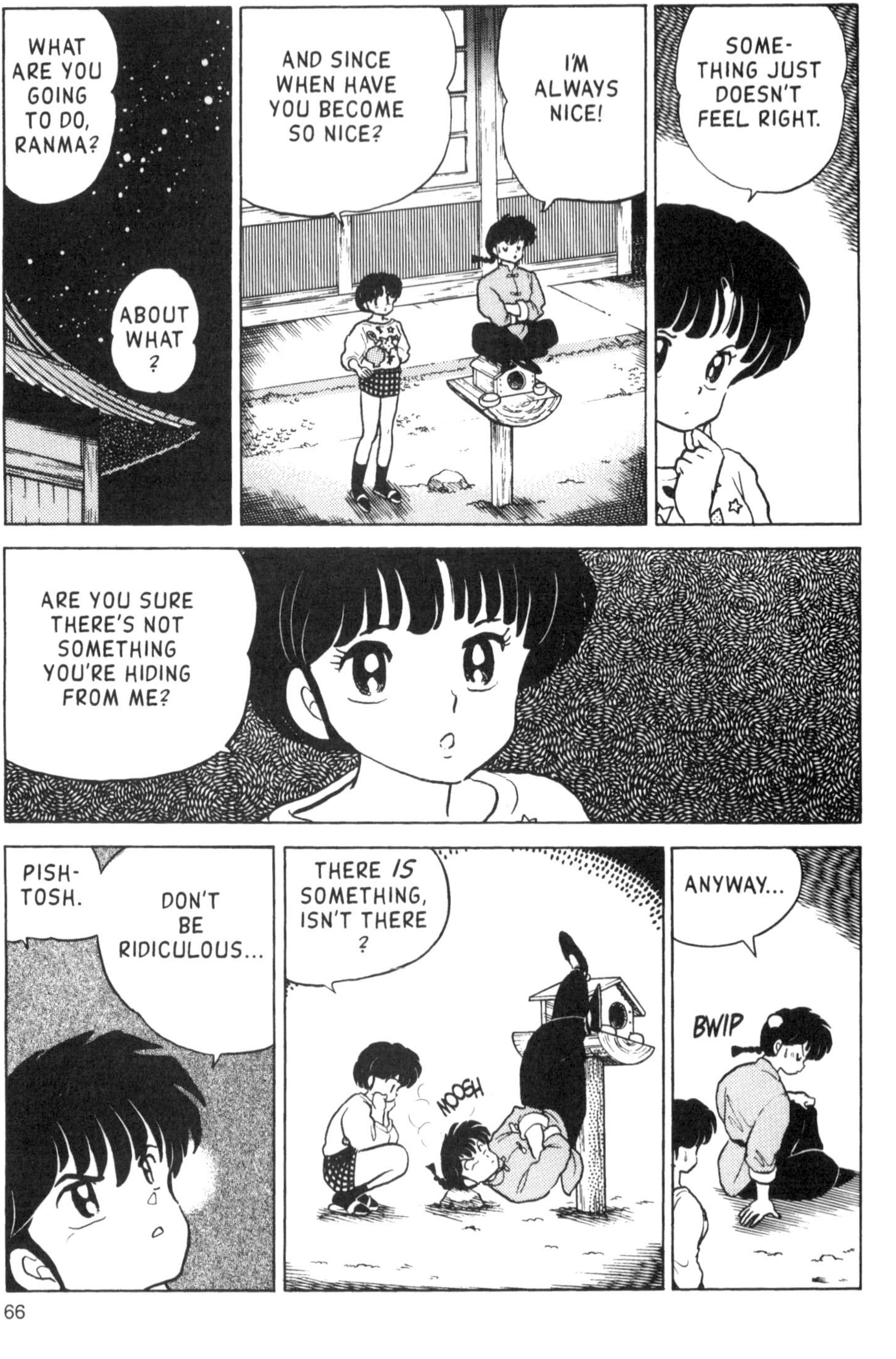
WHAT ARE YOU GOING TO DO, RANMA?
ABOUT WHAT ?
AND SINCE WHEN HAVE YOU BECOME SO NICE?
I'M ALWAYS NICE!
SOME-THING JUST DOESN'T FEEL RIGHT.
ARE YOU SURE THERE'S NOT SOMETHING YOU'RE HIDING FROM ME?
PISH-TOSH.
DON'T BE RIDICULOUS...
THERE *IS* SOMETHING, ISN'T THERE ?
ANYWAY...
BWIP

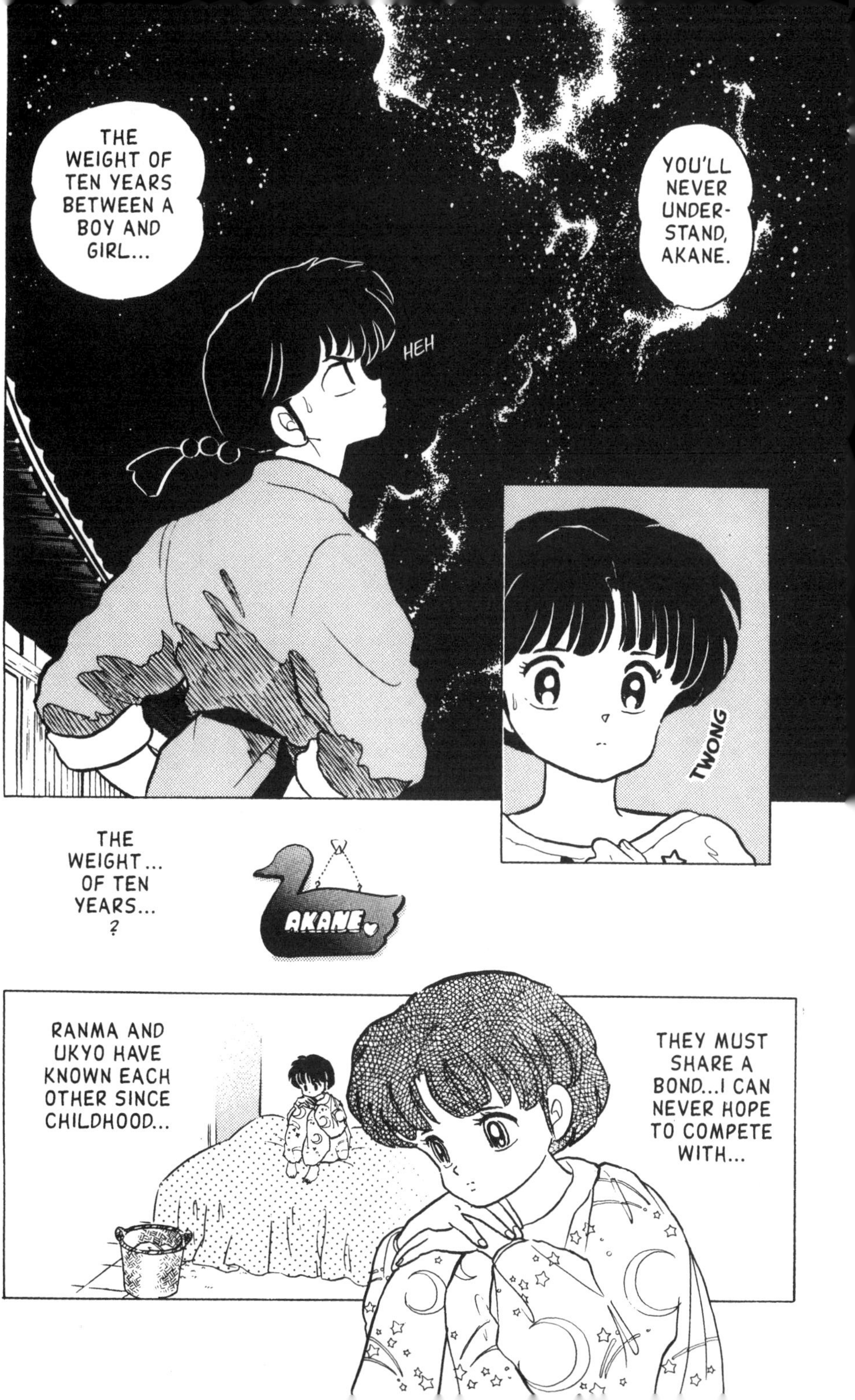
THE WEIGHT OF TEN YEARS BETWEEN A BOY AND GIRL...
YOU'LL NEVER UNDER-STAND, AKANE.
HEH
TWONG
THE WEIGHT... OF TEN YEARS...?
AKANE
RANMA AND UKYO HAVE KNOWN EACH OTHER SINCE CHILDHOOD...
THEY MUST SHARE A BOND...I CAN NEVER HOPE TO COMPETE WITH...

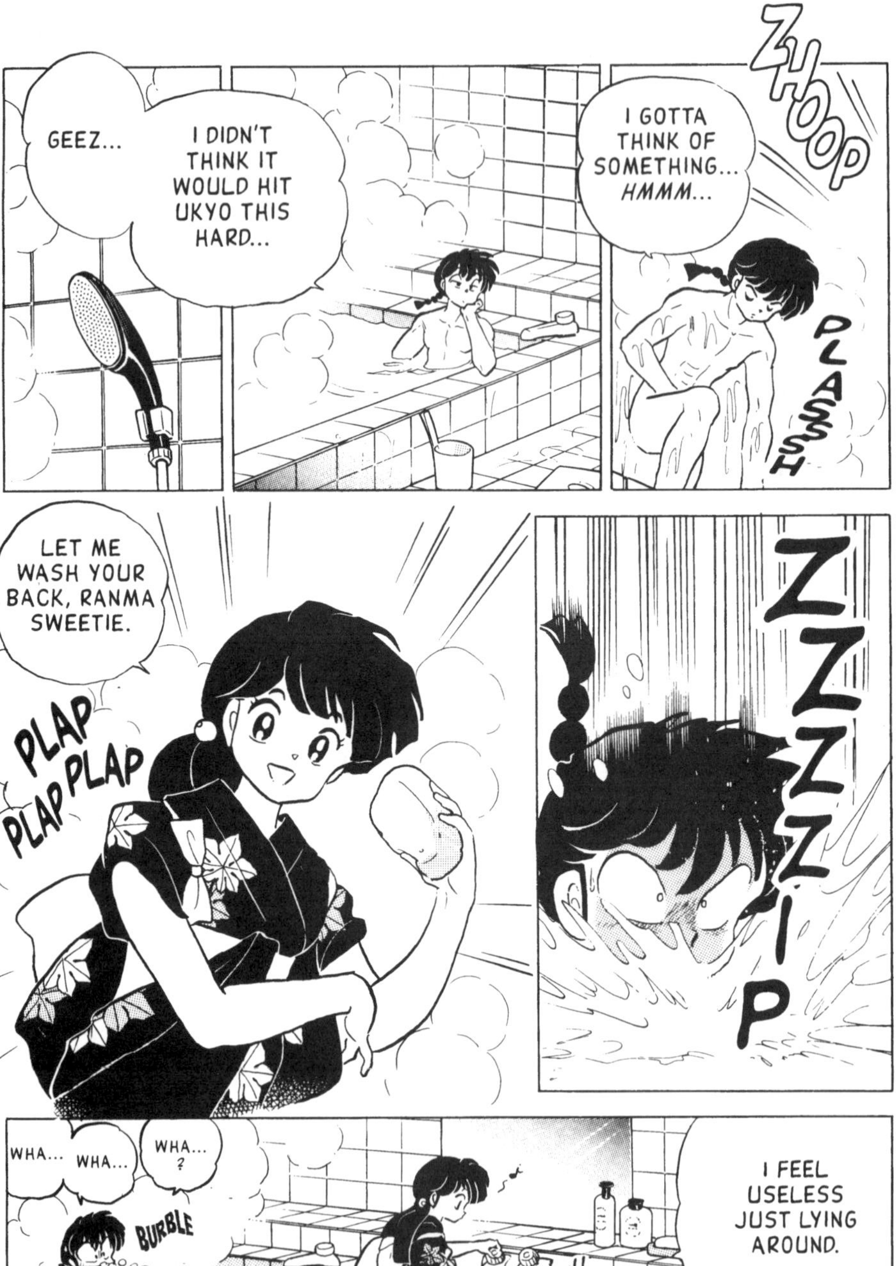
GEEZ...
I DIDN'T THINK IT WOULD HIT UKYO THIS HARD...
I GOTTA THINK OF SOMETHING... *HMMM...*
ZHOOP
PLASSHH
LET ME WASH YOUR BACK, RANMA SWEETIE.
PLAP PLAP PLAP
ZZZZZIP
WHA...
WHA...
WHA...?
BURBLE
SSHHH
I FEEL USELESS JUST LYING AROUND.

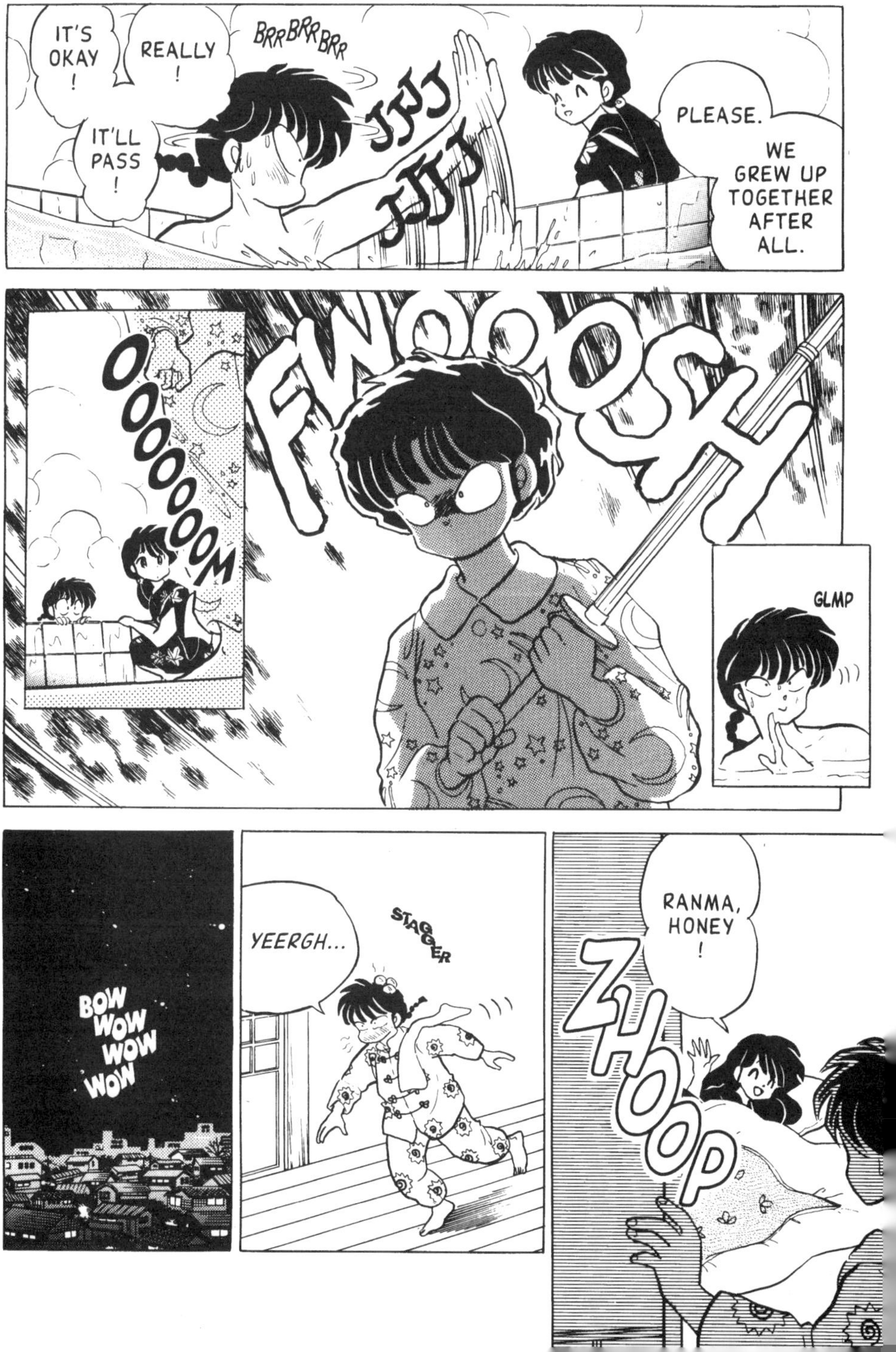
IT'S OKAY !
REALLY !
IT'LL PASS !
BRRBRRBRR
JJJ JJJ
PLEASE.
WE GREW UP TOGETHER AFTER ALL.
FWOOOSH
OOOOOOOOM
GLMP
BOW WOW WOW WOW
YEERGH...
STAGGER
RANMA, HONEY !
ZHOOP

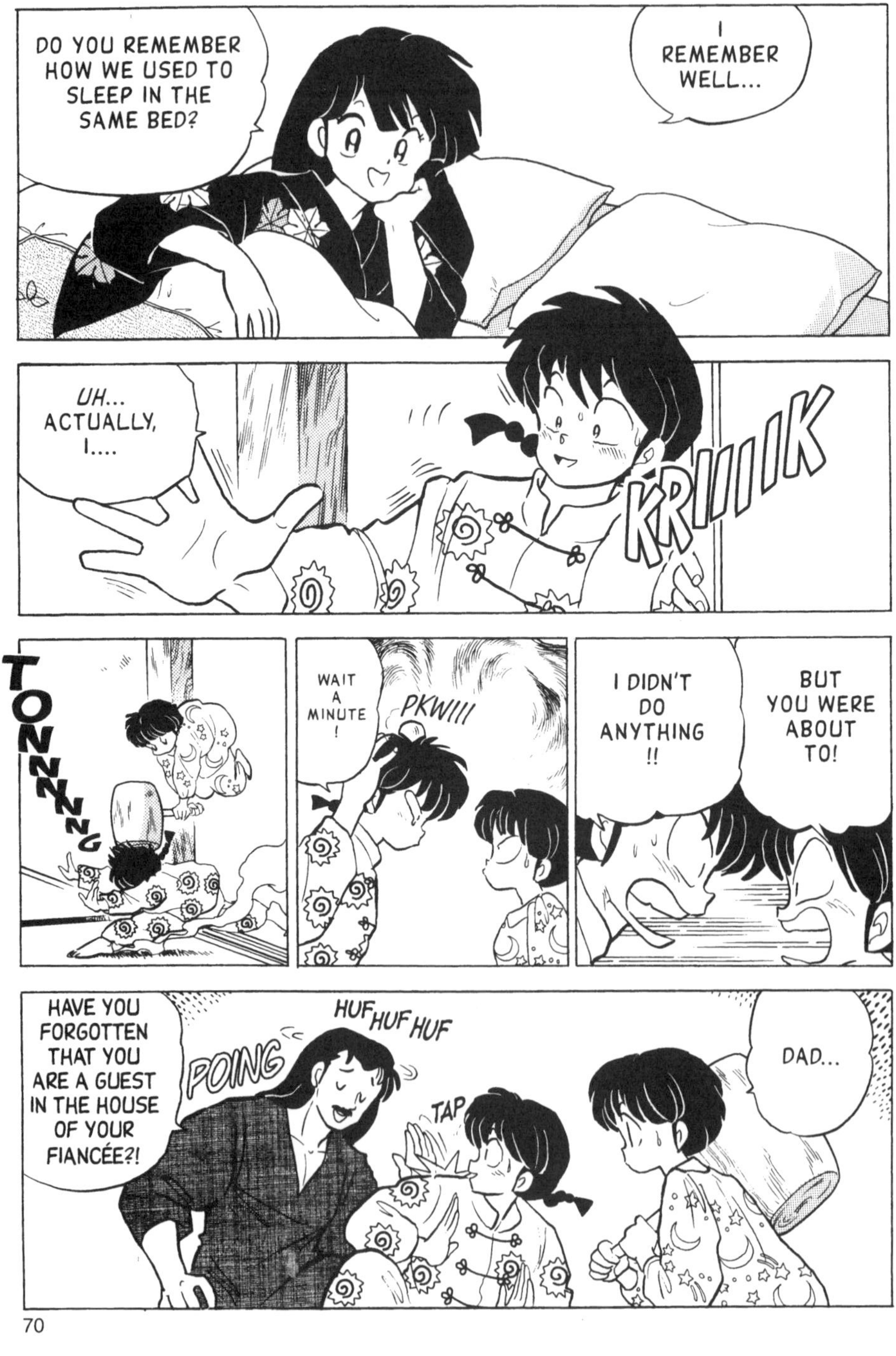
DO YOU REMEMBER HOW WE USED TO SLEEP IN THE SAME BED?
I REMEMBER WELL...
UH... ACTUALLY, I....
KRIIIIK
TONNNNNG
WAIT A MINUTE!
PKWIII
I DIDN'T DO ANYTHING!!
BUT YOU WERE ABOUT TO!
HAVE YOU FORGOTTEN THAT YOU ARE A GUEST IN THE HOUSE OF YOUR FIANCÉE?!
HUF HUF HUF
POING
TAP
DAD...

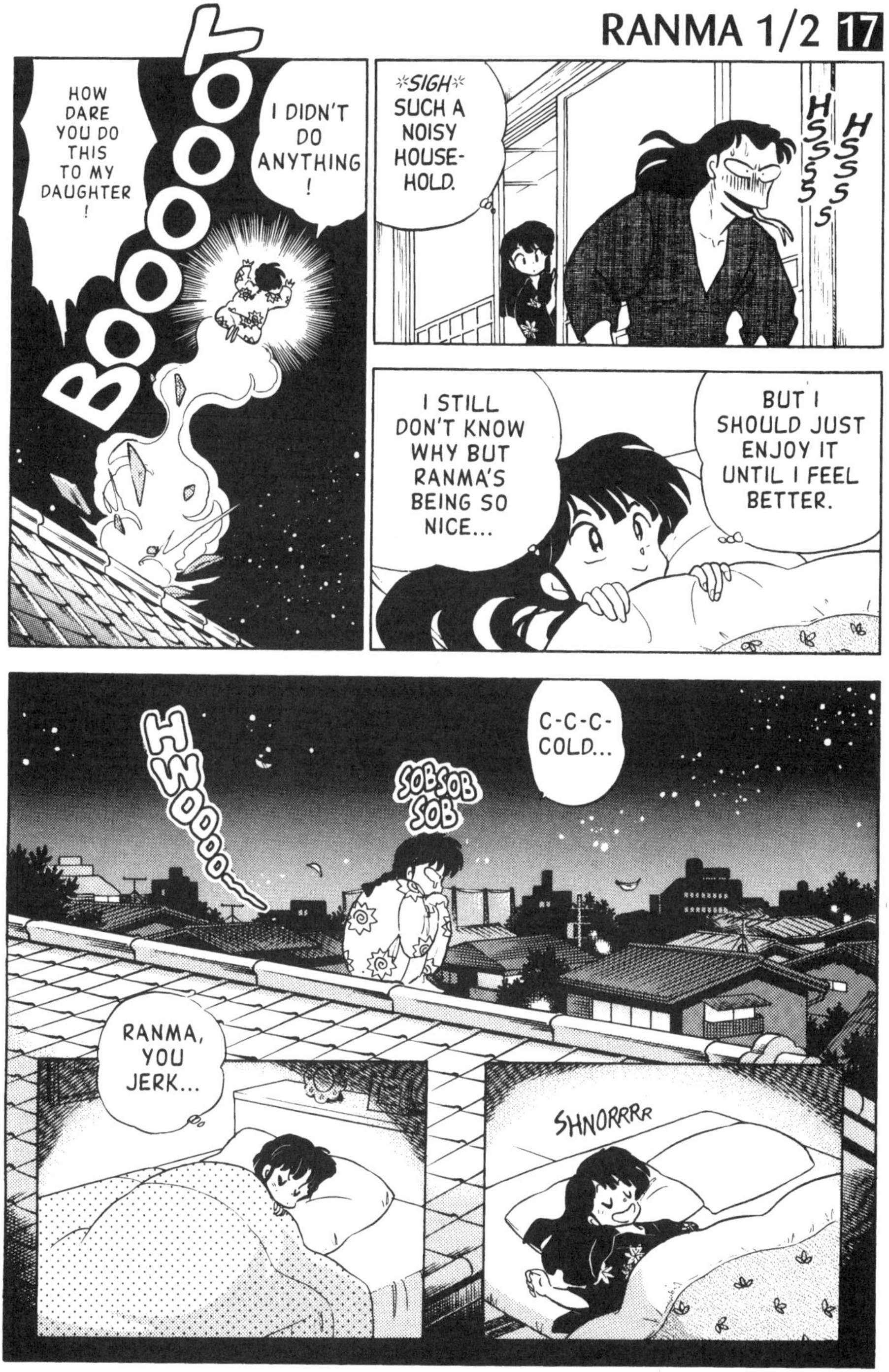
HOW DARE YOU DO THIS TO MY DAUGHTER!
I DIDN'T DO ANYTHING!
BOOOOOOY
SIGH SUCH A NOISY HOUSE-HOLD.
HSSSS HSSSS
I STILL DON'T KNOW WHY BUT RANMA'S BEING SO NICE...
BUT I SHOULD JUST ENJOY IT UNTIL I FEEL BETTER.
HWOOOO
SOBSOB SOB
C-C-C-COLD...
RANMA, YOU JERK...
SHNORRRR

Part 5
FOR THE LOVE OF SAUCE

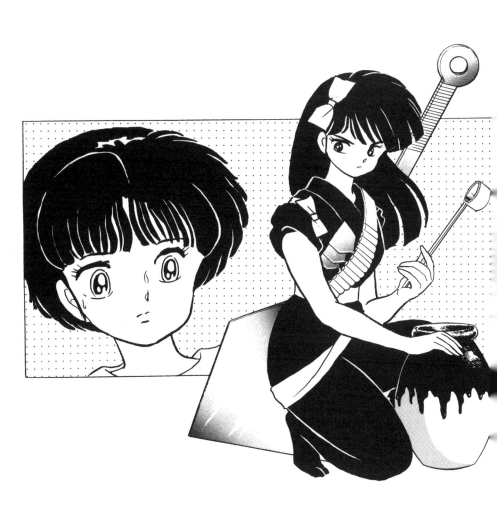

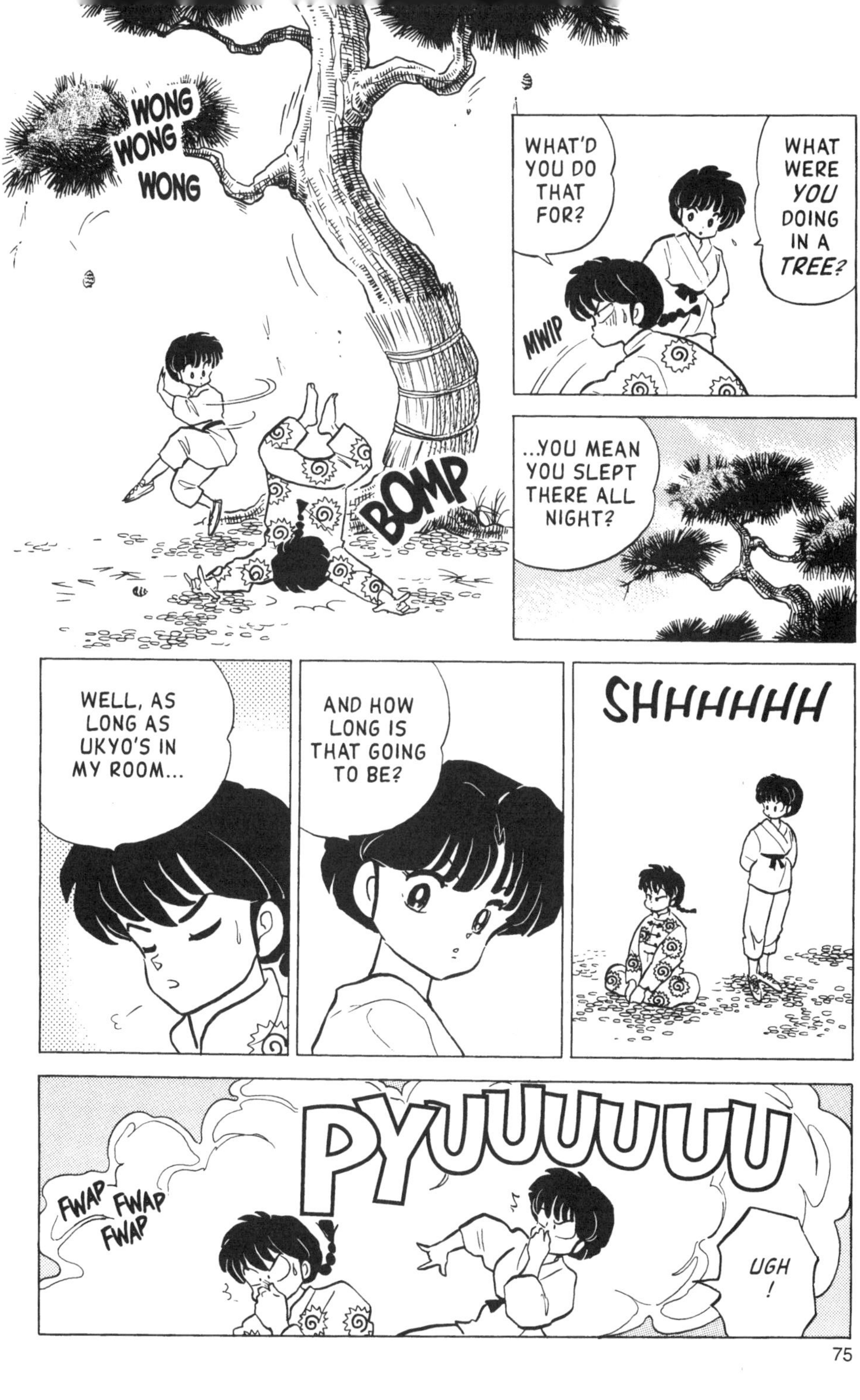
WONG WONG WONG
BOMP
MWIP
WHAT'D YOU DO THAT FOR?
WHAT WERE YOU DOING IN A TREE?
...YOU MEAN YOU SLEPT THERE ALL NIGHT?
WELL, AS LONG AS UKYO'S IN MY ROOM...
AND HOW LONG IS THAT GOING TO BE?
SHHHHHH
PYUUUUUU
FWAP FWAP FWAP
UGH!

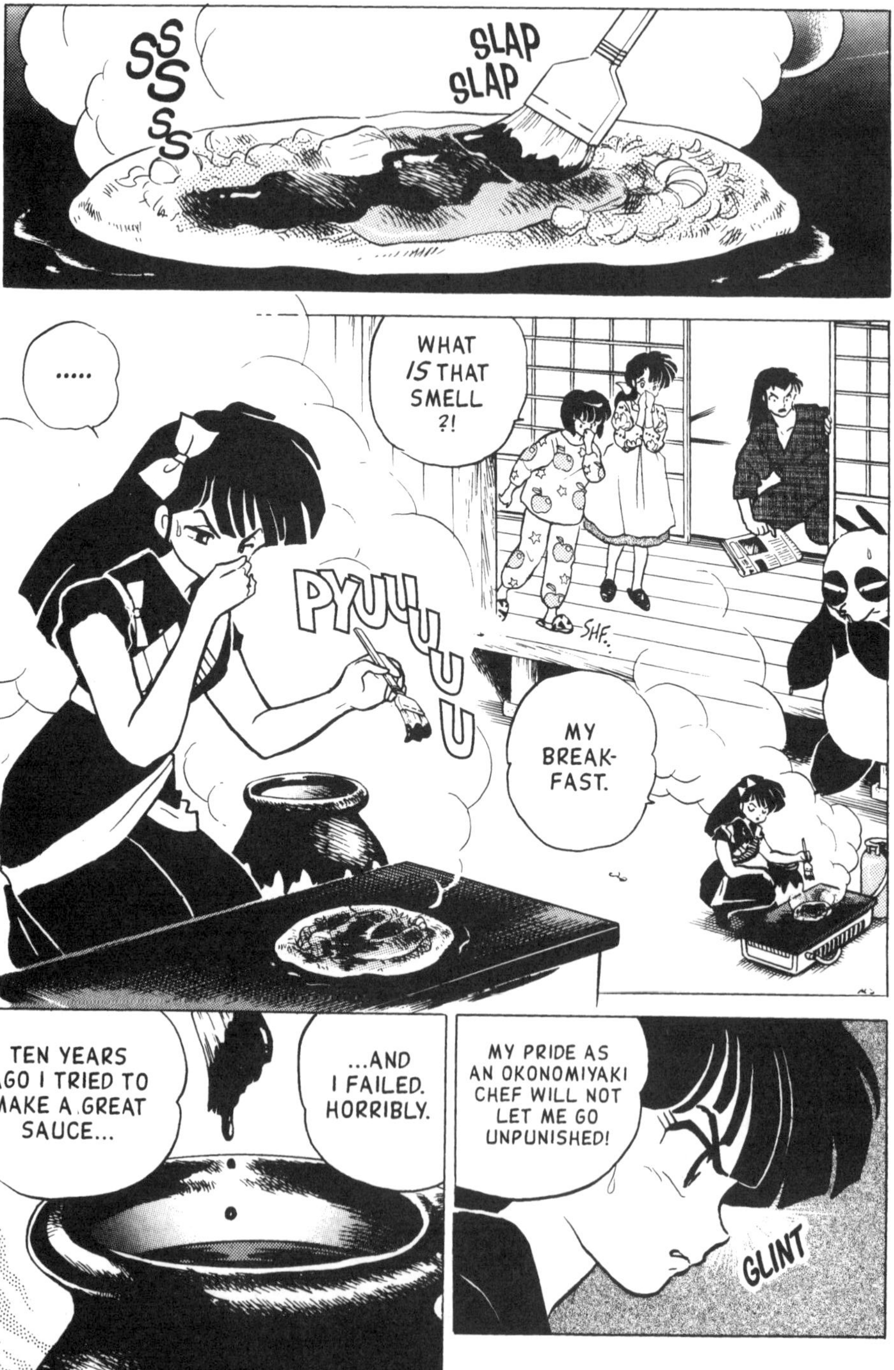
SSSSS
SLAP SLAP
.....
WHAT *IS* THAT SMELL ?!
PYUUUUUU
SHF..
MY BREAK-FAST.
TEN YEARS AGO I TRIED TO MAKE A GREAT SAUCE...
...AND I FAILED. HORRIBLY.
MY PRIDE AS AN OKONOMIYAKI CHEF WILL NOT LET ME GO UNPUNISHED!
GLINT

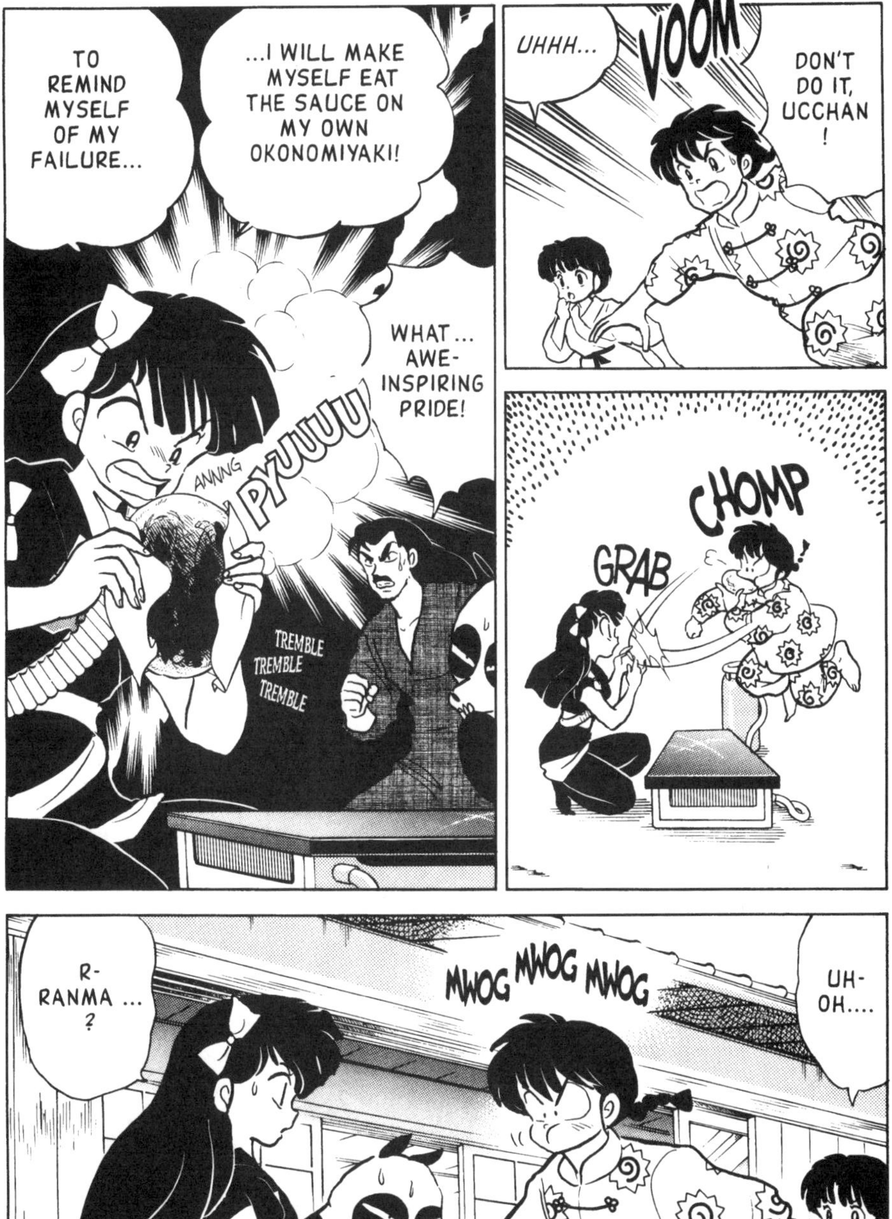
TO REMIND MYSELF OF MY FAILURE...
...I WILL MAKE MYSELF EAT THE SAUCE ON MY OWN OKONOMIYAKI!
WHAT... AWE-INSPIRING PRIDE!
ANNNG
PYUUUU
TREMBLE TREMBLE TREMBLE
UHHH...
VOOM
DON'T DO IT, UCCHAN!
CHOMP
GRAB
!
R-RANMA ...?
MWOG MWOG MWOG
UH-OH....

GLOMP

EEEEEEP

CHEEP

CHEEP

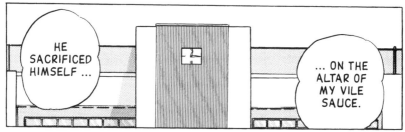

HE SACRIFICED HIMSELF ...

... ON THE ALTAR OF MY VILE SAUCE.

OH, RANMA HONEY...

SIIIIIGH

WHY ARE YOU BEING SO NICE TO ME?

RANMA, WHAT HAPPENED TO YOUR FACE?

I GUESS IT'S KIND OF TOO LATE...

TO ADMIT *I'M* THE ONE WHO MADE THAT SAUCE...

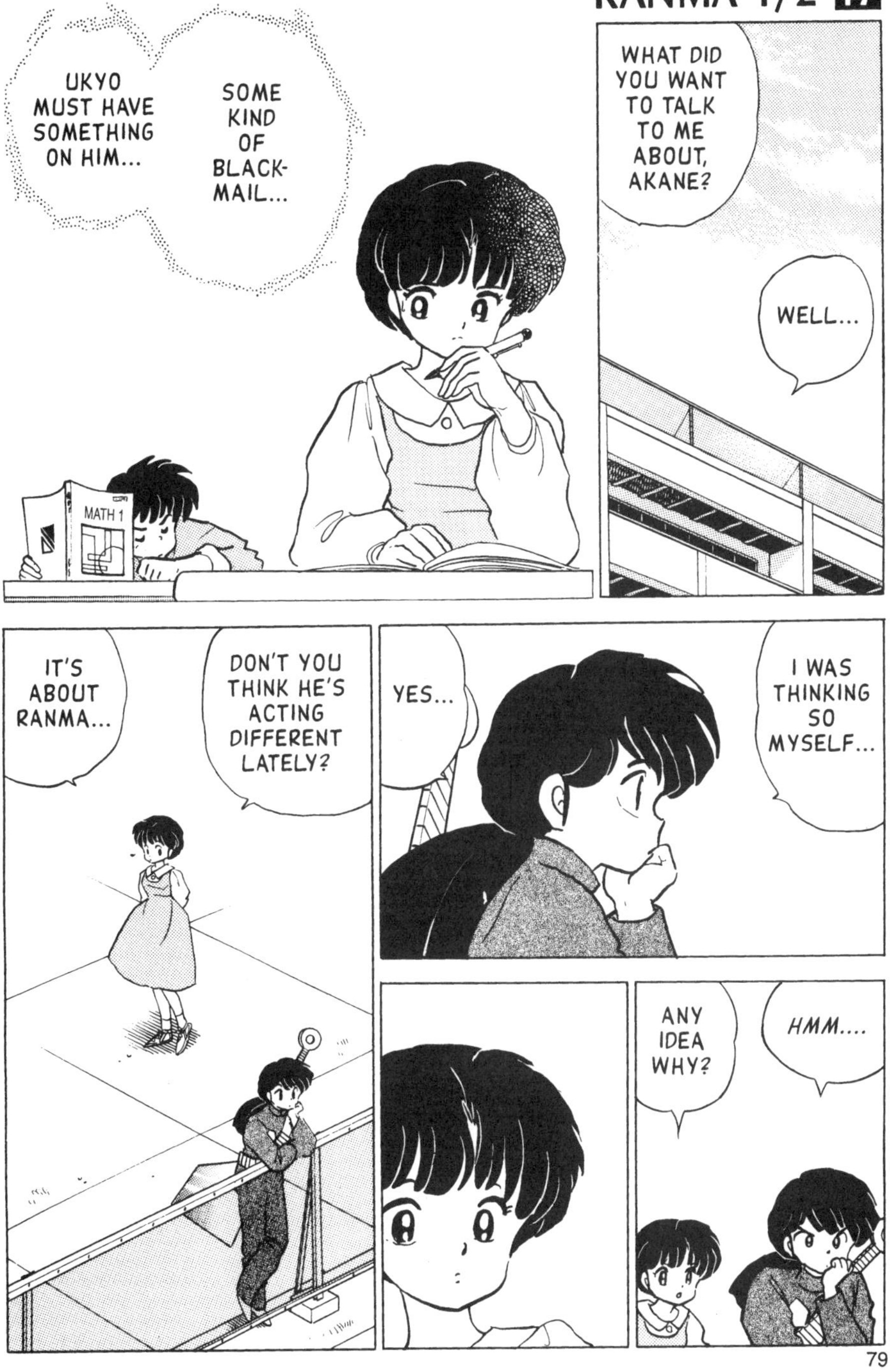
UKYO MUST HAVE SOMETHING ON HIM...
SOME KIND OF BLACK-MAIL...
WHAT DID YOU WANT TO TALK TO ME ABOUT, AKANE?
WELL...
MATH 1
IT'S ABOUT RANMA...
DON'T YOU THINK HE'S ACTING DIFFERENT LATELY?
YES...
I WAS THINKING SO MYSELF...
ANY IDEA WHY?
HMM....

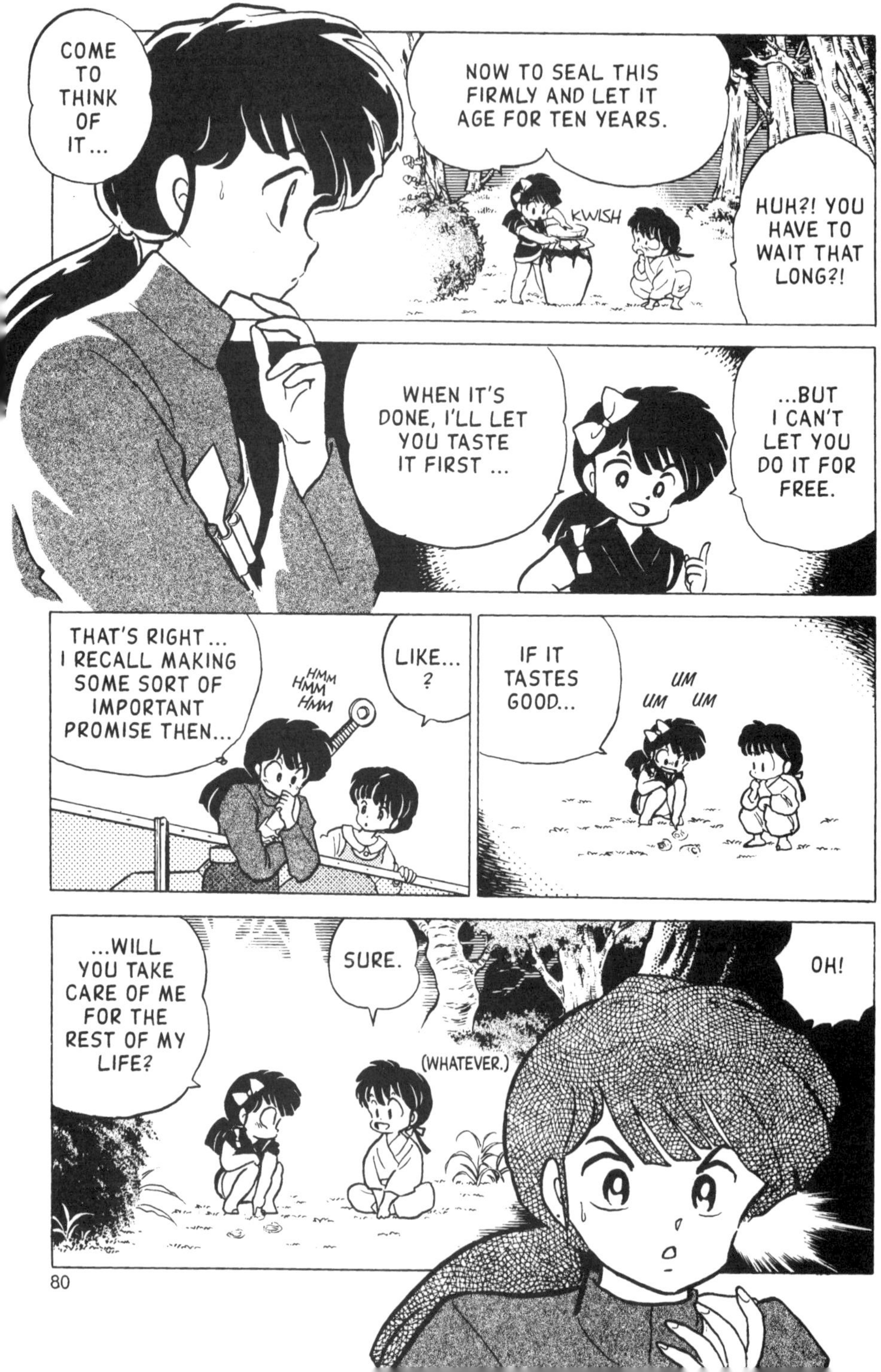

COME TO THINK OF IT...
NOW TO SEAL THIS FIRMLY AND LET IT AGE FOR TEN YEARS.
KWISH
HUH?! YOU HAVE TO WAIT THAT LONG?!
WHEN IT'S DONE, I'LL LET YOU TASTE IT FIRST ...
...BUT I CAN'T LET YOU DO IT FOR FREE.
THAT'S RIGHT... I RECALL MAKING SOME SORT OF IMPORTANT PROMISE THEN...
HMM HMM HMM
LIKE... ?
IF IT TASTES GOOD...
UM UM UM
...WILL YOU TAKE CARE OF ME FOR THE REST OF MY LIFE?
SURE.
(WHATEVER.)
OH!

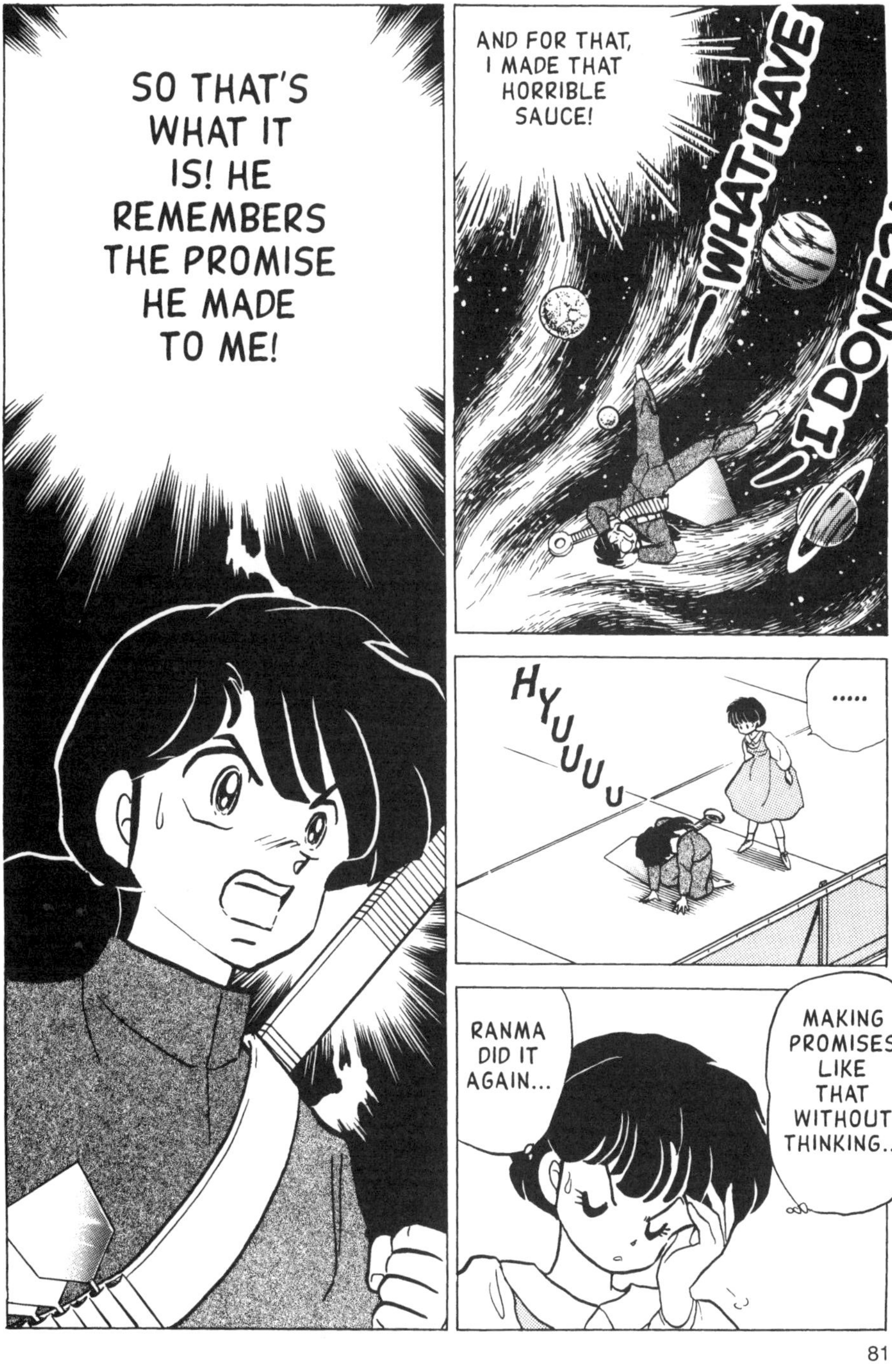
SO THAT'S WHAT IT IS! HE REMEMBERS THE PROMISE HE MADE TO ME!
AND FOR THAT, I MADE THAT HORRIBLE SAUCE!
—WHAT HAVE I DONE?!
HYUUUUU
.....
RANMA DID IT AGAIN...
MAKING PROMISES LIKE THAT WITHOUT THINKING...

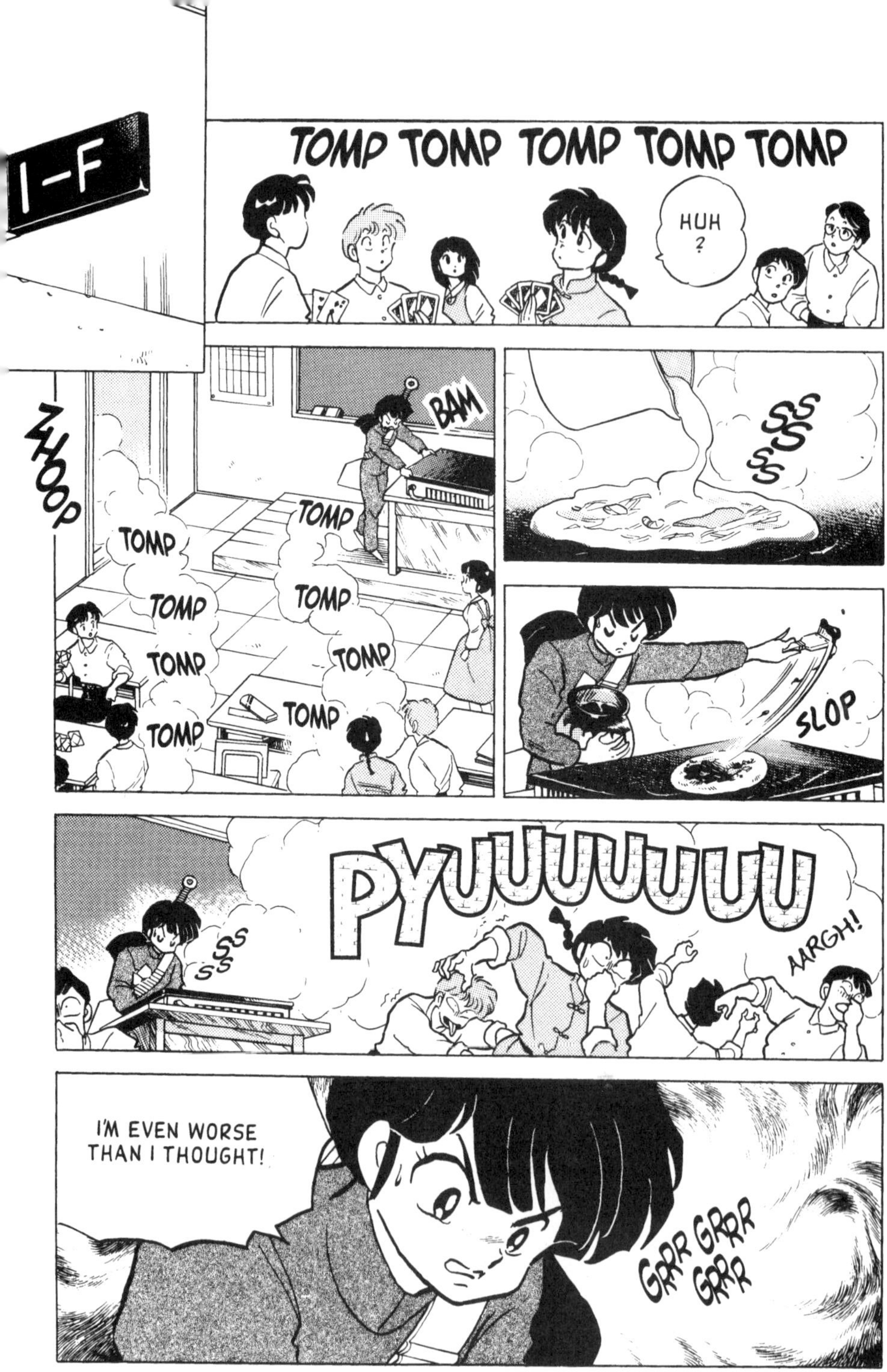
1-F
TOMP TOMP TOMP TOMP TOMP
HUH ?
ZHOOP
BAM
TOMP
TOMP
TOMP
TOMP
TOMP
TOMP
TOMP
TOMP
SSSSS
SLOP
SSS
PYUUUUUUU
AARGH!
I'M EVEN WORSE THAN I THOUGHT!
GRRR GRRR GRRR

83

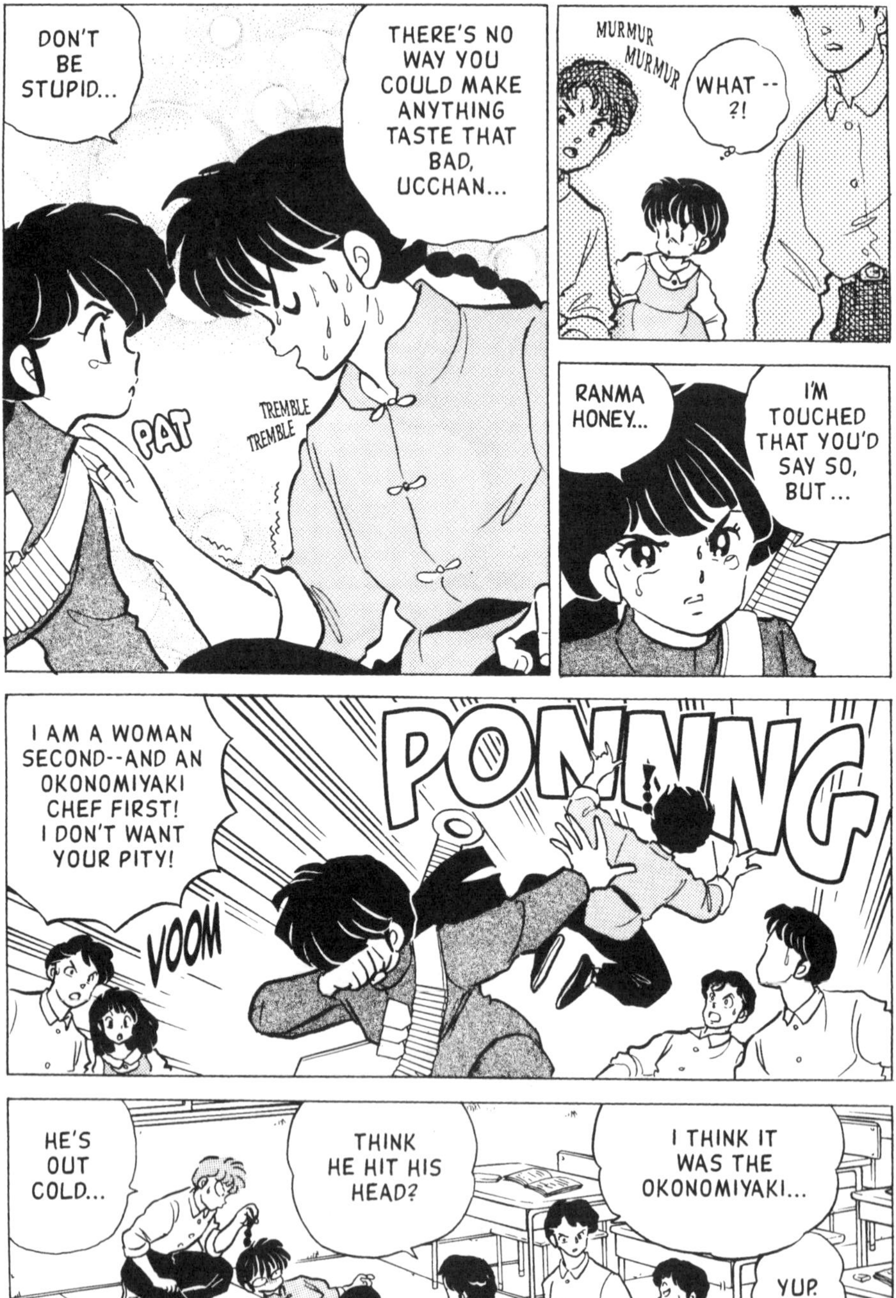
DON'T BE STUPID...
THERE'S NO WAY YOU COULD MAKE ANYTHING TASTE THAT BAD, UCCHAN...
PAT
TREMBLE TREMBLE
MURMUR MURMUR
WHAT --?!
RANMA HONEY...
I'M TOUCHED THAT YOU'D SAY SO, BUT...
I AM A WOMAN SECOND--AND AN OKONOMIYAKI CHEF FIRST! I DON'T WANT YOUR PITY!
PONNNG
VOOM
HE'S OUT COLD...
THINK HE HIT HIS HEAD?
I THINK IT WAS THE OKONOMIYAKI...
YUP.

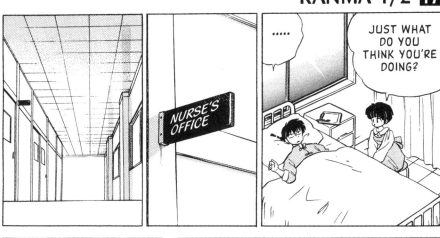

JUST WHAT DO YOU THINK YOU'RE DOING?

.....

IS THERE SOME REASON YOU CAN'T TELL HER THAT IT TASTES *BAD?*

HUH?

WHAT DO YOU MEAN BY THAT...?

"IF IT TASTES GOOD...WILL YOU TAKE CARE OF ME FOR THE REST OF MY LIFE?"

SURE.

SOME-THING...

...THAT HAPPENED TEN YEARS AGO?

BLUP BLUP

JABB

85

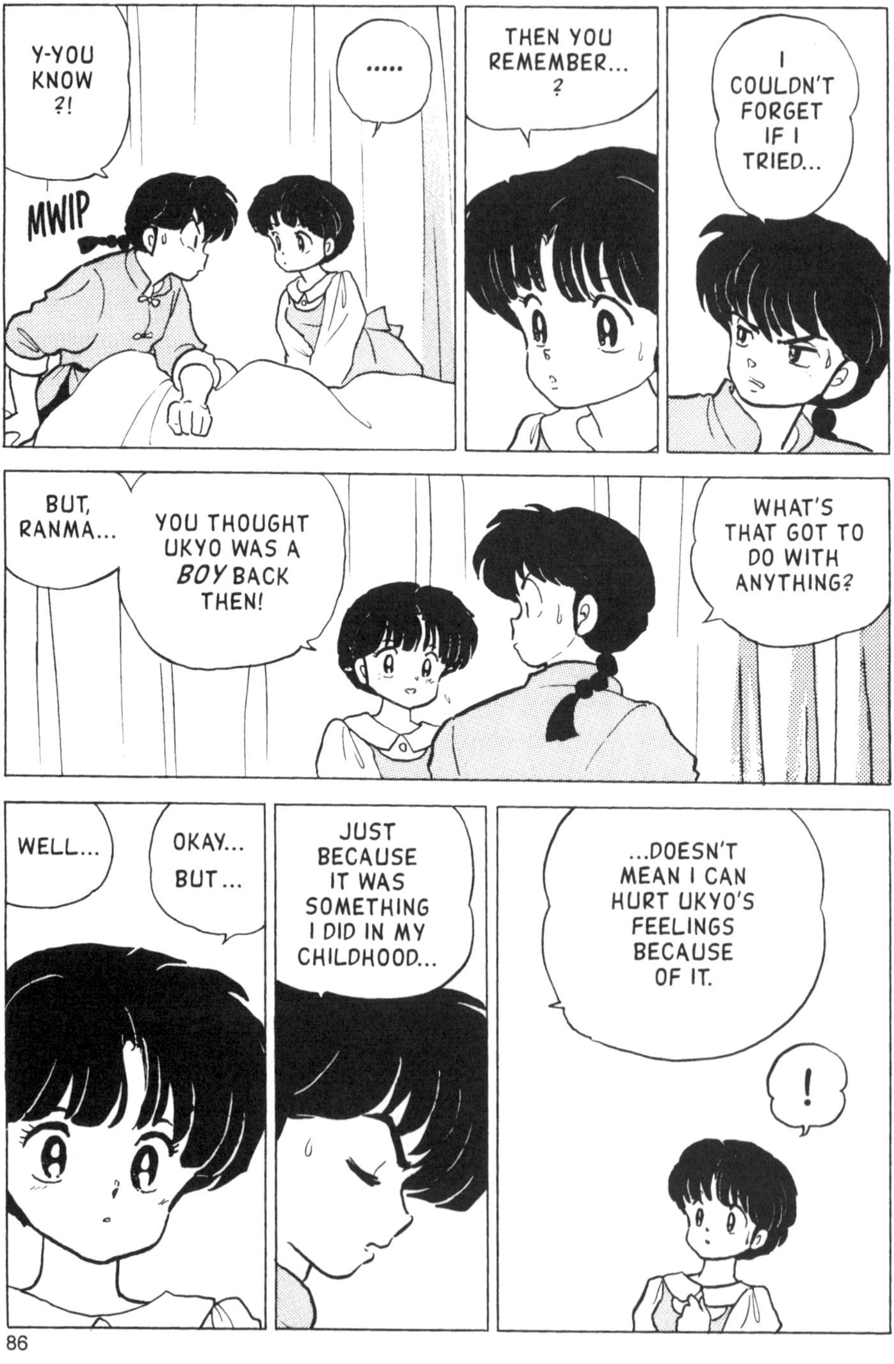
Y-YOU KNOW ?!
MWIP
.....
THEN YOU REMEMBER... ?
I COULDN'T FORGET IF I TRIED...
BUT, RANMA...
YOU THOUGHT UKYO WAS A BOY BACK THEN!
WHAT'S THAT GOT TO DO WITH ANYTHING?
WELL...
OKAY... BUT...
JUST BECAUSE IT WAS SOMETHING I DID IN MY CHILDHOOD...
...DOESN'T MEAN I CAN HURT UKYO'S FEELINGS BECAUSE OF IT.
!

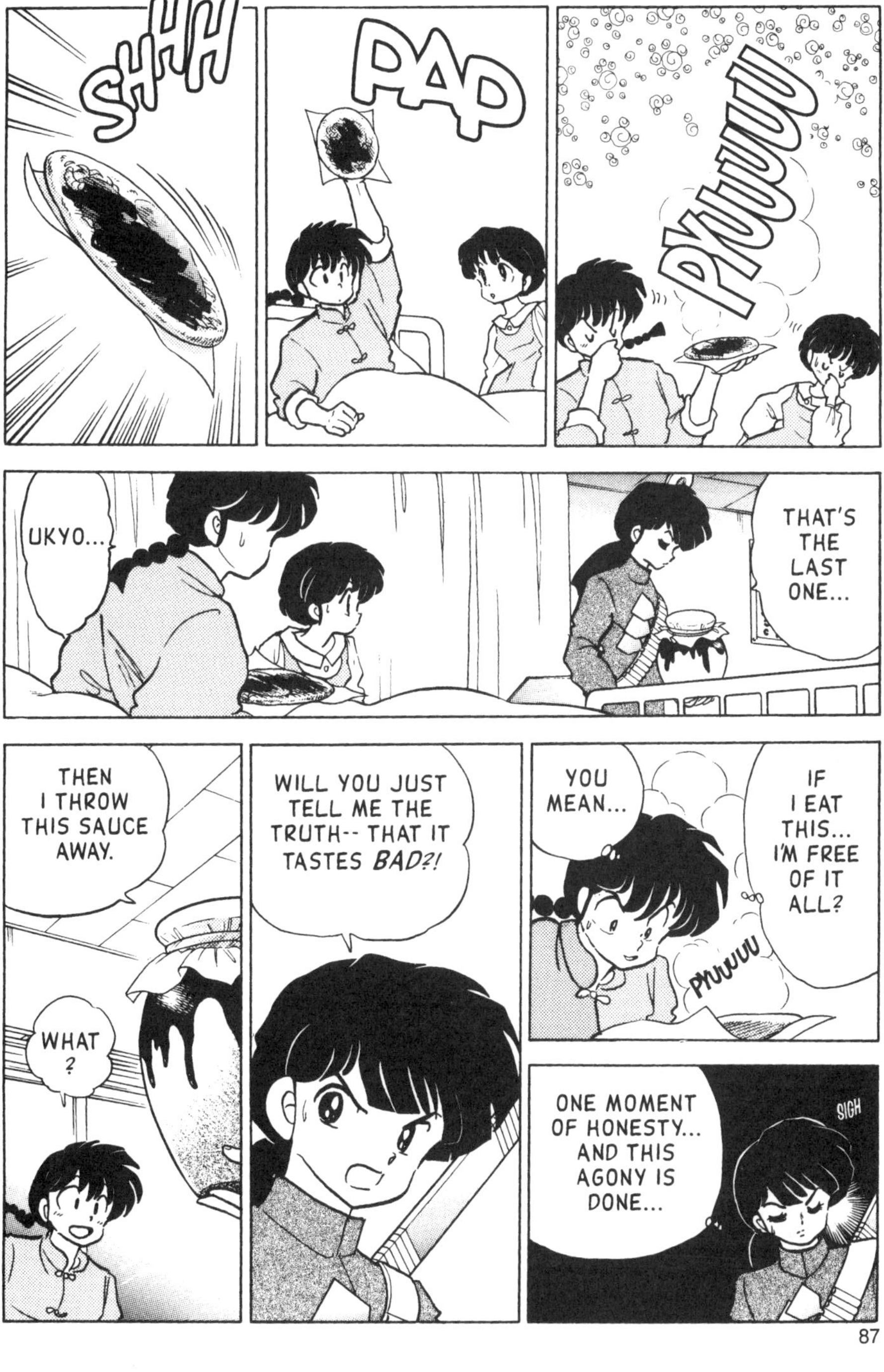
SHHH
PAP
PYUUUU
UKYO...
THAT'S THE LAST ONE...
THEN I THROW THIS SAUCE AWAY.
WHAT?
WILL YOU JUST TELL ME THE TRUTH-- THAT IT TASTES *BAD*?!
YOU MEAN...
IF I EAT THIS... I'M FREE OF IT ALL?
PYUUUU
ONE MOMENT OF HONESTY... AND THIS AGONY IS DONE...
SIGH

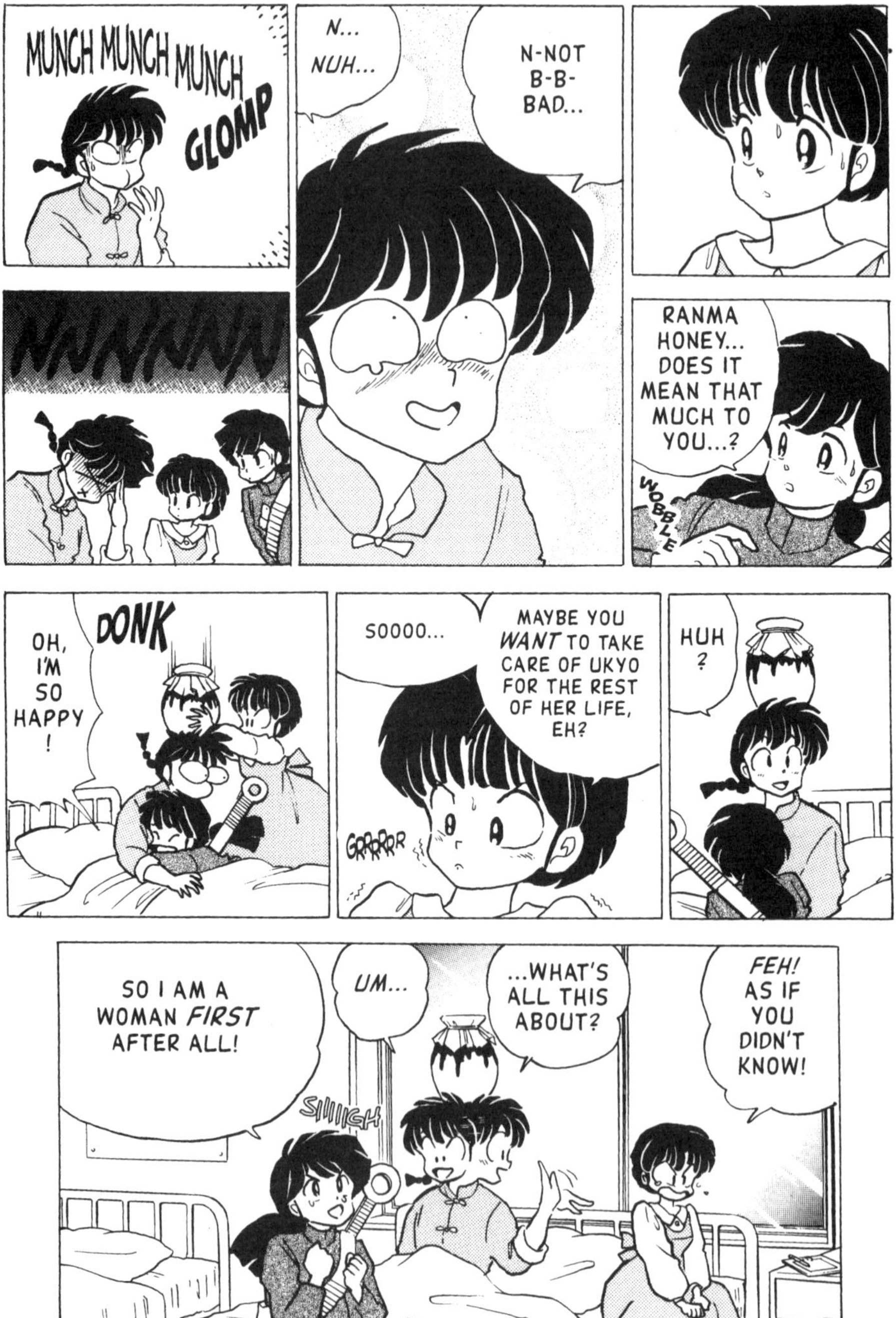
MUNCH MUNCH MUNCH
GLOMP
N... NUH...
N-NOT B-B-BAD...
NNNNNN
RANMA HONEY... DOES IT MEAN THAT MUCH TO YOU...?
WOBBLE
OH, I'M SO HAPPY!
DONK
SOOOO...
MAYBE YOU *WANT* TO TAKE CARE OF UKYO FOR THE REST OF HER LIFE, EH?
GRRRRRR
HUH?
SO I AM A WOMAN *FIRST* AFTER ALL!
SIIIIGH
UM...
...WHAT'S ALL THIS ABOUT?
FEH! AS IF YOU DIDN'T KNOW!

Part 6
THE TRUTH ABOUT THE TRUTH

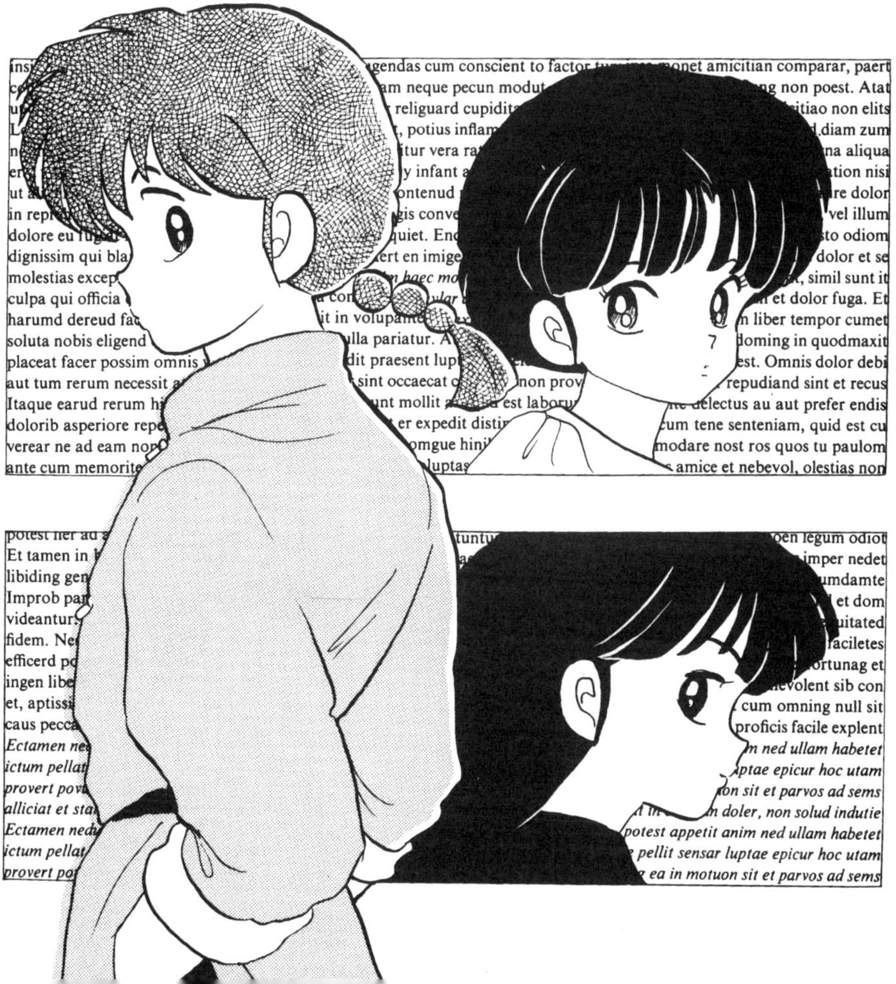

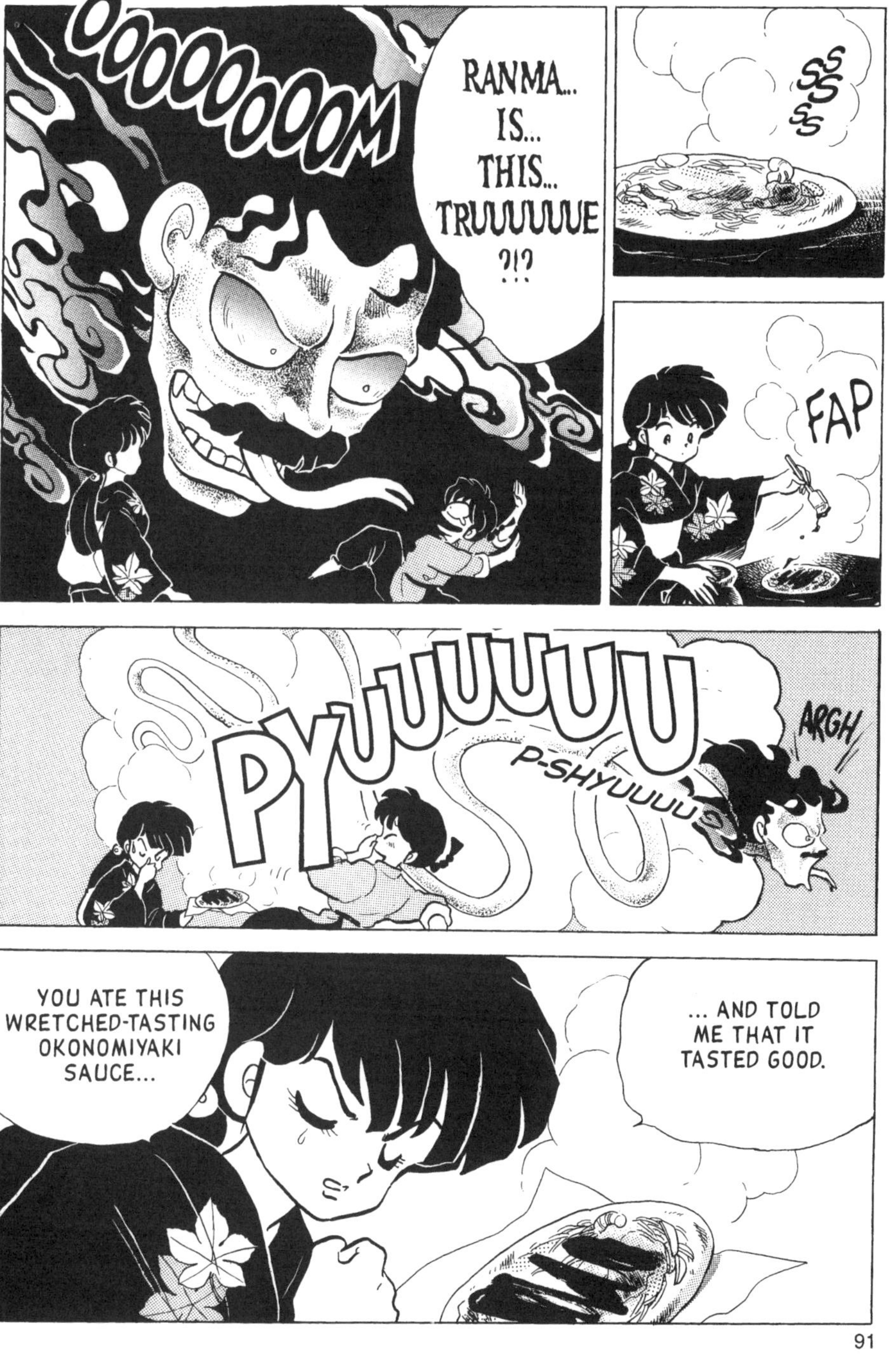
OOOOOOOOM
RANMA... IS... THIS... TRUUUUUE ?!?
SSSSS
FAP
PYUUUUUU
P-SHYUUUUU
ARGH
YOU ATE THIS WRETCHED-TASTING OKONOMIYAKI SAUCE...
... AND TOLD ME THAT IT TASTED GOOD.

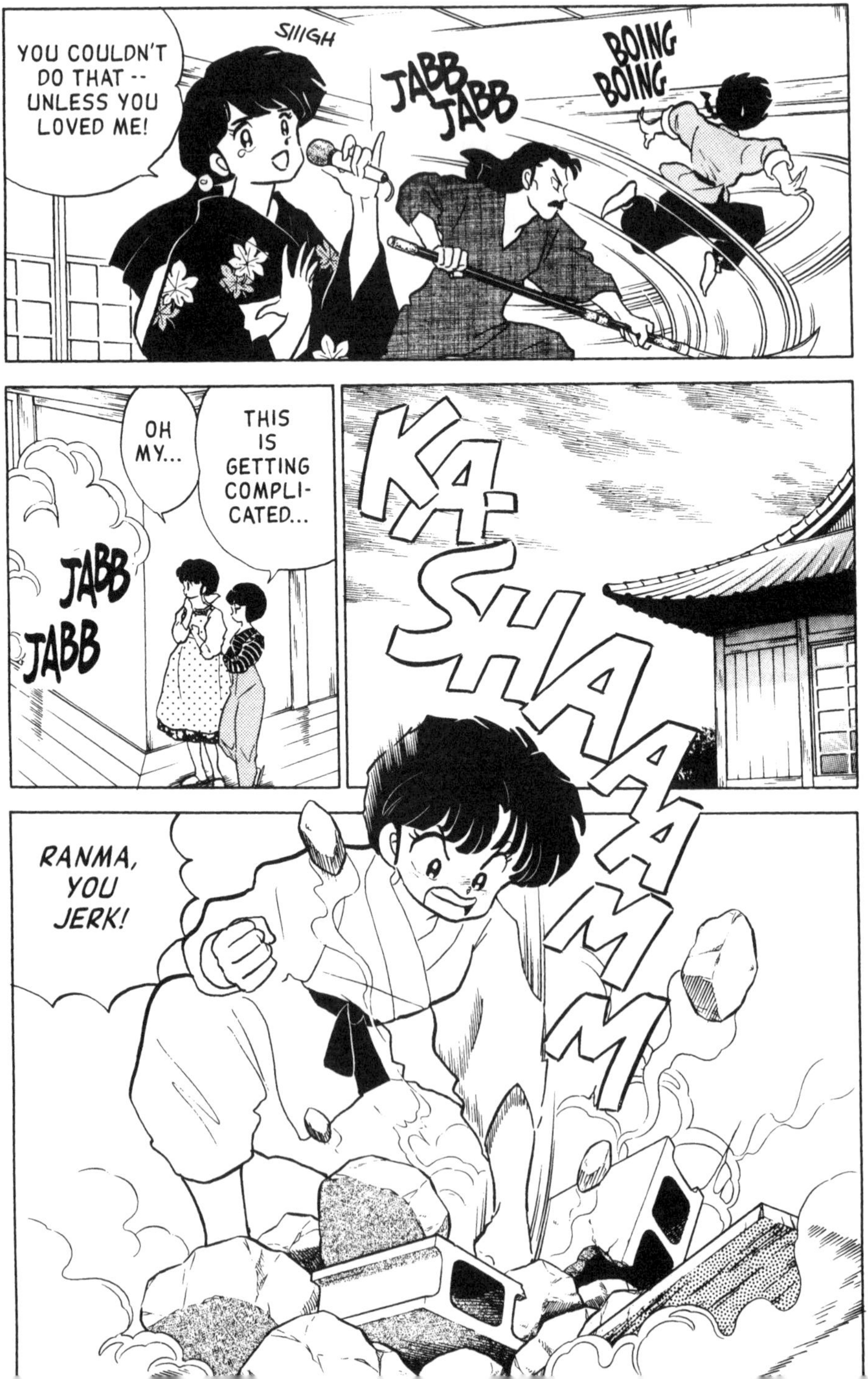
YOU COULDN'T DO THAT -- UNLESS YOU LOVED ME!
SIIGH
JABB JABB
BOING BOING
OH MY...
THIS IS GETTING COMPLICATED...
JABB JABB
KA-SHAAAAMMMM
RANMA, YOU JERK!

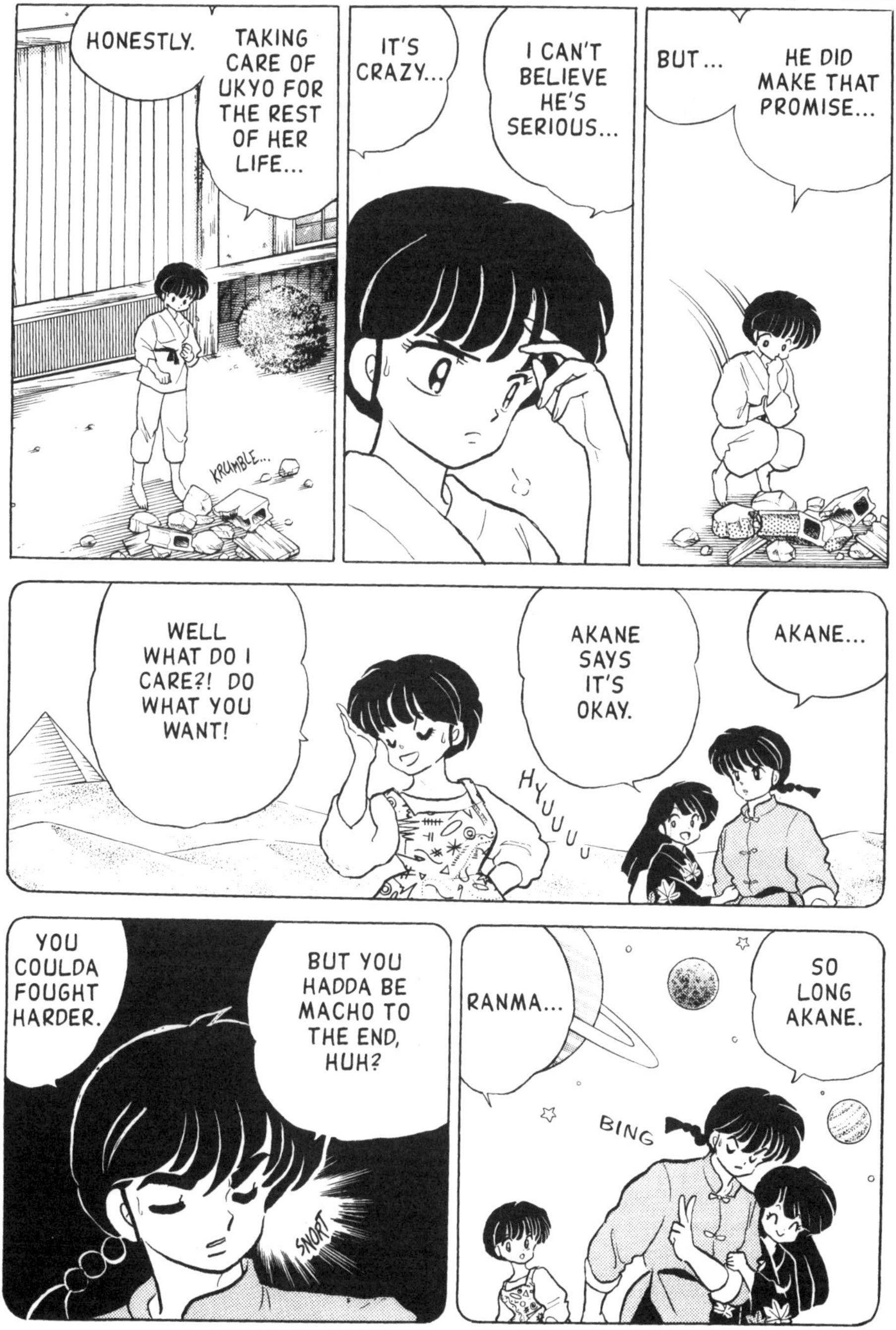
HONESTLY.
TAKING CARE OF UKYO FOR THE REST OF HER LIFE...
KRUMBLE...
IT'S CRAZY...
I CAN'T BELIEVE HE'S SERIOUS...
BUT...
HE DID MAKE THAT PROMISE...
WELL WHAT DO I CARE?! DO WHAT YOU WANT!
HYUUUUU
AKANE SAYS IT'S OKAY.
AKANE...
YOU COULDA FOUGHT HARDER.
BUT YOU HADDA BE MACHO TO THE END, HUH?
SNORT
RANMA...
SO LONG AKANE.
BING

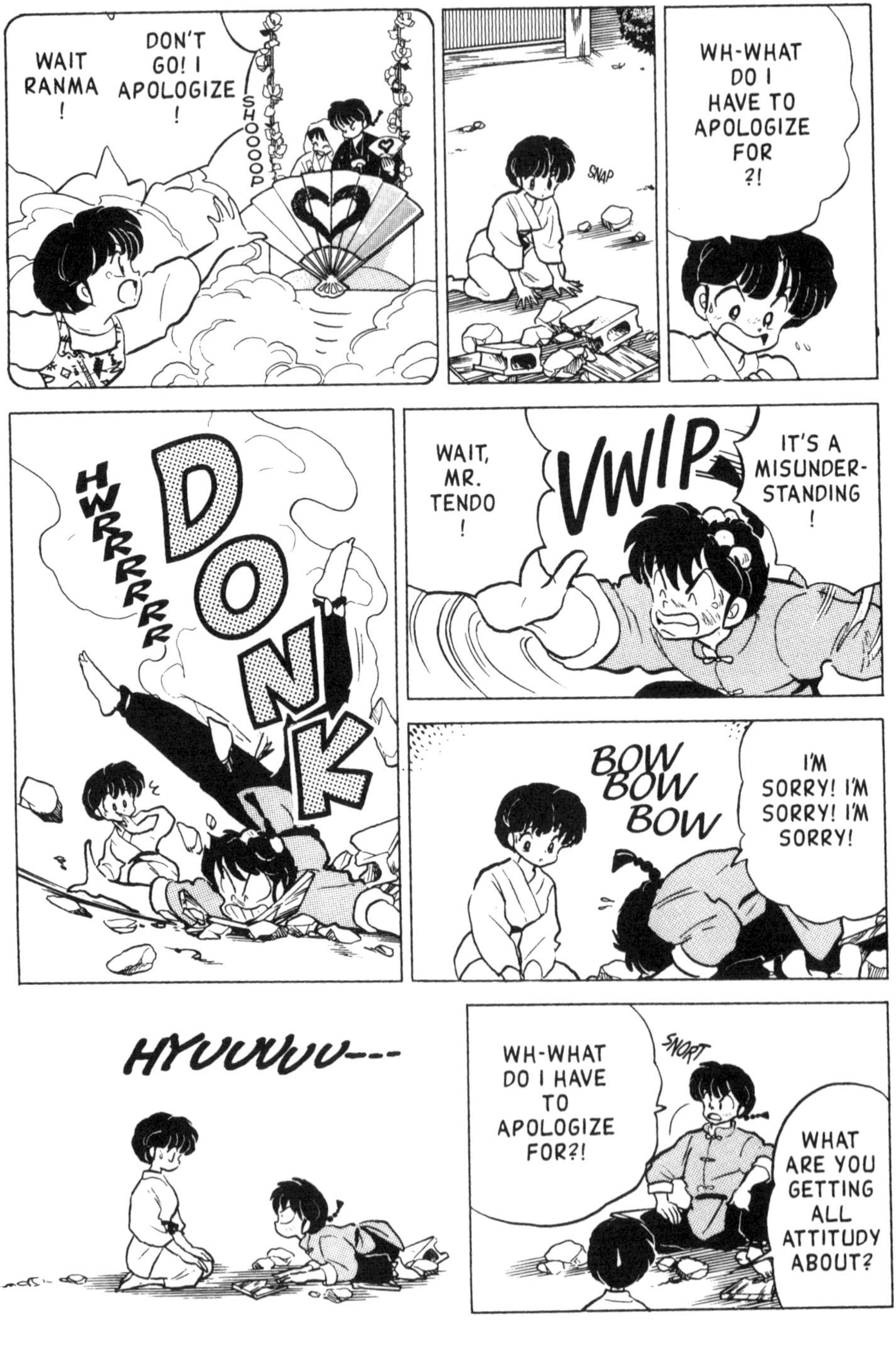
WAIT RANMA!
DON'T GO! I APOLOGIZE!
SHOOOOP
SNAP
WH-WHAT DO I HAVE TO APOLOGIZE FOR?!
HWRRRRRR
DONK
WAIT, MR. TENDO!
VWIP
IT'S A MISUNDERSTANDING!
BOW BOW BOW
I'M SORRY! I'M SORRY! I'M SORRY!
HYUUUUU---
SNORT
WH-WHAT DO I HAVE TO APOLOGIZE FOR?!
WHAT ARE YOU GETTING ALL ATTITUDY ABOUT?

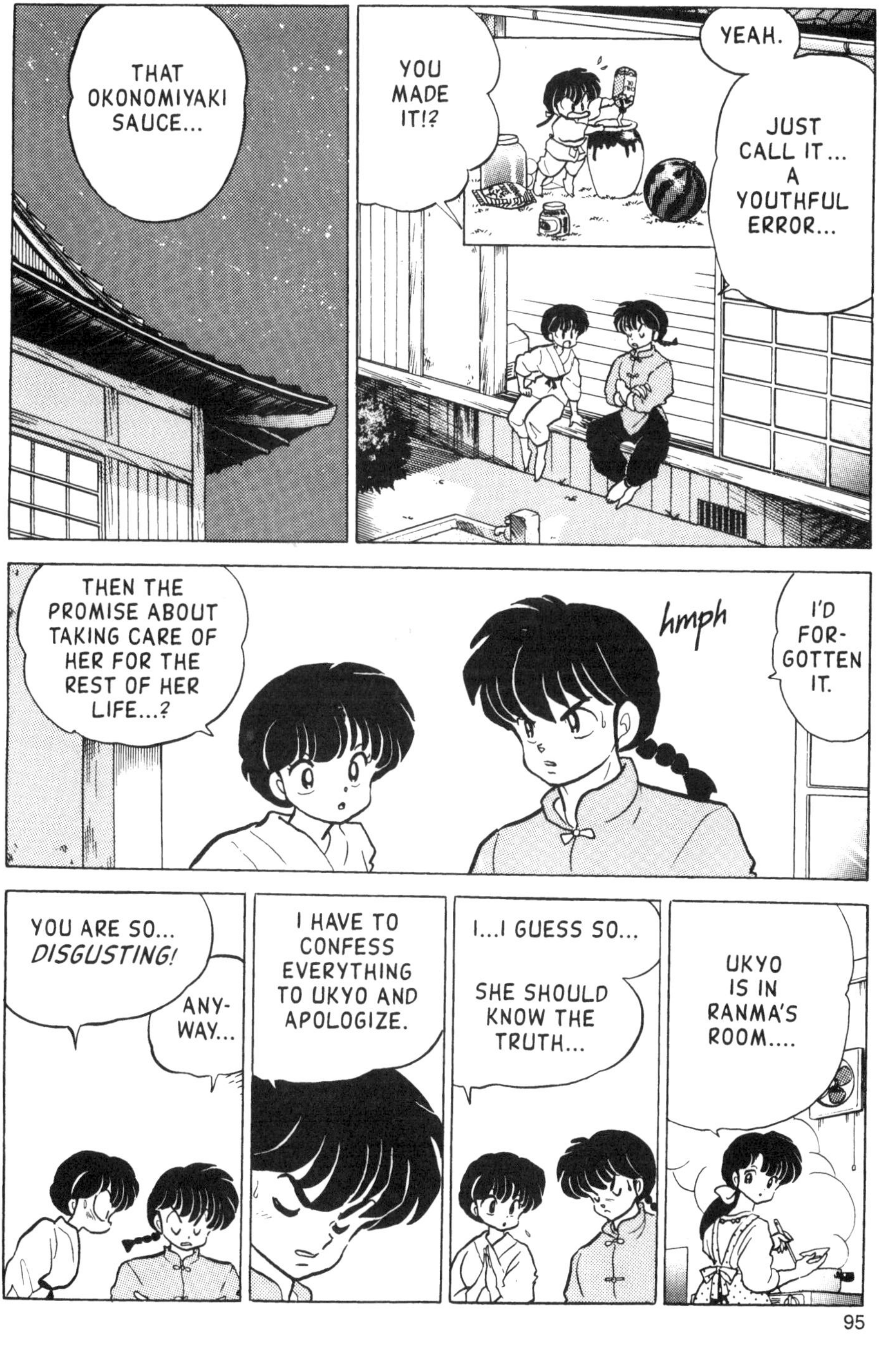
THAT OKONOMIYAKI SAUCE...
YOU MADE IT!?
YEAH.
JUST CALL IT... A YOUTHFUL ERROR...
THEN THE PROMISE ABOUT TAKING CARE OF HER FOR THE REST OF HER LIFE...?
hmph
I'D FOR-GOTTEN IT.
YOU ARE SO... *DISGUSTING!*
ANY-WAY...
I HAVE TO CONFESS EVERYTHING TO UKYO AND APOLOGIZE.
I...I GUESS SO...
SHE SHOULD KNOW THE TRUTH...
UKYO IS IN RANMA'S ROOM....

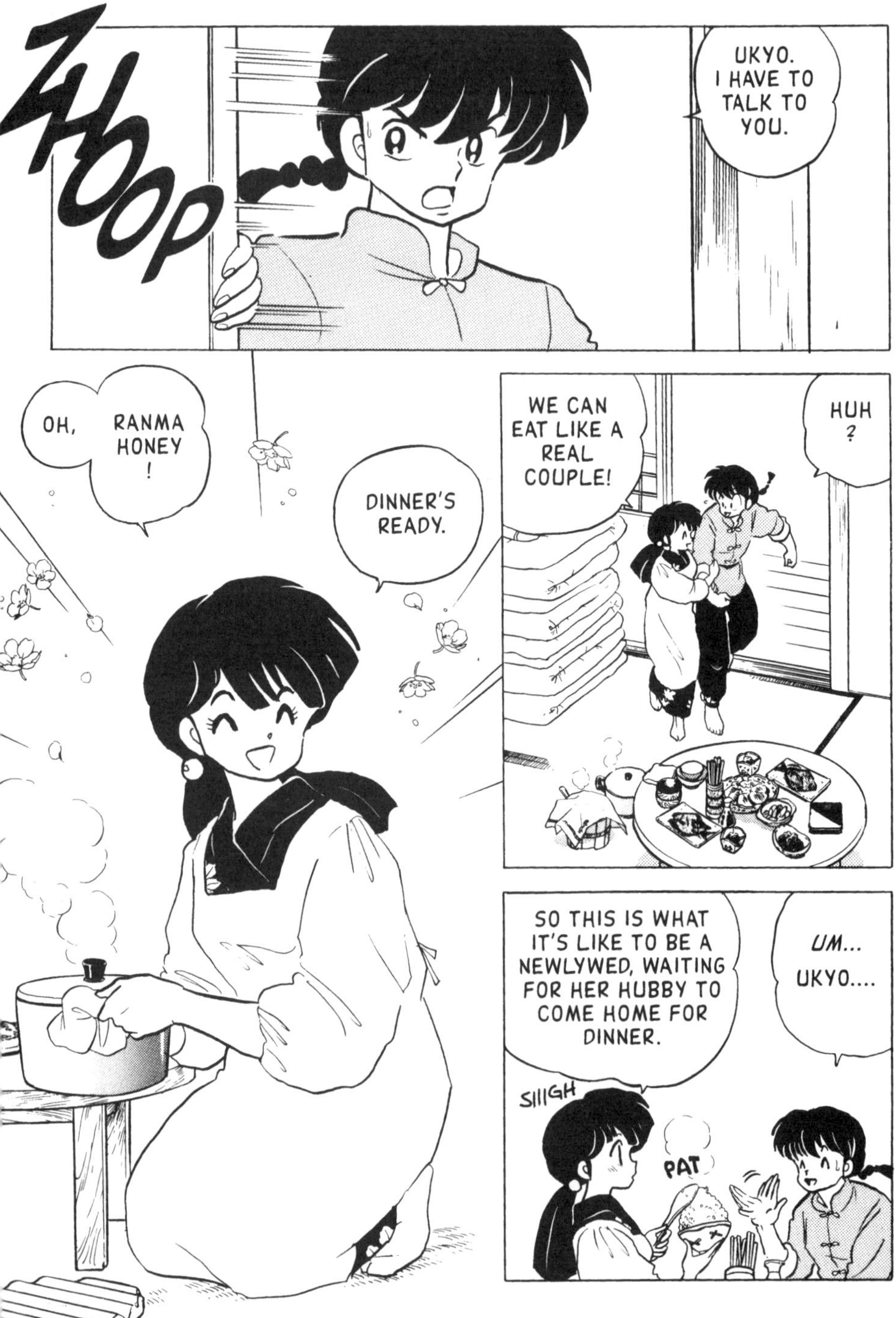
ZHOOP
UKYO. I HAVE TO TALK TO YOU.
OH, RANMA HONEY!
DINNER'S READY.
WE CAN EAT LIKE A REAL COUPLE!
HUH?
SO THIS IS WHAT IT'S LIKE TO BE A NEWLYWED, WAITING FOR HER HUBBY TO COME HOME FOR DINNER.
UM... UKYO....
SIIIGH
PAT

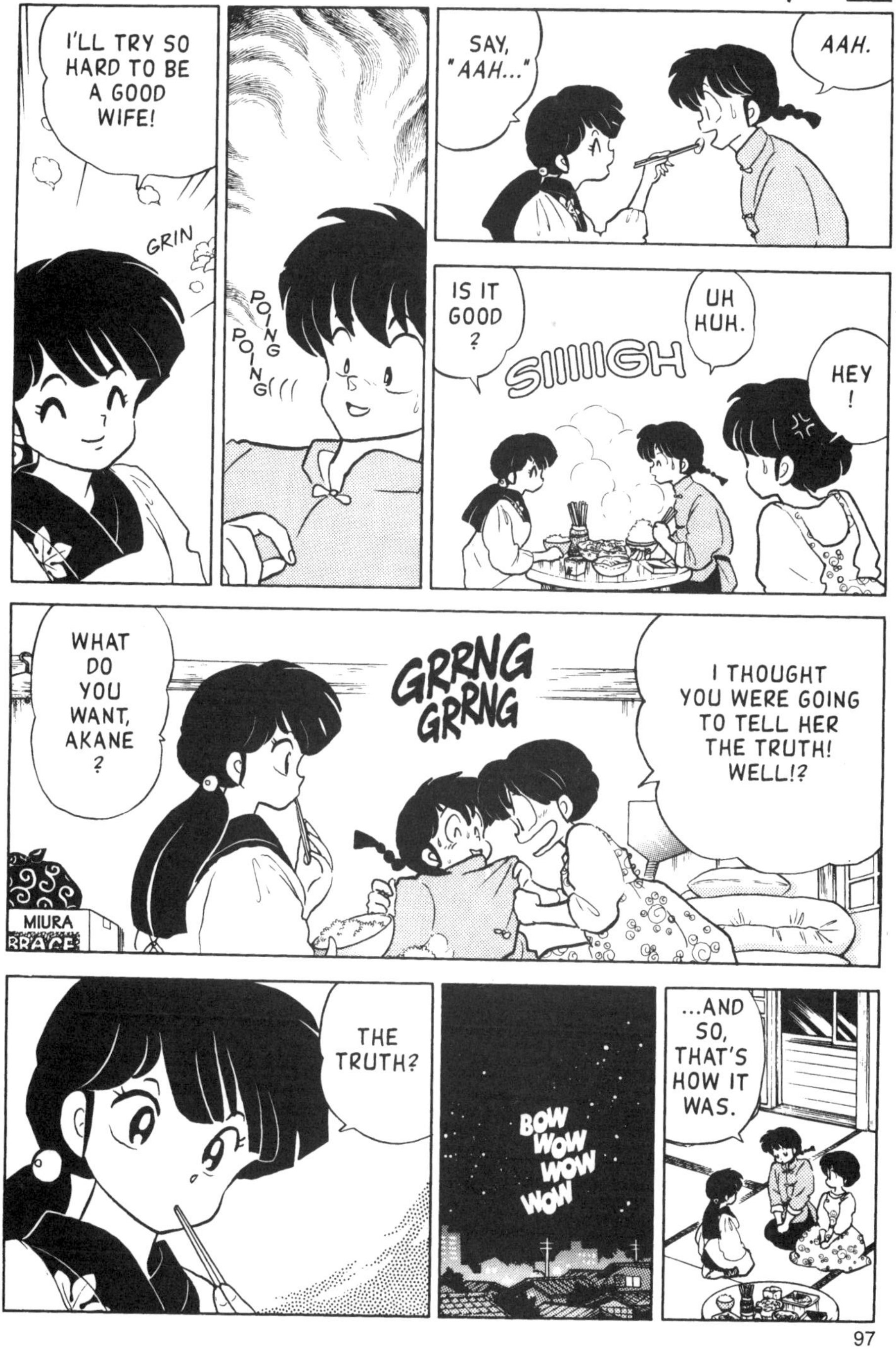
I'LL TRY SO HARD TO BE A GOOD WIFE!
GRIN
POING POING
SAY, "AAH..."
AAH.
IS IT GOOD?
UH HUH.
SIIIIIGH
HEY!
WHAT DO YOU WANT, AKANE?
GRRNG GRRNG
I THOUGHT YOU WERE GOING TO TELL HER THE TRUTH! WELL!?
MIURA
THE TRUTH?
BOW WOW WOW WOW
...AND SO, THAT'S HOW IT WAS.

I'M THE ONE WHO RUINED YOUR OKONOMIYAKI SAUCE.

HE WAS BEING NICE TO YOU BECAUSE HE FELT GUILTY ABOUT WHAT HE DID.

RANMA ...

I'M SORRY UCCHAN!

BOW

YOU CAN HIT ME UNTIL YOU FEEL BETTER.

SHHHHHH

hmph

POOR RANMA HONEY.

AKANE TOLD YOU TO SAY THAT, DIDN'T SHE?

HUH?

WHAT!?

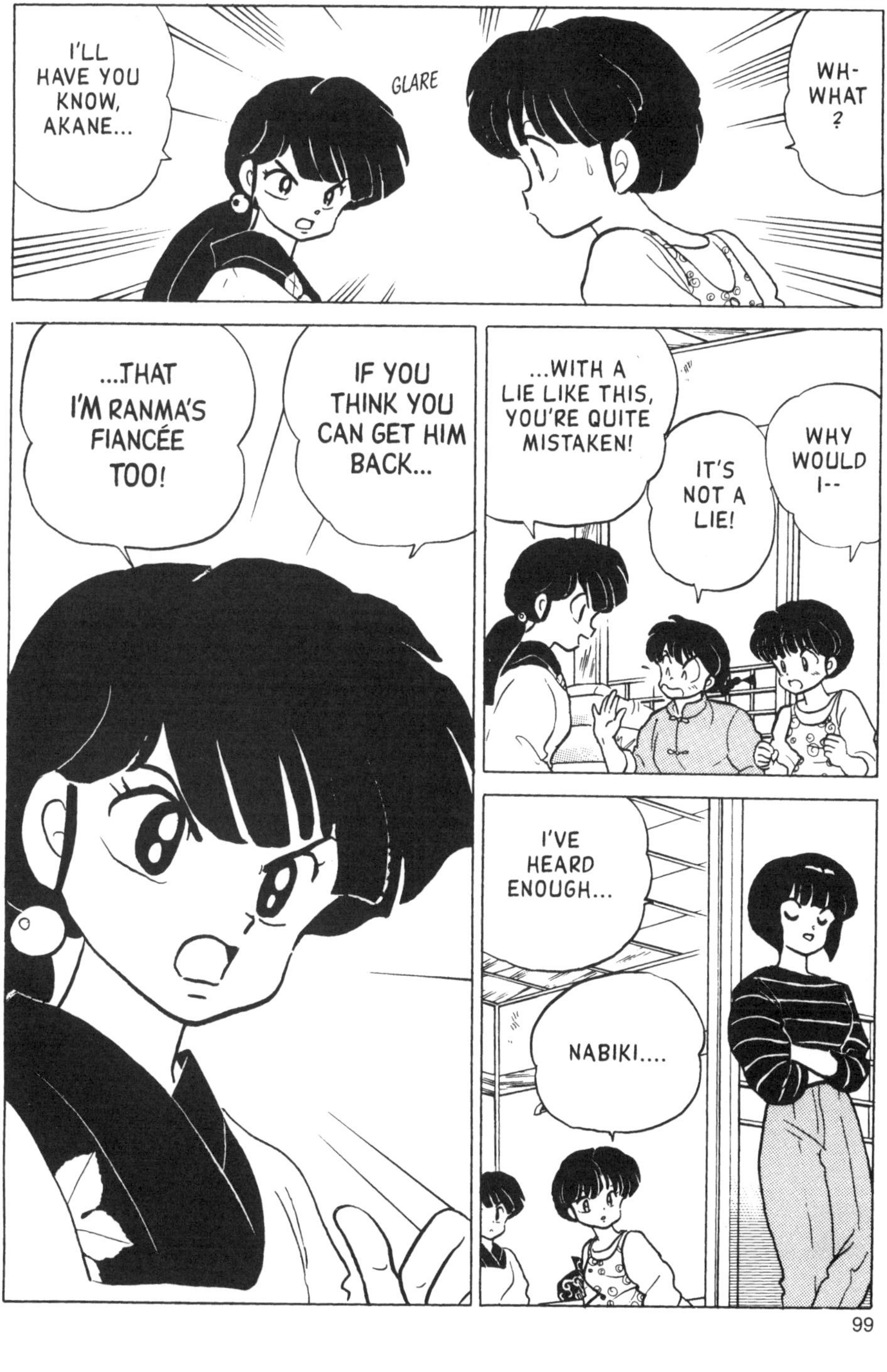
I'LL HAVE YOU KNOW, AKANE...
GLARE
WH- WHAT ?
...THAT I'M RANMA'S FIANCÉE TOO!
IF YOU THINK YOU CAN GET HIM BACK...
...WITH A LIE LIKE THIS, YOU'RE QUITE MISTAKEN!
IT'S NOT A LIE!
WHY WOULD I--
I'VE HEARD ENOUGH...
NABIKI....

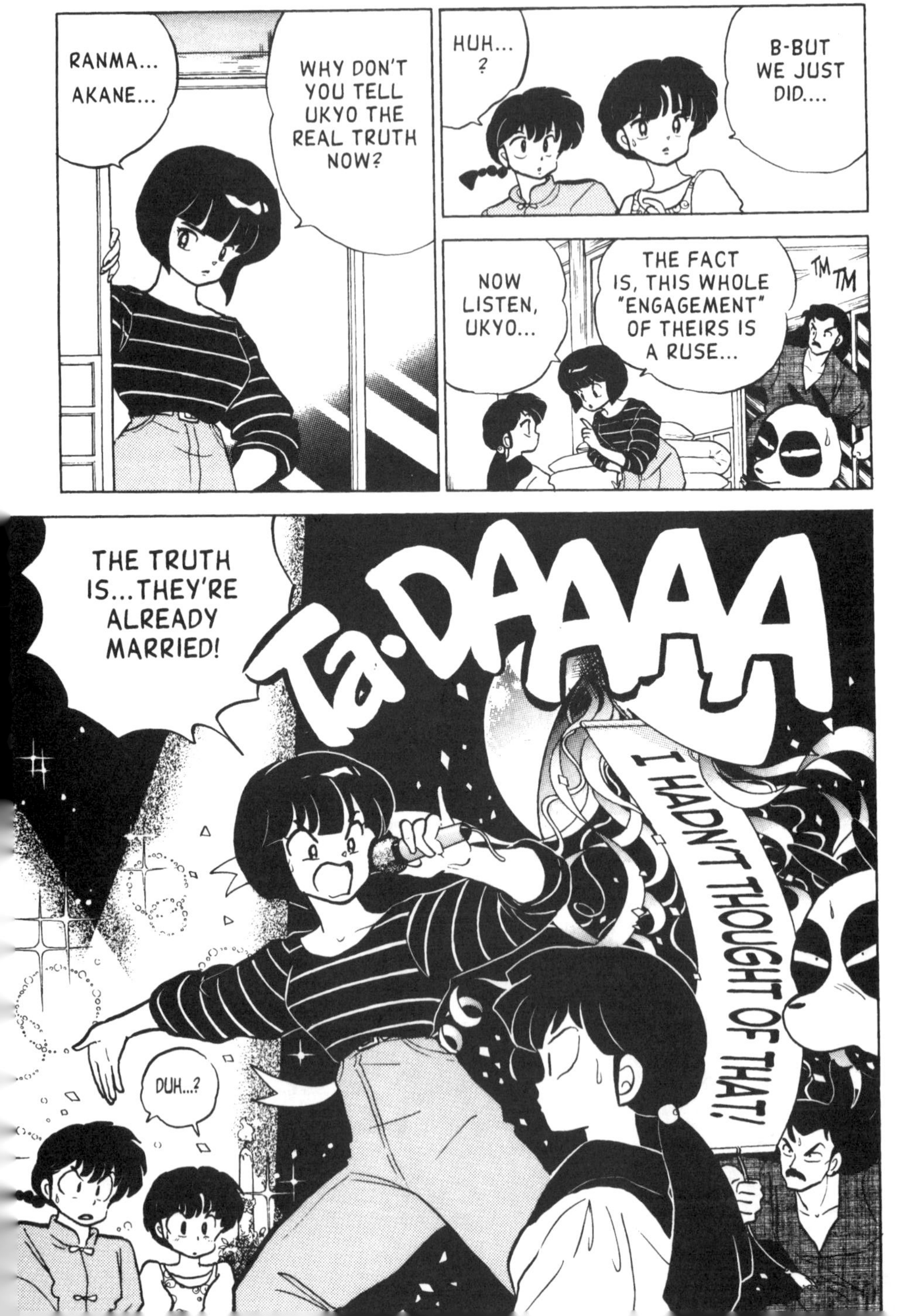
RANMA... AKANE...
WHY DON'T YOU TELL UKYO THE REAL TRUTH NOW?
HUH... ?
B-BUT WE JUST DID....
NOW LISTEN, UKYO...
THE FACT IS, THIS WHOLE "ENGAGEMENT" OF THEIRS IS A RUSE...
TM TM
THE TRUTH IS...THEY'RE ALREADY MARRIED!
Ta-DAAAA
I HADN'T THOUGHT OF THAT!
DUH...?

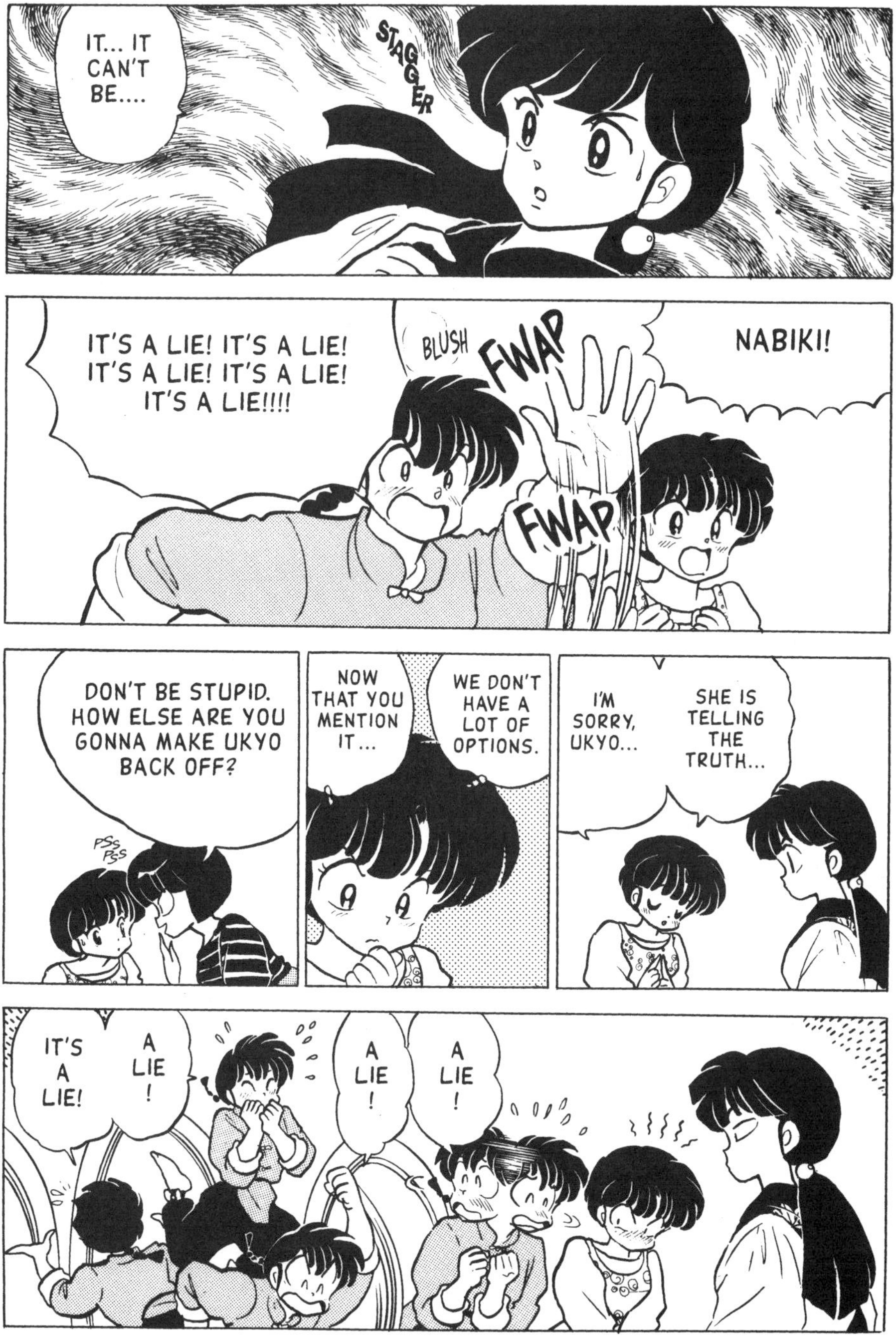
IT... IT CAN'T BE....
STAGGER
IT'S A LIE! IT'S A LIE! IT'S A LIE! IT'S A LIE! IT'S A LIE!!!!
BLUSH
FWAP
FWAP
NABIKI!
DON'T BE STUPID. HOW ELSE ARE YOU GONNA MAKE UKYO BACK OFF?
PSS PSS
NOW THAT YOU MENTION IT...
WE DON'T HAVE A LOT OF OPTIONS.
I'M SORRY, UKYO...
SHE IS TELLING THE TRUTH...
IT'S A LIE!
A LIE!
A LIE!
A LIE!

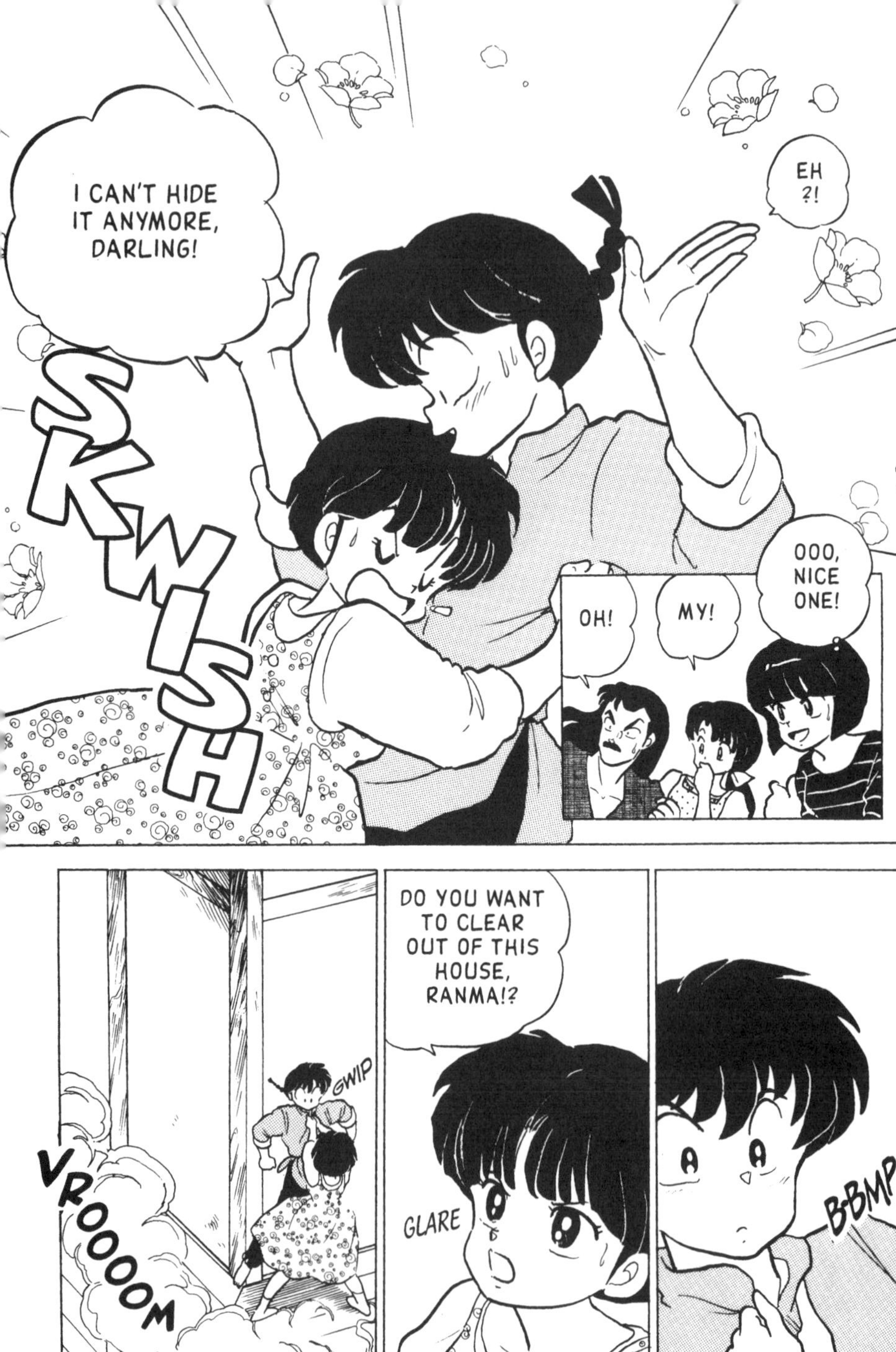
I CAN'T HIDE IT ANYMORE, DARLING!
EH ?!
SKWISH
OH!
MY!
OOO, NICE ONE!
VROOOOM
GWIP
DO YOU WANT TO CLEAR OUT OF THIS HOUSE, RANMA!?
GLARE
B-BMP

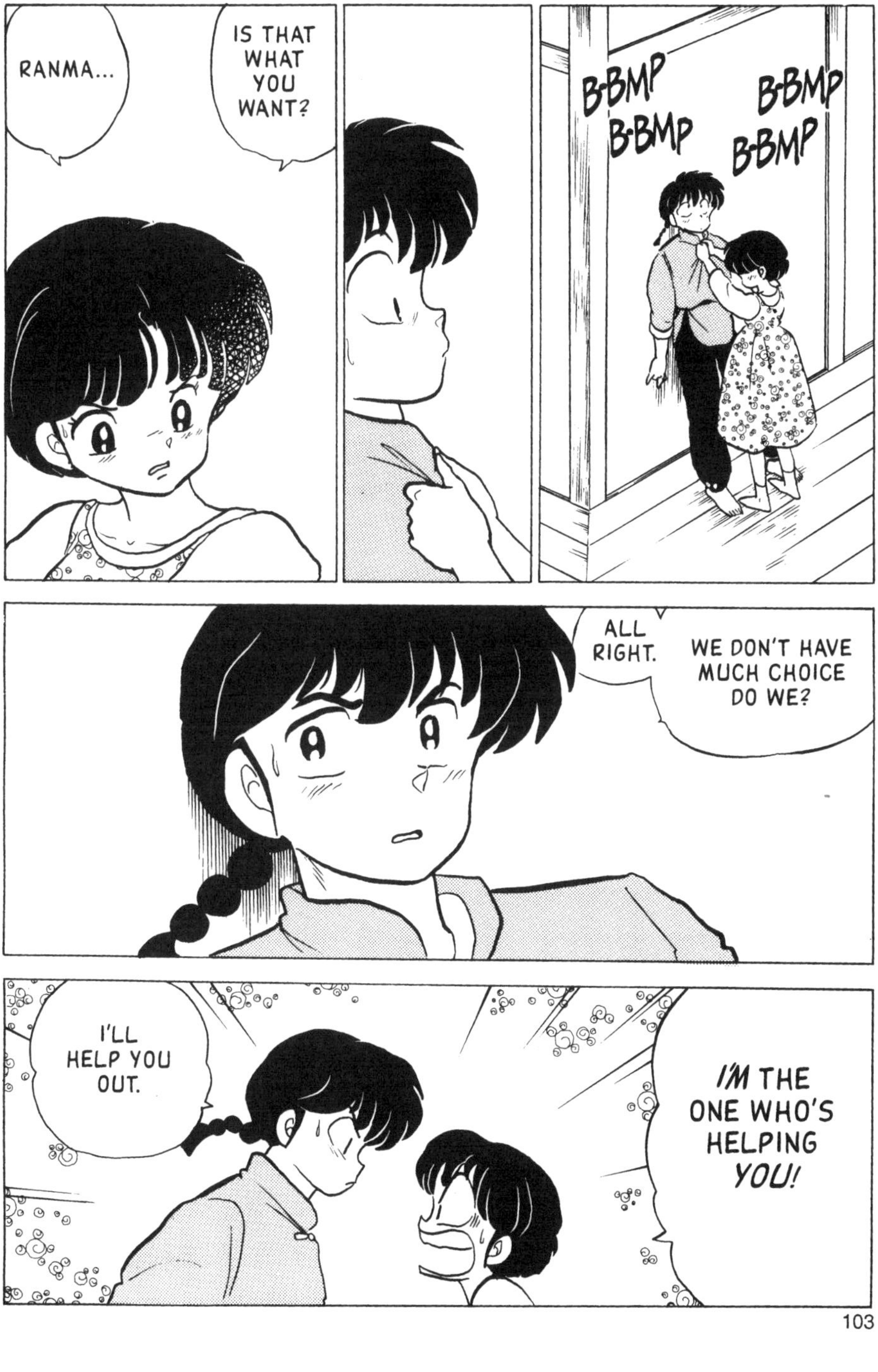
B-BMP
B-BMP
B-BMP
B-BMP
IS THAT WHAT YOU WANT?
RANMA...
ALL RIGHT.
WE DON'T HAVE MUCH CHOICE DO WE?
I'M THE ONE WHO'S HELPING YOU!
I'LL HELP YOU OUT.

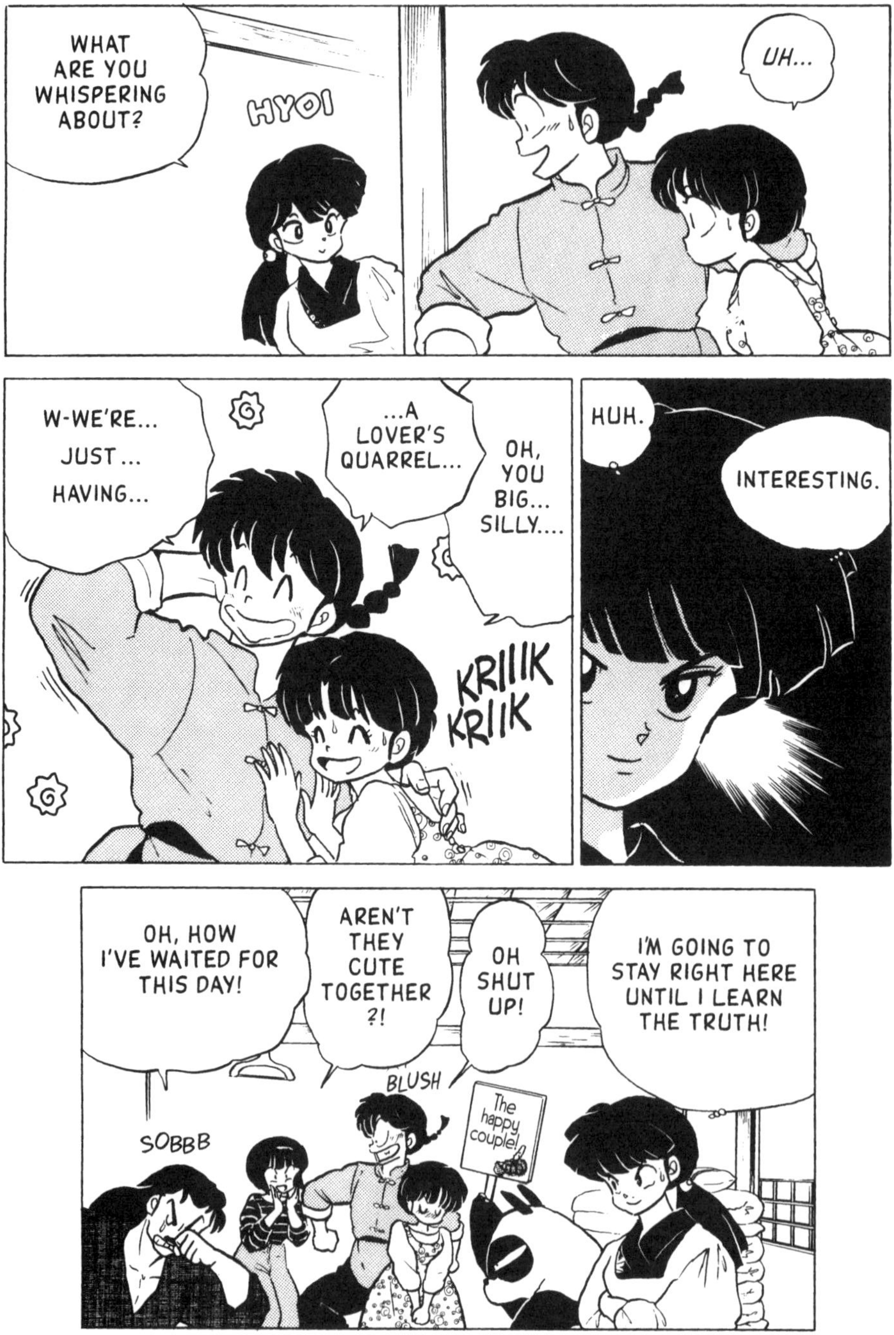
WHAT ARE YOU WHISPERING ABOUT?
HYOI
UH...
W-WE'RE... JUST... HAVING...
...A LOVER'S QUARREL...
OH, YOU BIG... SILLY....
KRIIIK KRIIK
HUH.
INTERESTING.
OH, HOW I'VE WAITED FOR THIS DAY!
AREN'T THEY CUTE TOGETHER ?!
OH SHUT UP!
I'M GOING TO STAY RIGHT HERE UNTIL I LEARN THE TRUTH!
BLUSH
SOBBB
The happy couple!

Part 7
THE HONEYMOON PERIOD

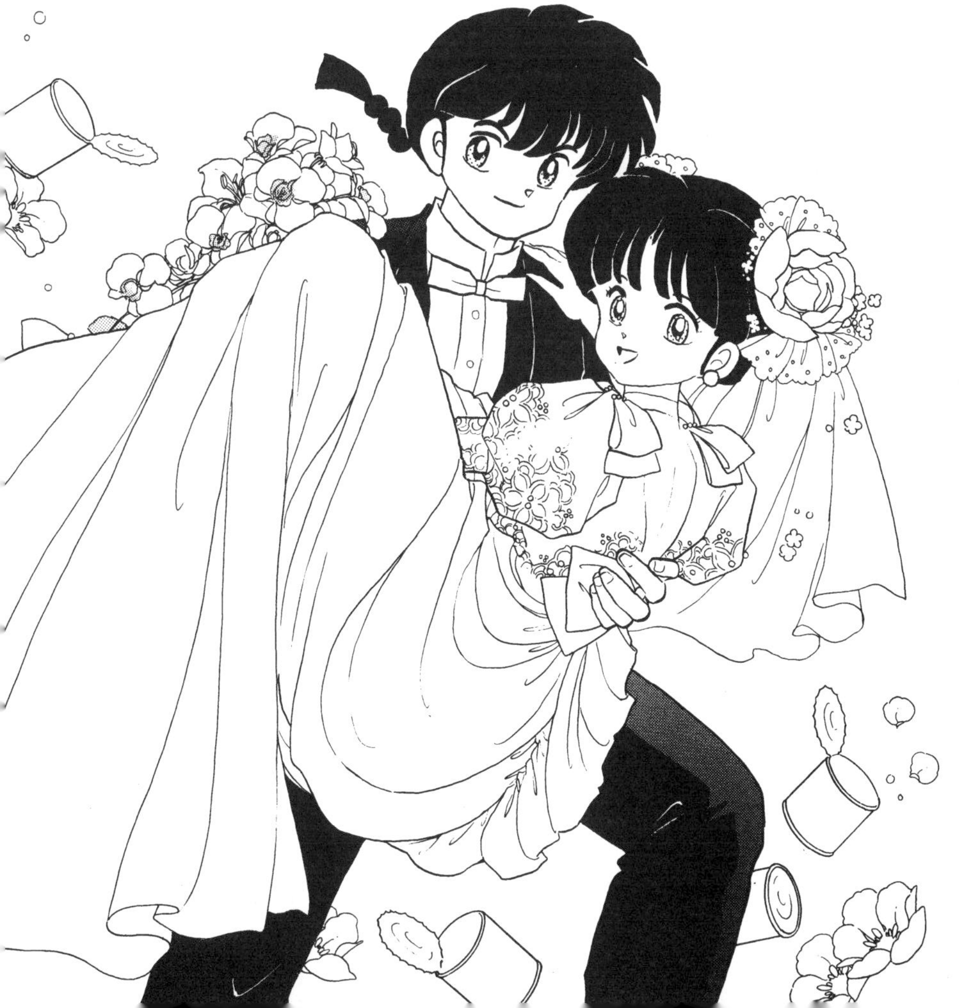

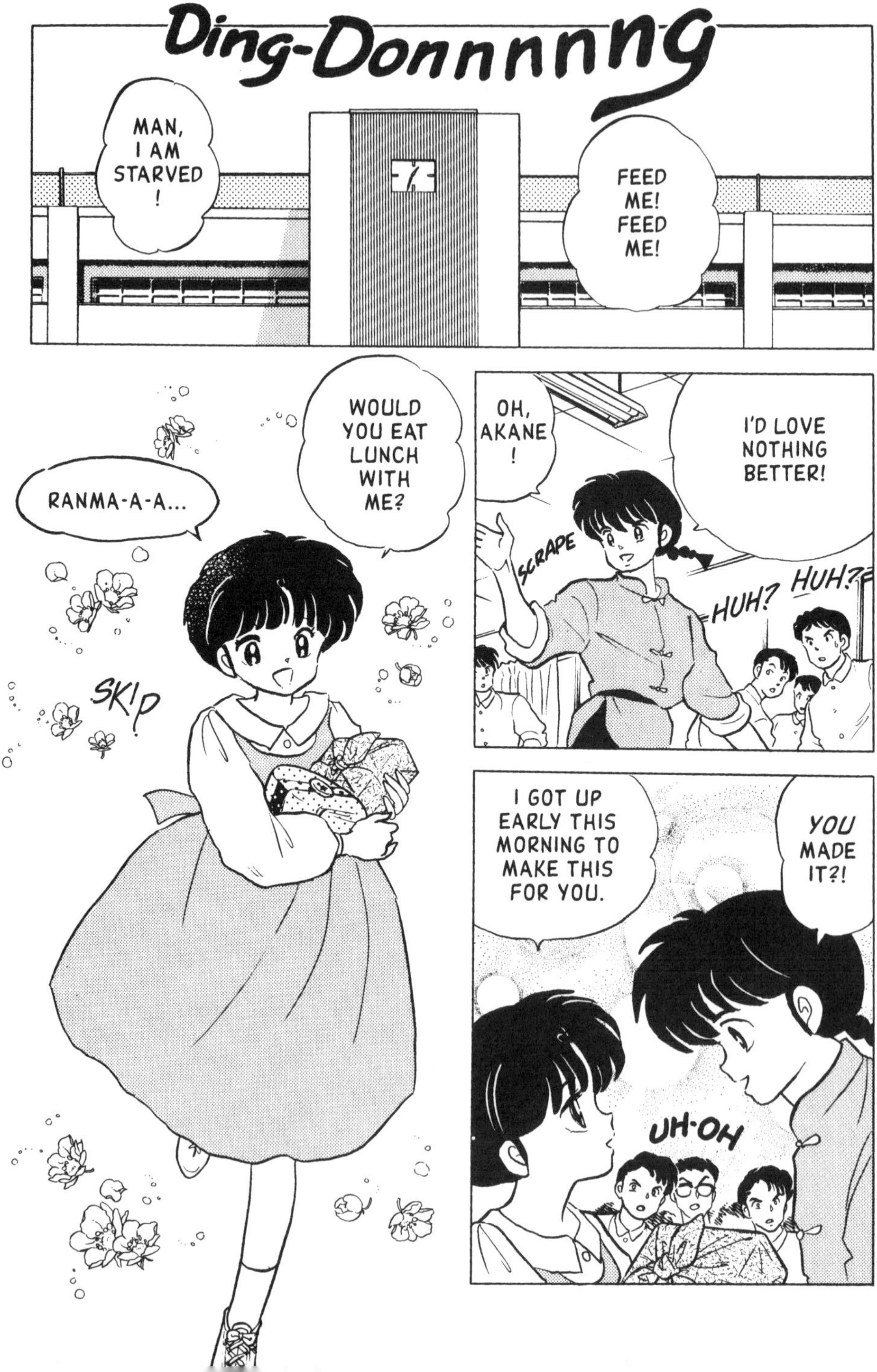
Ding-Donnnnng
MAN, I AM STARVED!
FEED ME! FEED ME!
RANMA-A-A...
WOULD YOU EAT LUNCH WITH ME?
SKIP
OH, AKANE!
I'D LOVE NOTHING BETTER!
SCRAPE
HUH? HUH?
I GOT UP EARLY THIS MORNING TO MAKE THIS FOR YOU.
YOU MADE IT?!
UH-OH

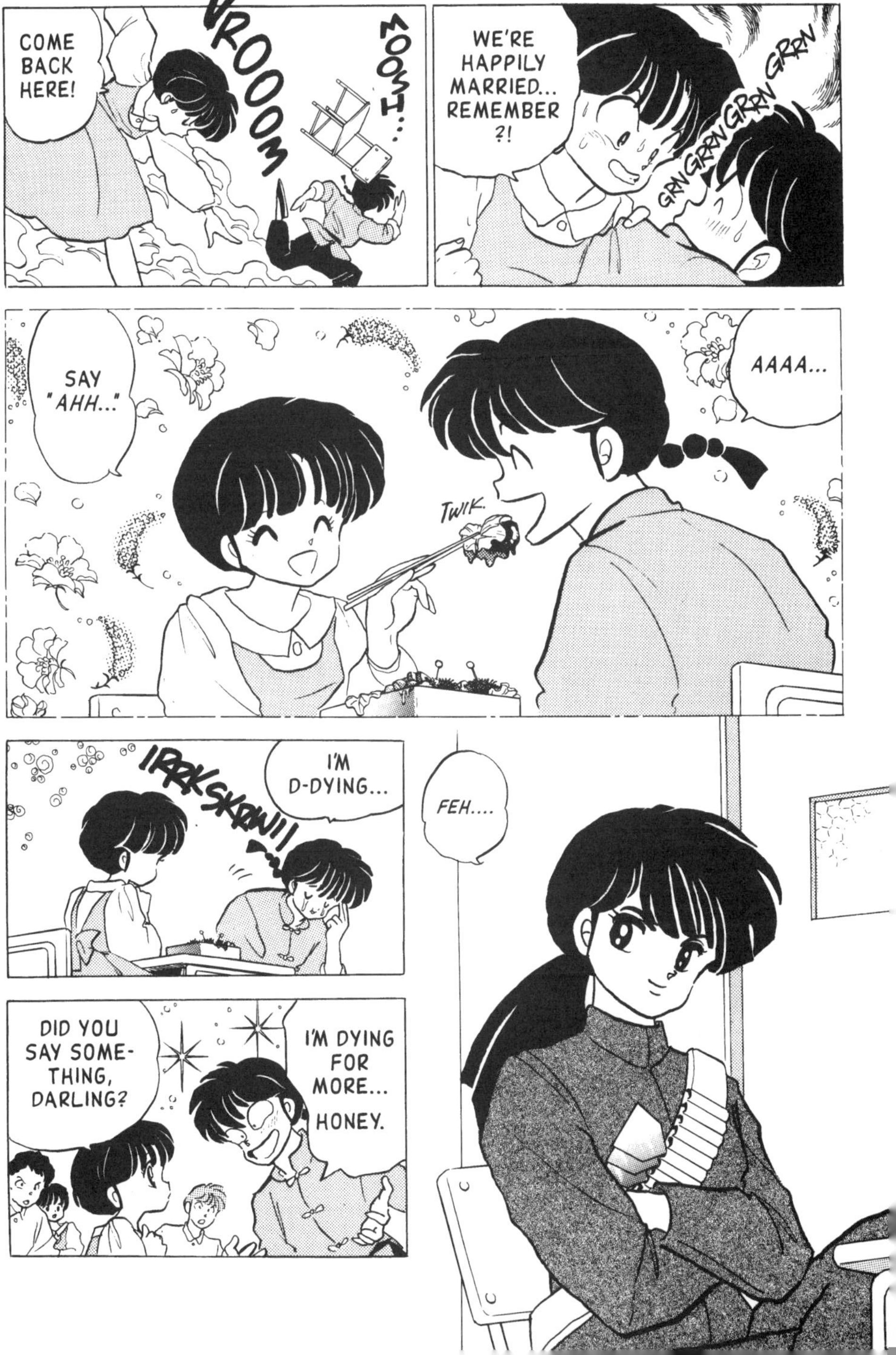
COME BACK HERE!
VROOOM
WOOSH...
WE'RE HAPPILY MARRIED... REMEMBER?!
GRRN GRRN GRRN GRRN
SAY "AHH..."
TWIK.
AAAA...
IRRKSKRAW!!
I'M D-DYING...
DID YOU SAY SOME-THING, DARLING?
I'M DYING FOR MORE...
HONEY.
FEH....

THEY SAY THE MORE THEY FIGHT, THE HAPPIER THE COUPLE.

HMM HMM

SO DOES THAT MEAN RANMA AND AKANE...

...ARE REALLY MEANT FOR EACH OTHER?

WE WERE ONLY PRETENDING THAT WE WERE ENGAGED!

THE TRUTH IS...WE'RE ALREADY MARRIED!

RANMA'S JUST AFRAID OF BEING KICKED OUT OF THE TENDO HOUSE.

I KNOW HE'S BEING FORCED TO GO ALONG WITH WHATEVER AKANE SAYS.

I'M GOING TO FIGHT THIS TO THE BITTER END.

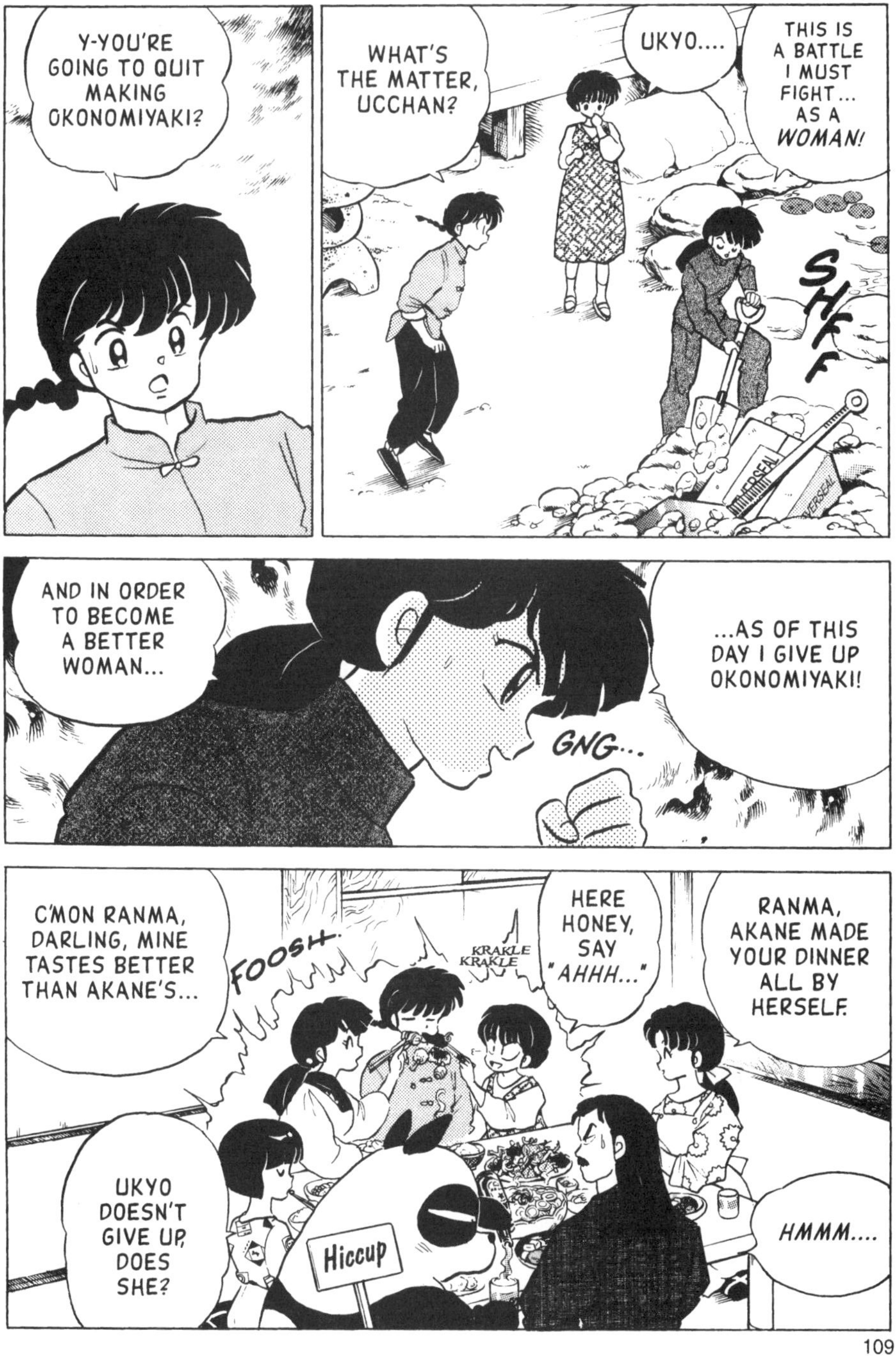
Y-YOU'RE GOING TO QUIT MAKING OKONOMIYAKI?
WHAT'S THE MATTER, UCCHAN?
UKYO....
THIS IS A BATTLE I MUST FIGHT... AS A WOMAN!
SHFF
AND IN ORDER TO BECOME A BETTER WOMAN...
...AS OF THIS DAY I GIVE UP OKONOMIYAKI!
GNG...
C'MON RANMA, DARLING, MINE TASTES BETTER THAN AKANE'S...
FOOSH
KRAKLE KRAKLE
HERE HONEY, SAY "AHHH..."
RANMA, AKANE MADE YOUR DINNER ALL BY HERSELF.
UKYO DOESN'T GIVE UP, DOES SHE?
Hiccup
HMMM....

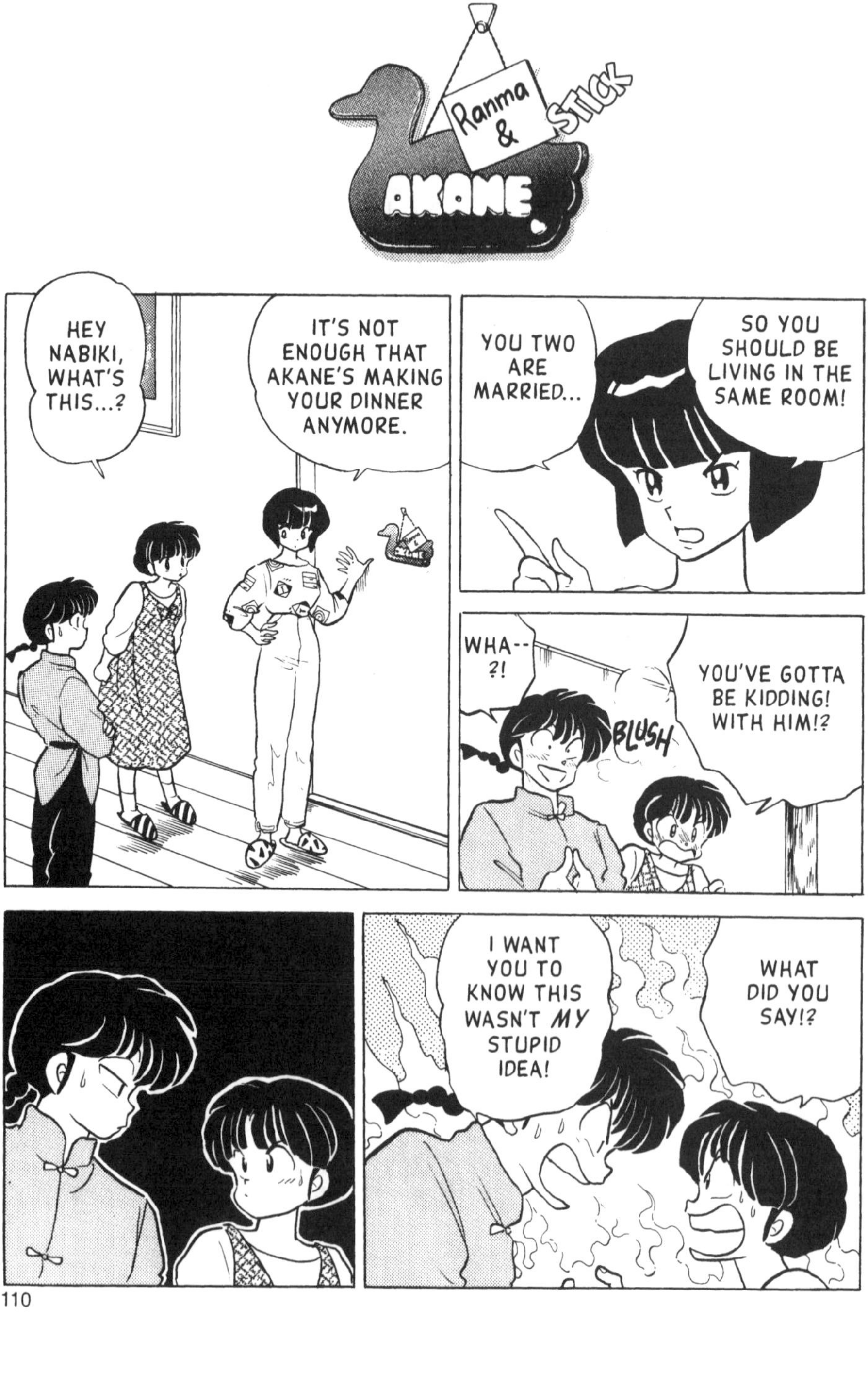
Ranma & AKANE STICK
HEY NABIKI, WHAT'S THIS...?
IT'S NOT ENOUGH THAT AKANE'S MAKING YOUR DINNER ANYMORE.
YOU TWO ARE MARRIED...
SO YOU SHOULD BE LIVING IN THE SAME ROOM!
WHA-- ?!
BLUSH
YOU'VE GOTTA BE KIDDING! WITH HIM!?
I WANT YOU TO KNOW THIS WASN'T MY STUPID IDEA!
WHAT DID YOU SAY!?

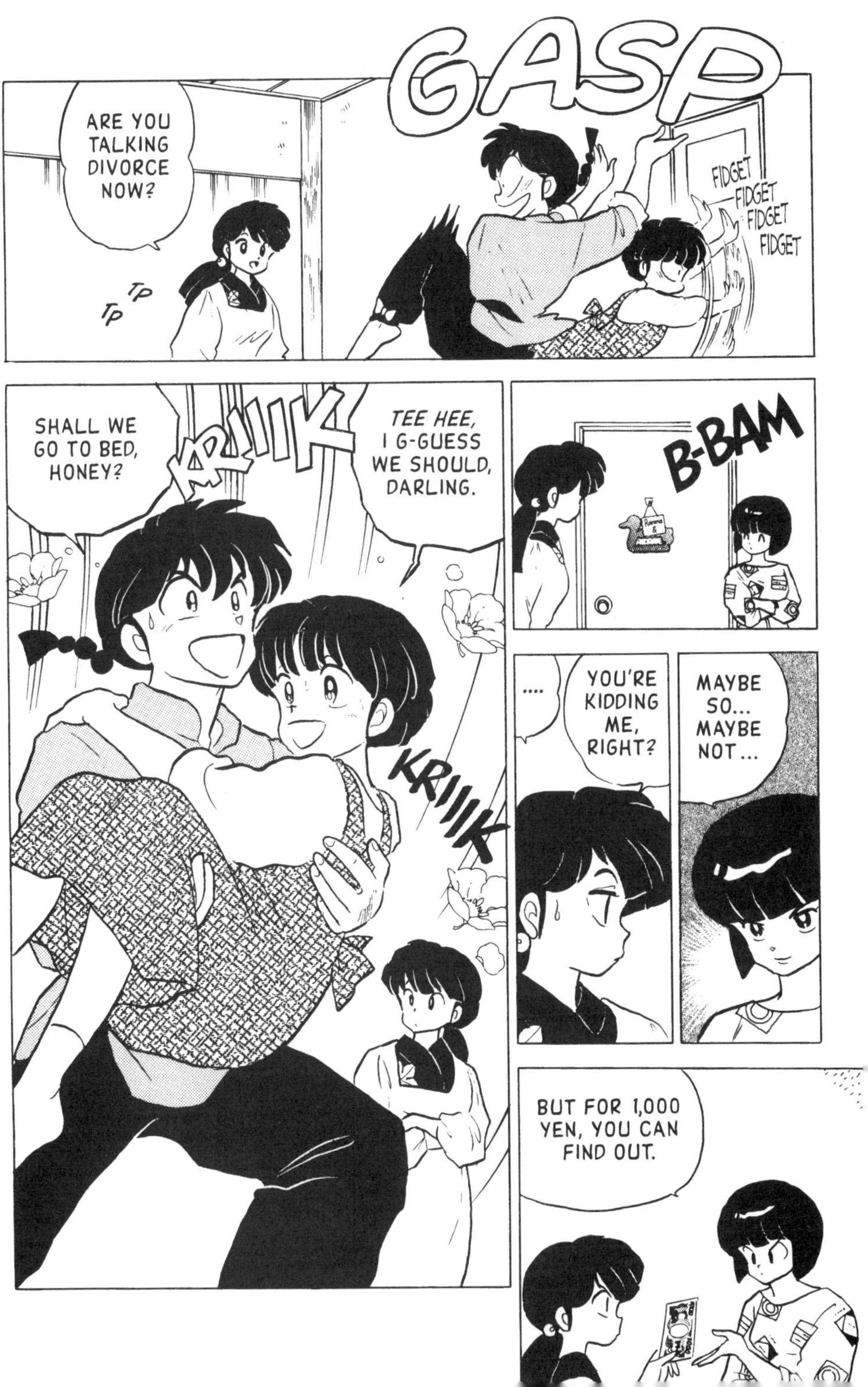
ARE YOU TALKING DIVORCE NOW?
TP TP
GASP
FIDGET FIDGET FIDGET FIDGET
SHALL WE GO TO BED, HONEY?
KRIIIK
TEE HEE, I G-GUESS WE SHOULD, DARLING.
KRIIIK
B-BAM
....
YOU'RE KIDDING ME, RIGHT?
MAYBE SO... MAYBE NOT...
BUT FOR 1,000 YEN, YOU CAN FIND OUT.

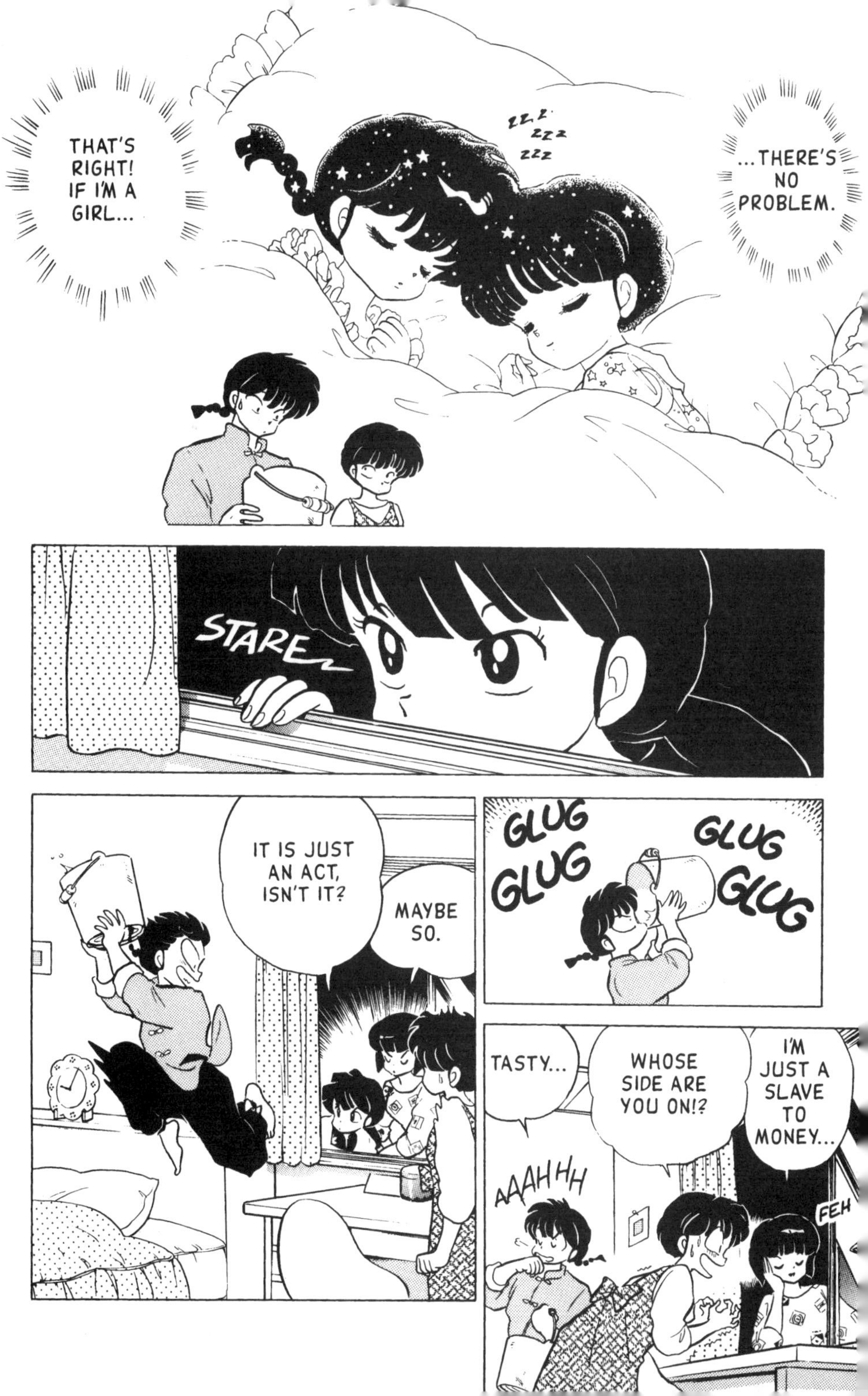
THAT'S RIGHT! IF I'M A GIRL...
ZZZ ZZZ ZZZ
...THERE'S NO PROBLEM.
STARE
IT IS JUST AN ACT, ISN'T IT?
MAYBE SO.
GLUG GLUG
GLUG GLUG
TASTY...
WHOSE SIDE ARE YOU ON!?
I'M JUST A SLAVE TO MONEY...
AAAHHH
FEH

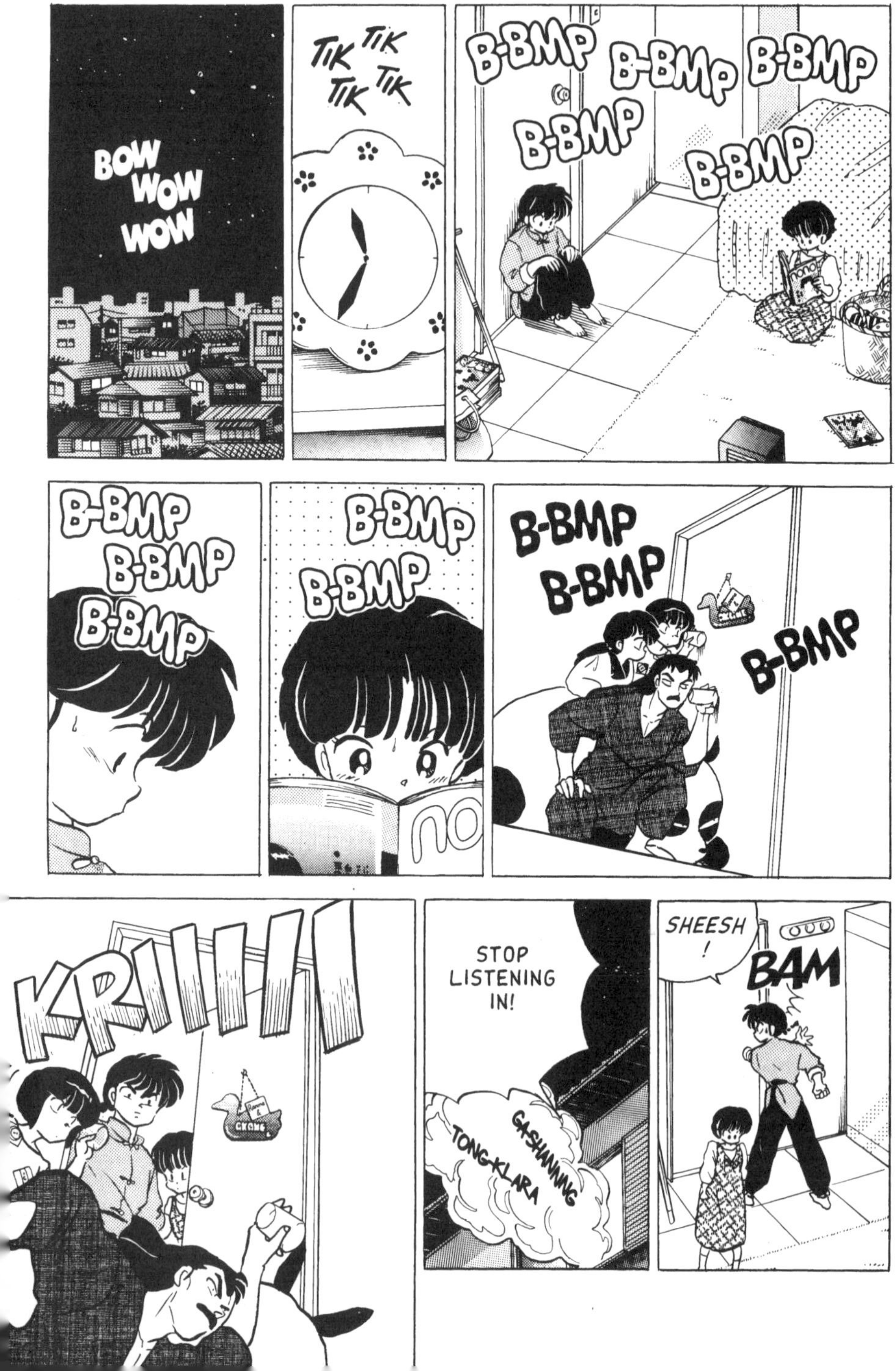

BOW WOW WOW
TIK TIK TIK TIK
B-BMP B-BMP B-BMP B-BMP B-BMP
B-BMP B-BMP B-BMP
B-BMP B-BMP
B-BMP B-BMP B-BMP
KRIIIII
STOP LISTENING IN!
GASHANNNG TONG-KLARA
SHEESH!
BAM

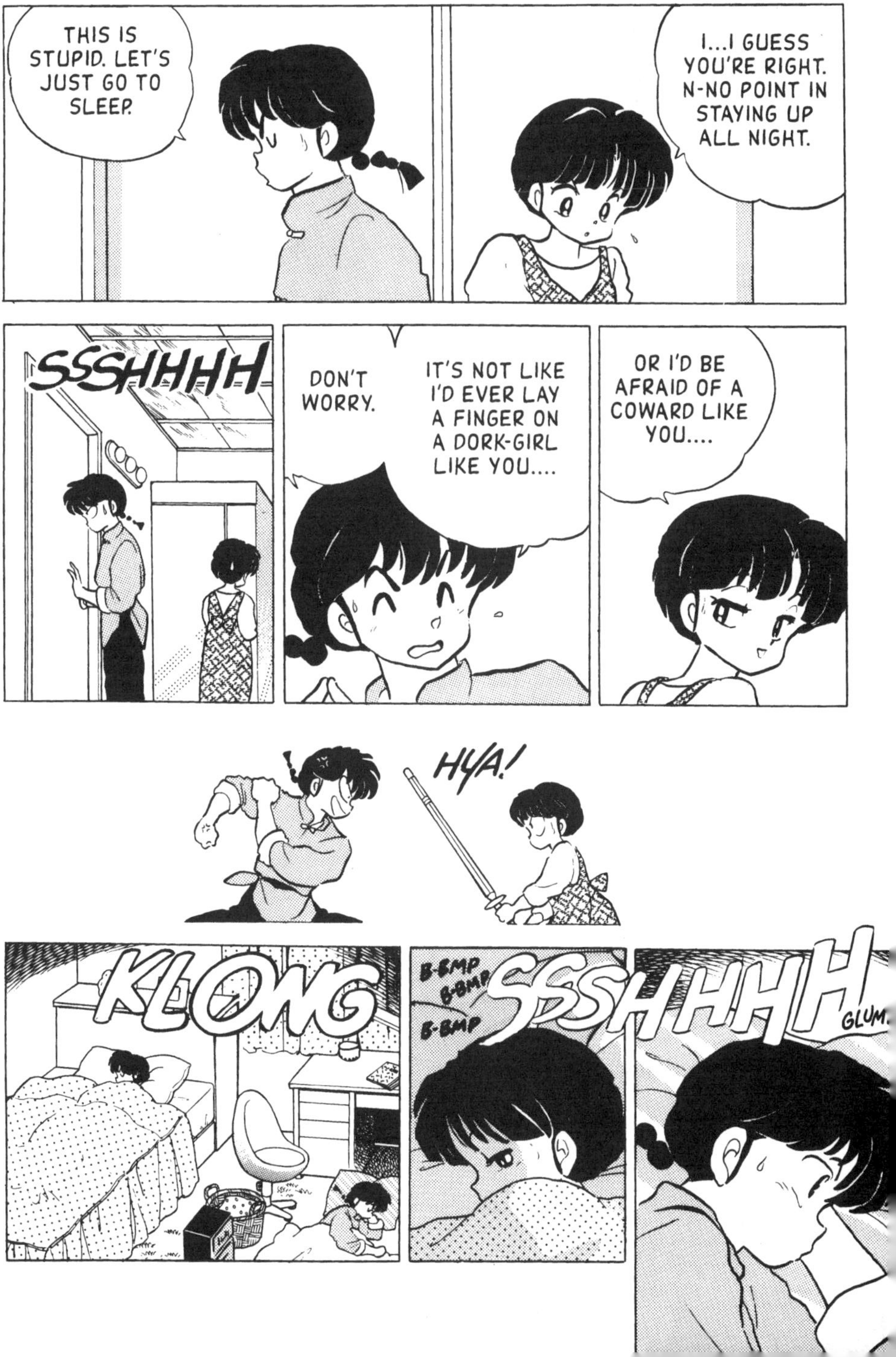
THIS IS STUPID. LET'S JUST GO TO SLEEP.
I...I GUESS YOU'RE RIGHT. N-NO POINT IN STAYING UP ALL NIGHT.
SSSHHHH
DON'T WORRY.
IT'S NOT LIKE I'D EVER LAY A FINGER ON A DORK-GIRL LIKE YOU....
OR I'D BE AFRAID OF A COWARD LIKE YOU....
HYA!
KLONG
B-BMP B-BMP B-BMP
SSSHHHH
GLUM.

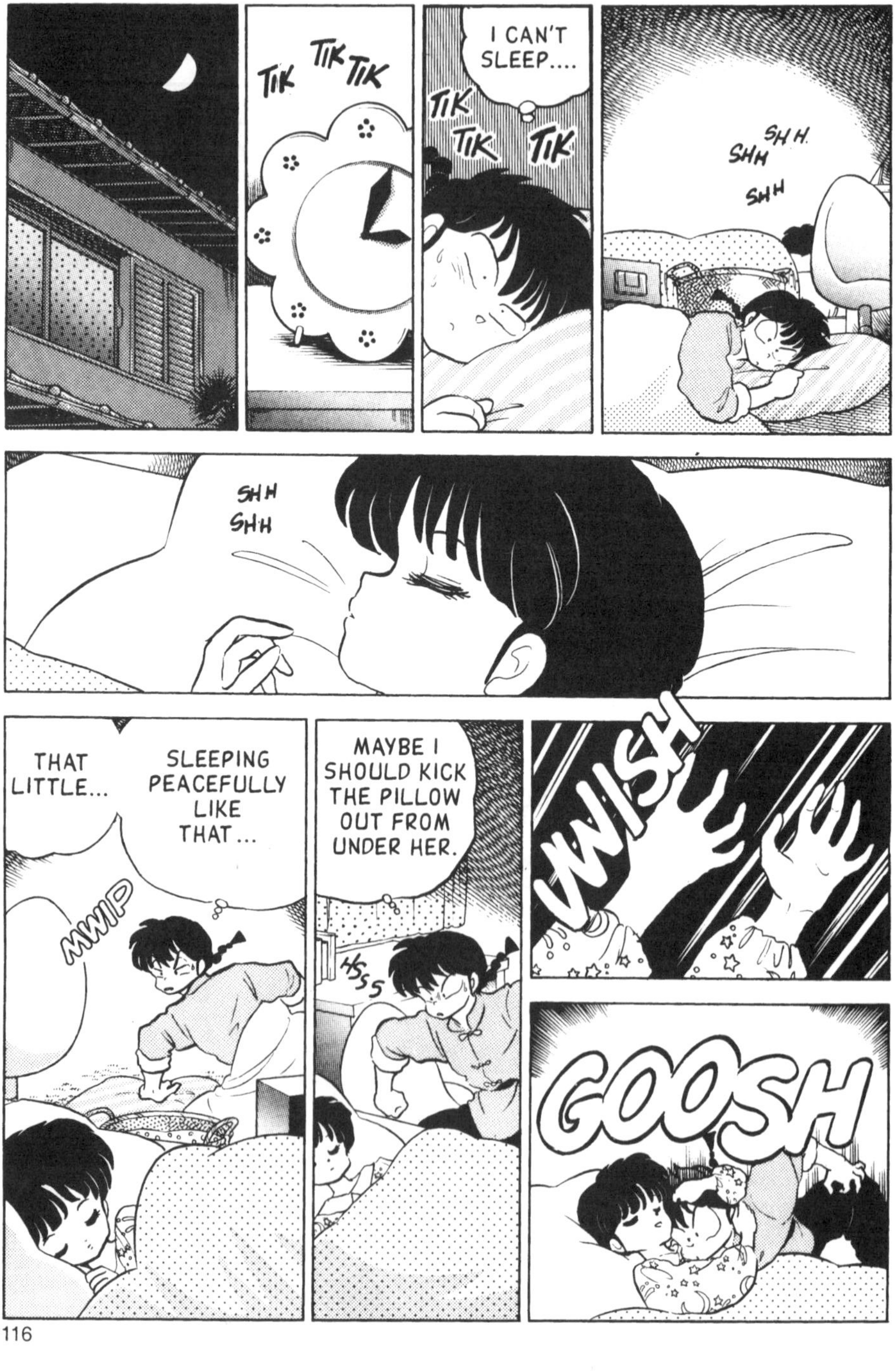

TIK
TIK TIK
I CAN'T SLEEP....
TIK
TIK
TIK
SHH
SHH
SHH
SHH
SHH
THAT LITTLE...
SLEEPING PEACEFULLY LIKE THAT...
MWIP
MAYBE I SHOULD KICK THE PILLOW OUT FROM UNDER HER.
HSSS
WISH
GOOSH

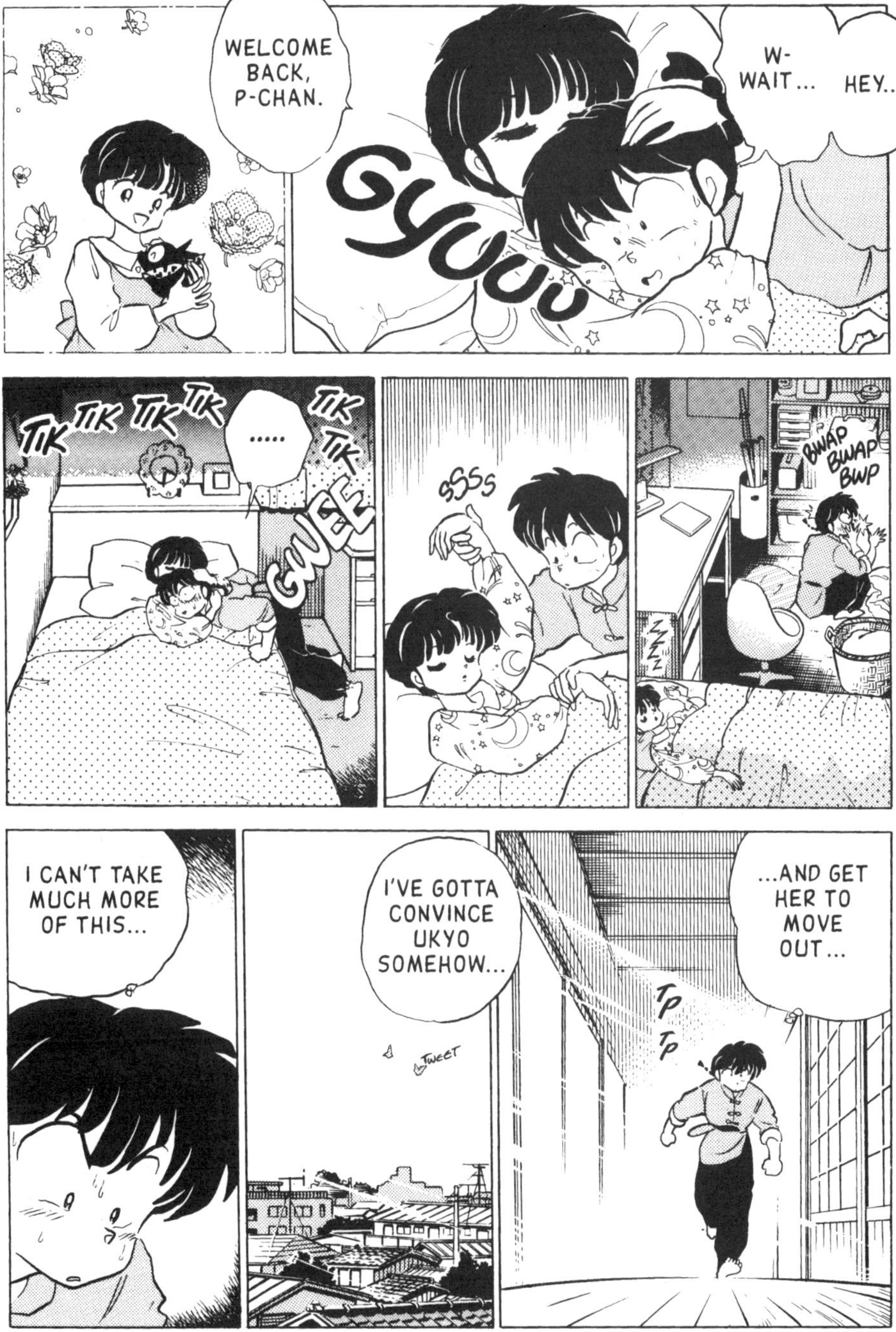
WELCOME BACK, P-CHAN.
GYUUU
W- WAIT...
HEY....
TIK TIK TIK TIK
.....
TIK TIK
GWEE
SSSS
BWAP BWAP BWP
I CAN'T TAKE MUCH MORE OF THIS...
I'VE GOTTA CONVINCE UKYO SOMEHOW...
TWEET
...AND GET HER TO MOVE OUT...
TP TP

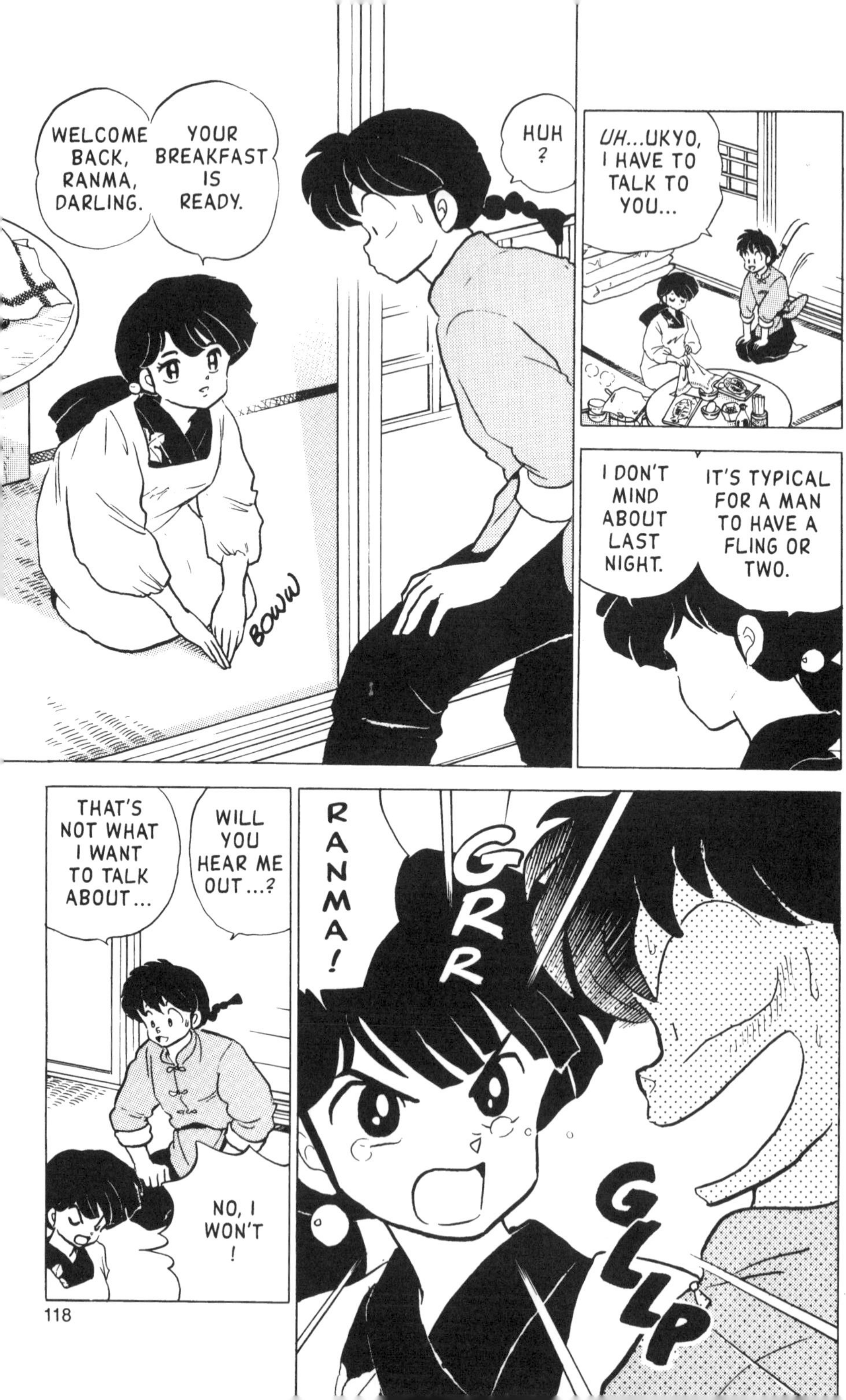
WELCOME BACK, RANMA, DARLING.
YOUR BREAKFAST IS READY.
BOWW
HUH ?
UH...UKYO, I HAVE TO TALK TO YOU...
I DON'T MIND ABOUT LAST NIGHT.
IT'S TYPICAL FOR A MAN TO HAVE A FLING OR TWO.
THAT'S NOT WHAT I WANT TO TALK ABOUT...
WILL YOU HEAR ME OUT...?
NO, I WON'T !
RANMA!
GRR
GLLP

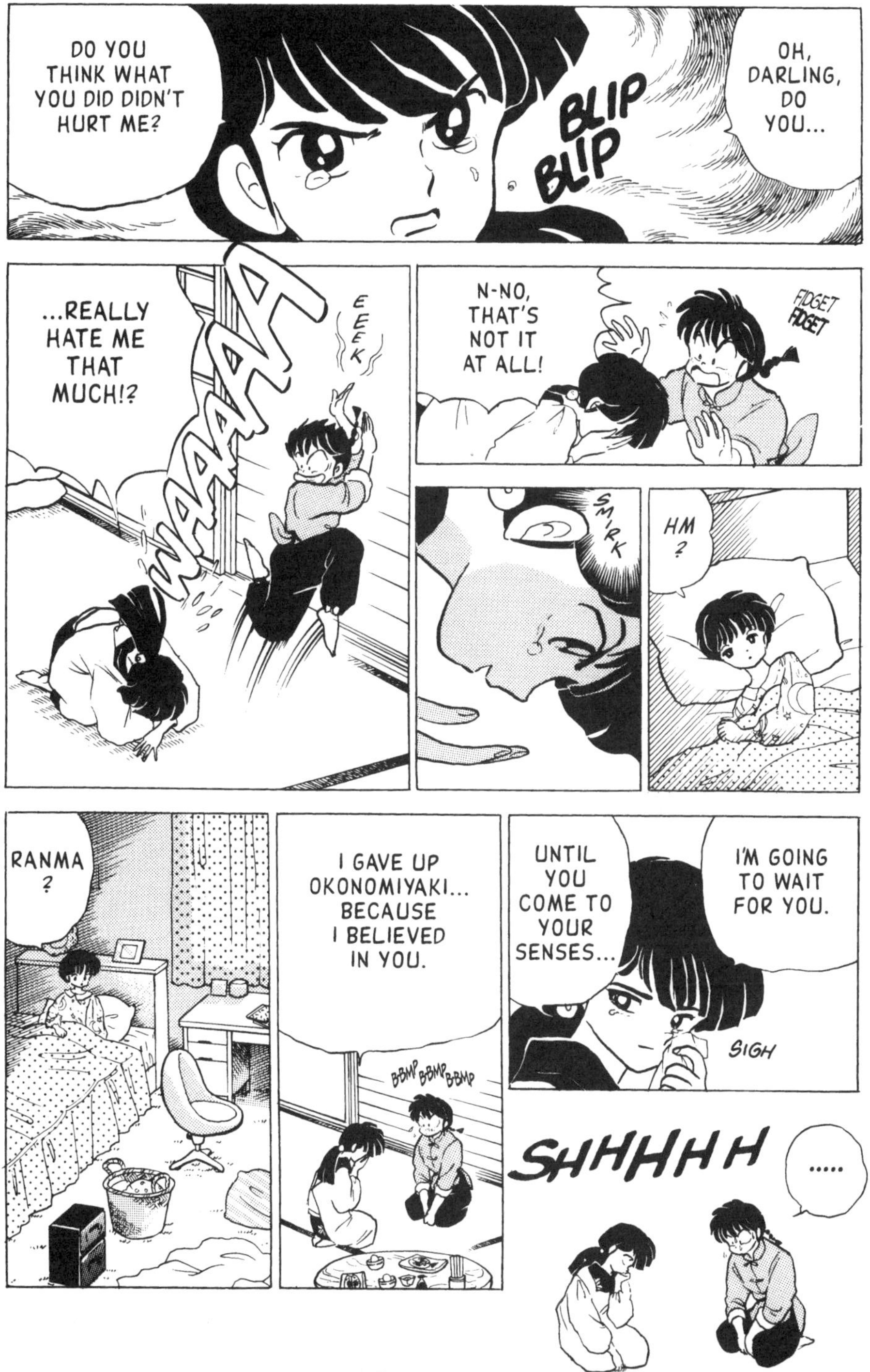
DO YOU THINK WHAT YOU DID DIDN'T HURT ME?
BLIP BLIP
OH, DARLING, DO YOU...
...REALLY HATE ME THAT MUCH!?
WAAAAA
EEEK
N-NO, THAT'S NOT IT AT ALL!
FIDGET FIDGET
SMIRK
HM?
RANMA?
I GAVE UP OKONOMIYAKI... BECAUSE I BELIEVED IN YOU.
B-BMP B-BMP B-BMP
UNTIL YOU COME TO YOUR SENSES...
I'M GOING TO WAIT FOR YOU.
SIGH
SHHHHH
.....

Part 8
PLEASE HATE ME

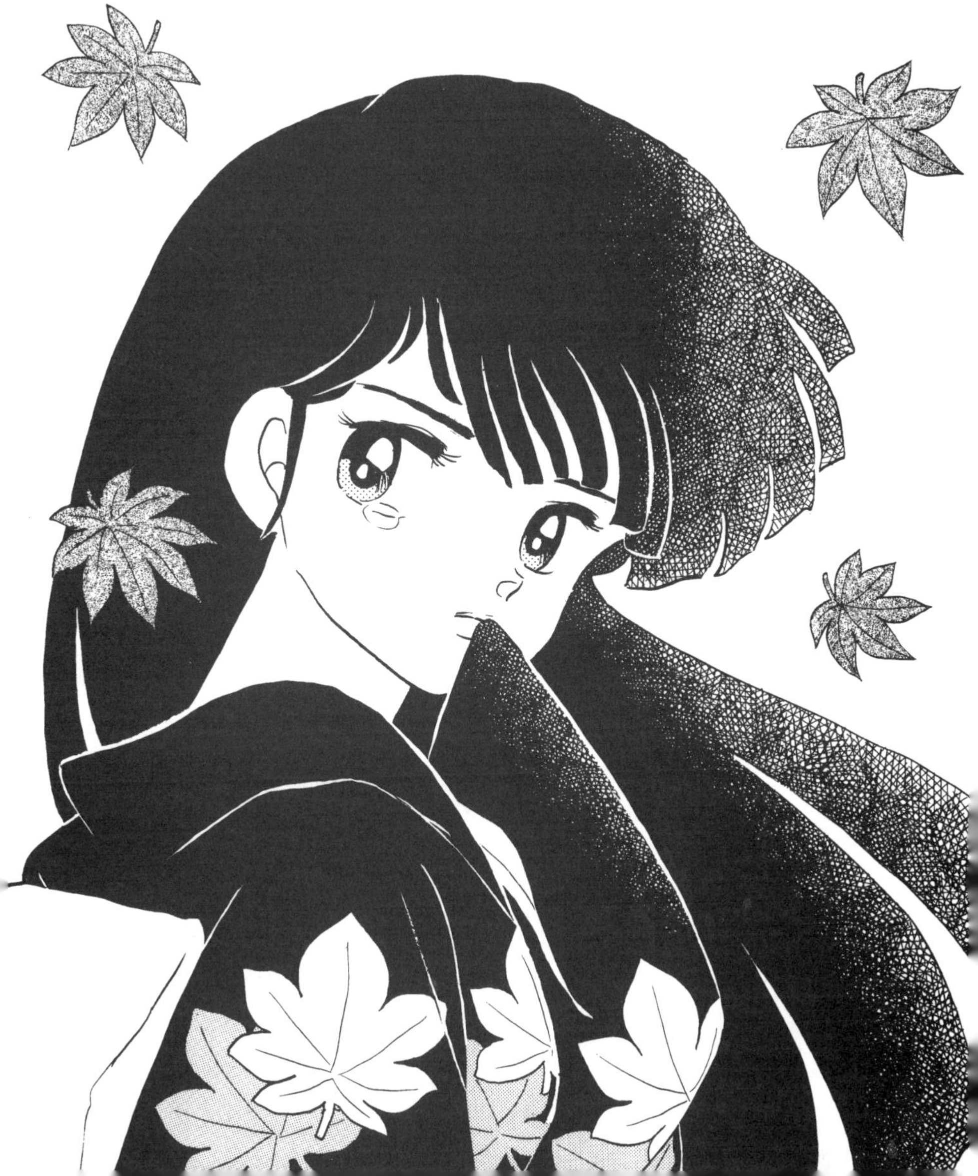

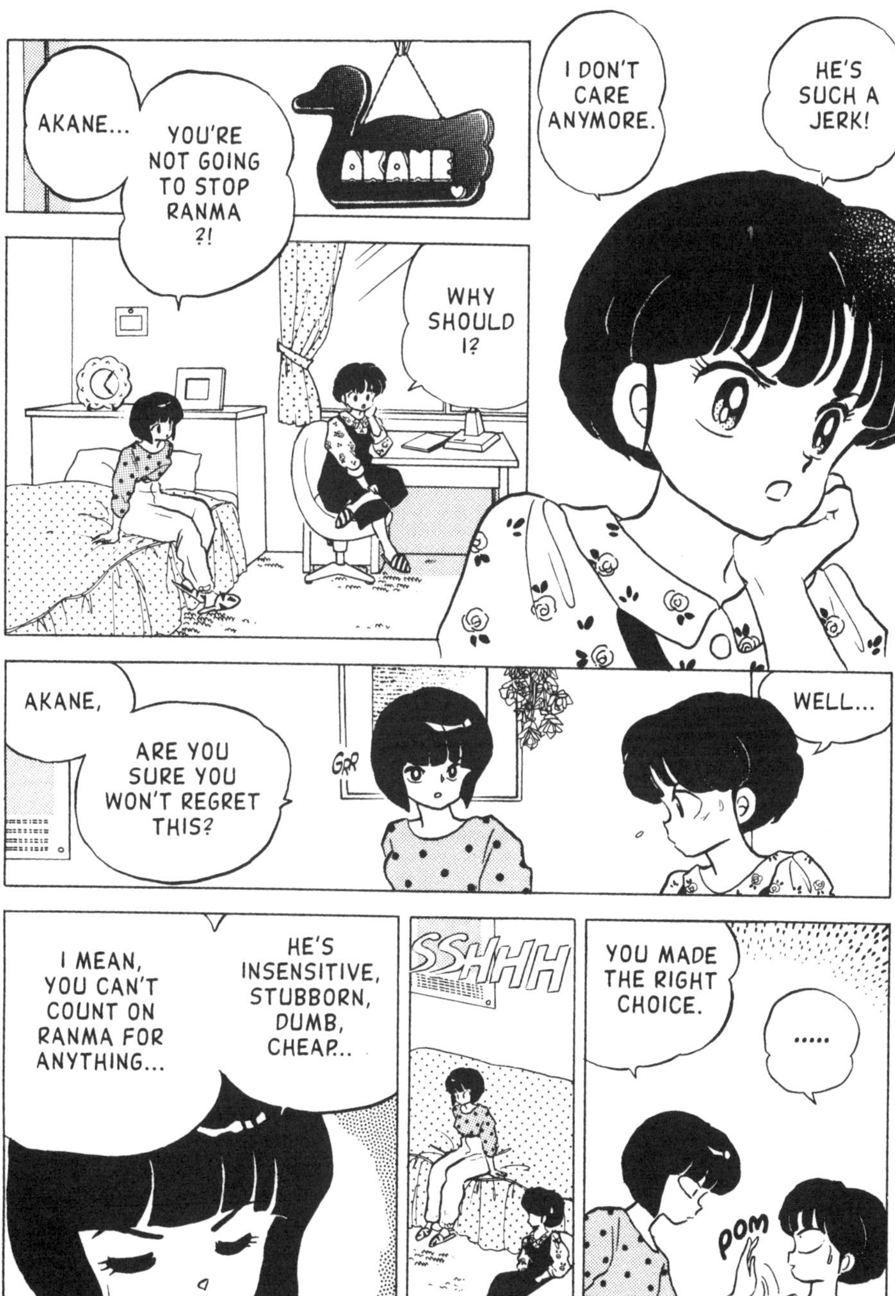
AKANE...
YOU'RE NOT GOING TO STOP RANMA ?!
AKANE
WHY SHOULD I?
I DON'T CARE ANYMORE.
HE'S SUCH A JERK!
AKANE,
ARE YOU SURE YOU WON'T REGRET THIS?
GRR
WELL...
HE'S INSENSITIVE, STUBBORN, DUMB, CHEAP...
I MEAN, YOU CAN'T COUNT ON RANMA FOR ANYTHING...
SSHHH
YOU MADE THE RIGHT CHOICE.
.....
POM

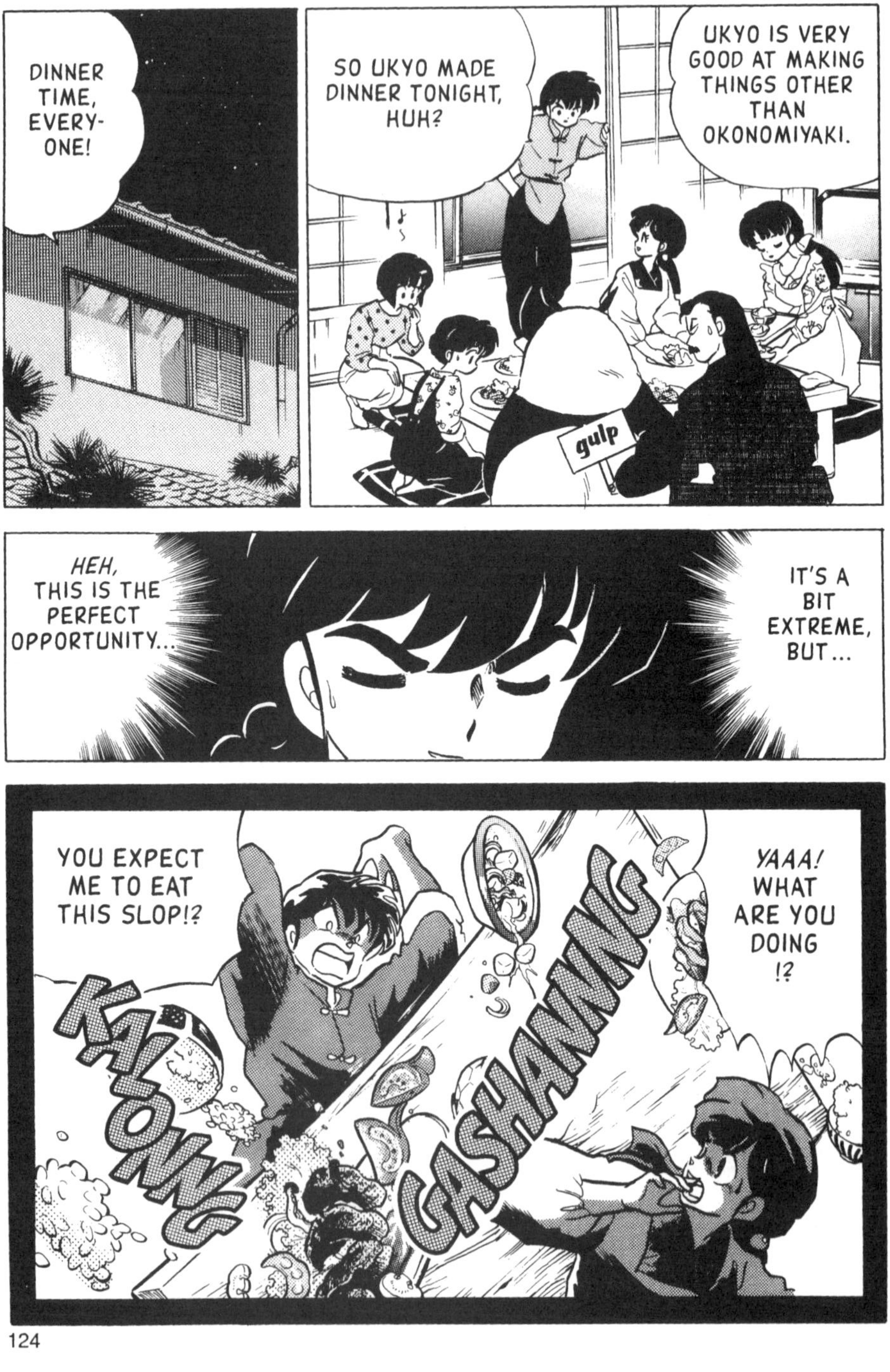
DINNER TIME, EVERY-ONE!
SO UKYO MADE DINNER TONIGHT, HUH?
UKYO IS VERY GOOD AT MAKING THINGS OTHER THAN OKONOMIYAKI.
gulp
HEH, THIS IS THE PERFECT OPPORTUNITY...
IT'S A BIT EXTREME, BUT...
YOU EXPECT ME TO EAT THIS SLOP!?
KALONNG
GASHANNG
YAAA! WHAT ARE YOU DOING !?

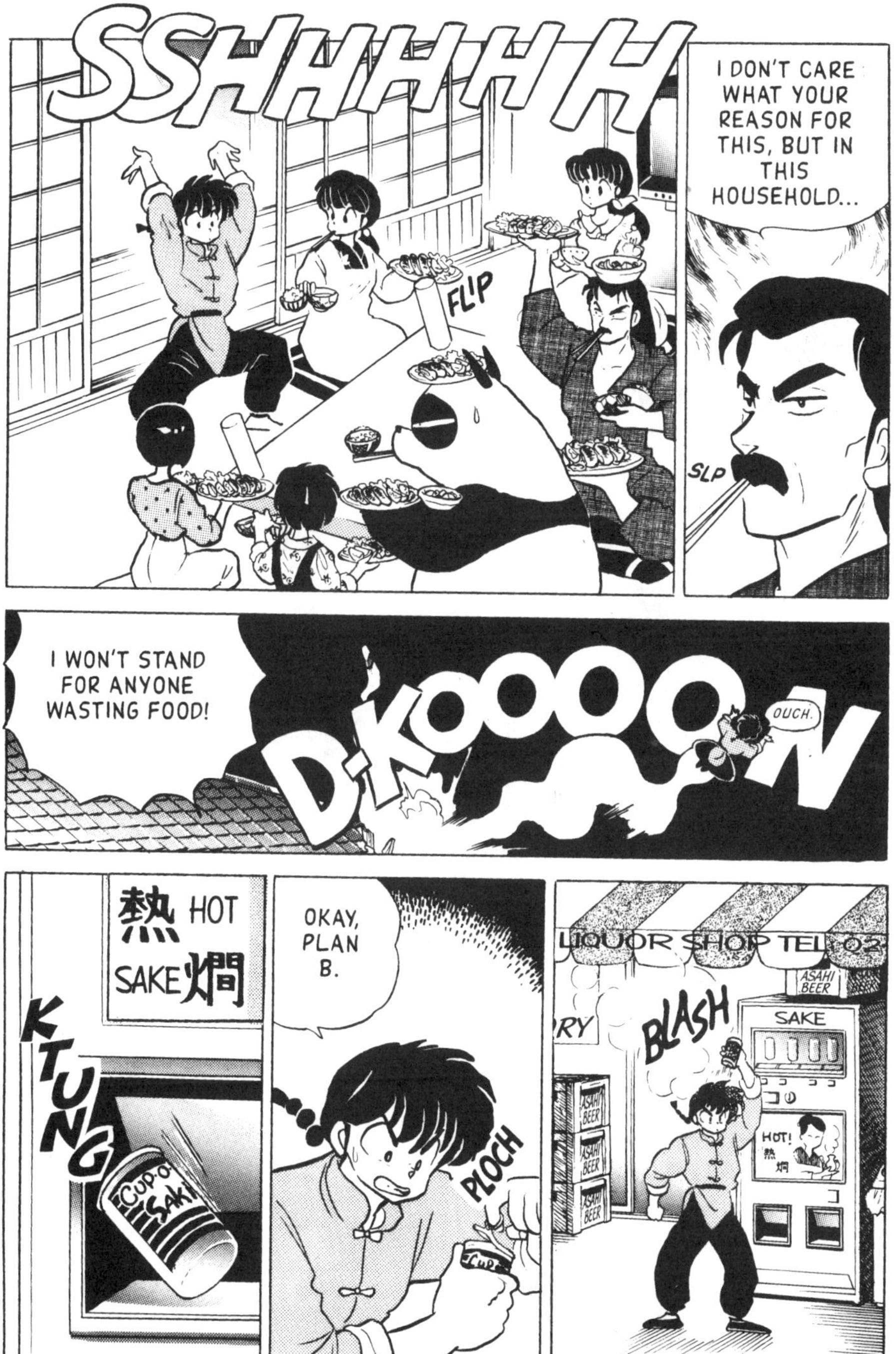
SSHHHHHH
FLIP
I DON'T CARE WHAT YOUR REASON FOR THIS, BUT IN THIS HOUSEHOLD...
SLP
I WON'T STAND FOR ANYONE WASTING FOOD!
D-KOOOOOOW
OUCH.
熱 HOT
SAKE 燗
KTUNG
CUP-O-SAKI
OKAY, PLAN B.
PLOCH
CUP
LIQUOR SHOP TEL 02
ASAHI BEER
SAKE
BLASH
RY
ASAHI BEER
ASAHI BEER
ASAHI BEER
HOT! 熱燗

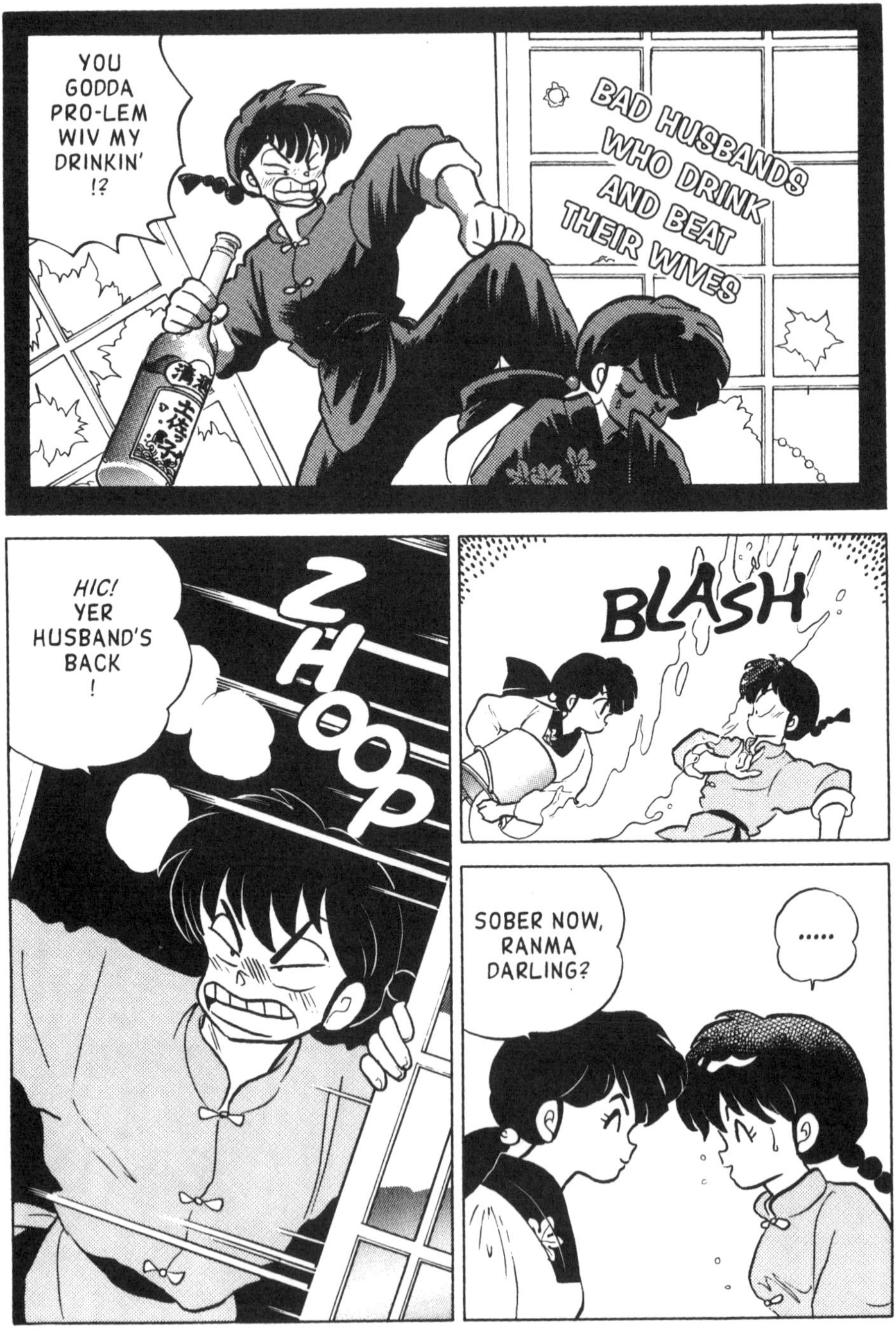

YOU GODDA PRO-LEM WIV MY DRINKIN' !?
BAD HUSBANDS WHO DRINK AND BEAT THEIR WIVES
HIC! YER HUSBAND'S BACK !
ZHOOP
BLASH
SOBER NOW, RANMA DARLING?
.....

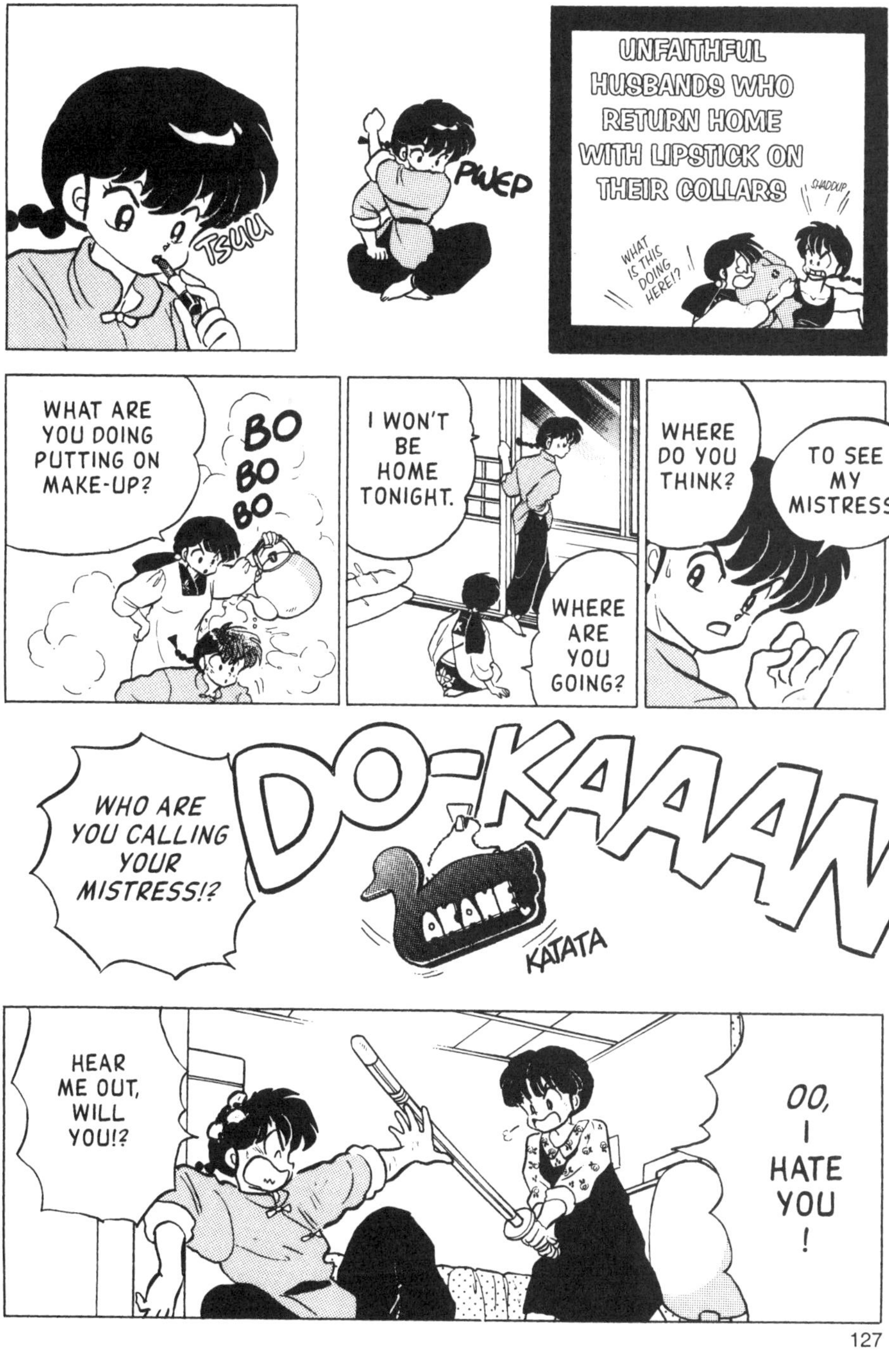
TSUU
PWEP
UNFAITHFUL HUSBANDS WHO RETURN HOME WITH LIPSTICK ON THEIR COLLARS
WHAT IS THIS DOING HERE!?
SHADDUP
WHAT ARE YOU DOING PUTTING ON MAKE-UP?
BO BO BO
I WON'T BE HOME TONIGHT.
WHERE ARE YOU GOING?
WHERE DO YOU THINK?
TO SEE MY MISTRESS.
WHO ARE YOU CALLING YOUR MISTRESS!?
DO-KAAAAN
AKANE
KATATA
HEAR ME OUT, WILL YOU!?
OO, I HATE YOU!

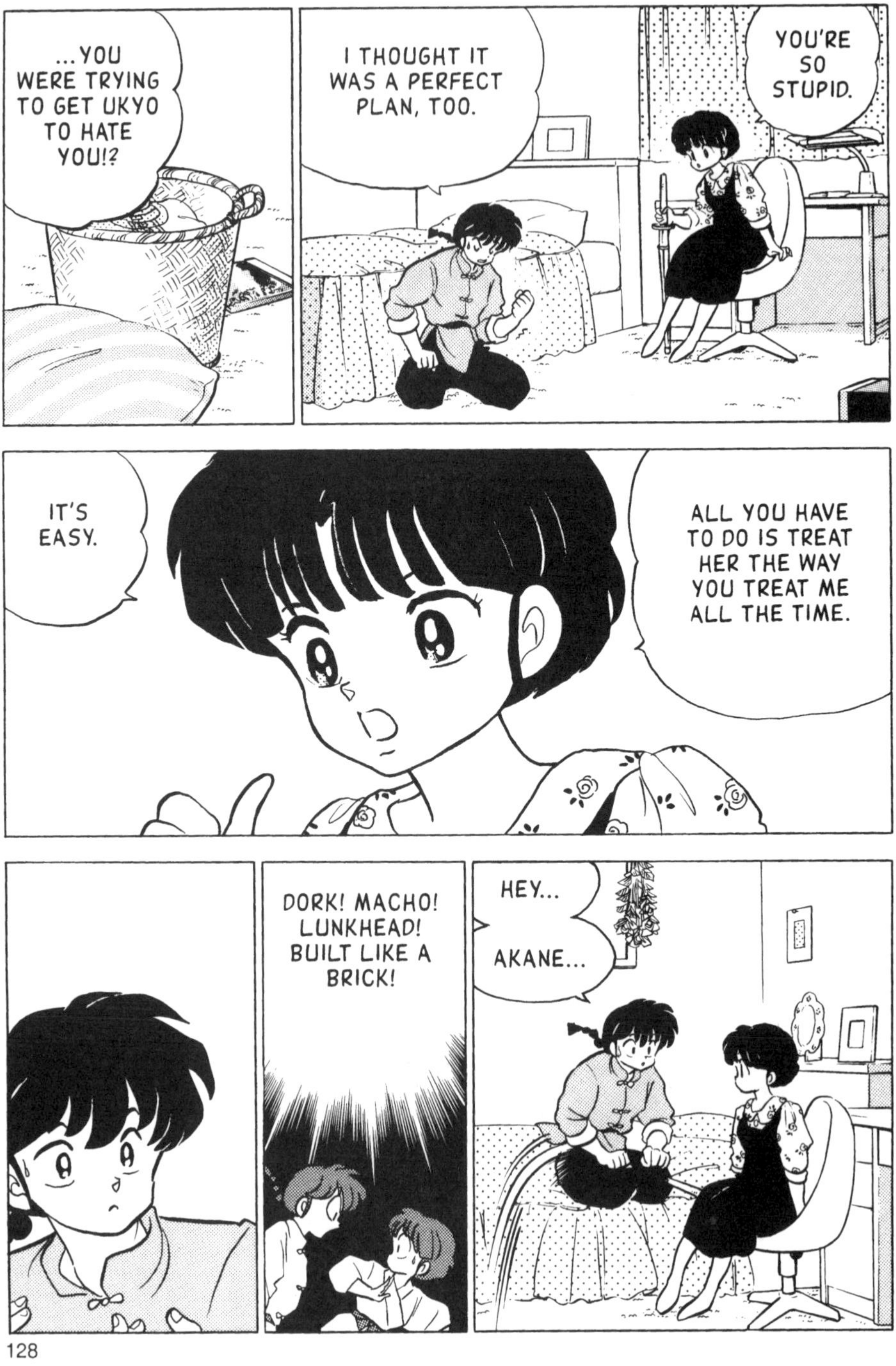
...YOU WERE TRYING TO GET UKYO TO HATE YOU!?
I THOUGHT IT WAS A PERFECT PLAN, TOO.
YOU'RE SO STUPID.
IT'S EASY.
ALL YOU HAVE TO DO IS TREAT HER THE WAY YOU TREAT ME ALL THE TIME.
DORK! MACHO! LUNKHEAD! BUILT LIKE A BRICK!
HEY...
AKANE...

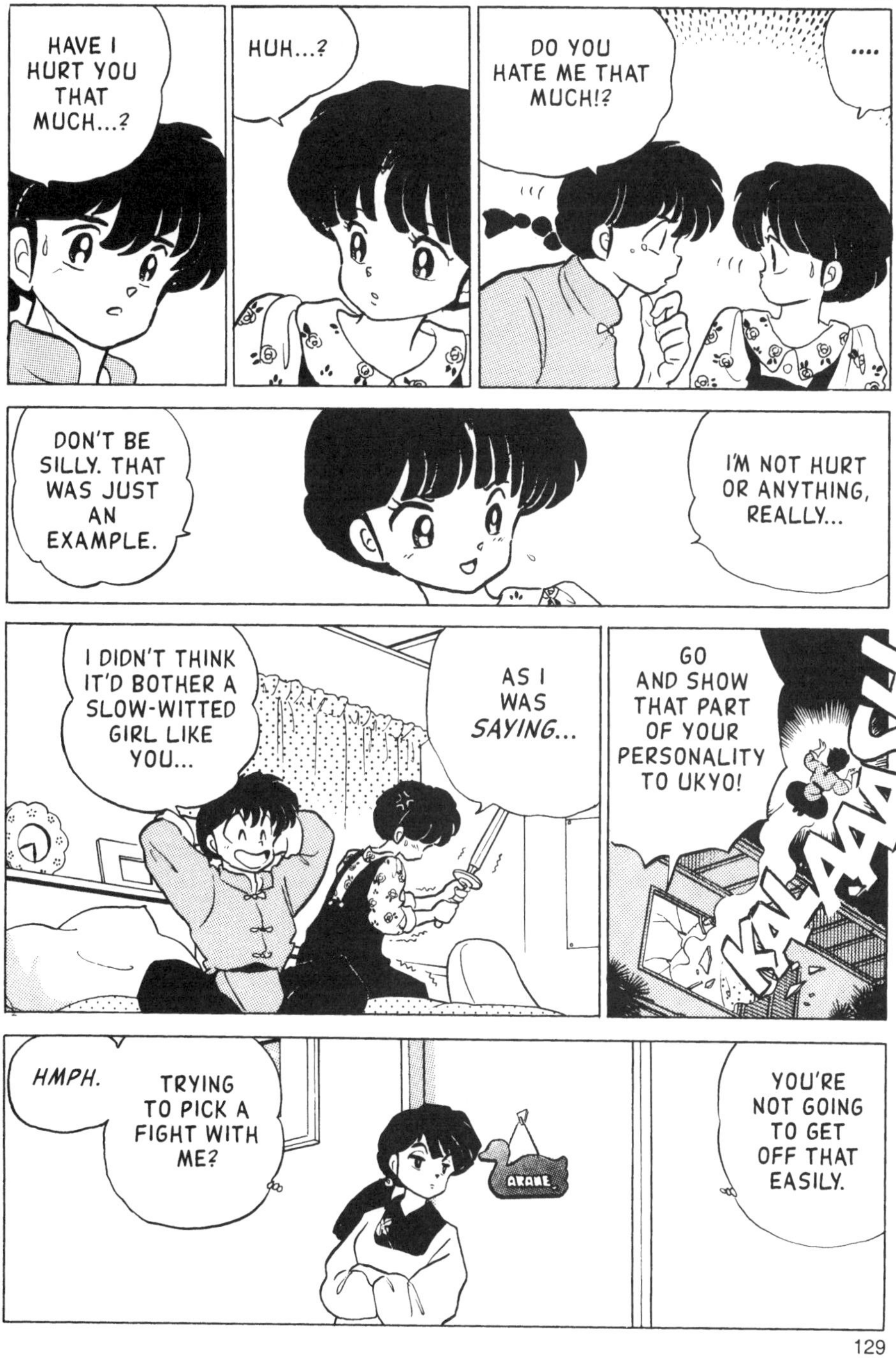
HAVE I HURT YOU THAT MUCH...?
HUH...?
DO YOU HATE ME THAT MUCH!?
....
DON'T BE SILLY. THAT WAS JUST AN EXAMPLE.
I'M NOT HURT OR ANYTHING, REALLY...
I DIDN'T THINK IT'D BOTHER A SLOW-WITTED GIRL LIKE YOU...
AS I WAS *SAYING*...
GO AND SHOW THAT PART OF YOUR PERSONALITY TO UKYO!
KAAAASH
HMPH.
TRYING TO PICK A FIGHT WITH ME?
AKANE
YOU'RE NOT GOING TO GET OFF THAT EASILY.

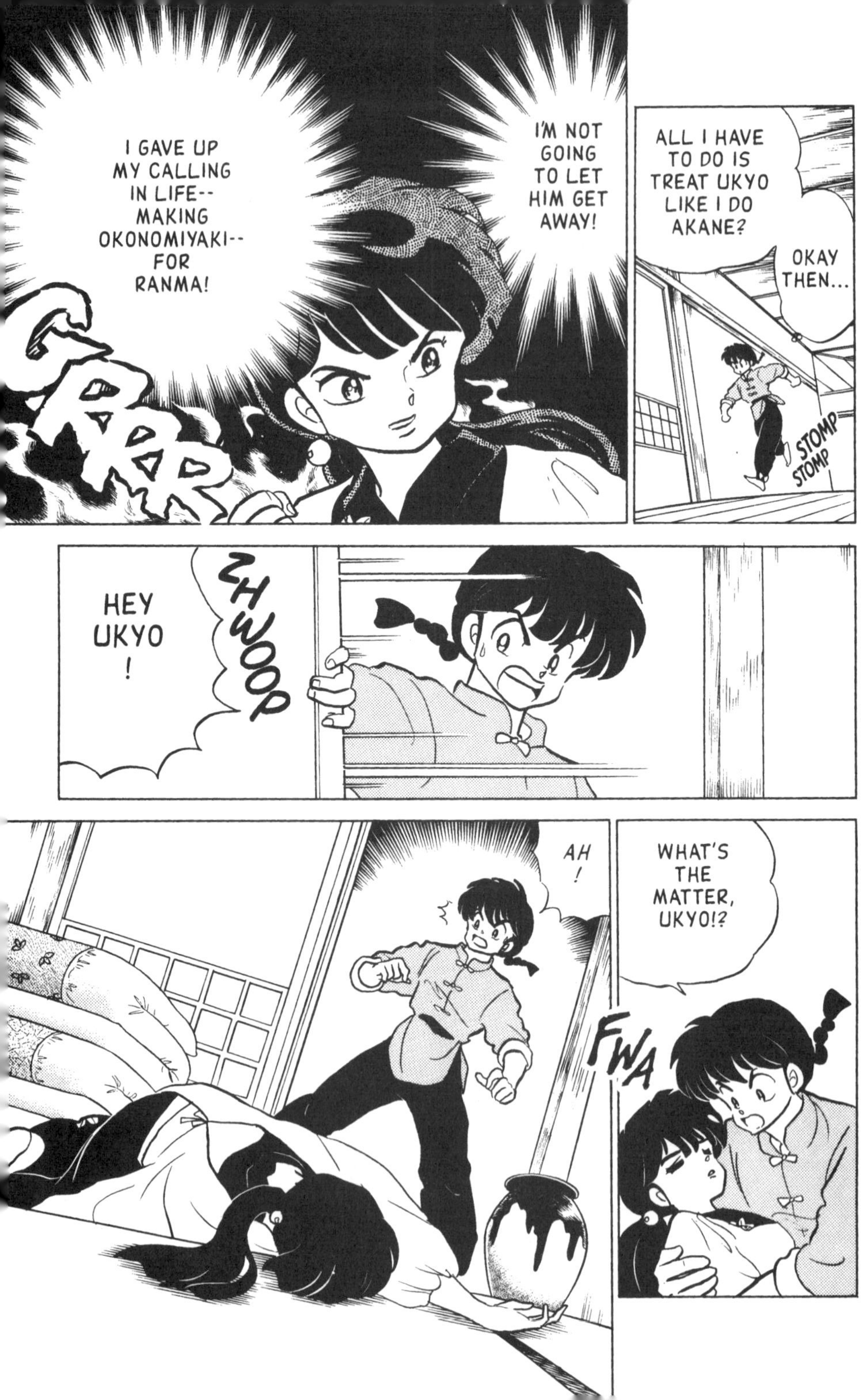
I GAVE UP MY CALLING IN LIFE-- MAKING OKONOMIYAKI-- FOR RANMA!
I'M NOT GOING TO LET HIM GET AWAY!
ALL I HAVE TO DO IS TREAT UKYO LIKE I DO AKANE?
OKAY THEN...
STOMP STOMP
HEY UKYO !
ZHWOOP
AH !
WHAT'S THE MATTER, UKYO!?
FWA

HUH
!?

THE SAUCE...
I THOUGHT
YOU THREW
THAT AWAY...

I-IT'S THE SAUCE...
THAT BROUGHT...
YOU AND ME...
TOGETHER.
I CAN'T...JUST
THROW IT...OUT...

ZHEE
ZHEE

YOU MEAN
YOU TASTED
SOME OF IT
AGAIN...?

NOD

DON'T BE
STUPID. I
TOLD YOU
ALREADY.

I WAS THE
ONE WHO
MADE THIS
SAUCE!

HOW-
EVER
VILE
IT MAY
BE...

IT IS
STILL
THE
TASTE OF
HAPPI-
NESS....

SIGH

K'RAAK

UKYO...
YOU LOVE
ME THAT
MUCH...
?

ARGH!
I CAN'T
WATCH
THIS
ANYMORE
!

BAM
BAM

WHY DO YOU ALWAYS WIMP OUT WHEN THE CHIPS ARE DOWN?

GRRR GRRR GRRR

I AGREE.

IT'S TIME WE SETTLED THIS.

poik

GRRR

SHHHH

OKAY.

I'LL PUT AN END TO THIS...

WHAT...?

B-BMP

IT'S BECAUSE OF THIS SAUCE.

THERE'S ONLY ONE WAY TO MAKE UP FOR WHAT I DID IN THE PAST...

GRABB

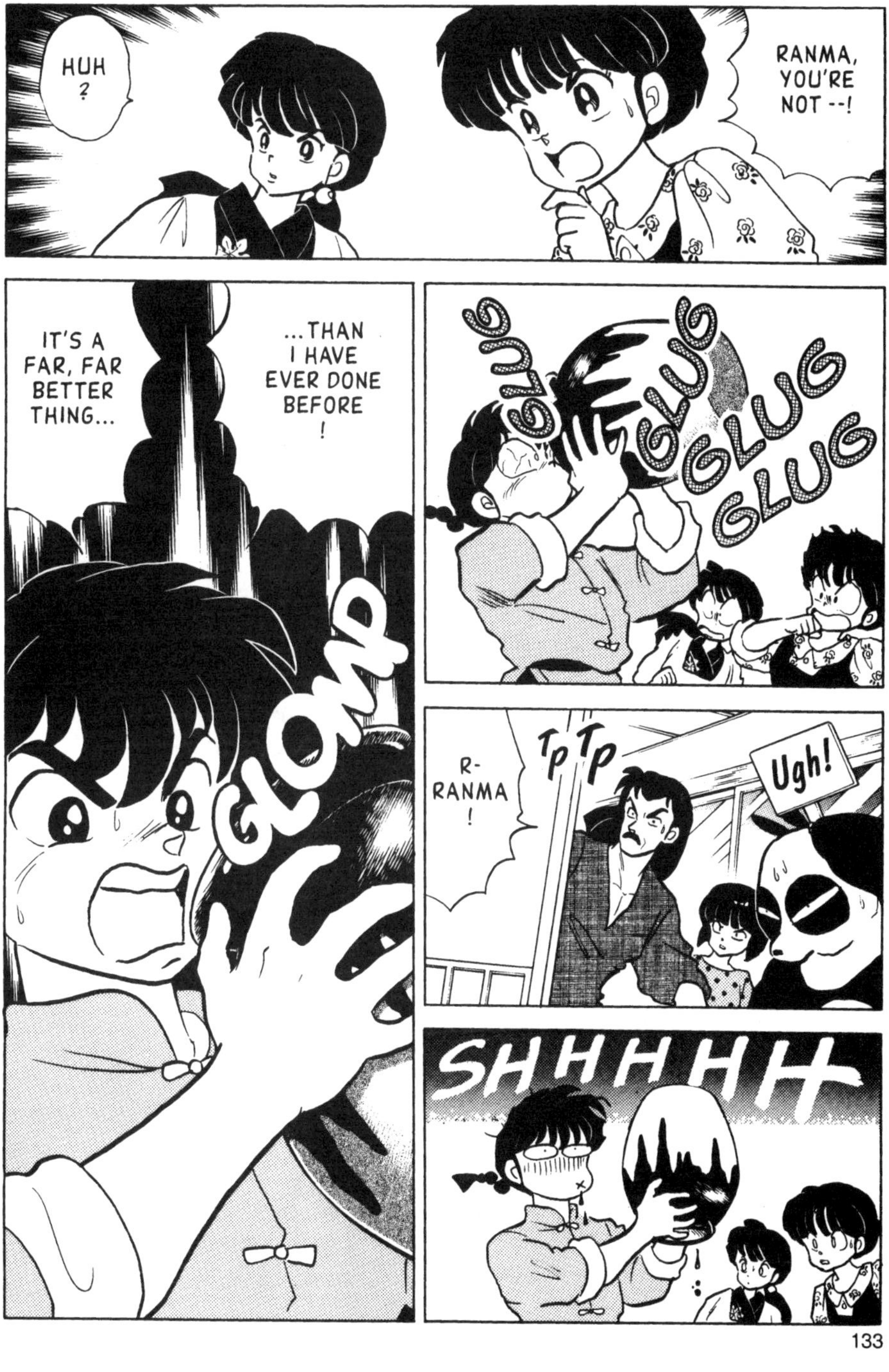
HUH ?
RANMA, YOU'RE NOT --!
IT'S A FAR, FAR BETTER THING...
...THAN I HAVE EVER DONE BEFORE !
GLOMP
GLUG GLUG GLUG GLUG
R-RANMA !
TP TP
Ugh!
SHHHHHH

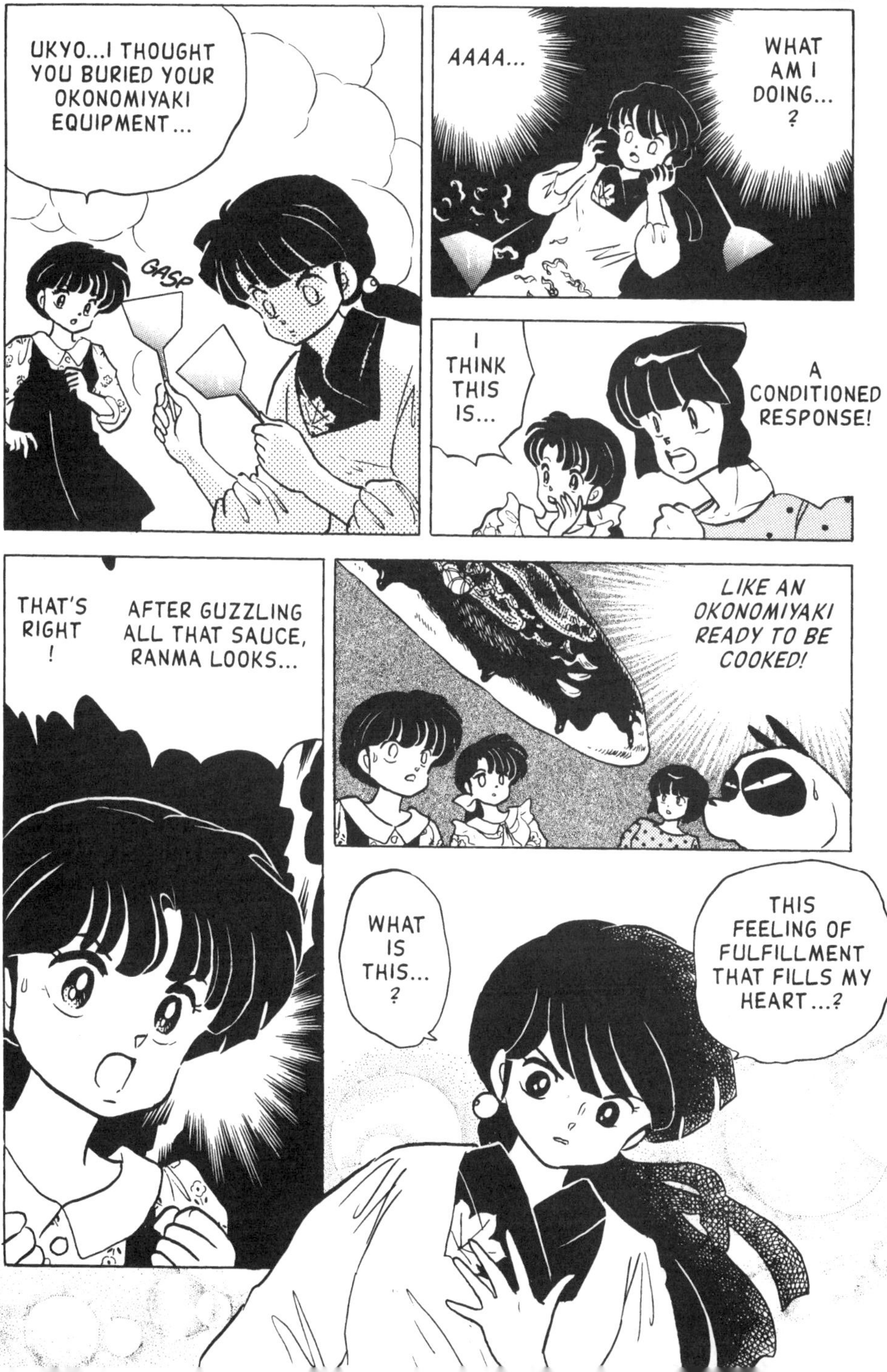
UKYO...I THOUGHT YOU BURIED YOUR OKONOMIYAKI EQUIPMENT...
GASP
AAAA...
WHAT AM I DOING...?
I THINK THIS IS...
A CONDITIONED RESPONSE!
THAT'S RIGHT!
AFTER GUZZLING ALL THAT SAUCE, RANMA LOOKS...
LIKE AN OKONOMIYAKI READY TO BE COOKED!
WHAT IS THIS...?
THIS FEELING OF FULFILLMENT THAT FILLS MY HEART...?

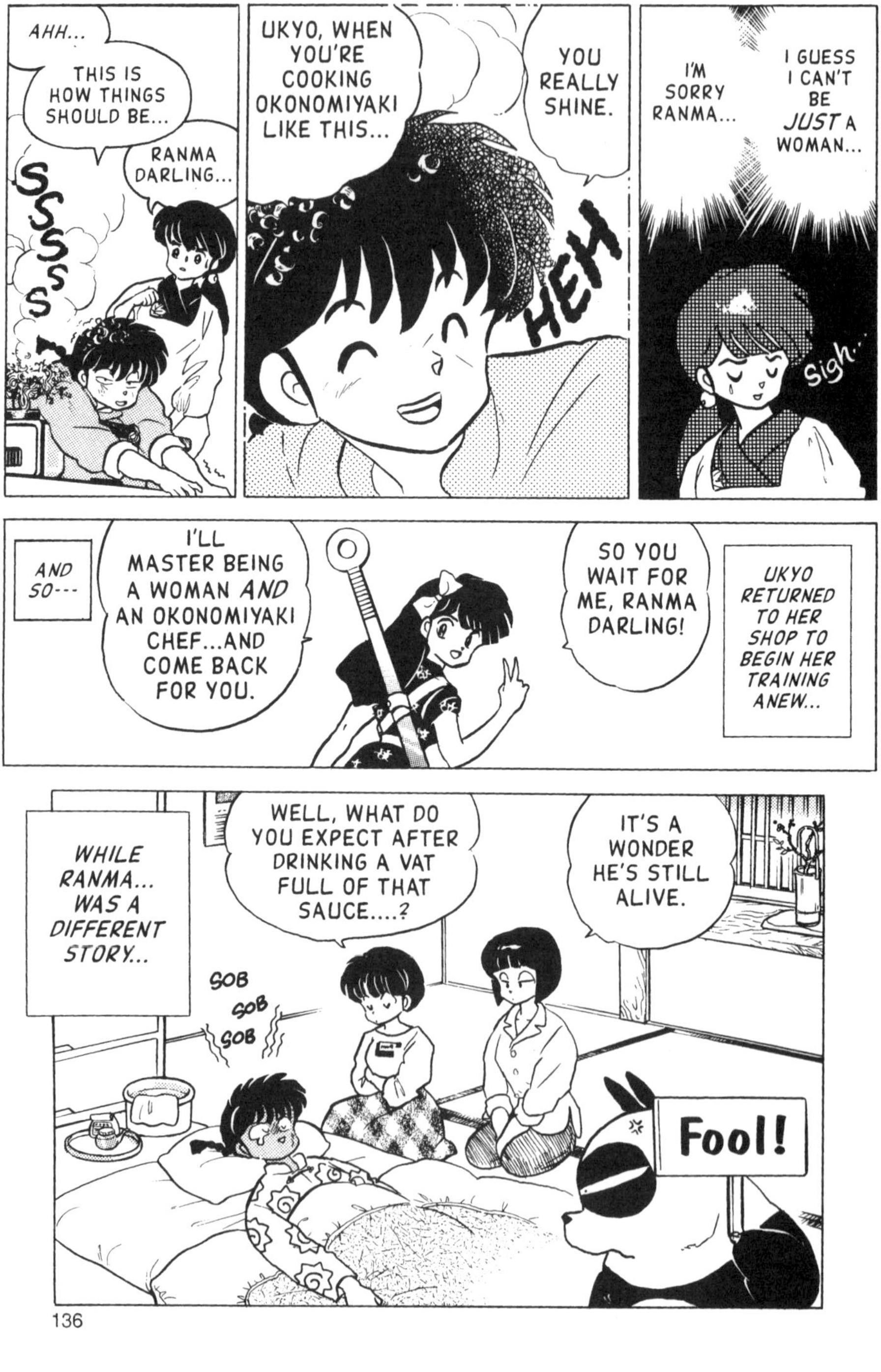
AHH...
THIS IS HOW THINGS SHOULD BE...
RANMA DARLING...
SSSSS
UKYO, WHEN YOU'RE COOKING OKONOMIYAKI LIKE THIS...
YOU REALLY SHINE.
HEH
I'M SORRY RANMA...
I GUESS I CAN'T BE *JUST* A WOMAN...
Sigh...
AND SO---
I'LL MASTER BEING A WOMAN *AND* AN OKONOMIYAKI CHEF...AND COME BACK FOR YOU.
SO YOU WAIT FOR ME, RANMA DARLING!
UKYO RETURNED TO HER SHOP TO BEGIN HER TRAINING ANEW...
WHILE RANMA... WAS A DIFFERENT STORY...
WELL, WHAT DO YOU EXPECT AFTER DRINKING A VAT FULL OF THAT SAUCE....?
IT'S A WONDER HE'S STILL ALIVE.
SOB SOB SOB
Fool!

SHP

SHP

GLP GLP GLP

BRING BACK THAT BARBECUE !

DM DM DM DM DM DM DM

LIVING... OCTOPUS... TRAP...?

OCTOPUS TRAP:

AN URN DROPPED INTO THE SEA TO TAKE ADVANTAGE OF THE OCTOPOD'S INSTINCT TO HIDE IN SMALL SPACES.

OCTOPUS

OCTOPUS TRAP

GONG

GING

GONG

SINCE THAT OCTOPUS TRAP FIRST APPEARED...

HEADQUARTERS HOT SPRINGS HOTEL ASSOCIATION

...IT HAS BEEN RELENTLESS IN ITS MISCHIEF...

SNIFF SNIFF SOB

...STEALING FOOD, ANNOYING COUPLES, AND TERRIFYING OUR HONORED VISITORS!

IF TOURISM CONTINUES TO DROP AT THIS RATE...

...THIS RESORT COMMUNITY COULD BE IN SERIOUS TROUBLE!

FEAR NOT. DEFEATING MONSTERS IS A MARTIAL ARTIST'S DUTY.

WE SHALL VANQUISH THIS CREATURE FOR YOU!

DOOM

THANK YOU SO MUCH!

WE'RE COUNTING ON YOU!

SOB SOB SOBB

SOB SOBB SOB

SHLURP SHLURP

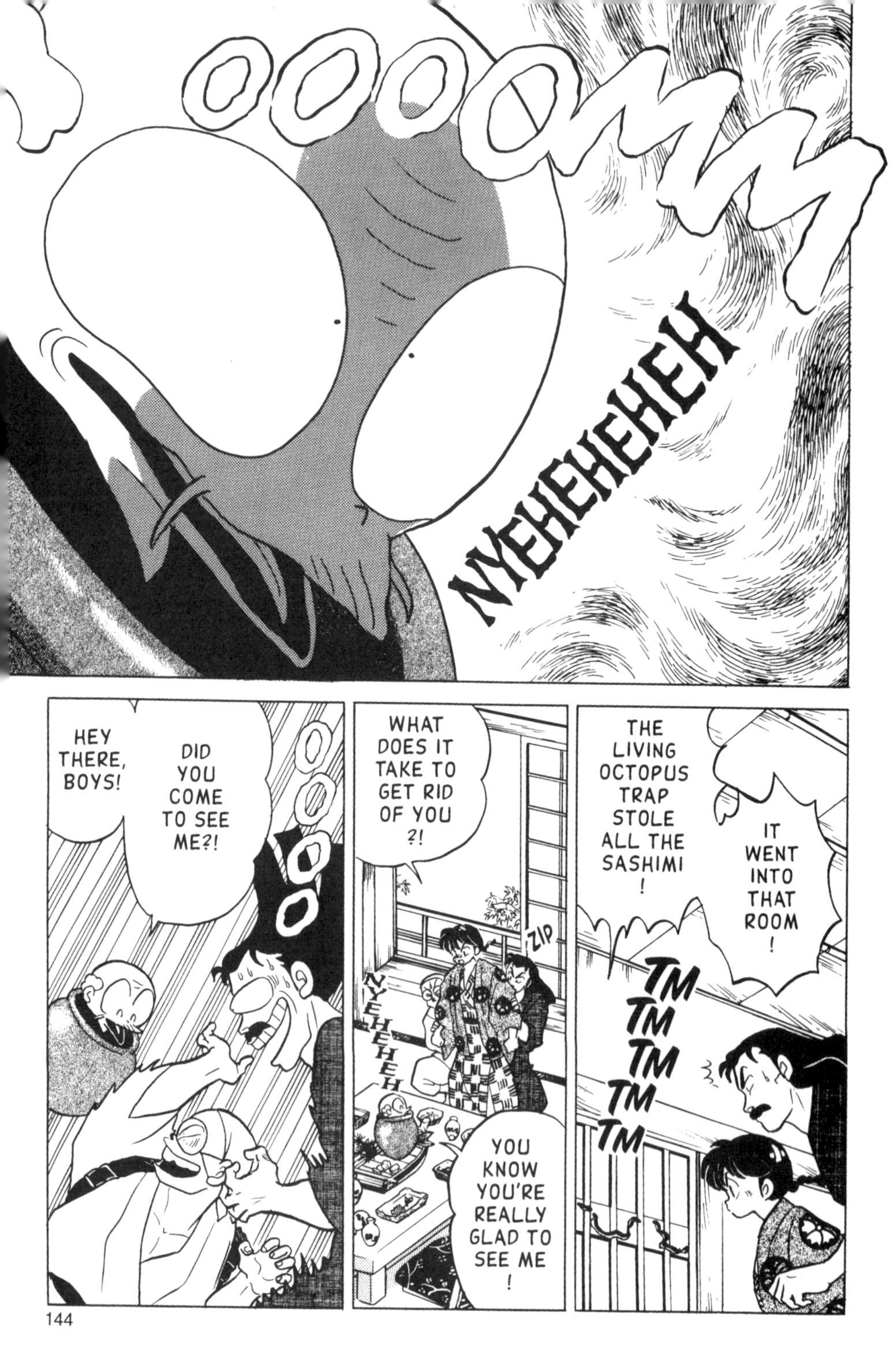
OOOOMM
NYEHEHEHEH
HEY THERE, BOYS!
DID YOU COME TO SEE ME?!
WHAT DOES IT TAKE TO GET RID OF YOU?!
ZIP
NYEHEHEH
YOU KNOW YOU'RE REALLY GLAD TO SEE ME!
THE LIVING OCTOPUS TRAP STOLE ALL THE SASHIMI!
IT WENT INTO THAT ROOM!
TM TM TM TM TM

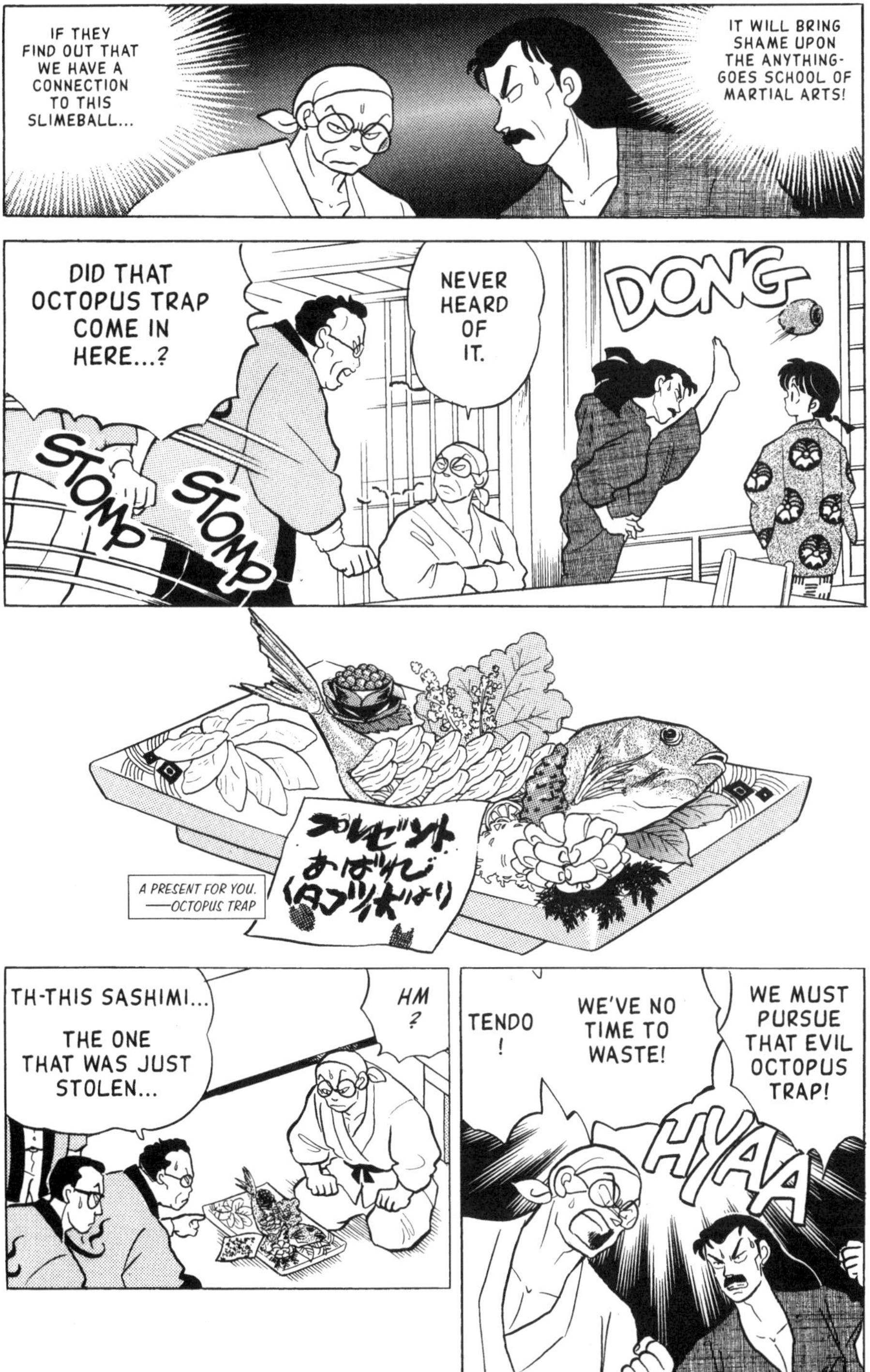
IF THEY FIND OUT THAT WE HAVE A CONNECTION TO THIS SLIMEBALL...
IT WILL BRING SHAME UPON THE ANYTHING-GOES SCHOOL OF MARTIAL ARTS!
DID THAT OCTOPUS TRAP COME IN HERE...?
NEVER HEARD OF IT.
DONG
STOMP
STOMP
A PRESENT FOR YOU. ——OCTOPUS TRAP
TH-THIS SASHIMI...
THE ONE THAT WAS JUST STOLEN...
HM?
TENDO!
WE'VE NO TIME TO WASTE!
WE MUST PURSUE THAT EVIL OCTOPUS TRAP!
HYAA

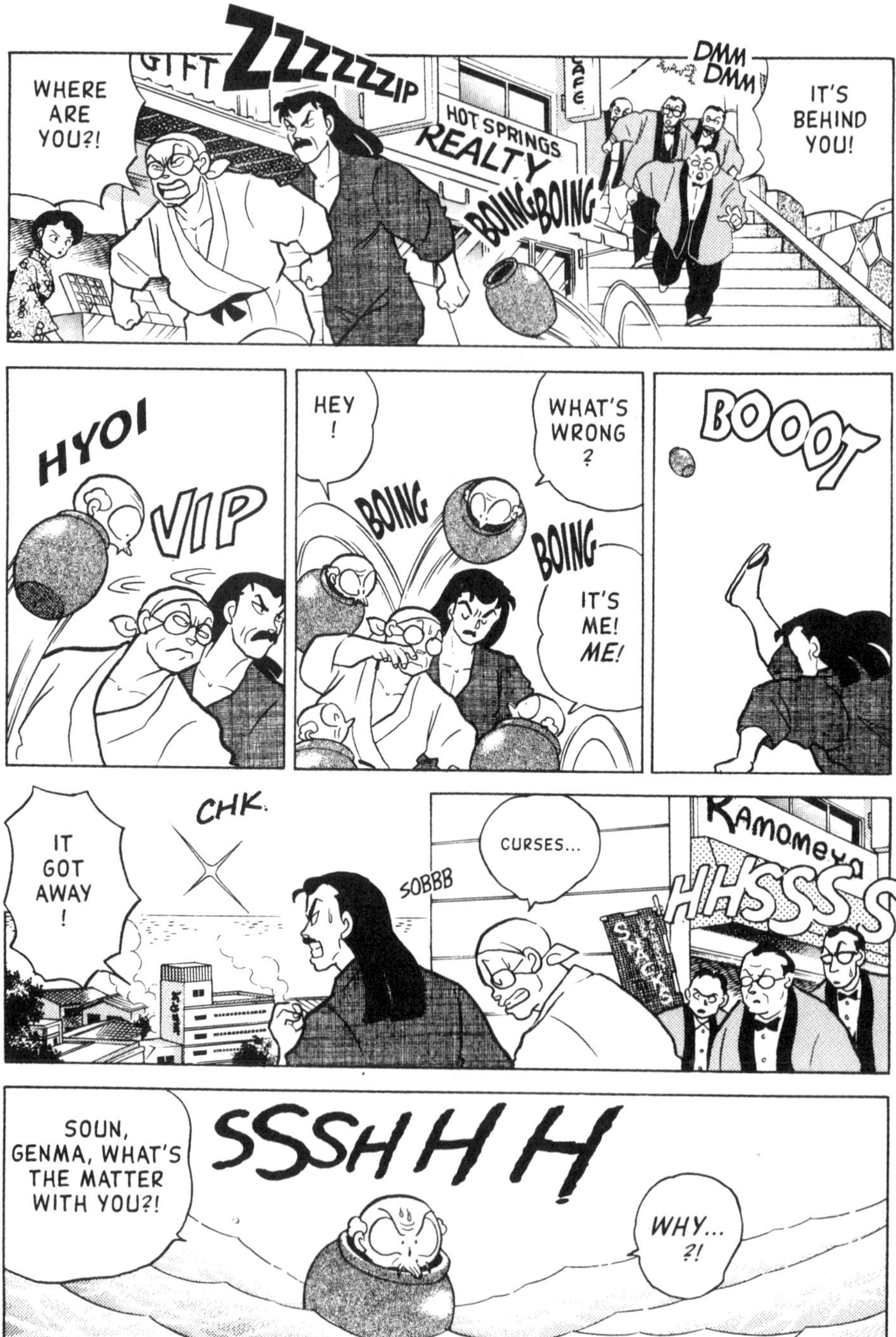
WHERE ARE YOU?!
GIFT
ZZZZZZZIP
HOT SPRINGS
REALTY
BOING BOING
CAFE
DMM DMM
IT'S BEHIND YOU!
HYOI
VIP
HEY!
BOING
BOING
WHAT'S WRONG?
IT'S ME! ME!
BOOOT
IT GOT AWAY!
CHK.
SOBBB
CURSES...
Kamomeya
HHSSSS
SOUN, GENMA, WHAT'S THE MATTER WITH YOU?!
SSSHHH
WHY...?!

MASTER, WHAT IS ALL THIS?

THEY'RE GIFTS.

I CAN'T GO HOME EMPTY HANDED, CAN I?

SO! IT WAS ALL A TRICK!

SWOOOOP

CAW CAW

KLATTA KLATTA

USELESS INGRATES.

OH! WELCOME HOME.

SO, DID YOU GET THAT MONSTER AT THE HOT SPRINGS?

OH, WE *GOT* IT, ALL RIGHT...

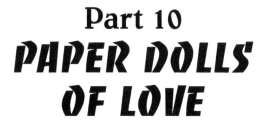

Part 10
PAPER DOLLS OF LOVE

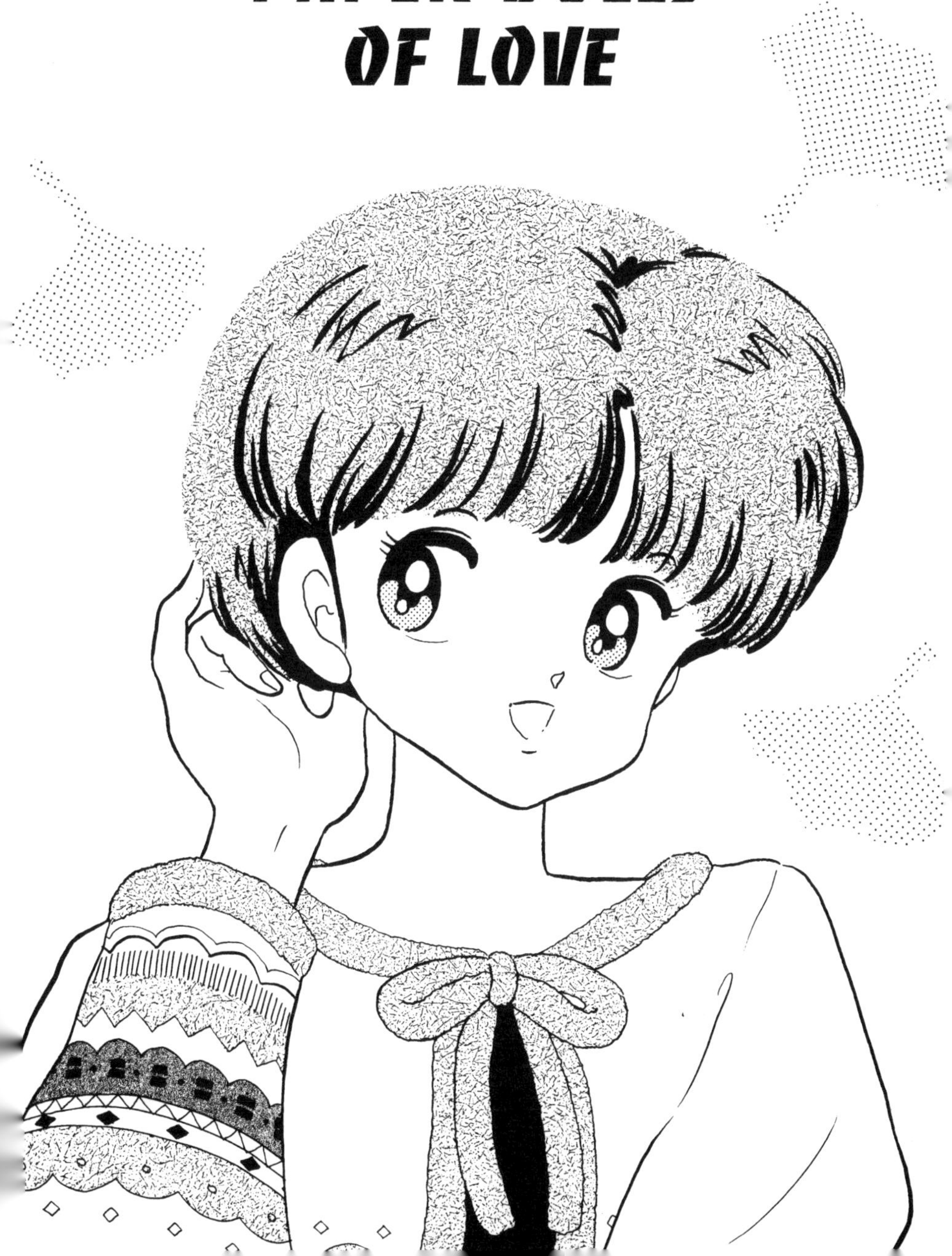

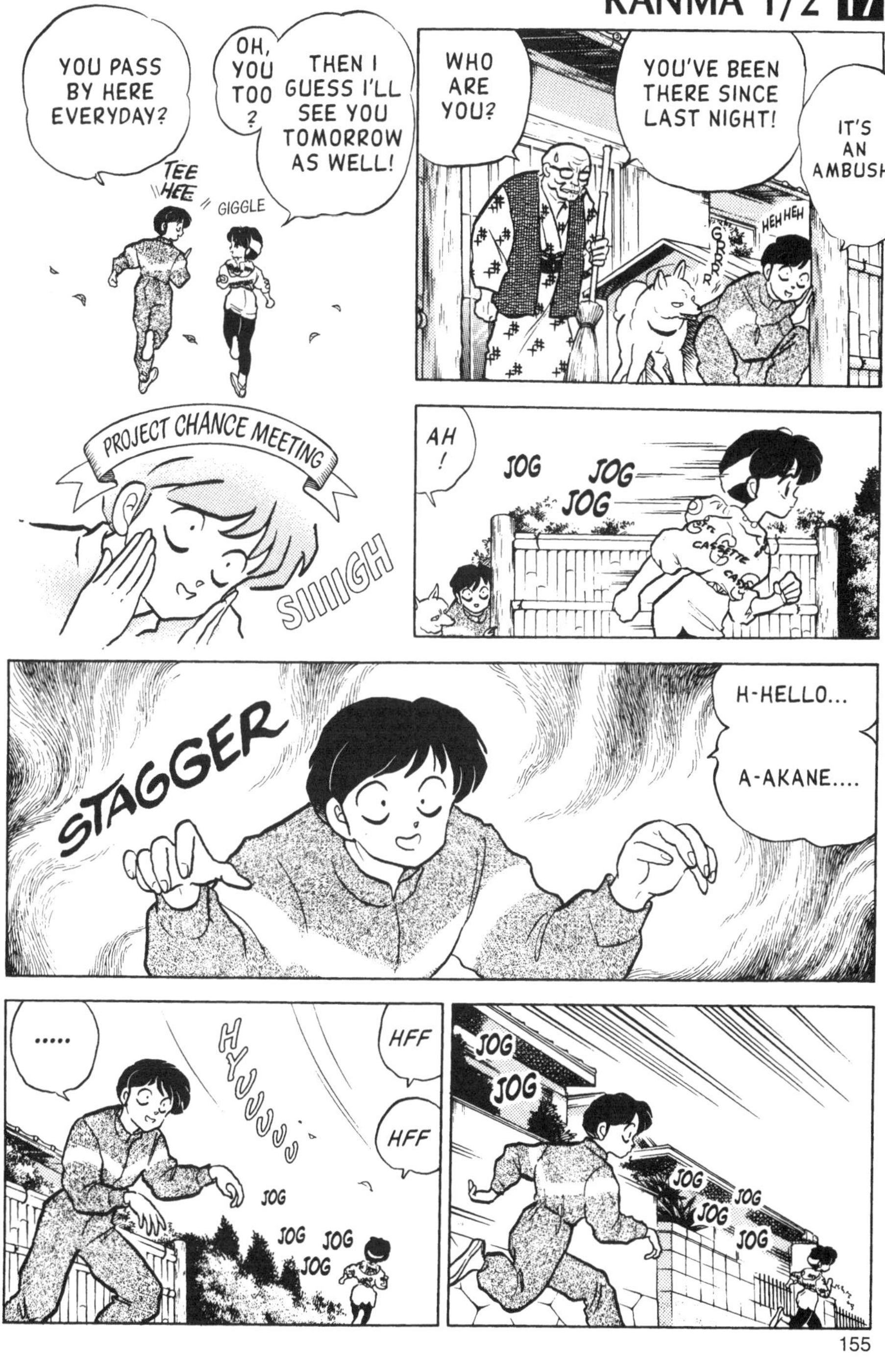
YOU PASS BY HERE EVERYDAY?
OH, YOU TOO?
THEN I GUESS I'LL SEE YOU TOMORROW AS WELL!
TEE HEE
GIGGLE
WHO ARE YOU?
YOU'VE BEEN THERE SINCE LAST NIGHT!
IT'S AN AMBUSH.
GRRRR
HEH HEH
PROJECT CHANCE MEETING
SIIIIGH
AH!
JOG
JOG
JOG
STAGGER
H-HELLO...
A-AKANE....
......
HYUUUUU
HFF
HFF
JOG
JOG
JOG
JOG
JOG
JOG
JOG
JOG
JOG
JOG

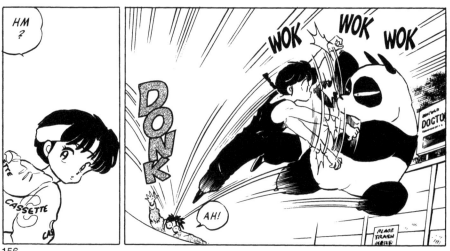

156

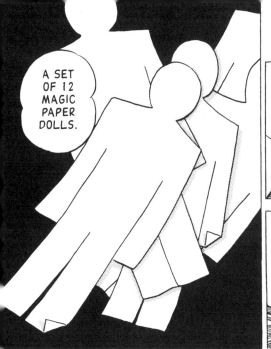

A SET OF 12 MAGIC PAPER DOLLS.

WHEN YOU WRITE A COMMAND ON IT AND SLAP IT ON SOMEONE'S BACK...

FLP

THE WEARER DOES EXACTLY WHAT YOU WROTE...?

SCRATCH SCRATCH

Give it to me for free.

ZIP

JAB

JAB

Pay 10,000 yen

ZIP

ZIP

ZIP

HYUUUUU

RRRR RRRR

HHH HHH HHH

RRR RRR

158

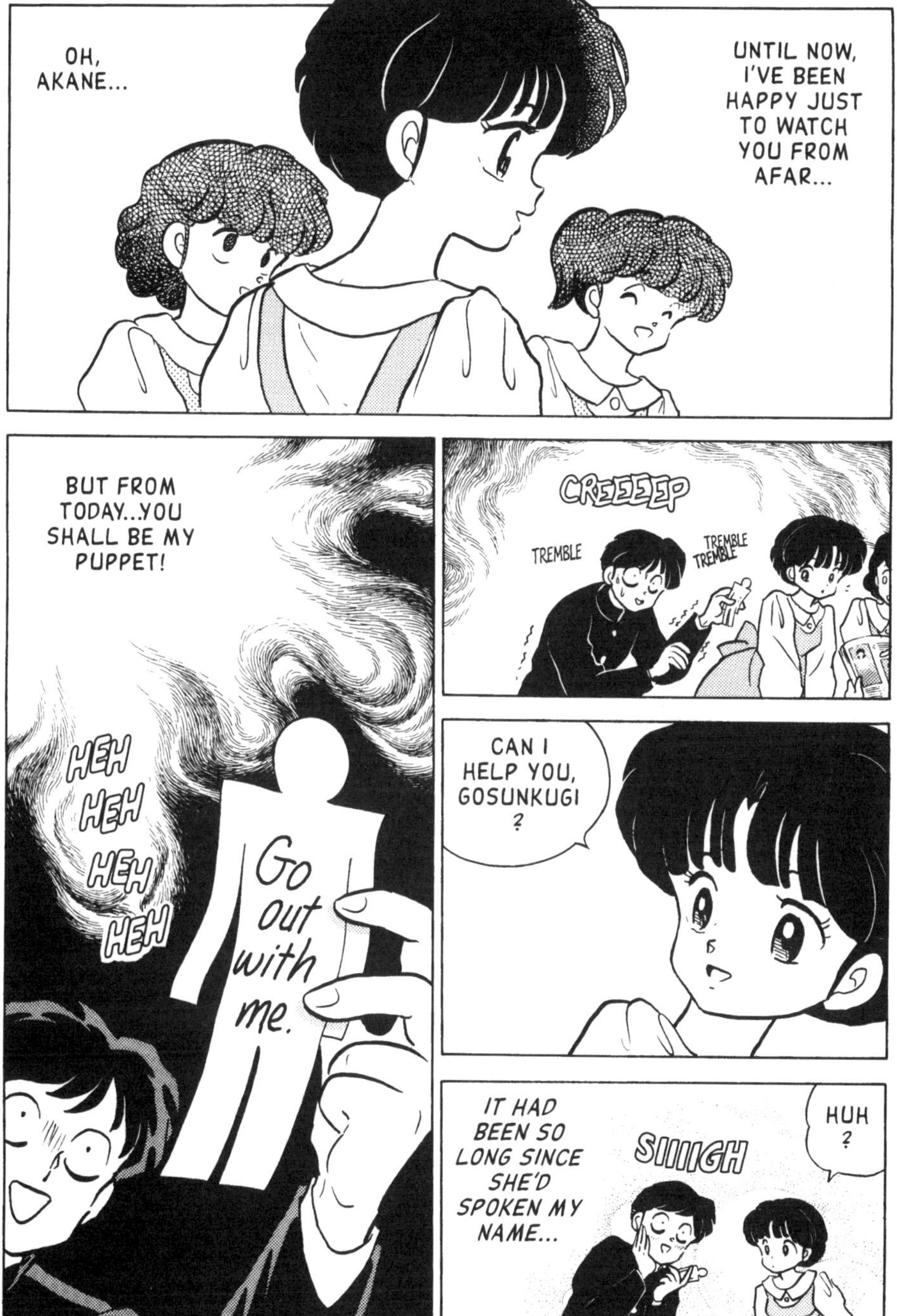
OH, AKANE...
UNTIL NOW, I'VE BEEN HAPPY JUST TO WATCH YOU FROM AFAR...
BUT FROM TODAY...YOU SHALL BE MY PUPPET!
HEH HEH HEH HEH
Go out with me.
CREEEEP
TREMBLE
TREMBLE TREMBLE
CAN I HELP YOU, GOSUNKUGI?
IT HAD BEEN SO LONG SINCE SHE'D SPOKEN MY NAME...
SIIIIGH
HUH?

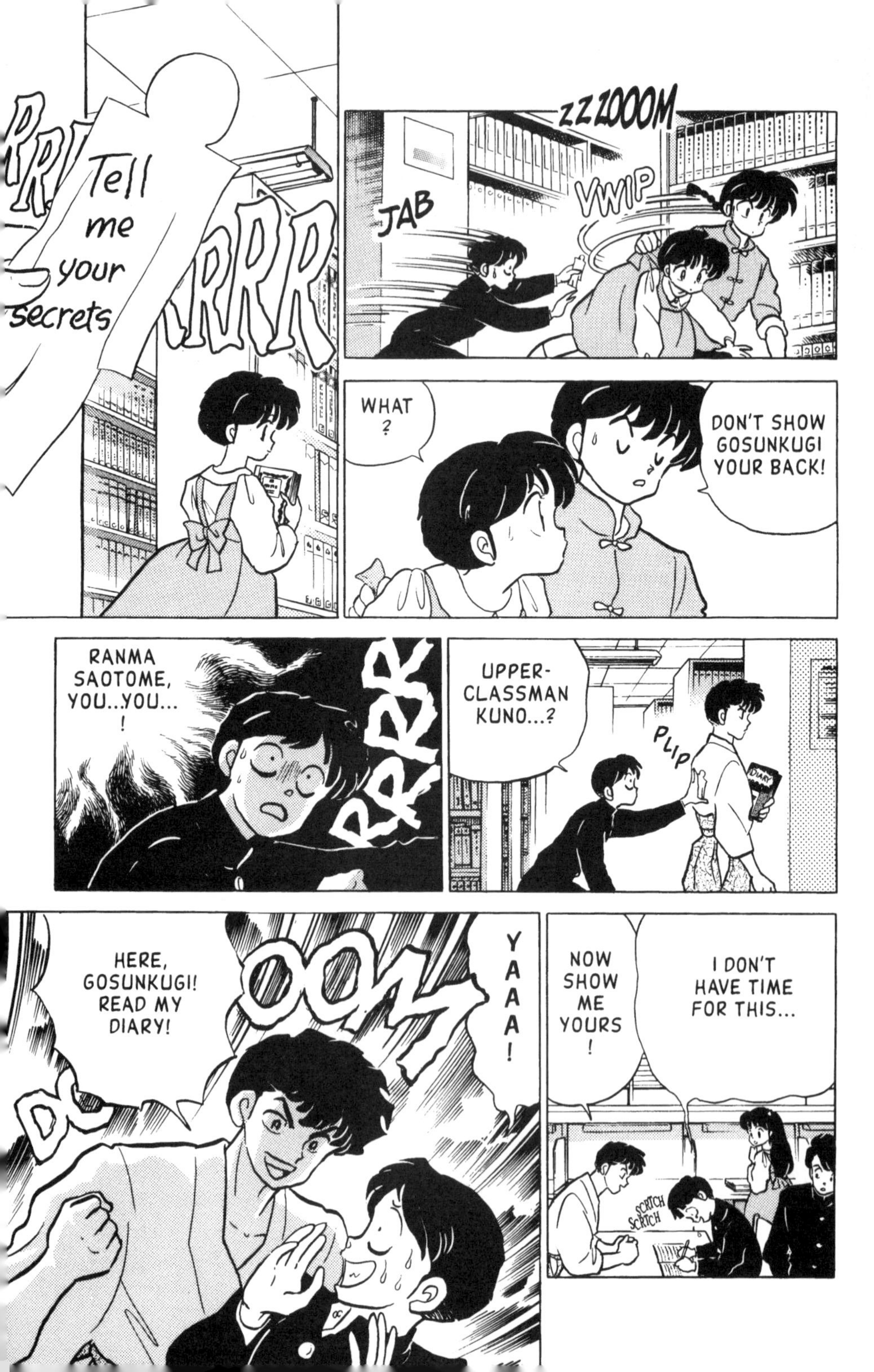
RRRRRR
Tell me your secrets
ZZZOOOM
JAB
VWIP
WHAT?
DON'T SHOW GOSUNKUGI YOUR BACK!
RANMA SAOTOME, YOU...YOU...!
RRR
UPPER-CLASSMAN KUNO...?
PLIP
DIARY
HERE, GOSUNKUGI! READ MY DIARY!
DOOOM
YAAAA!
NOW SHOW ME YOURS!
I DON'T HAVE TIME FOR THIS...
SCRITCH SCRITCH

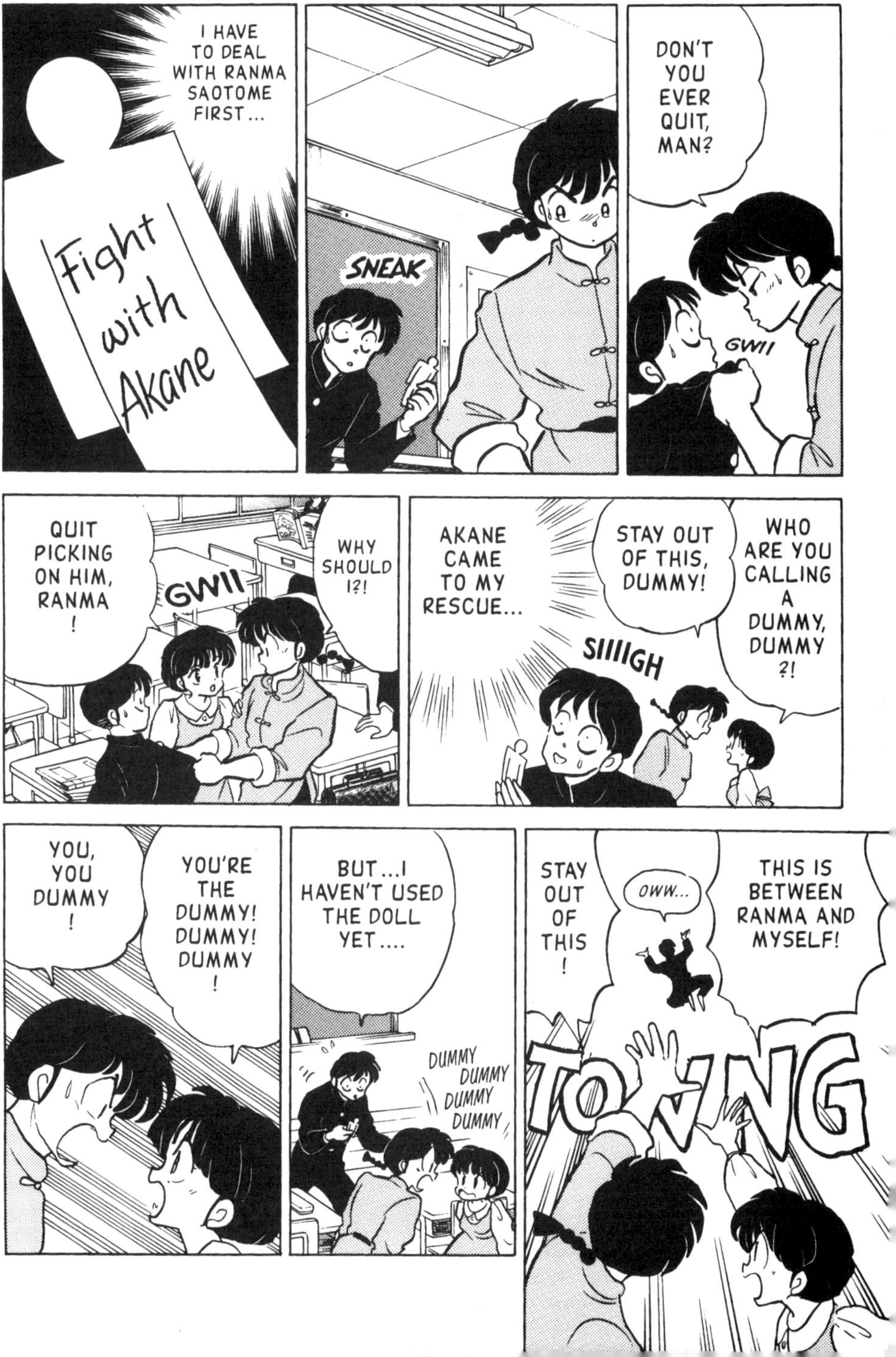
I HAVE TO DEAL WITH RANMA SAOTOME FIRST...
Fight with Akane
SNEAK
DON'T YOU EVER QUIT, MAN?
GWII
QUIT PICKING ON HIM, RANMA!
GWII
WHY SHOULD I?!
AKANE CAME TO MY RESCUE...
STAY OUT OF THIS, DUMMY!
WHO ARE YOU CALLING A DUMMY, DUMMY?!
SIIIGH
YOU, YOU DUMMY!
YOU'RE THE DUMMY! DUMMY! DUMMY!
BUT...I HAVEN'T USED THE DOLL YET....
DUMMY DUMMY DUMMY DUMMY
STAY OUT OF THIS!
OWW...
THIS IS BETWEEN RANMA AND MYSELF!
TO NG

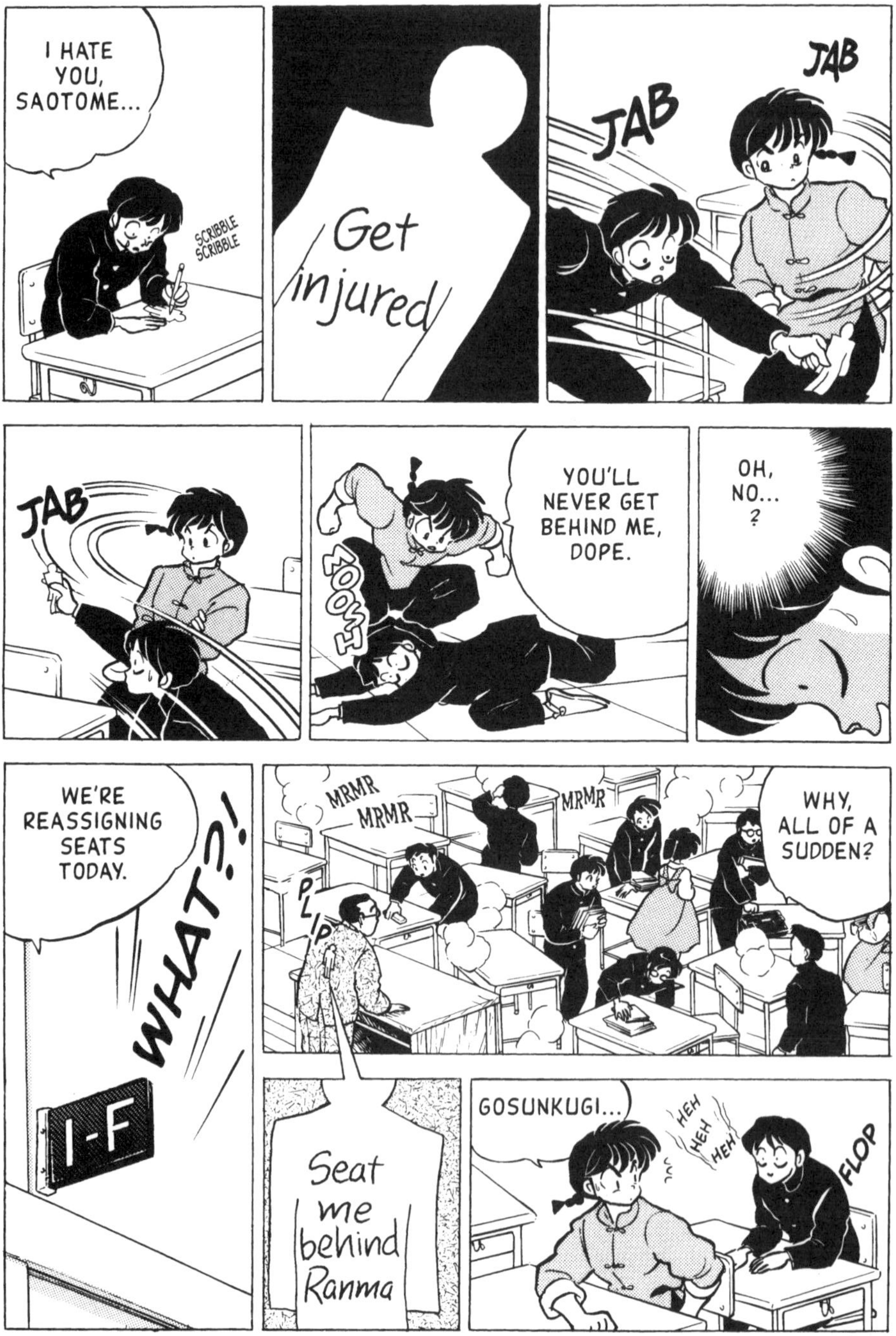
I HATE YOU, SAOTOME...
SCRIBBLE SCRIBBLE
Get injured
JAB
JAB
JAB
ZOOM
YOU'LL NEVER GET BEHIND ME, DOPE.
OH, NO...?
WE'RE REASSIGNING SEATS TODAY.
WHAT?!
I-F
MRMR
MRMR
MRMR
PLIP
WHY, ALL OF A SUDDEN?
Seat me behind Ranma
GOSUNKUGI...
HEH HEH HEH
FLOP

POOR RANMA SAOTOME.

YOU CAN'T ESCAPE ME NOW...

HEH HEH HEH HEH

RANMA....

WHAT, YOU'RE NEXT TO ME, AKANE?

AGH!

SCRA APE

CURSE YOU, SAOTOME!

GETTING A SEAT NEXT TO AKANE LIKE THAT!

I'LL DEAL WITH YOU YET!

AWP!

FLIP

NOOOOO!

I'VE ONLY GOT ONE LEFT!

Part 11
THE PILL OF OBEDIENCE

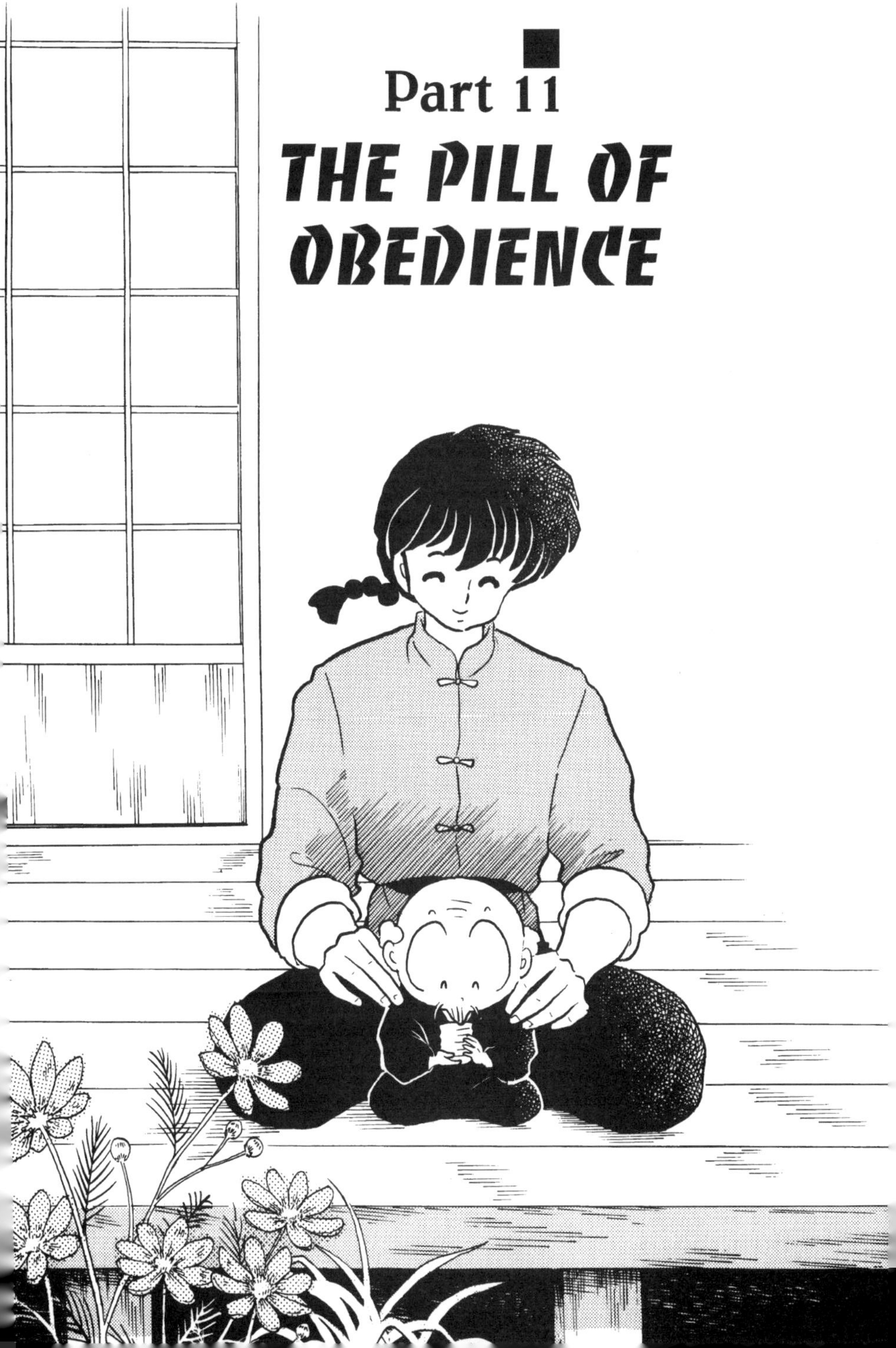

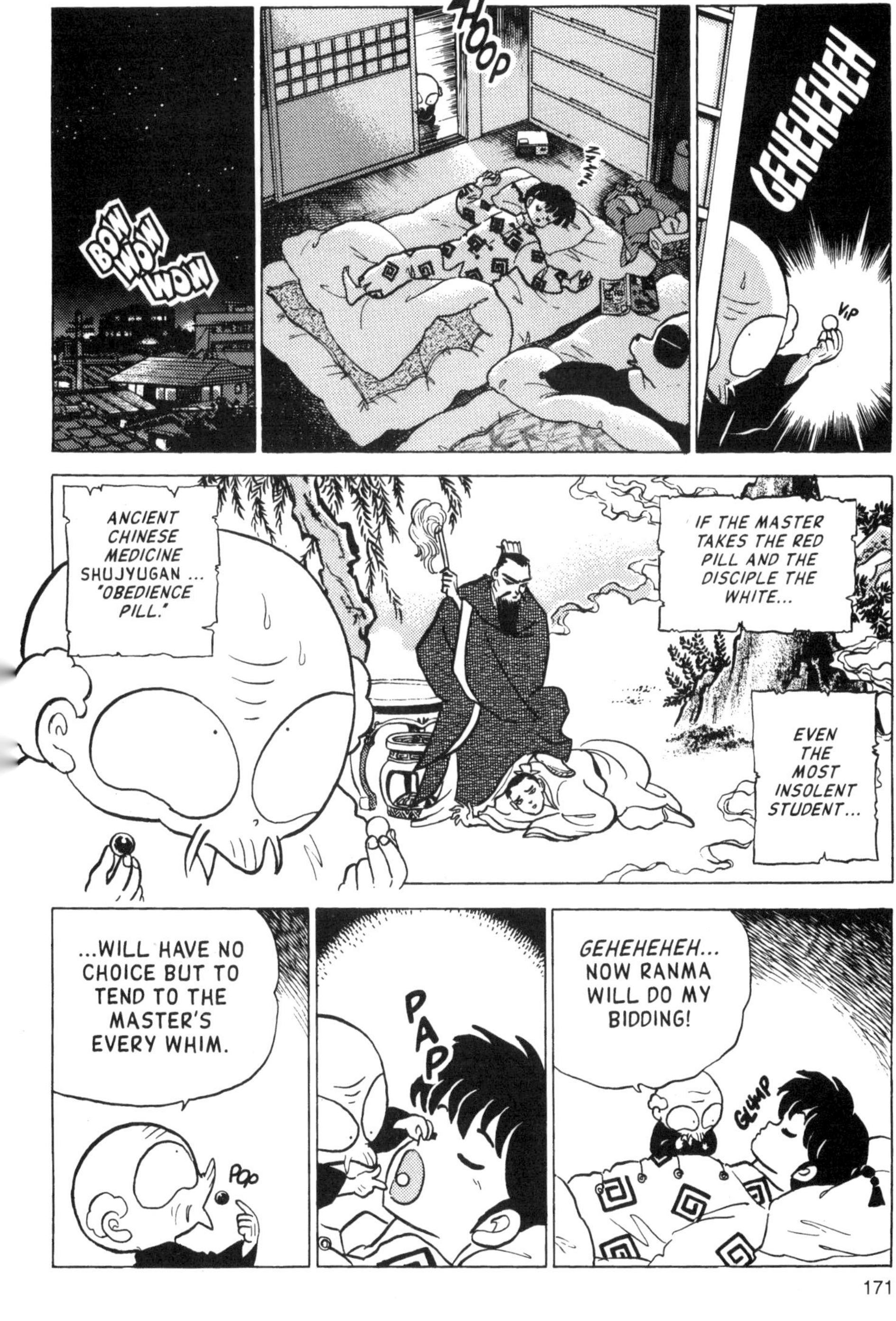
BOW WOW WOW
ZHOOP
Z-Z-Z-Z
GEHEHEHEH
VIP
ANCIENT CHINESE MEDICINE SHUJYUGAN ... "OBEDIENCE PILL."
IF THE MASTER TAKES THE RED PILL AND THE DISCIPLE THE WHITE...
EVEN THE MOST INSOLENT STUDENT...
...WILL HAVE NO CHOICE BUT TO TEND TO THE MASTER'S EVERY WHIM.
POP
PAP
GEHEHEHEH... NOW RANMA WILL DO MY BIDDING!
GLUMP

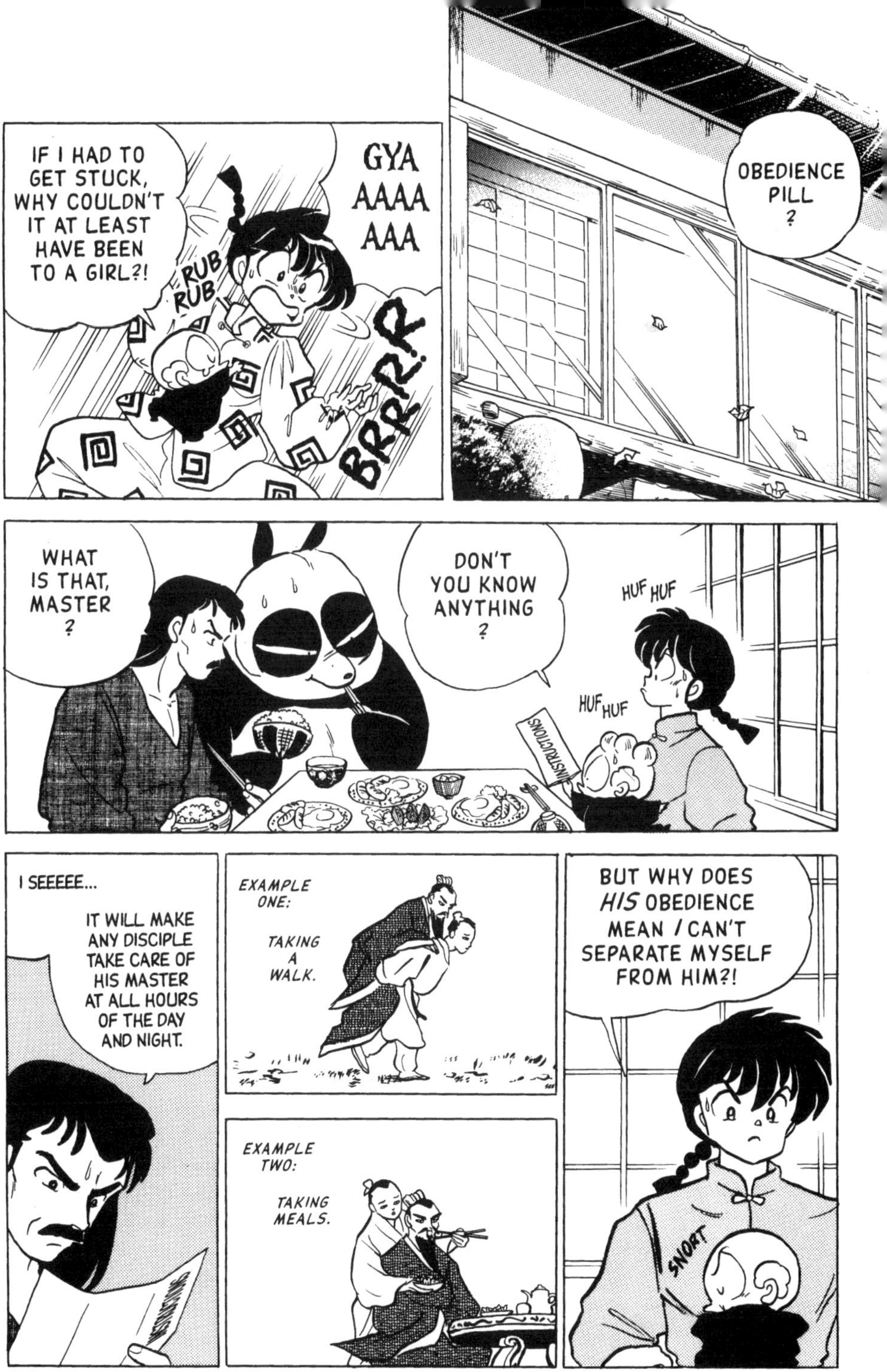
IF I HAD TO GET STUCK, WHY COULDN'T IT AT LEAST HAVE BEEN TO A GIRL?!
GYA AAAA AAA
RUB RUB
BRRRR
OBEDIENCE PILL?
WHAT IS THAT, MASTER?
DON'T YOU KNOW ANYTHING?
HUF HUF
HUF HUF
INSTRUCTIONS
I SEEEEE...
IT WILL MAKE ANY DISCIPLE TAKE CARE OF HIS MASTER AT ALL HOURS OF THE DAY AND NIGHT.
EXAMPLE ONE:
TAKING A WALK.
EXAMPLE TWO:
TAKING MEALS.
BUT WHY DOES HIS OBEDIENCE MEAN I CAN'T SEPARATE MYSELF FROM HIM?!
SNORT

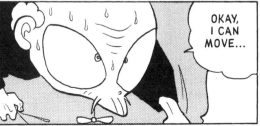

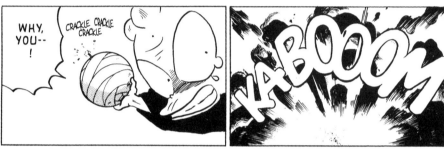

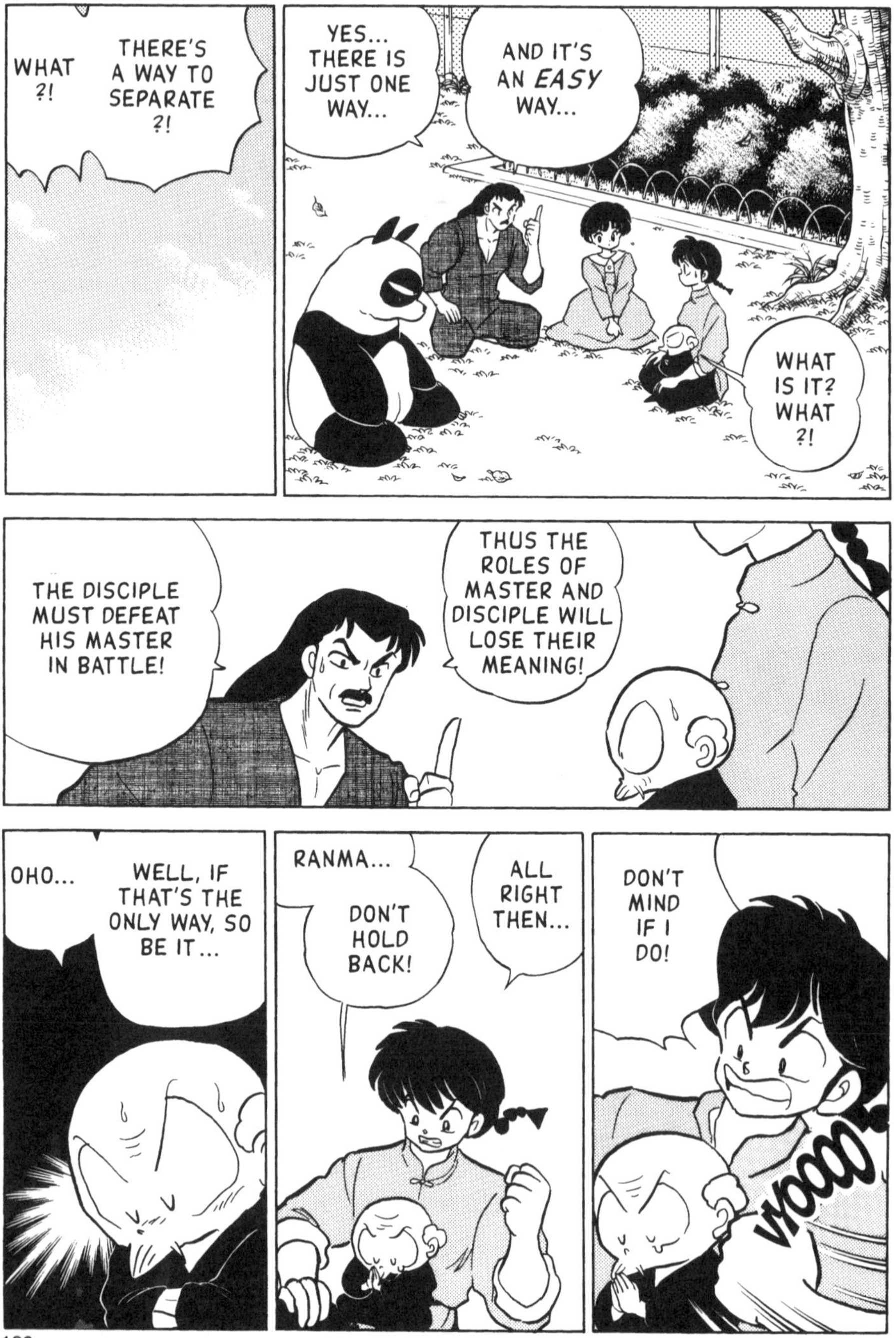
WHAT ?!
THERE'S A WAY TO SEPARATE ?!
YES... THERE IS JUST ONE WAY...
AND IT'S AN *EASY* WAY...
WHAT IS IT? WHAT ?!
THE DISCIPLE MUST DEFEAT HIS MASTER IN BATTLE!
THUS THE ROLES OF MASTER AND DISCIPLE WILL LOSE THEIR MEANING!
OHO...
WELL, IF THAT'S THE ONLY WAY, SO BE IT...
RANMA...
DON'T HOLD BACK!
ALL RIGHT THEN...
DON'T MIND IF I DO!
VYOOOO

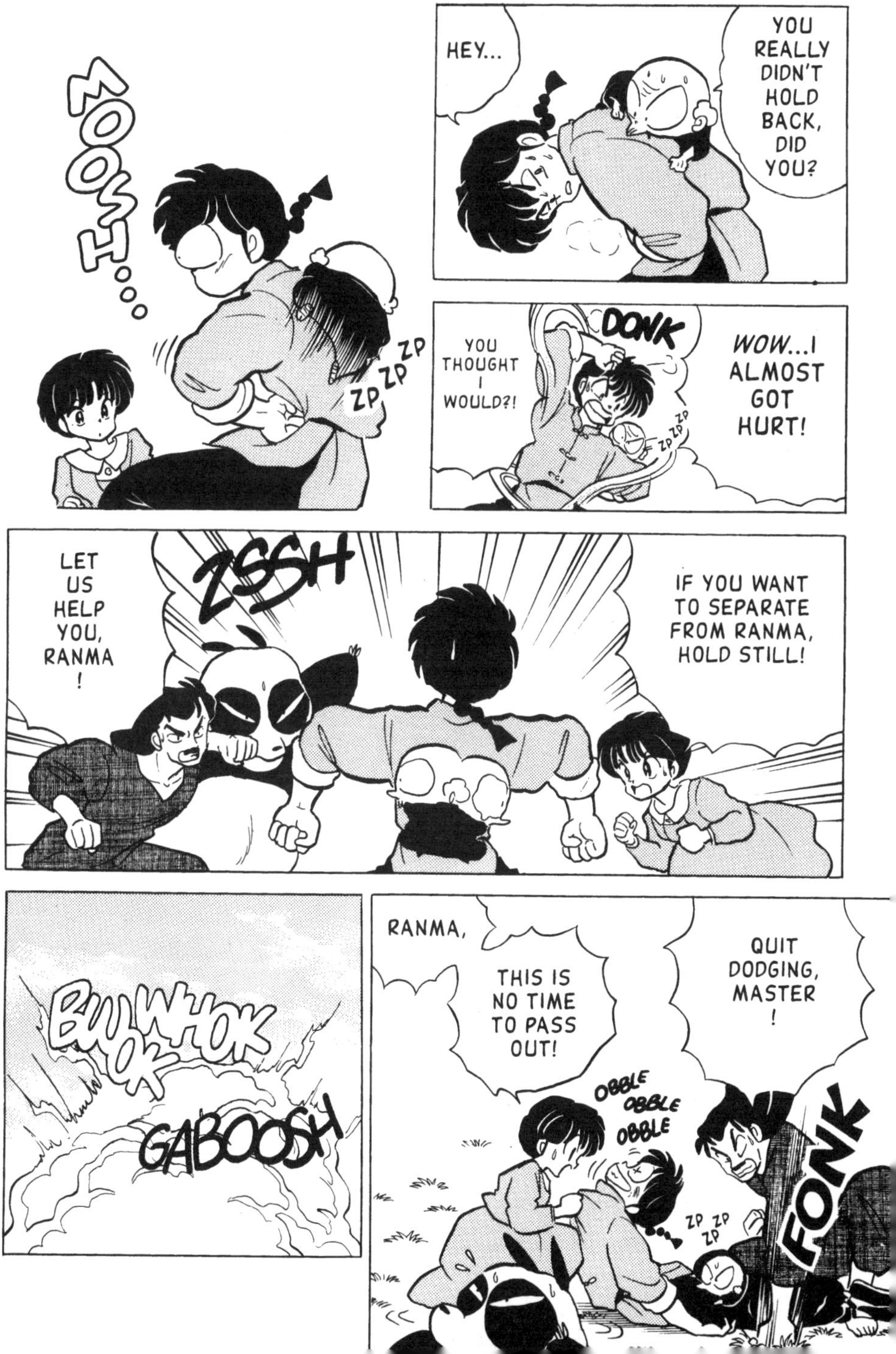
WHOOSH...
ZP ZP ZP
HEY...
YOU REALLY DIDN'T HOLD BACK, DID YOU?
DONK
YOU THOUGHT I WOULD?!
WOW...I ALMOST GOT HURT!
ZP ZP ZP
ZSSH
LET US HELP YOU, RANMA!
IF YOU WANT TO SEPARATE FROM RANMA, HOLD STILL!
BUWHOK
WHOK
GABOOSH
RANMA,
THIS IS NO TIME TO PASS OUT!
QUIT DODGING, MASTER!
OBBLE OBBLE OBBLE
ZP ZP ZP
FONK

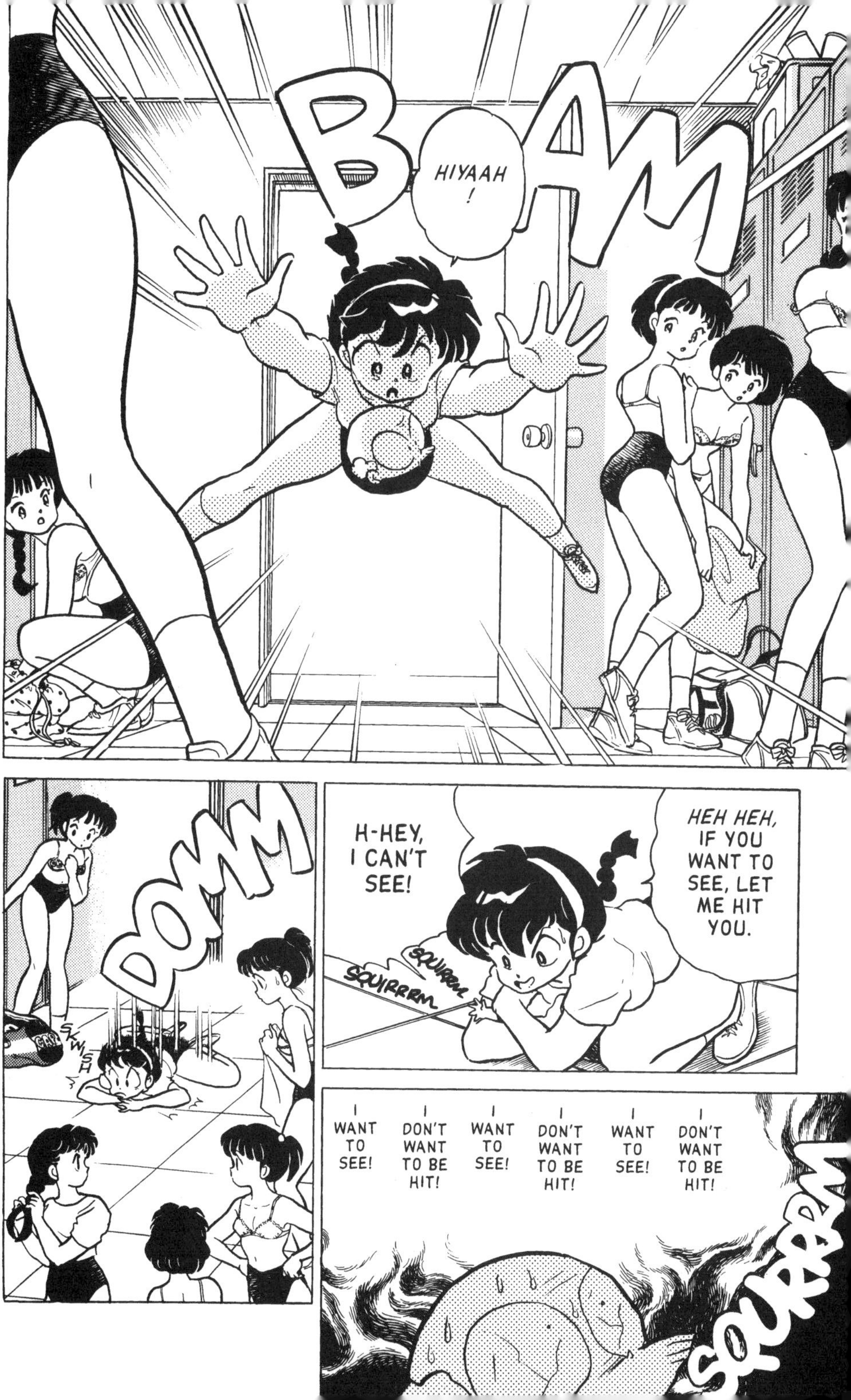
BAM
HIYAAH!
DOMM
SKWISH
H-HEY, I CAN'T SEE!
HEH HEH, IF YOU WANT TO SEE, LET ME HIT YOU.
SQUIRRM
SQUIRRRM
I WANT TO SEE!
I DON'T WANT TO BE HIT!
I WANT TO SEE!
I DON'T WANT TO BE HIT!
I WANT TO SEE!
I DON'T WANT TO BE HIT!
SQUIRRM

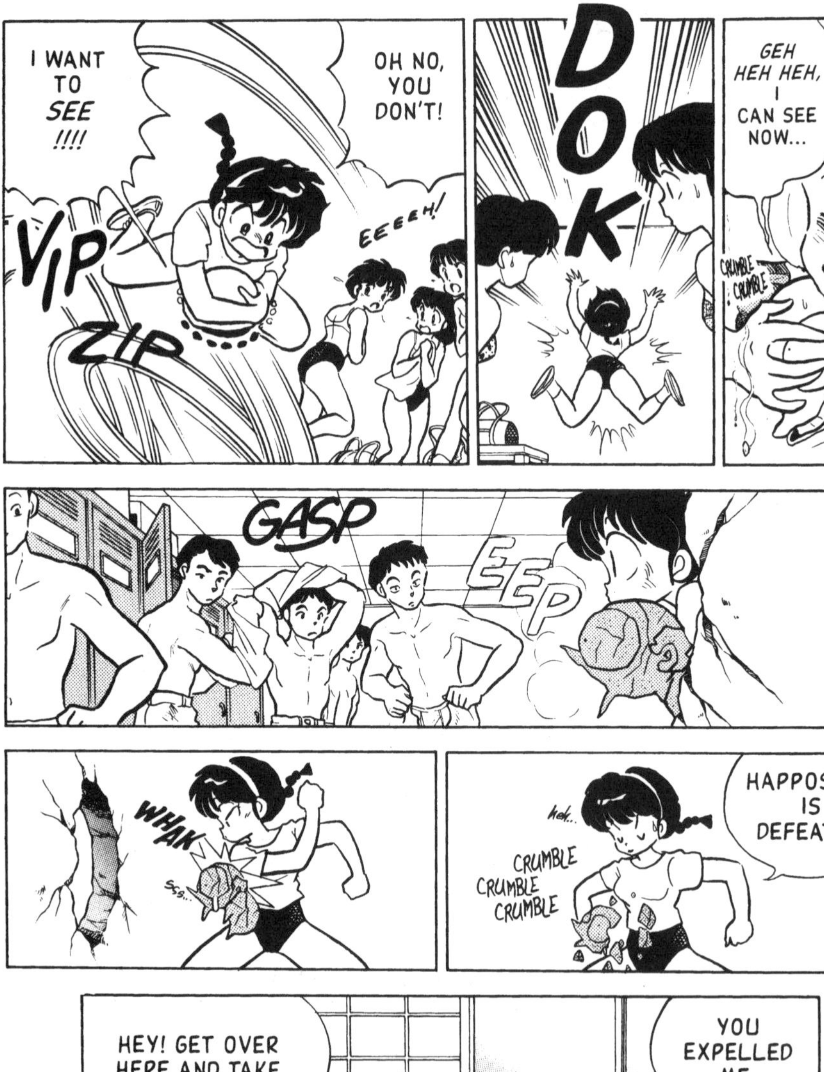
I WANT TO SEE !!!!
OH NO, YOU DON'T!
VIP
ZIP
EEEEEH!
DOK
GEH HEH HEH, I CAN SEE NOW...
CRUMBLE CRUMBLE
GASP
EEEP
WHAM
HAPPOSAI... IS DEFEATED.
heh...
CRUMBLE
CRUMBLE
CRUMBLE
HEY! GET OVER HERE AND TAKE CARE OF YOUR MASTER!
YOU EXPELLED ME, REMEMBER ?